Buffy drew her leg b[...]
It flew inward and landed at the feet of three
men standing in the ornate hallway.

The man in the middle held a snarling, maddened animal at the end of a heavy chain leash.

Although mostly doglike in appearance, the animal had a wedge-shaped skull and tiny greenish black scales that covered its gaunt frame instead of fur. The eyes were fiery, downturned crescents that wept flames. The fires dropped from the creature's saliva-coated muzzle but winked out of existence only inches above the carpet. Scarring marred the scales, mapping out a history of violent abuse. Huge talons stuck out from feet the size of pie plates.

"Liondog," Angel said quietly. "It's supposed to be one of the three creatures that made up the ancient Chimera."

The liondog bayed anxiously, sounding haunting and insane. Flames belched from its throat, lashing out nearly six feet.

Buffy leaned back from the heat. "Boy, I bet he's no picnic to be around when he's got indigestion."

"Beware of dog," the man holding the leash said. Then he released it.

Buffy the Vampire Slayer™

Available from ARCHWAY Paperbacks and POCKET PULSE

Buffy the Vampire Slayer adult books

Available from POCKET BOOKS

BUFFY THE VAMPIRE SLAYER™

REVENANT

MEL ODOM

An original novel based on the hit TV series created by Joss Whedon

POCKET BOOKS

New York   London   Toronto   Sydney   Singapore

HISTORIAN'S NOTE

This story takes place during the third season.

An *Original* Publication of POCKET BOOKS

POCKET BOOKS, a division of Simon & Schuster, Inc.
1230 Avenue of the Americas, New York, NY 10020

ISBN: 0-7434-0035-6

First Pocket Books printing January 2001

10 9 8 7 6 5 4 3 2 1

POCKET and colophon are registered
trademarks of Simon & Schuster, Inc.

Front cover illustration by John Vairo, Jr.

Printed in the U.S.A.

For Sherry—
You complete me and make me
more than I ever was alone.

Acknowledgements to . . .

Lisa Clancy, who makes this one of the greatest jobs ever!

Micol Ostow, who keeps all things schedule rolling along with grace and charm!

Annette and Matt Price, big Buffy fans and owners of Speeding Bullet Comics in Norman, Oklahoma.

Lesley Alison Craven, because cousin Michael T. Leslie asked me to.

Chapter 1

"SHE WAS AFRAID," WILLOW ROSENBERG SAID AS SHE carefully made her way through the graveyard. Full night had descended an hour ago, and moonlight cast harsh black shadows of tombstones and crypts on the gray-lit cemetery grounds. Except for the places where families with flashlights and lanterns were gathered around the graves and tombs.

She pulled at the dark green sweater she wore in an effort to ward off the chill sweeping in across Sunnydale from the Pacific Ocean. It didn't help. Goosebumps still formed on top of goosebumps, and she didn't really think it was just the cold wind.

Part of the fear that filled her was from the graveyard. *No matter how well-kept and clean looking a graveyard is,* she thought, *the whole* Better Homes & Gardens *thing just kind of goes out the window when you know a vampire or some other creepy creature could be clawing its way up from a grave at any moment to suck your blood or try to steal your soul.*

The instant she realized that, Willow felt a little ashamed, especially when she noticed all the light from the flashlights and lanterns scattered around them in the graveyard. The families were all so busy. Tonight was a special night for the family members visiting the cemetery, a night of respect and love. The thought of a bereaved ancestor equipped with talons and fangs actually popping up from one of the crypts was just—just—

Willow giggled—a high, thin, nervous sound—before she clapped a hand over her mouth. She whipped her head around and glanced at her companions to see if they'd noticed.

Buffy Summers, blond and petite and wearing a to-die-for black calf-length leather coat, looked at her friend with concern. "Are you okay, Will?"

"I did that out loud, didn't I?" Willow asked, face burning with embarrassment under her hand. She could face down vampires and dread demons, but a social faux pas could still unnerve her.

Buffy hesitated and glanced at Angel, obviously not wanting to be the bearer of bad news.

Angel hesitated, then shrugged and gave a quick nod. "Yeah. Maybe a little."

"Oh. Sorry."

"It's okay," Angel said. "No harm done. I don't think anyone heard you but us." Tall and broad-shouldered, Angel's dark eyes reflected far-off thoughts and a total familiarity with guilt and pain.

After all, Willow thought, *being a vampire for over two hundred years, killing hundreds of people, then getting your soul back doesn't contribute to a happy, care-*

2

free existence. Or even a happy, carefree nonexistence. Or after-existence. Whatever.

"It's just this place," Willow said, "and all these people out here cleaning graves." She indicated all the families working on different grave sites. It was the first time she'd ever seen 409 and Fantastik spray cleaners, dishwashing gloves, and mops at a graveyard, and it was jarring. Some of the visitors just used brooms to sweep the grave sites and rake the leaves.

Buffy looked around and nodded. "All this neat-freakishness is really creeping me out. Earlier, a little old grandmother behind me pulled out a spray bottle and *hiss-hissed* a couple times and I almost clocked her before I realized she wasn't a vampire."

"That would have been not good," Willow agreed.

Buffy seemed a little perturbed at making the mistake, which Willow understood completely. Making mistakes equals unfun.

"You never really notice how much a spray bottle sounds like a vampire till you hear it in a graveyard," Buffy said. She knew a lot about vampires, and she was still learning about demons and other things that hunted, haunted, and otherwise lurked around the Hellmouth that Sunnydale had been built on.

She was the Slayer, the girl born to be the Chosen One, equipped with powers and abilities that allowed her to combat vampires and other deadly creatures. Those powers, however, didn't keep her from getting killed. Slayers, as a general rule, didn't die of old age.

The grave cleaning went on around them, with appropriate sounds of scrubbing and sweeping and raking. The activity filled the cemetery with unaccustomed noise, which somehow made it creepier. Most cemeteries Willow visited were quiet—at least until all the growling and gnashing of teeth started as vampires dug their way out of their graves before they went out hunting for victims.

"You said your friend was afraid," Angel reminded her.

"Well, she is," Willow confirmed, brushing a lock of auburn hair from her face.

"She told you that?" Angel asked.

"No. I could just tell."

Angel glanced around, appearing uneasy.

Willow knew he was looking for the thing to be afraid of. "She didn't tell me what she was afraid of. Exactly."

Angel looked back at her, obviously waiting.

"You know how you can just kind of tell things about a person?" Willow asked, trying to defend her statement. "Like when someone says they broke up with their boyfriend, but you know they're not telling the truth? That really he dumped her?"

A total lack of comprehension showed in Angel's dark eyes.

"Don't worry about it," Buffy said to Willow, then turned to Angel. "It's not a guy power."

Angel nodded, then glanced at Willow again. "So your friend told you she *wasn't* afraid to come to the cemetery tonight? Only you knew that she was?"

"Not quite." Willow took a deep breath. *Why is it guys just never can get the easy things in life? Like basic uncommunicated communication? The things you aren't supposed to know, but do, but also understand you're not supposed to talk about. At least, not with that person who told you, but really didn't tell you.* "She told me she *was* afraid."

"Which means she wasn't," Angel said, trying desperately to catch up to the logic.

"No," Willow replied, "Jia Li told me she was afraid,

4

trying to let me think it was all a big joke so I wouldn't notice she was trying to act like she wasn't afraid when she really was."

Angel gave her a crinkly-eyed, crooked-lipped *huh?* expression that sort of reminded Willow of a confused, whipped puppy. Not that Willow would ever whip a puppy, but she'd seen them scared before. Oz, her boyfriend, got that look every now and then right before he turned into a werewolf. It was always a moment of serious cuteness that was cut short by the *I'm-a-ravenous-beast-gonna-swallow-your-head* growl.

"Look, guys, at this rate I'm going to need a scorecard." Angel was definitely lost, but he didn't sound aggravated, which was way cool in Willow's book.

Buffy smiled up at him and put her arm through his. "We're here to check on Willow's friend. Just to make sure nothing weird or creepy is out here to get her."

Angel nodded. "Okay. I can deal."

"We," Buffy corrected. *"We* can deal. I asked you along, remember? So technically this is my party."

"Sure," Angel said.

Buffy grinned at him. "But don't worry. Tonight I'm feeling generous. I promise to share any creepy things we come across."

"Vampires aren't exactly party favors," Willow pointed out, not feeling as confident as her friend. But that was the Buffy she knew, the one always ready with a joke or a comeback. *Well, ready most of the time, and funny most of the time.*

"Oh, I don't know," Buffy said, taking her stake from her coat pocket. "When they meet Mr. Pointy and explode into dust, they kind of remind me of piñatas. Only without the treats." She returned the stake to its hiding place.

"Do you know where your friend is?" Angel asked.

Willow pointed ahead. "At that end of the graveyard. I checked the graveyard plot location records on my computer when I got home from school. The family grave is down that way." She started walking again and they followed.

"What's your friend's name?" Angel prompted.

Willow let out her breath, thinking calm thoughts. "Jia Li."

"Jia Li what?"

"Jia Li Rong," Willow said. "That's why I thought I had the right grave."

"Because it was the only Rong one?"

Buffy waved at the dozens of graves around them. "If there's only one right grave, there's a whole lot of wrong ones."

"Willow looked up the Rong grave," Angel explained. "R-O-N-G. Rong."

Buffy blinked. "Oh."

"It's a Chinese name," Willow explained. "Jia Li is Chinese."

The Emerald Lotus Cemetery wasn't just for Chinese families, Willow knew from her research earlier. It wasn't even only for Asian families. But back when this section of Sunnydale was being built, there were a lot of Chinese families who worked on railroads in the nineteenth century and settled in the area. There had been a lot of prejudice back in those days and there had been separate graveyards. Now, the Emerald Lotus Cemetery was a historical landmark from early Sunnydale.

"Jai Li said she always liked the name Mandy," Willow said. "Her mom liked Barry Manilow and was always singing that song. Jia Li says the only reason her mother didn't name her Mandy was because of her father. Her father didn't like American names."

"Well, that kind of works out," Buffy said. "Mandy Rong just sounds that way. Jia Li Rong sounds way cooler."

"That's what I told her." Willow smiled, glad to find something they could agree on.

They walked through the graveyard, passing a number of graves that showed signs of cleaning. Several of them had imitation paper money, small rice cakes, and other items decorating the graves. Families stood around grave sites and sang or talked or prayed quietly. Candle flames on top of tombstones fluttered in the wind.

"What's with all the cleaning?" Buffy asked.

"It's April fifth," Willow replied.

"Okay, and . . ."

The path Willow was following dead-ended at a huge crypt constructed of gray and black stone. Going around to the left would have meant intruding on a family ceremony that included several weeping members. Willow guessed that this ancestor was recently departed. Choosing not to interrupt, she headed around the crypt to the right, toward the shadows at the back of the cemetery.

"April fifth this year," Willow explained, "is Ching Ming." At their identical, prompting looks, she went on. "Ching Ming is the traditional Chinese grave-sweeping day. Kind of like Memorial Day here. Only with cleaning and munchies." At the end of the crypt, the path wound around to the ten-foot tall honeysuckle-covered wrought iron fence. Dark forest lay beyond the fence, and farther beyond that were the lights of downtown Sunnydale.

"What is your friend afraid of?"

"She's never visited this ancestor's grave before." Willow turned and walked along the fence. The heady honeysuckle scent was almost overpowering.

"So?"

"So," Willow said, brushing some of the honeysuckle aside so she could pass more easily, "she's afraid."

"Of what?"

"Her ancestor."

"If this great-great-great-great-granduncle died one hundred and fifty years ago," Buffy said, "I don't think he's going to be much of a threat. Unless he's a vampire."

"Nope." At least, Willow was pretty sure he wasn't a vampire.

"And," Buffy went on, "why would he want to hurt Jia Li? They didn't even know each other."

"No, but Jia Li's ancestor was killed or murdered."

"Still in the dark here," Buffy said. "More than just the shadowy, crawling with honeysuckle, end of the graveyard dark, I mean."

"There's a Chinese belief," Angel put in quietly, "that if a person is murdered or dies an untimely death he or she will return as a hungry ghost, an orphan soul doomed to wander as a semiconscious entity."

"Now there's a real career goal," Buffy commented.

"But the bad part is," Willow said, "that hungry ghosts, also called *guei* in Chinese, are resentful and confused. They try to take out their frustration by injuring or possessing the bodies of family members because they haven't seen to it their souls are put to rest. The Chinese even have a special ceremony in October to deal with the *guei*."

"Getting a really gross picture of the *gooey* in my mind," Buffy said.

"They're not really a problem," Willow said. "At least, not after you exorcised them or conducted the ceremony of Universal Salvation." She shrugged. "I guess I researched a little extra on the Internet."

"Bonus points, overachiever. So Jia Li is afraid of visiting this ancestor's grave exactly why?"

"She didn't say, but I guess it's because she's afraid that he could turn out to be a hungry ghost. None of the family has ever been here before. They moved here just before Christmas."

"Really?"

"Yeah," Willow said. "Her brother, Lok?"

"I know Lok Rong."

The disgusted tone in Buffy's voice told Willow that her friend really had met Lok. He kind of left that impression on nearly everybody—especially girls. "Well, Lok was getting into some trouble over there and Jia Li's dad got the opportunity to set up business here. So they moved."

"That's cool. So what kind of business?"

"A restaurant. The Topaz Dragon."

"I've heard of it. Haven't been there."

Willow stepped over a pothole. "Oh, you should go there sometime. They've got really great food."

"I will."

Angel cleared his throat, which was kind of tricky, Willow thought, because as a vampire he didn't need to breathe, so probably throat clearing wasn't a thing he did very often.

"Maybe we could stick to the agenda here just a little longer," Angel suggested. "How did the ancestor die?"

"Don't know. Didn't ask. That seemed kind of personal. Just picked up on the fear factor I was getting from Jia Li and did a little snooping. I thought since you guys were going to be on patrol tonight anyway that it would be no big deal to swing by here, make sure everything was okay." Willow continued making her way along the fence, conscious of the fact that as carefully as she went, she was the only one making noise. Buffy and Angel moved as silently as shadows. "She's my friend."

9

"I'm always there for a friend, Will," Buffy said. "Even a friend of a friend. You know that."

Yeah, but I also know you were looking for some alone-time with Angel, Willow thought. She felt bad about interrupting that because her friends already had enough hardships in their lives without her asking them along on what might ultimately be a snipe hunt.

Since Angel's return to living—as living as living could be for a vampire cursed with having his soul returned along with the memory of all the terrible things he'd done while he'd been without it—and to Sunnydale, his relationship with Buffy had been tense at best. They loved each other without question, but they had to constantly be aware of what that love would do to them if they allowed it to take over their lives again.

"Did you tell Oz you were coming out here?" Buffy asked.

Oz and Dingoes Ate My Baby were playing at the Bronze tonight. "Yeah. If he'd been able to get free, he said he'd have come with me. He didn't want me to go by myself. I told him you guys were going with me and he chilled. He figured as long as I was with you, I'd be fine."

"Maybe not." A shadowy figure stepped from the honeysuckle where it had been hiding. He was over six feet tall, dressed in a mud-stained Pacific Gas & Electric uniform. His hard hat sat on his head at a rakish angle, but the predatory features beneath it were pure vampire.

Three other men, also dressed in torn and ragged PG&E uniforms, fell in behind the first. They grinned, and a flashlight wielded by one of the distant grave cleaners caught them full across the mouth for just an instant, illuminating the massive fangs.

Willow stopped abruptly only a few feet away, heart pounding in her chest. *No matter how many times you*

faced vampires, there was no way to really get used to it.
"Buffy, do you remember the power company workers
that got trapped in the mudslide a few weeks ago and
have been missing ever since?" She pointed. "I think we
found them."

"No way, girl," the lead vampire said. "We found you
first. I told my buddies that this old cemetery would be
jumping tonight with it being Ching Ming Day and all."
High ridges formed along his cheekbones and forehead,
and around his cruelly curved mouth. His eyes burned
with catlike intensity. "Figured we'd dig up something to
snack on."

"That's too bad," Buffy said, stepping up beside Willow with Mr. Pointy hidden at her side. "The kitchen is
closed."

Chapter 2

Buffy took another step, this one directly in front of Willow. The move put Buffy more or less within striking distance of the lead vampire. In the distance she could hear families singing, their voices raised enough that the conversation with the vampire went unnoticed.

The patch over the lead vampire's breast pocket read MORT. He glided to his right, stepping away from the fence, his hands held before him. His vampiric speed and strength lent him grace he didn't have when he'd been alive. Nothing human moved that well.

Buffy kept pace with him easily, showing him her open left hand and forearm raised to block. Her Slayer senses flared out, reading her opponents and the terrain she'd been given to fight on. At the moment, the confrontation remained out of sight of the families cleaning the graves of their ancestors.

Two of the vampires behind Mort carried fire axes, blades on one side with cruelly curved hooks on the other. The last of the four wielded a sledgehammer.

"Got a thing for one-liners, do you?" Mort asked.

Buffy shook her head. "Nope. No cool points. Strictly B-movie status. A time-killer till you start to make the biggest mistake you've made since crawling back out of the grave." She sensed Angel moving, knowing he was hustling Willow out of the way. The Slayer could feel him covering her back.

"Uh, Buffy," Willow called.

"Busy, Will," Buffy replied, watching the body language of the four vampires in front of her.

"Just wanted to remind you—" Willow started.

A gust of wind that pushed against the chill ocean breeze, too slight to be noticed by human senses, washed over Buffy, warning her that a large body flew toward her from the fence. She glanced up, already shifting her weight to the left, away from the approaching body.

The vampire sailed at the Slayer from the top of the cemetery fence like a missile. Behind the female vampire's outstretched hands tipped with sharp nails, her face was a mask of bloodlust. She wore a PG&E uniform as well. In life she'd been maybe thirty years old, maybe somebody's mom. But in death she was a monster bent on slaking her inhuman thirst.

"—that there were *six* PG&E employees that were lost in that mudslide," Willow finished.

Buffy swung her right foot back, bringing her body around and squaring up with the vampire hurtling toward her. She knew she couldn't hope to stand her ground against the female vampire, but she didn't want to go down and get her arms trapped on impact.

The female vampire—THERESA, read the patch—snarled angrily as Buffy ducked under her hands. Unable to completely escape her attacker or bring Mr. Pointy into play quickly enough, the Slayer gripped the female vampire's throat with her free hand. Buffy tightened her grip on her opponent's throat and yanked, dropping to her knees as the female vampire crashed into her.

The vampire's momentum bowled them both over and knocked them to the ground. However, with Buffy holding onto her, the vampire landed on her head with a bone-jarring thump that would have killed a normal person.

That's gotta hurt, Buffy thought, rolling from the impact and struggling to stay on top as they slid through the grass. She sensed Mort already in motion, closing in on her from the back. Then that sensation was gone, and Buffy knew Angel had waded into the fight.

The female vampire hissed and spat and snarled, thoroughly put out at the turn of events. The singing from the families was loud enough to cover any sounds of the struggle, but it was pretty bizarre fighting a vampire in a cemetery to a soundtrack that Buffy didn't recognize.

Buffy rolled and twisted, avoiding the snapping fangs and the gouging nails. They came to a sudden stop against a cross-shaped tombstone.

Hand still gripping the female vampire's throat, legs scissored around the creature's waist to pin her, the Slayer avoided the hands that reached for her and brought Mr. Pointy down hard. The wooden stake cracked the vampire's sternum and plunged through the dead, vampiric heart.

"No!" the vampire screamed in pain and disbelief as she gazed down at the stake.

"See ya," Buffy quipped. "Wouldn't want to be ya."

The vampire turned to dust.

Buffy caught a shadow rushing toward her from behind out of the corner of her eye. She moved, throwing herself into a short roll to the left that brought her to her feet.

Unfortunately, she dropped Mr. Pointy along the way.

One of the vampires with the fire axes brought his weapon down where she'd been only a heartbeat before. The keen ax blade split the hard ground of the old grave with a meaty smack.

While the vampire was trying to free his weapon from the ground, the Slayer seized his shirt and ran him head-first into the cross-shaped tombstone. The vampire's dead flesh cooked and sizzled, and he snarled pain-filled curses as smoke curled up around his head.

Buffy glanced over her shoulder and saw that Angel had engaged Mort and the other two vampires that had confronted them. The remaining vampire was after Willow, who was running for all she was worth.

"Bitch!" the vampire snarled, lashing out and catching Buffy on the jaw with the ax handle.

Pain exploded inside Buffy's skull as she fell back. For a moment she thought her jaw was broken. Black spots swirled in her vision, interrupted by the gleam of moonlight on the vampire's ax as he swung it at her head.

Buffy turned her head, narrowly avoiding the sharp edge, feeling the impact thrum through the ground. The vampire tore the ax free and raised it. Buffy kicked him in the crotch, driving him back.

As she rolled to her feet, Buffy remembered how close the ax had come to her head. She ran a hand through her hair. *Not the hair!* It was one thing to show up at school with the occasional color-clashing bruise or looking like she hadn't slept in days, but having her hair whacked off by an ax-slinging vampire would just be too much. Thankfully, it was still in place. Aveda could only fix so much.

The vampire came at her again, mouth open and hungry, the ax lifted high above his head.

Bouncing lightly on her toes, getting her balance, Buffy sprinted toward the vampire, totally locked into Slayer mode. Nothing else existed for the moment but the kill. She put one foot against the vampire's chest before he could bring the ax down, then kicked him in the face with her other foot. He brought the ax down even as his head snapped back.

Still in motion, Buffy took her foot from his chest and kicked the ax handle as the weapon came down. The ax handle splintered, leaving the vampire holding only a few inches of wood. She brought her hands together on both sides of the ax head, stopping it less than a foot in front of her face. She still managed to pull her knees in and, using the momentum she'd built by running up the vampire's body, managed to flip and land on her feet facing her opponent.

"You're not human," the vampire croaked in shocked surprise.

"Surprise," Buffy said. She reversed the piece of the fire ax she held, gripping the steel head in one hand and ramming the splintered end forward.

The wooden shards pierced the vampire's heart and he died a final death.

Pulling the axe handle back toward her, Buffy spotted Angel forced up against the cemetery fence. She sprinted through the swirling dust that had been the vampire. She found Mr. Pointy along the way, scooping the stake from the ground without slowing.

Angel swung an elbow in a hard, vicious arc that caught one of the vampires in the face with a sharp, bone-breaking crack. One of the vampires took advantage while Angel was off-balance and punched him in the throat. If Angel hadn't been a vampire himself, the blow would have killed him. Another vampire and the vampire with the remaining fire ax grabbed Angel's arms, pinning him for the vampire with the sledgehammer. The vampire raised the sledgehammer as Angel struggled to get free.

Before she reached Angel's side, Buffy saw the vampire chasing Willow suddenly catch her and drag her down, clapping a hand over her mouth to cut off any screams she might make.

Who to save?

That was a really big thing that a Watcher never trained a Slayer on. Not that the Watchers Council was exactly supervising the training Buffy was getting these days.

"Angel!" Buffy cried. She broke her stride, going into a baseball pitcher stretch, bringing the handle far behind her head. She let her momentum carry her forward in a short crow-hop, targeting the vampire with the fire ax because his back was presented most clearly to her. She rocked forward on her left foot and brought her right hand straight over her shoulder, releasing the handle at eye level, and dragging her knuckles across her boot toe on the follow-through.

The wood flipped through the air three times before burying between the fire ax-wielding vampire's shoulder blades. The vampire turned to dust even as Buffy recovered her balance.

"Go!" Angel said, dodging the sledgehammer and pulling the vampire holding his other hand off-balance.

Buffy ran. Normally, Willow might have had a chance against the vampire, and maybe she still did. But Buffy was unwilling to take the chance. Will was pretty much defenseless without a stake or the chance to get to the one she carried in her bag. That bag now sat on the ground back at the spot where they'd first been attacked.

By the time the Slayer reached Willow, Mort had straddled her, pinning her to the ground, holding her wrists together in one large hand above her head. The vampire pushed Willow's head up with the other hand, his fingers still clapped over her mouth.

Willow's eyes widened when she saw Buffy.

Tempering the anger that was unleashed inside her until it was as much a weapon as anything else in her arsenal, Buffy hooked an arm under Mort's throat, turned and slammed her hip into him, and flipped him away.

The vampire rolled, sprawled, then looked up at her with sheer hatred burning in his bestial gaze. "You're going to regret that."

"No," Buffy assured him, dropping into a loose stance, her hands curled into fists. "One shower and you're not going to leave as much of an impression as a bad dream."

Mort shoved himself up and came at her. He was more deliberate this time, setting up in a martial arts stance. He bounced athletically on his toes, his vampirism making the motions totally fluid. "Big mistake, little girl. I was champion at my tae kwon do dojo for five years running."

"Tae kwon do?" Buffy asked. "I've seen it. It's fun to watch." She exploded off her feet, taking the fight to him, the memory of Willow lying helpless under him making her strong. She punched and counter-punched, driving blows against his defense, battering him back, occasionally getting a punch or a jab inside that snapped his head back or connected with his midsection.

Buffy slowed her attack, setting him up, letting him become the aggressor. The confidence returned to him quickly. He punched and kicked at her, but she managed to stay just out of his reach. She had the rhythm now, even when he tried to escalate it. He was all about power and intimidation, skilled, but lacking in finesse.

Mort stamp-kicked at her, setting her up to move to the side, which she did. He swung a spinning backfist blow that he intended to crush her temple with. Instead, Buffy let the vampire's huge right fist skim by just over her head. She turned, corkscrewing her hips, elevating her left foot and bringing the heel down hard on the vampire's right shoulder.

Bone splintered and Buffy knew she'd broken the collarbone and maybe done some serious damage to the shoulder socket as well.

Some of the confidence deserted Mort then, leaving him wilted. He tried to set himself, unable to use his right arm.

Buffy spun again and kicked the vampire's right knee from the side. The joint shattered, going to pieces in rapid-fire pops. The Slayer mercilessly advanced, thinking of how Willow must have felt in those few heartbeats at being helpless in the vampire's grip, wondering how many others had felt that fear over the last few days.

"Buffy," Willow called. She stood only a couple feet away, holding a cross-shaped arrangement of plastic white roses. "Wood." She tossed the flowers over.

Buffy caught the arrangement just as Mort lunged desperately at her. The Slayer held the flowers in one hand and captured the vampire's injured arm by the wrist. She stepped forward and twisted it behind him, forcing him to the ground. In the next instant she brought the flower arrangement down. The wooden base penetrated the vampire's back and pierced his heart.

Mort opened his mouth to scream, but he turned to dust before he could cry out.

Brushing herself off as she got to her feet, Buffy stared at the flower arrangement quivering in the ground. She hadn't known she'd struck that hard. "Well," she said, "there's a sure indication that things have got to get better. Everything's coming up roses."

"Here comes Angel," Willow said.

Buffy nodded. She'd already known that. Even though Angel moved without making a sound, her personal sense of him had let her know he was approaching.

He looked only a little disheveled when he handed Mr. Pointy back to Buffy. "Well, that was fun."

"Told you I would share." Buffy smiled. When he smiled back, the far-off lantern and flashlights reflecting in his eyes, she could feel her heart *ker-thump!* in her chest. No one had ever made her feel that way before. She put a hand on Mr. Pointy tucked safely in her waistband. It was reassuring. "Well, come on and let's go find out if the Rong grave is."

The right grave *was* Rong, as it turned out.

"You know Jia Li from school, right?" Willow asked.

Buffy looked at the slender, petite Asian girl dressed in a black and red plaid skirt, red blouse and black jacket, and nodded. Jia Li was a junior, a grade level behind Buffy's class. "I've seen her in the halls, but I've never really talked to her," Buffy said.

"That's understandable," Willow whispered. "She's kind of shy. It's one of the things I like about her. And she's really good with computers."

Willow pointed out the other people. Shaozu Rong, Jia Li's father, was only a few inches over five feet tall, with a broad, lined face that had heavy worry wrinkles, and salt and pepper hair he kept neatly parted. He wore a black business suit. His wife, Bok-Hyun Rong, had her hair pulled up into a bun, fixed with traditional needles, gray showing at the temples. She wore a black dress and wore a long coat, holding her hands inside a muff. There were three smaller Rong children, two boys and a girl, also dressed in black.

Lok Rong stood apart from the rest of the family, the frown on his face telling Buffy he definitely wasn't there by choice. He was dressed in khaki convertible cargo pants, a bright red snowboarding tee shirt, scuffed Doc Martens, and a bright yellow nylon jacket. He wore his short-cropped hair in a skater cut, dyed scarlet on the ends.

A sophomore at the local college, Lok was an explosive basketball player, Buffy had heard, with enough talent and skill to walk onto the court and get the attention of every coach there. That talent and skill had put Lok at odds with most of the players, and his abrasive personality had guaranteed problems.

Buffy knew that he'd already been suspended from the university twice for three days for fighting. The coaches had stepped in and made sure the punishment was nothing more than a slap on the wrist even though one of the guys Lok had fought had ended up in the emergency room. Buffy had seen Lok a few times when he had picked up Jia Li from Sunnydale High. Lok never failed to go out of his way to antagonize someone. Xander Harris didn't care for Lok at all, and even Oz, who had the coolest head of anyone Buffy knew, avoided him.

Jia Li and her family gathered around a plot marked only by a small stone plaque set squarely in the ground. Mr. Rong knelt with a pair of pruning shears, delicately cutting the grass away from the plaque. Mrs. Rong held the Chinese lantern to light the area for her husband.

"Their relative," Willow whispered as they stood down the hill from the Rong family under a small pine tree, "came to America during the gold rush. Jia Li said he worked on the railroad. I don't know if he was murdered. I just know he died before his time."

"His ghost would return and haunt the family because he died accidentally?" Buffy had a sudden vision of all the accidental deaths that happened every year ganging up on the living. That would be nothing less than total chaos.

"That's what they believe," Willow said. "Maybe it doesn't really happen. Or maybe it only happens sometimes and they don't want to take chances. It has been a hundred and fifty years."

Buffy glanced around at all the families cleaning the different grave sites in the cemetery. "Whether it does happen or it doesn't, there are a lot of people out here who believe it can." Since she'd stepped into her role as the Slayer, she'd learned any number of impossible things happened.

"It does happen," Angel stated quietly.

Buffy looked at him.

"I saw a *guei* once, but I didn't know what she was until later."

"*She?*" Buffy asked, trying to keep her voice light. With a two hundred-plus year history, Angel had known a number of women—in all senses of the word. But as Angelus, he hadn't cared for any of them, except perhaps his sire, Darla, the vampire who had turned him.

Willow and Angel both looked at her sharply.

Okay, Buffy thought, *so maybe the voice wasn't the lightest it could have been.* She smiled, waiting impatiently, and not daring to speak.

"I never even got her name," Angel said.

And, yes, I like that even less. Buffy felt her chest constrict. Despite best intentions and wishes since Angel's return, things hadn't been the same. Somehow they were closer than ever, while at the same time being more aware than ever of the rift between them and what they wanted.

It had been a bad thing for a Slayer to love a vampire,

kind of going against everything the Watchers Council believed should happen, but even worse for Angel to express that love physically. Nobody had counted on his return to the pure evil that was Angelus.

Some days when they talked, it seemed like they would never get past that. Just being close to each other drove them crazy, setting off sparks that would ignite fireworks that turned into nuclear bombs. But for the last couple days, being together had been great, almost stress-free. Kind of like turning the clock back and forgetting about all the Really Bad Things that could happen if they didn't keep their hands to themselves.

Buffy didn't want to let go of the warm glow she felt. She didn't know how long it might last, and there were so many things that threatened their relationship besides the curse that kept Angel in check.

"I saw the *guei* on a Chinese freighter while I was in Singapore," Angel went on. "She didn't smell like anything I'd ever been around before. I remember there was this scent, like bitter almonds and sweet rot all rolled into one."

Now that's positively stomach churning. Buffy felt better already. *No warm fuzzies there. Unless it was a fungus or mold.*

Up at the Rong grave site, Mr. and Mrs. Rong and Jia Li all lit candles on the gravestone while Lok and the three children watched, then knelt and held hands. Mr. Rong led them in singing as the children burned imitation money. Orange cinders rose into the night and flickered out.

"One of the vampires I was with told me she was a hungry ghost," Angel said quietly, "and that she was haunting one of the men aboard ship."

"Was she?" Willow asked, obviously entranced by the story.

"I don't know," Angel replied. "The ship sailed a couple hours later and I never saw her again."

Buffy continued watching the ceremony that Mr. Rong conducted. Mrs. Rong laid out rice cakes bound in dark scarlet napkins. Mr. Rong poured a small cup of wine and placed it on the grave, then added three loose cigarettes. Jia Li took out four candles and set them in wooden holders at the corners of the grave. Her hands shook and her face looked tight.

"Isn't it beautiful?" Willow whispered. "I mean, in between all the sheer creepiness of it?"

"Yeah," Buffy agreed.

Jia Li's hand kept shaking as she lit the candles. Mr. Rong knelt again and placed his hands together before him. He spoke in Chinese and the only thing Buffy understood was Lok's name.

Still outside the family, Lok snorted and spoke in English. "Not me. You can pray all you want to an empty grave, but I'm not joining you."

Mr. Rong's voice came back sharply, but he didn't look up at his son.

"No," Lok argued, "I'm not offering disrespect to the dead. There is no dead in that grave."

Mr. Rong spoke again.

"*You* be afraid of the *guei* all you want. I'm not going to."

Gracefully, Mr. Rong got to his feet. Serious intent lined his face. He spoke again, barking syllables.

Jia Li took one of her father's hands and talked to him softly. Her father shook her hands away, chastising her abruptly. Jia Li bowed her head and pulled her hands back.

"Look at them," Lok demanded, pointing to his mother and siblings. "You've got them scared of an empty grave. You should be the one who's ashamed."

Mr. Rong glanced around briefly, aware that other people were watching them now. He growled an order at his son.

Moving with the same easy grace he exhibited on a basketball court, Lok crossed over to the grave. He snatched up two of the cigarettes, sliding one behind his ear and taking up one of the candles to light the one between his lips.

"All this talk about this ancestor," Lok stated harshly, "and you're making no move to find out what really happened to him." He puffed on the cigarette and blew smoke in his father's face.

Mr. Rong spoke again.

"I'll be respectful when I feel like there's something to respect. And I'll speak English if I damn well feel like it. It's a new country. Learn the language. It's what they speak over here."

Without warning, Mr. Rong stepped forward and slapped his son's face.

Chapter 3

LOK'S HEAD TURNED WITH THE FORCE OF HIS FATHER'S blow. The cigarette flew from his mouth to the ground, leaving a spiraling trail of orange cinders.

Willow started forward but Buffy caught her friend by the shoulder. "Not our fight, Will," Buffy said gently.

"You know Lok's temper," Willow said. "And he's a lot bigger than his father."

At the graveside, Lok jerked his head back around. His eyes narrowed and he placed a palm against his cheek. He trembled with rage. "You protest so much to try to hang on to the old ways, yet you come here to this damned sacrilege the wealthy and privileged of this town have caused to be created to mollify our family."

Mr. Rong's gaze was steely and hard, but he didn't say anything.

"Our ancestor doesn't lie at rest in this grave," Lok continued. "His body was never recovered so it could be properly buried or returned to his family. To *our*

26

family. None of their bodies were. You know that's true."

Mr. Rong spoke again, his voice like chipped ice.

Buffy didn't need a translation for that short speech. She knew a warning when she heard it.

"No," Lok argued. "I'm not going to shut up. You can fool yourself that what you're doing here tonight is going to put Mei-Kao Rong's spirit to rest, but I know it's not true. Mei-Kao and the other men killed with him while digging in those mines to line the pockets of the whites aren't going to rest until they've had their revenge against the descendants of those families."

Wordlessly, Mr. Rong pointed away from the graveside. The three smaller children were crying, their fearful voices carrying plaintively. Jia Li and her mother tried to comfort them.

"Fine," Lok snapped. "Terrorize our family with these stories and this make-believe restitution. But I can't do that." He spun angrily on his heel and walked away, cursing at the people he caught looking at him.

A pale sliver of moonlight shone down on the grave, lending silver highlights to Jia Li and her three young siblings. She talked softly and soothingly to them while Mrs. Rong tentatively approached her husband.

"They're a really close family," Willow said. "All of them, even the little guys, work at the restaurant. Lok is the only one who doesn't fit in with the rest of the family."

"I can't imagine Lok fitting in anywhere," Buffy said.

"It's the pride between a father and son," Angel said quietly. "The father has to learn to let go gradually, and the son has to accept responsibilities that he's given. The father fears that he hasn't taught the son enough to survive, and the son fears that he's going to grow up with all the responsibilities of his father. When they don't agree on who is doing what part, it complicates everything."

Buffy looked into Angel's eyes and saw the deep hurt locked within him. She knew he'd fallen into Darla's arms and been turned after another of the long arguments he'd had with his own father. Shortly after that, with no soul and no tender feeling to stay his hand, Angel had killed his own family.

When she'd first learned of the murders, Buffy had been horrified. Then, when she'd come to truly understand Angel and his painful need for redemption, she'd also realized what a tragedy it had been.

Without a word, Buffy took Angel's hand in hers and held it. He squeezed back tenderly, and some of the pain faded from his gaze.

Slowly, the Rong family went back to praying. There were no more songs. After a few minutes, the family gathered their things and blew out the candles. Mr. Rong herded them all back to the front of the Emerald Lotus Cemetery, talking quietly to a few of the people he passed.

"No ghost," Buffy said. "I guess Jia Li was afraid for no reason."

"Well," Willow said, "there could have been a ghost."

"True." Buffy patted her friend on the shoulder, knowing as empathetic as Willow was that she would worry about Jia Li anyway. "There's always next year."

Willow looked at her.

"Okay," Buffy admitted, "so maybe there aren't exactly many ha-has to go around tonight."

"It's not you," Willow said, gazing toward the front of the cemetery. "There may not have been any *guei*—or is it *gueis?*"

Buffy shrugged. "Beats me, Will. Still haven't had my first yet."

"Whatever. What I'm saying is that even though we

28

didn't have to save Jia Li from a hungry ghost, she might still need a friend tonight."

"You're probably right."

"And you guys could use some alone-time patrolling." Willow looked at them. "I mean, you think you'll—I mean, that everything will—" She appeared flustered.

"You mean alone-time as in patrolling, staking the occasional vampire, and not giving in to a case of raging hormones?" Buffy asked.

"Yeah," Willow replied. "If it's polite to mean that. And I do, in the kindest, nonprying way I know how."

Buffy hugged her friend and smiled. Alone-time with Angel would be hard, but she felt she needed it so badly. "We've got more going for us than raging hormones. Right, Angel?" She glanced over her shoulder then saw that Angel had wandered delicately out of conversation range. "Guess we were getting a little too *Cosmo* for him."

"Embarrassed." Willow smiled, glancing at Angel.

"Yeah," Buffy agreed.

"Modesty's kind of nice to find in a guy these days."

"I know," Buffy said, smiling.

"Uh-oh."

"Uh-oh?" Buffy echoed.

"You've got a twinkle in your eye," Willow warned. "It could be the only warning you get before the raging hormones' preemptive strike."

"No preemptive strikes." Buffy held up a hand. "Promise."

"If you feel you're weakening, you'll call?"

"Yes."

"Pinkie swear?"

Buffy rolled her eyes. "If I have to."

Willow held up a pinkie.

Buffy swore, feeling kind of dumb but glad she had

someone like Willow who cared enough to be silly and serious. "Maybe you could get Jia Li out of the house and go down to the Bronze long enough to see Oz and the band playing."

Willow pulled her sweater tight again. "Don't think so. Jia Li's dad isn't big on Western culture. A club like the Bronze wouldn't even come close to being acceptable." She waved good-bye to Angel and turned to go.

"Willow," Angel called.

"Yeah?"

Angel nodded toward the Rong grave. "Do you know if it's really empty?"

"No. I didn't look that closely at the cemetery records. I can, if you think it's that important. Is it?"

Angel shook his head. "Curiosity, mostly."

"Okay." Willow said good-bye to him, hugged Buffy and left.

Buffy and Angel walked out of the cemetery to resume patrol on foot. "I guess we could stop by the Bronze in a little while," Buffy said. "Take in a song or two, then get back to patrolling."

"And if the vampires bite someone while you're listening to the band?"

Buffy frowned. "All work and no play makes Jill a dull girl?"

Angel shook his head.

"Spoilsport."

"Not entirely," Angel said. "We can still hold hands while we're on patrol."

"Hand-holding goes better with music," Buffy suggested as they passed through the cemetery gates.

"I'll hum."

Buffy rolled her eyes in mock fright. "Oh no! Anything but that."

"That kind of attitude will lose you the hand-holding privileges."

Buffy laughed, and the sound of it, even inappropriate as it was so close to the cemetery, felt good. She felt Angel take her hand, his flesh much more chilly than hers.

"We should develop a direction for the patrol," Angel suggested.

"I thought we had one," Buffy replied. "There's the convenience store on Maple that's selling the blood cones, then hit Willy's after the blood cone quick-stop."

"Okay," Angel agreed.

Buffy squeezed his hand and they kept walking like they could do it all night.

"No evil alien suit out to kill him?" Xander Harris asked suspiciously, tapping the colorful cover of the comic book he held.

"Nope," Matt Barker said, sliding another comic book into a plastic sleeve with a backer board. He wore a maroon shirt that advertised MATT'S COMICS on one side and a *Star Trek* communicator on the other. He was over six feet tall, with short-cropped black hair, a goatee, and glasses.

"No clones popping out of the closet?" Xander asked.

"No clones." Matt placed the protected comic on one of the shelves of the display counter where he kept his cash register. The comics shop was small and compact, narrow across and straight back. Comics hung from thumbtacks on the walls and filled boxes sitting on tables. An inflatable Wolverine hung in the front window facing the street, air-filled claws exposed and ready for action. The place just smelled like adventure, secret identities, and superpowers.

"Don't tell me he's got six arms again." Xander flipped through the comic, intent on finding the fatal flaw the new writer had picked for the series. "Although I don't know how they missed the deodorant commercials with that stunt."

"Nope," Matt said. "Just the two arms. Of course, in this incarnation, they're both on the same side."

Xander looked up, an *aha!* already on his lips and forefinger ready to emphasize.

"Kidding," Matt said.

"Not funny." Xander put away his unused forefinger.

"I guess it depends on which side of the counter you're standing on." Matt leaned on the counter. "I mean you, you're looking at the series again, now that it's gotten a new number one, and thinking, maybe I should buy this. Me, I'm watching you read my comic and thinking, maybe he should buy this, then take it home and read it."

Feeling a little guilty, Xander closed the comic and dropped it onto the counter. He pulled at the blue tee shirt with a large white star on the chest he wore under a Hawaiian shirt. "Look, over the years you've sold me comics that didn't live up to my expectations."

"They were good stories," Matt said.

"Yeah."

"But the resale value sucked."

"Right."

Matt shook his head. "Comics are no longer a speculator's market. They never were. Only now people are admitting it."

"I was going broke keeping up with the alternative covers," Xander agreed.

"Like I tell people," Matt said, "you only need the one copy to read and enjoy. If you don't like it, don't buy it. And reading it for free in my shop is not a great option. At least, not for me."

Xander glanced at the comic again, noting the action pose the red and blue clad hero struck. "I don't know. I remember reading this guy a couple years back, before he married M. J. supermodel. His life was always screwed up, which made him my kind of guy. I always thought of myself as him, only without the cool powers."

"His life is still screwed up."

"He's married to a supermodel pulling down really big bucks," Xander argued. "How screwed up can his life be?"

"He's not happy about it. He doesn't feel like he's pulling his own weight and M. J.'s gone a lot."

"I could think of worse things to be unhappy about," Xander said. "Like maybe living in your parents' basement because they fight all the time and they don't want to see you and you don't want to see them." *Do they do autobiographical comics?*

"What kind of power?"

"What?"

"Lives in the basement, can't stand his parents," Matt explained, "you've got me hooked so far. Now this guy needs a power, a thing he does."

"Hero stuff."

"Exactly."

Xander thought for a moment. "He fights evil."

"Evil's pretty generic," Matt pointed out. "Gimme a specific kind of evil."

"Demons," Xander said, thinking quickly. "Really mean, nasty demons the rest of the world denies is even there. He's like the last bastion of hope against these mighty demon hordes."

"Fine, so he fights demons. What does he fight them with?"

"A crystal ball," Xander said, warming to the subject.

"One that kind of floats around and follows him everywhere. It has demon-zapping powers."

Matt shrugged. "Maybe. Needs more work."

"You think?" Xander felt a little more excited than he had in days. High school graduation seemed right around the corner these days, and he couldn't really stand the thought of college. And what did that leave: *Would you like fries with that?* Nope, that thought just made his teeth ache. *But a comic book writer? Man, I could do that.*

"Definitely needs more work," Matt said. "With all the maybes in the comics industry right now, who knows?"

Xander turned his attention back to the comic. "Remember when they introduced the clone story line a while back? Then everybody started panicking because it was like they'd never had the original hero, just this fake the writers pulled out of a hat twenty years ago."

"I remember." Matt pointed back to the boxes. "Still have a few copies I can sell you."

"No way." Xander tapped the comic. "But that's how I feel when they roll out a new number one. Get out a new number one, squeeze out a few more bucks."

"That was part of the deal they cut with the writer," Matt said. "He wanted his own number one. Plus, Aunt May is back in this issue."

"You're kidding!" Xander opened the comic and started flipping through the pages again.

"You're the reason comics need to come to the store in sealed bags," Matt said pointedly.

Xander ignored the sarcasm. "The last time I read this book, Aunt May was dead." *Of course, about this same time last year, Angel was dead, too. Now look at him.* "How did they bring her back?"

"No explanation."

Xander scanned the comic panels. "Wonder if Aunt

May's the clone this time. Or maybe she was the clone last time." He glanced up. "You can drive yourself crazy thinking about this stuff after what we've been through with this guy."

"You could *buy* the issue and find out."

"You already told me it didn't reveal how Aunt May came back in this issue."

"It'll probably be revealed in the next issue," Matt said. "And how can you buy issue number two without owning issue number one?"

Xander closed the comic and looked at it. His part-time jobs pulled in some cash, but he couldn't go around spending it frivolously. The whole slayage thing with Buffy, Willow, Oz, Giles, and Angel again took up a lot of part-time job hours. Picking up a comic series at the moment was like a major responsibility. "How much?"

"Five bucks."

"That's more than the cover price and it just came out."

"That's the going price," Matt countered. "The publishers underprinted. That's a first edition."

Xander dickered a little more, but he knew he wasn't going to get anything but exercise. When Matt set a price, it wouldn't move one bit. Xander paid for the comic and negotiated a protective bag and backer board thrown in for free.

"Enjoy the comic," Matt said.

"I'll let you know," Xander threatened.

"Aunt May has a new hairdo."

"Really?" Xander looked at the comic again. "Man, they just never leave anything alone anymore, do they?"

Matt grinned at him, then pointed through the front glass of the comics shop. "Your friend is back."

Xander looked and saw Rupert Giles standing on the other side of the glass looking up at the air-filled

Wolverine figure. The Watcher wore a dark suit with a sweater vest. The light from the MATT'S COMICS sign sparkled on his gold-rimmed glasses. He looked like he'd stepped out of an upscale coffee ad instead of being the Sunnydale High School librarian.

"Yeah. Guess I gotta roll."

"I have to tell you," Matt told him, "that you're keeping different company these days." Matt had graduated Sunnydale High before Buffy and Giles had arrived there.

"You don't know the half of it," Xander promised. "But he's an okay guy."

"He went into Zolton's Mystic Tomes next door, right?" Matt shook his head. "Man, I've never understood that. That guy sells books on how to eviscerate corpses and store the organs in canopic jars in your backyard, and he's never once had the police invade *his* premises and search through *his* stock."

"That's because most of his books don't have full-color pictures." *Plus, most of the Sunnydale cops have learned to leave the really weird stuff alone out of self-preservation.*

"Interesting that you should know that."

"It's just that I sometimes help Giles look for stuff," Xander explained. "I'm a—a research assistant."

"And what do you research?"

"How to kill demons or send them back to whatever otherworld slimy pit they crawled out of to get here."

"There it is!" Matt exclaimed.

Xander looked over his shoulder and was ready to start moving in case it was closer than he thought. "There what is?"

"Your comic idea."

"It is?"

"Yeah," Matt said enthusiastically. "Kind of a Caped Crusader/Boy Wonder kind of thing about a school librarian and student moonlighting as demon hunters. Hey, I'd buy it if you made it fun enough."

"There's no fun in demon-hunting," Xander said. "It screws up your social life. Every girl you meet only wants one thing." He hesitated. "Well, actually one of three things." He ticked them off on his fingers. "Your blood, your heart, or your soul. The only lasting relationship they have in mind is some pact they made with a demon a thousand years ago or so. Trust me on that, okay?"

"Hey, I'm telling you, that's a great idea for a comics series. You should think about it."

I do, Xander thought. *Every night. That's why I sleep with a stake under my pillow.*

The bell over the door rang as Giles entered the store. "Xander, we really need to be going."

"I'm on my way." Xander said good-bye to Matt and joined Giles outside. They walked back toward Giles's ancient foreign car parked a couple blocks down. "You find what you were looking for?"

Giles shook his head. "Not really." He looked at Xander more closely. "You look depressed."

"I am," Xander admitted. "Totally. We're talking crying-in-my-Doritos bummed."

"Anything I can—?"

Xander shook his head. "Nothing. It's just that the end of everything is coming much sooner than I thought."

"The end of everything?" Giles looked alarmed, though Xander knew it wasn't because he thought the possibility remote.

"No, nothing to do with the Hellmouth," Xander explained.

"Then what is it?"

"Graduation is going to tear us apart."

Giles took his glasses off and cleaned them. "Perhaps

you're overreacting to this somewhat. I mean, a little paranoia and fear is normal at this time."

"I don't know if this is a little," Xander admitted. "I think about Buffy, Willow, and Oz going off to college—and me—" He shrugged. "And me—well—*not* going to college. It drives me crazy."

"I see." Giles cleared his throat, as if preparing to say one of the profound things he was really good at.

Xander waited hopefully.

"Graduation," Giles said finally, "can be a very traumatic thing."

"What?" Xander demanded. "No solution? No pat words of advice? Nothing to make me feel better?"

"Any solution," Giles said, "is going to have to come from within you, Xander."

"And what if all that's inside me is this scared teenager that I am now?" Xander couldn't believe he'd just said that, but that was what he'd been thinking and couldn't stop himself. "What if this is as good as it gets and the rest of my life is just a downward spiral?"

"It's not," Giles assured him.

"You don't know that."

"Yes, I do. I was there once, too, you know. It's a phase that passes, then you get on with the rest of your life."

Xander felt totally frustrated. "I'm so frustrated right now I could scream."

A scream echoed along the street.

Xander touched his lips and looked at Giles. "I didn't do that, did I? I mean, that sounded kind of high-pitched and . . . well, *feminine.*"

"It wasn't you." Giles stared past Xander. "It came from that alley." The Watcher ran toward the darkened mouth of the shadow-filled alley beside the soup-and-sandwich café next to Matt's Comics.

Xander shoved his comic down the back of his waistband and followed Giles closely.

The narrow alley held several Dumpsters, overflowing from the businesses on either side. A sour stench filled the still air in the alley. Feline shapes moved liquidly along the fire escape ladder and the Dumpsters. Their yellow and orange eyes glowed like dulled lamps.

At the end of the alley, a heavyset man stood over a woman lying prone on the ground. A small boy hunkered down beside her, pulling at her and trying to get her up. "Mommy, Mommy!" the little boy cried. "Come on! The bogeyman is going to get you! Mommy!"

Xander started forward, moving stealthily.

"We'll want to be careful," Giles whispered.

"Yeah," Xander replied, "and maybe quiet should figure in there, too." Cats hissed at them as they passed but the hulking shape towering over the fallen woman didn't seem to notice.

The heavyset man yanked the unconscious woman up easily, then turned her head to give him easier access to her neck.

The little boy cried and pulled on his mother's arm. "No! No! Please! Leggo, leggo!"

Moved by the little boy's passionate cries, Xander yelled, "Hey, you repugnant chunk of ambulatory pus! Let go of that woman!"

The heavyset man swung around like he was on swivels. His face looked like a gray-blue blob in death, but the vampiric ridges stood out starkly. He held the woman by the blouse in one massive hand. He grinned, baring his fangs. "You talking to me, blood bag?"

Chapter 4

XANDER SWALLOWED HARD AS HE STARED AT THE VAM-
pire in the alley before him. *Man, he's big. Besides becoming a vampire, he must have been bitten by a
radioactive rhino.*

"Would you mind telling me," Giles whispered at his
side, "when it was exactly that you decided the stealth
approach wasn't working?" He searched through the
refuse bin beside him and found a broken mop handle.

"He was going to bite her," Xander said defensively.
"I had to do something."

"I think we might have had time to get to him, without
being seen, before then." Giles swung the four-foot
length of wooden mop handle experimentally.

The little boy continued trying to free his mother and
calling out to her.

"You made a big mistake," the vampire suggested.
"Maybe it's not too late for you to leave."

Xander started digging through the Dumpster next to

him, looking desperately for a weapon. He pulled out a slimy banana peel and threw it to the ground. *Yuck! For a minute there, that felt like a severed ear. God, and am I sorry that I know for a fact what one of those feels like.* "Maybe it's not too late for *you* to leave." He tried to sound convincing.

"I'm not leaving," the vampire said.

"Neither are we," Xander declared bravely.

The vampire grinned and tilted his head. "Good. More for me."

"You have no idea who you're messing with," Xander stated. Styrofoam fast food cartons spilled out onto the ground at his feet. *Wood! Wood! There's gotta be something in here made out of wood!*

"This time of night," the vampire said, "you'd be dinner. First course or second course, that's up to you and your friend."

"We're friends of the Slayer." *Oh boy, now that sounds tough.*

"Never heard of him."

Xander felt slightly shocked. "You must be new at this."

The vampire left the unconscious woman and approached fearlessly. Giles brought the creature up short by jabbing the mop handle at him. The vampire swung a fist, but the Watcher quickly dodged backward.

"Xander," Giles called.

"Coming, coming. Keep your shirt on." Xander dug through the garbage faster, finally touching a wooden surface. Only when he pulled it up, it was a flimsy vegetable crate containing rotting lettuce. He started to throw it away in disgust, then noted the framing one-by-ones that were thick enough to be used as stakes.

Stepping to the side of the Dumpster, Xander swung the vegetable crate at the metal, smashing it. Wire bound the shattered remnants for an instant till he clawed free a piece nearly two feet long.

"Xander!"

Giles's warning came just in time. Xander ducked, throwing himself to one side and rolling. He pushed to his feet with the wooden stick in front of him. This wasn't working out so badly. It hadn't been all that long ago that he'd taken on Jack O'Toole and his merry band of zombies and put them away by himself. "Now," he crowed triumphantly, "we're gonna see whose—"

The vampire spun and yanked the stick from Xander's hand.

"Owwww!" Xander yelled, grabbing his hand. "Splinters!"

"Now we'll see who is gonna be the pincushion around here," the vampire taunted. He stabbed the stick at Xander.

Xander stumbled backward, windmilling his arms in an attempt to keep his balance. He crashed into a couple of old galvanized trash cans blotted with rust. He went down as the vampire came for him.

Giles rushed the creature from the back, but the vampire turned quickly and backhanded the Watcher across the alley.

Taking advantage of the brief respite, Xander flailed around and snared one of the metal trash can lids. He fit his hand through the dented handle and raised it just as the vampire stabbed at him again.

KA-LANG!

The stick punctured the rusted lid a full eight inches, coming to a stop only a couple inches from Xander's face. Xander swept the vampire's feet out from under him and shoved himself to his feet. By the time he stood, the vampire was on top of him again, raining blows with his massive fists. The trash can lid bent and twisted, quickly becoming misshapen. Ignoring the stinging splinters in his hand, Xander gripped the stick and pulled it free.

The vampire froze suddenly and looked down at the mop handle sticking through his chest. Then he got a really mad look on his face.

"Drat and damnation," Giles muttered, pulling it out, "I missed his heart."

"I won't!" the vampire roared. He whirled, grabbing Giles's jacket in one beefy paw before the Watcher could slip away.

"No," Xander said, stepping forward, "we're going to play nice." He swung the trash can lid into the vampire's face and was bummed when the metal only dented into a semiprofile of the creature's face.

The vampire smiled. "Got plenty of hurt to go around, blood bag." He reached for Xander.

Stepping behind the shield again, Xander batted the vampire's hands away, deflecting and defending to the best of his ability. His arms and shoulders ached from the punishing blows, and his ears throbbed with the metallic thunder of the blows against the metal lid.

Putting his weight behind the blow, the vampire punched the trash can lid, knocking Xander backward. Before the creature could move in for the kill, Giles attacked again from behind, putting the broken mop handle through the vampire's stomach from the back. The vampire pulled the mop handle on through, pulling Giles flush against his own back. The mop handle stuck out of his stomach. Before Giles could step back, the vampire seized him and spun him around in front of them. He bent the Watcher's head back, baring his throat.

Xander got to his feet and whipped the trash can lid behind him like an oversize Frisbee. "Hey, buttface!"

The vampire snarled and turned from Giles.

Torquing his body, rolling his arms and shoulder so he could put as much weight into it as possible, Xander threw the trash can lid. The heavy metal lid sailed across the distance and thudded into the vampire's face, knocking him backward.

Off-balance, the vampire released Giles and fell on his butt. His face was broken and blood-smeared, smashed in from the trash can lid. The lid caromed from the alley wall, waffling like an out of control UFO from an old *Lost in Space* episode, and clanked to the ground a few feet from Xander.

Giles retreated, frantically searching for a weapon.

"That hurt," the vampire snarled, pushing at his face as he got up. The dead flesh gradually resumed the shape it was in. "Time to die." He rushed at Xander.

Xander swept the trash can lid from the ground and flung it Frisbee-style at the pavement in front of the vampire's feet. Dented up as it was, the trash can lid proved hard and unwieldy to throw. Still, the lid clanked against the ground, kicked out a small shower of sparks, then arced back up into the vampire's ankles.

The vampire tripped, falling facedown onto the pavement in front of Xander. Knowing he couldn't leave the unconscious mother and her young son to their fates, Xander dove on the stunned vampire, locked his hands around the mop handle and wrenched it free from under the creature's body. The fall had snapped the mop handle off, leaving little more than a foot intact.

On his knees, both hands wrapped around the wood, Xander waited till the dazed vampire rolled over onto his back. The hellish eyes gazed up at Xander, and Xander knew the grin he was wearing was the last thing the vampire was going to see. Xander brought the stake down, pushing on through the vampire's heart.

The vampire opened its mouth to scream, then promptly turned to dust.

Xander turned his face away from the noxious clouds, breathing hard and covered with perspiration despite the chill that hung over Sunnydale. He staggered to his feet and headed for Giles. "Are you all right?"

"Well," the Watcher said. "I've certainly been better. Did you get him?"

"*We* got him. He's dust." After helping Giles to his feet, Xander walked over to the little boy. The mother was only unconscious, a bruise already forming on her chin.

"My mommy," the little boy sobbed. "He hit her."

"I know," Xander said calmly as he hunkered down on the other side of the woman and took the little boy's hand. "But it's going to be all right. I promise." He pulled the boy's hand in front of his mother's face. "See? Your mom's breathing fine. Feel her breath? She's going to be okay. She's just sleeping now. She'll wake up in just a little while. Until then, we're going to get some help for her, okay?"

The little boy quieted a little and nodded. "I knew everything was going to be okay when I saw you."

Xander was stunned. "You did?"

"Uh huh." The little boy touched the white star on Xander's blue shirt. "I read all your comics. The bad guys never win when you're around."

Suddenly, Xander understood. "I'm not that guy. This is just a tee shirt."

"It's okay." The little boy still held onto Xander's hand with one of his but used the other to brush his tears away. "I know all about secret identities and how important they are. I guess you didn't have time to change all

45

the way into your costume before you came to save me. But don't worry, I won't tell anybody."

The complete trust Xander saw in the little boy's gaze unnerved him. He couldn't use his voice for a moment. He swallowed hard. "I'm going to need to go find help. I'm going to leave you with my friend for a second."

"No!" The little boy looked up at Xander. "Please. My mommy has a cell phone in her purse. You can call 911. She won't mind, honest."

"I've got it," Giles said, picking up the woman's purse. He took the phone out and made the call, telling the dispatcher that there'd been a mugging.

Quietly, the little boy stepped over his mother and nestled inside Xander's arms. Xander suddenly felt awkward and inept, but at the same time there was a sense of satisfaction and well-being.

Xander looked up at Giles. "It's going to go on, isn't it?"

"The fight against darkness and all the evil things that dwell in it?" Giles's gaze turned soft and sympathetic. "Did you think it was going to end on graduation day?"

"I don't think I've been thinking much past graduation day," Xander admitted.

"You've been inadvertently caught up in something, Xander. And once you're in it, it doesn't let go."

"So there's always something out there for me," Xander realized.

"Yes, well, I suppose that is one way of looking at it," Giles admitted after a moment. "You have to remember that whatever it is waiting out there, it isn't waiting with your best interests in mind."

"That's cool," Xander said. "It probably sounds pretty sicko, but it's kind of nice to know that something's out there."

"Something's always out there for all of us," Giles said. "It's just that most people don't realize that."

Willow stood in front of the Topaz Dragon restaurant in downtown Sunnydale. The restaurant closed its doors at nine sharp during weekdays, and with this being Easter Monday and a long weekend for some people, business was a little quieter than normal.

An amber neon dragon blazed on the sign in front of the restaurant, rearing in fierce glory. Fire blew from its nostrils every few seconds, captured in red, pulsing neon light. The landscaping in front of the restaurant was beautiful, designed and primarily cared for by Mrs. Rong. In between vampire hunting and homework and seeing Oz, Willow had helped out in the gardens a few times.

A police cruiser whipped by with its lights on and siren going full-blast, startling Willow. It wasn't an uncommon occurrence in the town, so it only worried her for a moment even after the confrontation at the Emerald Lotus Cemetery.

She took another deep breath and released it, then glanced around the well-lit parking lot. *Okay, there's nothing there. Let's go.*

She kept her purse open so she could easily get to the stake inside. The flight of stairs at the back of the Topaz Dragon led up to the floor where the Rong family lived.

When they'd moved into the building, Mr. Rong had built a tiny receiving area before the front door, then put in a postage stamp-size rock garden with a small pool stocked with colorful goldfish. Pots held camphor trees, bleeding hearts, tulips, and jasmines. Oriental lanterns hung from the thatched roof. People who were impressed by the restaurant, Willow often thought, would be so blown away by the residence few of them ever got to see.

Soft, golden light seeped through the delicate windows on either side of the door. Willow stopped and took a deep breath. *I could really be stepping over my boundaries tonight.* The Rongs were a private family, and usually guests had to be announced well in advance.

Willow pressed the doorbell, listened to it *bong* cheerily within, then waited nervously.

The lantern by the door flashed on. Mr. Rong opened the door but left the screen door closed. Surprise registered on his face. "Good evening, Willow. Is something wrong?"

"No."

Mr. Rong gazed out the door, looking carefully to both sides. "Since I did not know you were coming, I thought perhaps there had been some trouble."

"No. Look." Willow reminded herself to breathe. It wasn't that the Rong parents were especially harsh, but she knew with them working at the restaurant all day and taking care of three small children that they depended on their schedules being observed. "I'm really sorry about coming by so late."

"Yes." Mr. Rong consulted his watch. "It is ten twenty-five. I would think you would be home with your studies." He looked back at her. "If you were up at all. School comes early."

Not as early for me as it does for Jia Li. Willow knew from past experience that her friend got up at six every day to help her family get the daily menu started at the restaurant. Of course, Jia Li didn't spend a lot of nights out staking vampires or stalking whatever new ghastly ghoulie decided to wander through Sunnydale.

"I had some questions about some homework," Willow began, feeling absolutely awful about lying. It was so hard to do, and got worse every time it had to be done. And then there was all that remembering of who was told what and when.

"Homework?" Mr. Rong repeated.

He knows I'm lying! Everyone always knows when I'm lying! Panic tightened Willow's throat. "Actually, that's not true."

"It isn't?"

"No. I feel really bad about this, but Jia Li seemed kind of nervous about going out to the cemetery today. I just wanted to make sure she was all right."

"She is quite all right. Thank you. But you should get along home now."

"Husband," Mrs. Rong called, approaching from the hallway behind Mr. Rong. "Who is at the door?"

Mr. Rong answered her, then they had a short conversation in Chinese. Mr. Rong seemed unhappy about the outcome, but took his hat from beside the door and clapped it onto his head.

"My wife," Mr. Rong said, "feels that your presence in our home tonight might serve as a balm for our oldest daughter. So please enter, Willow." He held the door open.

Willow stepped into the home, not knowing whether to feel invited or not. *Only a vampire would have known for sure,* she thought.

"I am going down to help with closing the restaurant," Mr. Rong said. "Good-bye." He went down the steps.

"My husband," Mrs. Rong said affectionately, leading Willow through the immaculately kept house, "still doesn't completely understand his daughter's heart even after all my counseling, which he wisely takes."

The living room just off the foyer was beautifully furnished in black and red sofa and lacquered table. Dozens of butterflies decorated the furniture and vases, and were pressed under glass picture frames on the wall.

Mrs. Rong paused at the door of the bedroom Jia Li shared with her five-year-old sister. She smiled gently at Willow. "My eldest daughter was disturbed by tonight's visit, though my husband might not acknowledge it. I think she wouldn't mind a little company."

"Thanks," Willow said. "I knew she looked really upset tonight."

Mrs. Rong looked at her curiously.

"I mean, she looked really upset in *school* today *about* tonight. That's what I meant. Really."

"Of course. She is lucky to have a friend like you who cares so much." Mrs. Rong knocked on the door.

Jia Li answered and there was another brief conversation Willow didn't understand except for her own name. Then Jia Li opened the door.

"Hi," Willow said, smiling. "Surprise."

"Only for a short time, though," Mrs. Rong admonished. She left them.

"Did I come at a bad time?" Willow asked.

Jia Li wore a jade nightgown and robe. "No. I'm just surprised that my father let you in." She opened the door and stepped back.

Willow entered the bedroom, familiar with the cramped space all neatly kept, and the narrow alley between the two beds. A computer, table, and chair filled one corner almost to overflowing. The only light came from a small reading lamp on the headboard of Jia Li's bed.

In her bed, swaddled in stuffed toys, five-year-old Oi-Ling looked at Willow with animated interest. Like her sister, her coal-black hair was carefully brushed back and she wore a jade nightgown.

"Hi," Oi-Ling said cautiously. Her English wasn't

quite as good as her older sister's, and she always acted shy around Willow. But she loved the games they sometimes let her play on the computer.

"Hi," Willow said. Both sisters looked at her expectantly. "I get the feeling I interrupted something."

Jia Li held up a familiar book as she sat on the edge of the bed. *"Where the Wild Things Are.* Oi-Ling likes the monsters."

"Ah." Willow looked at the little girl and sat on the bed beside Jia Li. "That used to be one of my favorite books, too." *Until I learned there really were monsters out there who weren't very friendly.*

Acid metal suddenly thumped to life out in the hallway, coming from a room farther down. Willow was so tense she jumped a little.

"Lok," Jia Li explained with a sigh. "He is mad. Again."

"Oh," Willow said.

"If my father were here now, Lok wouldn't be so rude."

"I can tell Mommy," Oi-Ling volunteered, starting to get out of bed.

"No," Jia Li stated firmly, taking her sister up in her arms and putting her back into bed. "I am certain Mommy already knows. We shall mind our own business."

Oi-Ling grumpily lay back in the bed. "Lok is being mean."

"Lok is troubled," Jia Li said. "We must try to help him through this time."

"I'm surprised he's home," Willow said, "after your dad sent him out of the graveyard tonight."

Jia Li looked at Willow sharply. "The graveyard?"

Oooops! Willow felt hot embarrassment color her face.

"You were there?" Jia Li asked.

Willow only hesitated for a moment. *It was easier to tell the truth, wasn't it?* "I was there. But only for a little while. Hardly any time at all. Not spying, not doing anything at all creepy. Just curious after everything you told me earlier today. And I wanted to make sure that you were okay."

"Why wouldn't I be okay?"

Willow searched Jia Li's face. *If she's mad, at least she's not too mad.* "In case, you know, your ancestor rose from the grave as a hungry ghost."

Oi-Ling laughed. "Silly Willow. *Guei* are made-up stories like in my book." She slapped a small hand down on *Where the Wild Things Are.*

"Right," Willow said, then shifted her attention back to her friend, "but I still wanted to be there for you."

The acid metal riffs continued to assault the hallway. Mrs. Rong passed by the open doorway and started banging on a door farther down the hallway. She called out Lok's name several times.

Lok snapped back at his mother. Willow might not have understood the words, but she understood the tone. The music level increased.

"Lok is being really mean tonight," Oi-Ling stated.

Jia Li looked terribly embarrassed, and Willow guiltily wished she'd gone to see Oz at the Bronze instead. Some days it didn't pay to be a caretaker. *Well, actually, hardly any days does it pay.*

"You saw what happened between my brother and father?" Jia Li asked.

Willow nodded. "He seemed pretty upset."

Mrs. Rong continued to call her son's name.

"Lok was upset," Jia Li admitted. "And he still is. He says he is angry at our father, but I know it is something more."

"What?" Willow asked.

Jia Li appeared uncertain and kept glancing out toward the hallway. "I know my father must seem like a traditionalist to you, but Lok believes more in the old ways than my father."

"Old ways?" Willow asked, suddenly feeling a little creeped out.

"Lok believes in the *guei*," Jia Li said. "And when he found out about our ancestor a few days ago, he became very excited."

"Why?"

"Because—" Jia Li started, then stopped when a door suddenly opened and the music thundered into the hallway.

Mrs. Rong's voice raised sharply, and Lok's name was repeated a number of times. Finally the music stopped. He yelled back at his mother in what Willow knew was a disrespectful tone. In the next instant, Lok strode by the bedroom door and shot Willow and Jia Li a hot, angry glance. He stopped and leaned into the doorway.

"Willow," he barked, eyes bright and hard under his scarlet-tipped hair, perhaps even not quite sane. "Hope your family wasn't one of those connected to the mining operations that killed my great-great-great-great granduncle, because they're all going to die. Their money isn't going to be able to save them." Then he was gone.

Willow glanced back at Jia Li.

"Lok," Jia Li said softly, "believes the *guei* can be raised to claim vengeance on those who caused his death."

Chapter 5

"Two BLOOD CONES," BUFFY ADDRESSED THE CONVE-
nience store clerk politely. Seeing the guy's look of confusion, she held up two fingers.

The clerk stood in the semi-gloom filling the estab-
lishment. Well into his forties, gray flecking his hair and
eyebrows, the man had heavily pockmarked pale, leathery skin. His eyes were blue with enflamed pools of pus-
yellow around them. He wore a gray coverall and a
stained white butcher's apron that covered him from
chest to knees. Most of his attention was on the closed-
circuit television over the counter that showed a black-
and-white cowboy movie.

Papers advertising various sales covered the iron-
barred windows, held up by gray duct tape that covered
the cracks in the glass. Buffy knew the papers were there
more to block view from the outside than to draw new
business. Set in the older section of Sunnydale, the convenience store was a squared-off cinderblock eyesore

that melted into the city's shadows. No cars were parked in the lot, and the gas pumps all had NOT WORKING signs on them.

"Don't have no blood cones," the clerk said apologetically. He pulled an unfiltered cigarette from his pocket, stuck it between his lips, and fired up. Smoke wreathed his head.

"Sure you do." Buffy smiled. "That guy has one." She pointed at the biker standing by the video game arcade. The biker lapped at his scarlet-drenched snow cone with slow deliberation. The other six guys playing the games with him laughed.

"That's Razz-Apple Appeal," the clerk said.

Buffy glanced at the photo ID on the guy's coverall. The picture was of a happy twenty-something-year-old guy who was probably toast. "Look, Ernie, I came here for a blood cone. I'm going to have a blood cone."

"Fine," the man said. He turned the crank on a hand-powered icemaker and filled a cup with shaved ice. When it was full, he shoved it under a flavor pump clearly labeled RAZZ-APPLE APPEAL, thoroughly soaked it, then handed it to Buffy. "There you go. A blood cone. That'll be three bucks."

Buffy sniffed the snow cone. "Smells like raspberries and apples."

"All the blood cones we serve do," Ernie said.

Pointing at the guy near the arcade, Buffy said, "Not his."

Ernie reached under the counter and brought out a sawed-off double-barreled shotgun. He leveled it at Buffy. "Maybe you need to breeze, little sister."

Buffy felt Angel move at her side but checked him with an open hand. "Or what?" Buffy challenged.

"You'll ventilate me? Let some daylight through me? Come on, let me hear the cliché."

"Sayonara, sweet cheeks." Ernie's finger tightened on the trigger.

Buffy moved like lightning, kicking the shotgun up and back. Both barrels went off, filling the convenience store with thunder. The double-ought buckshot took out the television in a spray of electronic fireworks.

The bikers erupted from the video game machines, surging toward Buffy and Angel. As they charged, the bikers' faces morphed, revealing their vampire natures.

Vaulting the counter, Buffy kicked Ernie in the face, knocking him out from the counter and into the aisle. The shotgun twirled up end over end. The Slayer caught the shotgun on the way up, broke it open and popped the spent, smoking casings out, then glanced under the counter. There, in a half-empty carton of cigarettes, was a scattered handful of shotgun shells. She grabbed two of them and shoved them into her captured weapon.

"Duck," Angel advised, grabbing the lead vampire by the shirtfront and hip-tossing him over the counter.

The vampire sailed through the air and hit the entry door on the other side of the counter, upside down. He crashed through, taking out the glass, advertisement, and iron bar rack.

Angel couldn't avoid the next vampire and got swept up in the biker's open grab. Holding Angel's feet off the ground, the vampire charged back toward the refrigerated cases and rammed Angel through the glass and into the stockroom behind.

"Grab the bitch!" one of the bikers yelled.

Buffy leaped up and rolled backward across the counter, landing on her feet on the other side. Ernie was just trying to get to his feet when she kicked him in the face. He crashed into the potato chip racks, taking them all down.

Still on the move, the biker vampires just behind her, Buffy skidded down the paper goods aisle. A cardboard cup held a fistful of pencils. She upended the shotgun and dropped pencils down both barrels. Whirling, she brought the shotgun around, pointed directly at the lead vampire's chest. She slid her finger into the trigger guard, feeling both triggers of the double-barreled weapon. Each trigger fired one of the barrels and it didn't matter to Buffy which one went first. Both of them took out whatever was directly ahead of the weapon.

The vampire held his hands up in mock surrender, smiling hugely. "Might hurt me some, little darling," he said in a heavy Texas accent, "but it ain't nothing gonna be permanent."

"Wrong," Buffy said, pulling the hammers back.

"With pencils? And the erasers pointed out at me to boot?" The vampire couldn't believe it. "What are you gonna do?"

Buffy smiled coldly. Only this morning she'd been told about the convenience store and the blood cones it was selling. Willow had checked the police records and found out several persons had gone mysteriously missing in the area.

"I'm going to close this place down," the Slayer promised, "and I'm going to rub you out." She pulled the first trigger.

Constructed without rifling, totally smoothbore, the shotgun was designed to push out everything in the barrel when it fired. The pencils, broken by the heated rush of gunpowder and buckshot, turned into splinter confetti that ripped through the vampire's chest, taking the heart out along the way.

Incredulous, not believing what had been done to him, the vampire glanced down at the huge hole in his chest where his dead heart had been. Then he turned to dust.

The next vampire held up, looking like he was considering other options. He started to run.

"Don't go," Buffy said. "I think I can pencil you in—or, out, rather." She pulled the trigger, sending pencil debris ripping through the vampire's chest and turning him to dust.

"She's out of rounds!" one of the vampires squalled. "Rush her!"

Buffy blocked with the shotgun, using it like a bo stick, then as a club. One of the vampires tried to sneak up on her but she heard the scuff of his shoe on the floor as he closed in from behind. The Slayer whirled, superhumanly fast, and rammed the shotgun's hot, smoking barrels through the vampire's chest. She didn't stop pushing until the shotgun went completely through the creature, including the wooden stock. The vampire turned to dust as well.

Glass shattered in the back again as Angel pushed his way out. He carried a plumber's helper with a huge rubber suction end. One of the vampires turned toward Angel only to catch a faceful of plumber's helper. The suction cup latched onto the vampire's face, but Angel's strength shot the wooden handle on through the rubber suction cup, down through the vampire's head, and into the creature's heart.

Slipping Mr. Pointy from her jacket, Buffy leaped high into the air, put a hand down on the head of the next vampire who charged at her, and landed on her feet. She struck with the stake as the vampire pulled up short, penetrating its heart from behind, hearing the sudden rush of dust falling to the floor as she whipped the stake back.

Angel attacked the last vampire in the room with the

broken stick left over from the plumber's helper, ducking under the lock-back knife the creature swung. He was dust by the time Angel stood again.

The store was a wreck. Overturned racks and shelving littered the floor with bags, cans, and boxes. Ernie was trying to crawl away on hands and knees.

Angel caught the man by the shirt collar and yanked him to his feet. Ernie only made token resistance, stopping entirely when Buffy pressed her stake against his chest.

"Where?" Buffy asked.

Ernie pointed, fingers trembling. "Back in the freezer section."

Buffy led the way, trusting Angel to control their prisoner. The door to the freezer was padlocked. The Slayer gripped the lock and yanked. The padlock and the locking mechanism tore from the door with a loud shriek.

Darkness filled the freezer room, but the salt-copper scent of blood lingered in the air.

Buffy kept her stake tight in her fist as she searched for the light switch.

Dim refrigerator lighting filled the small freezer section. A young woman in a light green windsuit hung suspended from a meat hook in the ceiling in the center of the room. A straitjacket bound her arms and a gag fitted her mouth. IV tubing ran from both sides of her neck, tapping the two carotid arteries that would be full of adrenaline freshly pumped from the heart. Surgical steel cut-off valves glittered at the other end of the tubing. Glazed fever dulled the woman's eyes and they tracked Buffy slowly. No hope lived there, and she'd obviously been there for a few days.

Buffy's eyes blurred with tears. *If only I'd come sooner,* she couldn't help thinking. But she hadn't known, and even when she had, she hadn't believed.

She'd expected to raid the convenience store only to find that the blood cones were from hospital blood bags, not a hostage.

"Buffy . . ." Angel said gently.

"I'm okay," she insisted.

"I can take care of this."

"No," Buffy said. "I'm the Slayer. This is my job." She turned to the vampire Angel held. "Bye, Ernie. Hope they burn you for a long time." She stabbed Mr. Pointy through his heart, moving at normal, human speed so he'd see it coming.

His dying scream broke off midway through as he turned to dust.

Buffy put the stake away and turned her attention to the hostage. The woman's dulled eyes didn't even show fear.

"It's okay," Buffy told her. "We're here to help." Gently, she started loosening the straitjacket from the meat hook. The vampires had wanted their prey to last for a while so they had slid the meat hook through the straitjacket and not into her flesh.

Angel took the woman in his arms when they had her free. "She's in shock," he said, "but if we get help for her quickly enough, she'll be okay."

Buffy shook her head. "She'll never be okay again, Angel. She might live, but she'll never be okay."

Buffy stood in the shadows across the street from the convenience store. She watched the paramedics load the woman onto a gurney, an IV already feeding lost fluids back into her body.

The Sunnydale police had cordoned off the area and tentatively poked around in the building. Only a handful of neighbors had turned out for the excitement. Most residents didn't venture out to rubberneck atrocities that took place after dark. By morning, it would be like none of this had ever happened.

"We're done here," Angel said quietly.

"I know." Buffy watched the scene a little longer. "I can't help thinking about how she must have felt while she was hanging there, having them siphon blood off her like she was nothing."

"You can't think about that," Angel whispered.

"I can't not think about it." Buffy turned to Angel and she didn't mean to let some of her anger out, but she did. "And if you're going to tell me that you're not going to go back to your home and not think about it, then maybe we don't share as much as I thought we did."

Angel was silent.

"Well?" Buffy demanded.

"I'll think about it."

"Why? Because I told you to?"

"No."

"Because it sounds like now that you're only going to think about her because I told you to."

"That's not it."

"Then what is it?"

"You're angry," Angel stated, "and I understand that."

A single tear slid down Buffy's cheek before she could regain control. She made her voice hard. "Then why did you tell me I couldn't think about it?"

Angel remained silent.

"Don't tell me what to think," Buffy said. "Don't think you can tell me what to not think about. I feel the way I do about things, Angel, and you can't change any of it. No matter how much you want to. Or I want to."

Hurt flared in his eyes, but he didn't break contact with hers.

"And I don't want to," Buffy said weakly at last.

Spike's words the last time they'd met still haunted her. And every now and again she still had nightmares about Angel trying to end his life on Christmas. Instead of the unexpected and unusual snowfall that had prevented the dawn that morning, in her nightmares she could only watch him burn.

Angel reached for her and pulled her close. She felt the smooth strength of his chest against her cheek, and he blocked the wind from her. She tried to ignore the chill that clung to him because his body couldn't maintain ninety-eight-point-six, but she knew she'd never feel the heat of him. She felt safe, protected.

"I just wish," Angel said, "that I had more to tell you than not to think about things like this. It's frustrating to know that telling you that is the best I can do and it's not going to work."

"I know." Buffy wrapped her arms around him tightly. "But that's not all you do, Angel. If I didn't have you, I don't know what I'd do." She stood on tiptoe and kissed him.

After a moment, he broke the kiss and stepped back. "Maybe we'd better keep moving," he said in a thick voice.

"Sure," Buffy said, taking his hand, her breathing slightly elevated while her sexual frustration level had buried the needle. "Let's go see what Willy has to say about waiting to tell us about Ernie. I'm really in the mood for him to lie to us."

Chapter 6

LESS THAN AN HOUR AFTER THEIR VISIT TO THE CONVE-
nience store, Buffy and Angel took a table at the back of
Willy's Alibi. Humans and demons rubbed elbows at the
tables and at the bar, laughing and joking, and watching the
basketball game on the television over the bar. The stench
of stale beer and cigarettes covered everything, given more
lasting power by the layer of grease from the microwave
Willy used to prepare nachos and other snacks for the tavern's patrons. Canned metal music hammered from the
cracked speakers, creating an undercurrent of total din.

When it came to social stratification in Sunnydale,
Willy's was an armpit. It was a place where socially er-
rant and uncivilized creatures, humans as well as demons,
met to compare notes, set up jobs or marks, or to hide
from the law. Everyone in Willy's was on the run from
someone, and no one ever gave his or her right names.

Seated in the shadows around the table, Buffy scanned
the crowd for new faces, or old faces showing new wor-

ries. None were in the offing. She sighed and checked her watch. It was almost eleven. Oz and Dingoes Ate My Baby would be playing the final set at the Bronze, and that sounded a lot better than vampire-hunting.

Only the image of the woman hanging in the convenience store wouldn't leave Buffy's head. Even though she knew she still had human weaknesses, it was hard not to realize that every moment she was sleeping could mean someone else's death.

She glanced at Angel.

"No one new," he said.

"Let's ask Willy," Buffy said, sliding up from the table. "He was so busy I bet he didn't even see us come in."

"He saw us come in," Angel responded. "He avoided us."

"Not nice." Buffy crossed the crowded floor, instantly drawing attention from the men seated around the stained, tilting tables. A handful of them tried to touch her as she passed. She left three broken fingers, a fractured wrist, and a broken cloven hoof in her wake. She turned at the sound of a meaty smack behind her.

Angel brought his leg back as one of the men at a nearby table sailed backward in his chair. The legs caught on the uneven flooring and spilled the guy onto the floor.

The demon started to get up, growling furiously, but a big man built like a pro wrestler put a heavy boot on his shoulder. "No, mate," the blacksmith said easily. "Yer done. I come here to have a quiet drink afore I ship again, and I mean to have it. Don't you be starting something what's gonna rile the whole bar up. Ye best be leaving that girl alone, or that man there'll have yer tripes out and be showing them to ye."

The demon struggled only a moment more, then nodded.

"Ye mind yer manners whilst yer in here," the big man added, "afore I smash yer kebob meself."

Buffy continued to the bar, knowing every eye in the place was on her—except for the Thurik demons in the corner that grew an extra one in the back of their heads.

"Bad pennies and Slayers," Willy muttered. "Always showing up at the wrong time. And unwanted." He was short and scrawny, a bar towel thrown over the shoulder of the soiled white shirt he wore. His dark hair hung in greasy locks.

"Gee, Willy," Buffy said brightly, "it's a good thing I don't rate the opinion of pond-feeding scum very highly. That could have hurt my feelings."

Willy's face tightened into a scowl. "I don't know nothing."

"Don't you be worrying about old Willy," the woman at the bar beside Buffy said in a soft, rolling Southern accent. "He never has an opinion. Unless someone gives him one, and permission to use it, of course."

"Thanks. I'll remember that." Buffy looked at the woman and tried not to stare.

"It's okay, sugah, I'm used to people paying me over-particular attention." Even seated on the barstool, the woman looked statuesque. She had a Pamela Anderson Lee post-op build and scaly, obsidian skin that glittered in the dim light. Her hands were long and tapered, with beautiful silver nails. Her age was indeterminate, but her face was indescribably beautiful, high cheekbones and a generous mouth. Her hair was bone-white, seeming to flow and move effortlessly. "But I'm sure a pretty girl like you is used to getting a lot of attention of her own as well."

"Yeah . . ." Buffy said, staring into the woman's hypnotic gaze. The woman's eyes were pale lavender and scarlet, with black irises shaped like a cat's. White limned the outer ring of her eyes.

"Cut it out, Treena," Angel ordered, stepping between the woman and Buffy.

An unfamiliar heaviness lifted from Buffy's mind and she felt like she was just waking. "What's going on?"

"Treena is a Medusa," Angel said. "Some of the stories in Greek myth were based on her. They said her gaze could turn men to stone, but it wasn't just men. It was anything human."

"And they weren't turned to stone, sugah," Treena stated. "They were delivered unto rapture, which is the gift of my kind."

"Medusa," Buffy said as thinking still clunked around in her head. "The snakey-haired woman?"

"Yeah." Angel put a menacing fist close to the Medusa's face.

Instantly, the hair strands lifted, coiled to strike, tiny mouths open to show fangs. Dozens of snakes stood revealed, hissing. The demon seated next to Treena cursed in disgust and abandoned his seat.

"Oh dahling," Treena said good-naturedly, "you're such a caution." She pushed at Angel's shoulder playfully, then smoothed her hands through her viper-hair, calming the snakes. "I didn't mean any harm. If you didn't have that pesky soul of yours, you might be a lot more fun."

"She's not really a she," Angel continued, taking his hand back down. "A Medusa is a symbiotic being. The snakes are a separate entity co-joined by a single brain."

Ugh! "So she's a *home* for those snake things?" Buffy stared   the snake hairs in sick fascination.

"Yeah," Angel answered.

"Oh sugah," Treena protested. "You say that like it's a bad thing." She scratched the back of her head. "Although the little boogahs *do* get a little rambunctious and wiggly from time to time. I assure you, the vhipurn have nothing but my well-being in mind."

"Except that they like to feed on human flesh," Angel pointed out. "They give Treena and her kind powers in return for habitat space."

"I guess," Buffy said, "that they must appreciate you always keeping them in mind."

Treena scowled into the mirror behind the bar. "A smart mouth on a beautiful girl is such an unlovely accessory." She sipped her drink, revealing her forked tongue striped in orange and black.

Willy placed another dish of beetles in front of Treena. The Medusa scooped them up irritably and dropped them into her mouth. Satisfied that none escaped, she crunched enthusiastically.

Okay, Buffy thought, feeling sick, *not even a Slayer's stomach is prepared for everything.* She turned her attention to Willy. The mirror behind the bar didn't show Angel or a couple dozen other vampires in the tavern.

"Willy," Buffy said, "we want to talk."

"I'm trying to run a business here," Willy protested. "Got some unexpected holiday traffic and I'm short-handed." He pulled two more draft beers and slid them across the counter to a truck driver who caught them in massive hands that each had seven fingers.

"I'm checking," Buffy said, paused for just a heartbeat, then added, "Nope. I don't feel any differently this time than the last. I guess we're down to the easy or hard option. Boy, we didn't waste any time there, did we?"

Willy looked at Angel, then back at Buffy. "I really hate you guys."

"I know," Buffy replied. "It's one of those security

things in our world we've come to rely on." She tapped her watch. "Tick-tock, tick-tock."

Willy sighed, bringing the heartfelt disappointment up from his shoe soles. "Come on down here." He walked to the opposite end of the bar from Treena.

Buffy and Angel followed, staying alert to the hostile gazes around them. No one in Willy's liked them, and it wasn't hard to remember that.

"Look," Willy said in a low voice, darting his eyes around the small storage room off the main bar, "I got nothing for you. And I'd have told you about Ernie if I'd remembered."

"Okay, Willy," Buffy said. "Thanks." She turned to go.

" 'Okay, Willy, thanks'? That's all you're going to do?" Willy looked incredulous. "You're not going to threaten me, bust up the bar, or rough me up a little?"

Buffy exchanged glances with Angel and found it hard to keep from busting out laughing. "Nope. We believe you."

"Why?" Willy demanded.

"Because you seem so sincere."

"I've given you sincere before. Buckets of sincere. You and Angel have never bought that before."

"We don't think you're lying to us now," Angel said.

Anger showed in Willy's shriveled little face. "Well, I'm not lying to you. So there!"

"Good," Angel said. "Then maybe the next time we drop by you'll remember that."

"You're not going to get information out of me easily," Willy threatened. "I've got a reputation to consider."

"See ya," Buffy called, walking back toward the door past Treena.

Willy ran behind the bar, following them. "I mean,

you can get information out of me, but it's just not going to be easy."

Before Buffy could make a reply, the front door to Willy's tavern swung open. A dozen young Asian men wearing sullen expressions, khaki cargo pants, and colorful tee shirts strode into the room. Their short, spiky hair was colored in green and white stripes that ran from front to back.

"What the hell do you want?" Willy called belligerently from behind the counter.

One of the young men stepped toward the counter. The men behind him fanned out. Before he reached the bar, he reached under his jacket and brought out an Uzi hanging from a shoulder strap. "Hand over the money and you won't get hurt." He pulled a black bag from his pocket and flipped it open.

"A robbery?" Willy asked. "You can't rob this place. You don't know who you're messing with."

"We're the Black Wind," the guy with the Uzi said. "We are death. Give me the money or I'll take it off your corpse."

Willy looked at the bar's patrons. "You aren't going to let him do this, are you?"

The question hung over the quiet that filled the room. The young men filled their hands with handguns, machine pistols, stakes, cut-down shotguns, and wrist-mounted devices that Buffy couldn't identify locked down into place on the backs of their forearms.

Then the patrons started laughing. "Looks like you're on your own, Willy!" someone yelled. "They've got us covered."

Buffy turned slowly, looking for a way out that didn't involve getting past the Asian youths.

The Black Wind gang leader shook the bag. "Fill it and live."

Cursing, hands shaking, Willy opened the cash register and started shoveling bills into the bag.

"All of it," the gang leader ordered. "Including the floor safe behind the bar."

Once the cash register was emptied, Willy knelt and opened the floor safe. The money that came from there was rubber-banded into neat stacks. The man walked behind the bar and checked the safe. He turned back to address the bar.

"All right," he said calmly. "Now the rest of you." Five other men opened cloth bags and started shoving them at the tavern patrons. "Jewelry, wallets, plastic."

"Hey," a horned demon protested, "now that's something you're not going to get away with. Robbing Willy's one thing, kind of fun to watch, but you're not robbing the rest of us without getting bloody."

Emotionlessly, the gang leader shot a dozen bullets into the demon's face, knocking him backward and shattering one of his horns. The demon's body landed on the table behind him, smashing it to the floor.

"Okay," the gang leader said, "he's bloody. Does anyone else want to be bloody?"

One of the men called for the leader's attention, then pointed Buffy out. The leader pushed his sleeve back and glanced at something on his wrist. When he glanced back at Buffy, his dark eyes were filled with conviction.

"Kill her," he ordered, raising the Uzi again.

"You're sure you don't want to come in and clean up?"

Xander glanced at Giles as they sat inside the Watcher's car. "Yeah. I'm sure. I'm good. After you get through picking up the bandages and stuff, we're probably going to call it a night, right?"

"You're in a hurry to get home?"

Xander shifted his gaze past Giles to the drugstore on the other side of the street. "Not especially, but I could watch a little *Discovery* channel, shower, and hit the hay early for a change." *And try to avoid being depressed that Cordelia won't have called.*

After the Sunnydale paramedics and police had arrived, their statements had been quickly taken and they'd been released. The woman was going to be fine and would be sent home after a quick trip to the ER.

"Well, I must say your ebullient mood after rescuing that woman and her son seems to have worn off quite quickly," Giles said.

"Must you?" Xander asked.

Giles shrugged. "Perhaps not, but I thought it worth mentioning as a bridge to anything else you might have on your mind that you might wish to talk about."

"Cordelia," Xander sighed.

"Must we?"

"No," Xander said, "that's why I suggested me staying here while you went in for the gauze and antiseptic."

"Right." Giles opened the door, waiting for a car to pass. He cleared his throat. "At your age, Xander, breaking up is hard to do."

"Yeah, I think I've sung that one a few times."

"It doesn't get any easier as you get older."

Xander suddenly understood. "You've been there a few times yourself."

Giles nodded. "A Watcher's life, unfortunately, is usually a solitary one."

"Solitary on a crossword puzzle fills exactly six spaces. L-O-N-E-L-Y."

"Yes, I'm afraid it does." Giles paused. "Buffy's relationship with all of you has made my life as a Watcher appear even more devoid of human companionship. She's shown me that it is possible to bring people into this calling, but they have to be the right people. And even then they are at risk."

Xander felt guilty as he realized that Giles was talking about Jenny Calendar. It was one thing to lose Cordelia and see her walking through the halls at Sunnydale High, but it would have been another to lose her forever.

"Hey," Xander said, "there's no use in both of us getting maudlin. You get the Band-Aids and I'll spring for tacos later."

"Okay. I'll only be a moment." Giles got out of the car and crossed the street to the drugstore.

Xander glanced at the comic he'd bought and just didn't have the heart to open it yet. *Maybe in the morning or between classes, at some point when I start thinking superpowers really will fix everything.*

He sighed, knowing he would check his answering machine again as soon as he got home and—again—there wouldn't be a message from Cordelia. And it was all his fault. When he and Willow had thought they were going to be killed by Spike while he'd been pining over Drusilla dumping him, they'd given in to their own attraction for each other. Of course, that had been the exact moment Cordy and Oz had come to the rescue.

Xander glanced at the comic book. *And you thought clones were hard to deal with. Man, if you only knew what teenage life was really like.*

He pushed out of the car, needing a breath of fresh air. Oz and Willow had gotten over the stumbling time, realizing their feelings for each other were very real. But he and Cordelia Chase hadn't made it. In a way, he didn't blame her. *Weird has always been a part of my life, but Cordy was new to it.*

"Hey, Harris," a booming male voice called.

Drawn out of his funk momentarily, Xander gazed at the dark park in front of him. A tall, chain link fence enclosed a basketball court lit by halogen lights. Five guys stood at one end of the court. Xander knew two of them. Chris Tyler and Dave Sawyer had been varsity basketball players at Sunnydale the year before. They'd barely known him well enough to ignore him in the hallways.

"Xander," Dave called again. He was nearly seven feet tall, with a shaved head, and sweat gleaming like diamonds against his dark skin. "Yo, Xander, we need a third man."

"Me?" Xander couldn't believe it. "You want *me* to play basketball with you?"

Dave threw up his hands as he and Chris jogged over to the car. "Got nobody else, man, and these fools say we gotta be three or they ain't gonna play us."

Dave Sawyer had been one of the strongest forwards Sunnydale High had ever turned out. Not good enough for USC, maybe, but good enough for college somewhere. Only Dave hadn't gone, choosing to stay in town and help take care of his family.

Chris Tyler was a six-three point guard who had an outside three-point conversion percentage that had been staggering. He had gone to college, then gotten kicked out, though the details hadn't yet filtered back to Sunnydale as to why. His blond hair stood out starkly against Dave and the three guys ready to play them.

"Nah, really," Xander said, conscious of the injuries he'd already picked up during the night, "you guys go on ahead without me. I appreciate the offer, though."

"Xander, man, you ain't listening," Dave said. "We need you or they ain't gonna play us. Me and Chris, we got some money up on this. I'm willing to pay you twenty bucks to come out here and *stand.*"

"Twenty bucks?" Xander asked, suddenly interested. Twenty bucks didn't just magically appear in his pockets. "How long are you going to need me?"

"Five, ten minutes," Dave replied. "Going to fifteen by ones, two for the three-pointers. Make-it, take-it. These guys got no game. Be an easy twenty for you for coming out here, standing around."

Xander glanced back at the drugstore. It looked like Giles was going to be a few minutes. Maybe playing basketball was a good idea. And twenty bucks was twenty bucks. He trotted over to the basketball court, stepping through the gate Chris held open for him.

"Who are we playing?" Xander asked.

"Street guys," Chris said. "Make their money hustling B-ball. They stung Dave's little brother last night for fifty bucks. Me and the D-man thought we'd come back here tonight for a little payback, get Anthony's money back, maybe some beer money. Didn't know they were going to try to stick us because there wasn't three of us."

The three guys on the other team were pure street, their skin blazed with blue gang-member tattoos and scars looking like pink and white weals. One of them had what looked like a scar from a gunshot wound on his upper right shoulder.

"We got three now," Dave declared. "You chumps gonna play, or are you gonna walk?"

The other team member holding the ball fired it at Dave. "Shoot the die, man."

At the top of the key, hardly pausing to look, Dave shot the ball, putting it high into the air so that it arced up, then plummeted back down through the chain net. "Looks like it's our ball."

Xander set up with Dave and Chris, then sprinted for the basketball goal when Chris broke and drove for the bucket. Holding his hand up, Xander cut across the lane. Chris fired the ball at him. Just as Xander reached for the ball, one of the opposing team members stepped in front of him and elbowed him in the mouth. He tasted coppery blood as his head exploded with pain.

"Come on, Xander!" Dave called. "Shake the lead out, buddy. Basketball's a full contact sport."

Xander shoved himself to his feet. *Twenty bucks, twenty bucks. And if I back out, Dave will have to forfeit. He'd probably kill me himself.* He made himself run.

At the other end of the court, Xander managed to block a pass with his face, dropping to his knees in pain. He watched through blurred vision as Dave swept the loose ball up, dribbled to the other end of the court, and slammed the ball home, clinking the net's chain links.

"Come on, Xander. Let's push 'em now!"

Xander waved a hand and got up slowly. He didn't know whether staking vampires or playing basketball was harder. He trotted groggily to the other end of the court, feeling the fiery pain lancing through his ribs. Then he noticed the two shadowy figures sitting on the bench at the side of the court.

Both of them wore letter jackets from a nearby high school. They watched the basketball players with hungry eyes. Then they licked their fangs in anticipation.

Where the hell is Giles? Xander wondered.

Chapter 7

"CAN I HELP YOU FIND SOMETHING?"

Startled, Giles looked up from the row of bandaging supplies and first-aid creams. "Thank you, no. I believe I can find what I'm looking for without assistance."

The drugstore clerk standing behind the counter looked like she was in her mid-fifties, deeply tanned and proud of her cleavage. The white smock top fit her like a glove. Her hair was frosted gold and her eyes were a brilliant aquamarine color. The nametag read BARBARA STYLES.

Giles wondered briefly if the name was real, or if it was one chosen to make a statement.

A concerned look lighted the woman's face as she looked more closely at the Watcher's face. Some of the bruises from the encounter with the vampire were already starting to show. "What happened to you?"

"A mugging, I'm afraid. Nothing to be alarmed about. I'm quite all right."

"For a minute there I thought you were one of the victims from Peppy's Miniature Golf."

"Victims?" *Miniature golf?* Watchers by their very nature were curious. The trait for caution had to be trained in.

"Yes," Barbara said. "They're covering it on the local news now." She pointed at the small television set on the counter.

Giles threw an extra box of gauze into the small basket he carried his selections in. *You can never have too much gauze.* He and the counter attendant were the only ones in the small drugstore.

Barbara turned the television so he could see it better.

Joining her at the counter, Giles watched as the news reporters showed the carnage that had taken place at the miniature golf course on the other side of Sunnydale.

"So far there have been only two fatalities confirmed." The reporter was in her early twenties, her red hair cut short and fluttering only slightly in the breeze. Excitement burned in her eyes. "No one knows what the gunmen were doing in this amusement park tonight, but already rumors of gang warfare have hit the streets. The Sunnydale Police Department will neither confirm nor deny these allegations."

Giles noted the LIVE legend in the bottom corner next to the reporter's name, GAYLE KENNEDY. "When did this happen?"

"Just a few minutes ago," Barbara answered. "Did the police come to your mugging?"

"Yes. I mean, it wasn't exactly my mugging."

"Well, whoever it was, you can bet it'll never make the news now."

"As you can see," Gayle Kennedy said on the television screen, "the Sunnydale PD is cordoning off the area." The television camera panned across the miniature golf course. Small fires still burned in some areas, and paramedic teams worked on people covered by blankets. An ambulance pulled to a stop near a fire truck, avoiding the firemen deploying the hose. "Emergency rescue teams are still arriving here as well."

"Gayle," a male voice said over the television, "how many victims are we talking about in tonight's shooting?"

"Bob," Gayle replied, speaking directly at the camera, building a rapport with her audience, anguish in her expressive eyes, "as of right now I've been given reports of between eighteen and twenty-three."

"Were any of them gang members?" A small picture-in-picture opened on the television screen, revealing Bob, the anchorman. He was thin and dark and very intense.

"None have been identified as gang members as yet," Gayle confirmed, "but nearly a dozen of the victims' names have now been released. We should know something in a little while."

Barbara nodded her head approvingly. "This kid is going to go far."

Giles looked at her. "I beg your pardon."

She nodded at the television. "These guys couldn't get more experience if they were living in a war zone."

They are *living in a war zone,* Giles couldn't help thinking, *and it's called the Hellmouth.*

"Bob," Gayle called, "I've just heard that Mayor Richard Wilkins was here at Peppy's Miniature Golf Park at the time of the shooting spree."

"Do you think there's any chance we could speak with the mayor?" Bob asked earnestly.

Gayle's eyes widened. "Bob, I believe that's Mayor Wilkins headed this way now. Yes, yes it is!" She waved, stepping toward the man off-screen, causing the camera to pan across a burning car and an EMS team administering CPR to a man in the background. "Mayor! Mayor Wilkins! Over here, sir! We know Sunnydale would like to hear your version of what happened here tonight."

That couldn't have been any more staged than if someone had yelled "roll camera," Giles thought.

Mayor Wilkins joined Gayle Kennedy on-screen as Bob the anchorman promptly vanished. "Mayor," the reporter said, thrusting the microphone into the mayor's face, "can you tell us what happened."

Giles trusted nothing the mayor said.

The mayor appeared to be slightly disoriented. "I'm sorry. I was wounded during the shooting. Shot, actually, it would appear." He pulled at a tattered coat sleeve to reveal a bloodied bandage wrapped around his forearm.

Too bad they missed your forehead, Giles thought.

"How badly are you wounded, Mayor?" Gayle asked.

"It's not much," the mayor said dismissively, pulling the sleeve back down. "Just a flesh wound. There are people here who are injured much more grievously than I am."

"Can you tell us what happened?" Gayle repeated.

"I was over in Circus Circus," the mayor said, pointing with his wounded arm and flinching as if in pain, "my personal favorite course here at Peppy's—and, as you will remember—the location of my orphan fundraising charity last year. I was in a business meeting/getting-to-know-you tête-à-tête, so to speak, when the attack began. Mr. Chengxian Zhiyong of China—who has graciously agreed to open a new division of his business in Sunnydale, which will provide a number of well-paying jobs for our fair populace—pulled me to the safety of his car after the attack began. Were it not for Mr. Zhiyong's quick actions, I might have perished tonight."

"It's fortunate for us that you didn't," Gayle Kennedy said. The camera panned back on her.

"If I may say one more thing," the mayor interrupted, plucking the microphone from the reporter's hand and signaling for the camera to turn back to him. "Citizens of Sunnydale, I know you share my outrage that this, one of the more pleasant and family-oriented areas in our fair burg, was subject to this kind of activity. I promise you, I promise you with all my heart, that I will spare no power that lies within my grasp to leave no rock unturned till we find those responsible for this—this *outrage*." He passed the microphone back.

Gayle took it and checked her earpiece, taking a few steps away from the mayor. "Bob, I've just been told that one of the visitors at Peppy's had a camcorder and filmed part of the attack. We're going to show you an exclusive now. Our camera technicians are ready to go on the air with the footage." She stood, waiting expectantly.

A small screen opened to her right, then ballooned up to fill the whole television screen. At first, the camcorder operator had been filming a small boy chopping industriously with his golf club, missing the ball again and again. Then the camera jerked and showed a man's hand shoving the boy down. Voices, torn and splotchy from disbelief and the wind, shouted. "Someone's shooting! Someone's shooting! Oh, God, everybody get down!"

Then the camera angle turned around, blurred and out of focus for just a moment before the autofocus tightened up. A quartet of young Asian men showed for just a moment. The most prominent thing about them was the green and white striped hair.

A Sunnydale police officer, probably working security at the miniature golf course, rushed out with a pistol in his hands. He fired without a warning yell, a nicety that had become something of a moot point in Sunnydale. The policeman got off at least four rounds before the gang member he was shooting at turned and shot him down.

The screen cleared and returned to Gayle Kennedy.

"Did the police officer just miss the gunman?" the anchorman asked.

Gayle Kennedy shook her head. "The man that filmed that violent exchange insists that the officer's bullets all struck their target. He believes the gunmen were wearing Kevlar armor and shooting cop-killers."

"Cop-killers?" the anchorman asked. "Those are the armor-piercing rounds some gang members have been using for a time against law enforcement agencies."

But Giles didn't think the Asian men were wearing Kevlar. There was also something very familiar about their faces. Before he could get very far in his train of thought, the front door to the drugstore opened, ringing the bell.

Three Asian youths dressed in khaki pants and neon-colored tee shirts stepped through the door, their hair striped green and white.

Well, Giles thought sourly, *this can't be any good at all.*

For one frozen second, Buffy watched the gang members turn their weapons toward her. Then Angel bumped into her, knocking her behind the wooden bar.

"Move!" Angel commanded. He stepped toward Treena and grabbed a double fistful of the writhing snakes from her head.

Still in motion, Buffy watched as Angel yanked the snakes from Treena's head, leaving pockmarked openings in her skull. The snakes hissed and drew back to strike, but Angel's speed was too much. He flung them toward the intruders while Treena screamed in painful indignation.

The snakes, most of them no more than a foot long, sailed through the air and spread out. When they struck the gang members, the snakes sank their barbed heads into exposed flesh, then quickly slithered out of sight into their victim's bodies. Seven of the gunmen dropped, their bodies knotted up in agony as the snakes crawled through them.

Five of the gang members showed no reaction at all to the snakes invading their bodies. They lifted their weapons and raked the bar with bullets. The mirror on the wall and several of the bottles on the shelves shattered, throwing gleaming shards in all directions. Other rounds punched holes in the bar.

Buffy had no doubt they were gunning for her, but they showed no qualms about blasting any human or demon that got in their way. The intruders met stiff resistance from the crowd at Willy's, though. Most of the clientele at the tavern didn't come unarmed.

Willy cowered behind the bar, arms wrapped over his head.

Buffy grabbed Willy along the way and hustled him toward the back of the tavern. Other regular patrons had the same idea, so the way was jammed when Buffy and Angel got there. She didn't hesitate about going, yanking Willy to his feet and shoving him into the mass of men, women, and demons trying to get through the door all at the same time.

Heart pounding, Buffy glanced around the stock room, noting the nearly bare shelves that occupied the walls. Then the back door alarm buzzed as someone ripped the locks out and hurried through.

The door let out into the alley behind the tavern. Rough asphalt, buckled in several places, stretched only a scant ten feet before butting up into the next building. Dumpsters and trash cans lined the walls.

Buffy hung onto Willy with one hand, her Slayer senses alive and thrumming within her. Both ends of the alley were open, but both let out into a street.

"You saved me!" Willy screamed, holding onto Buffy's wrist for dear life.

Then car lights and the thunder of a powerful motor filled the alley. A ten-year-old black sedan fought for traction against the sideways slide the driver had thrown it into. Gray smoke poured from the tires as they spun, then they gripped the street and hurtled the car forward.

"This way!" Angel yelled, pulling on Buffy's arm.

Willy craned his head around, looking over his shoulder, legs slapping the asphalt as he tried to keep up with the Slayer's quick motion. "You've killed me! You've killed me!" He fought against Buffy's grip but couldn't break it.

The sedan roared into the alley, swerving from side to side to hit the people fleeing from the tavern. A Dumpster slowed the vehicle for just a moment, filling the alley with the thunderous boom of the collision. The Dumpster shot ahead of the car, knocking down two horned demons.

One headlight gone now, the car smashed into the Dumpster again and drove the garbage container sideways before it. Metal shrilled as the Dumpster crumpled inward, squeezing trash out like toothpaste from a tube. The Dumpster banged against both sides of the alley, showering orange sparks and scarring the brick walls.

Buffy glanced at the other end of the alley, knowing she'd never make it before the car and Dumpster overtook her. *Who are these guys and what do they want with me?* Willy was trying to run with her again, but she had to slow down even as she was helping him. She looked frantically for a way out of the alley, then glanced over her shoulder.

A slender demon with a triangular face and a prehensile tail hanging below her trench coat turned toward the sports car. The she-demon waited until the last possible moment, then vaulted high into the air. She would have cleared the car and Dumpster easily if her timing had been right. Instead, her foot smacked against the Dumpster's lip and flipped her through the air. Even then she almost recovered, would have probably landed safely, but a man leaned out the passenger window and sprayed her with bullets, dropping her broken and bloodied corpse in a pile behind them.

Angel leaped up, inhumanly high, and caught the bottom rung of the retractable fire escape ladder. He held on and brought it crashing down into the asphalt. When he landed, he turned to Buffy, his face a tight mask of concern and anger. He took Willy from her, gripping the man by the throat and the crotch, and swung him up.

Willy landed with a bone-jarring thump on the first landing.

"Go!" Angel cried hoarsely.

Buffy didn't hesitate, knowing Angel wouldn't leave her side until he knew she was safe. She leaped halfway up the ladder then began pulling herself up. "Come on, Angel!"

Angel started up after her, but the sedan came on too fast.

Buffy pulled herself onto the landing with Willy. She turned around with quick desperation, extending a hand down toward Angel and anchoring herself with her other hand. "Angel! Grab my hand!"

Angel stretched forward, setting himself to push upward. In the next instant, the Dumpster slammed into the bottom of the ladder, tearing it free. The ladder fell back over the Dumpster and Angel toppled with it.

"No!" Buffy screamed, watching helplessly as Angel smashed against the sedan's windshield and spiderwebbed the safety glass. In the next instant, the vehicle roared out into the street, but Buffy saw the man in the passenger seat raising to aim his weapon point-blank at Angel's head.

"Why would Lok believe the *guei* could come back to life?" Willow asked Jia Li. They sat in front of the Rong household near the trickling pond, each of them wrapped in a blanket from Jia Li's room. Mr. and Mrs. Rong had gone out searching for Lok in the family car, leaving Jia Li in charge of the three younger children.

Jia Li fidgeted nervously, staring constantly into the parking lot at the side of the restaurant. "My brother has always been different."

"Different is good," Willow said. "At least, different is good when it gets into an environment where sameness isn't trying to kill it all the time." Her skin still prickled from the cool night air.

"From the time he was very young, Lok has talked to . . . *things.*"

"What kinds of things?" *Okay, now there's an announcement of potential ominous dread,* Willow thought.

"No one knows."

"Hasn't anyone ever asked him?"

"Plenty of times, but Lok never knew how to talk about it. It was like those experiences were things he never could explain."

Willow remained quiet for a moment, then asked, "Have you seen Lok talk to things?"

Three small faces pressed against the window behind them. Jia Li spoke sharply in Chinese and the three children vanished. She sighed. "Yes, but I haven't seen him do anything like that since we were kids."

"What did you see him talking to?"

"Shadows mostly. Usually in corners of the room where it was darkest. Occasionally he would talk to fires."

"What did he talk to them about?"

Jia Li shrugged. "Any time he knew someone else was in the room with him, he stopped speaking. He knew my father didn't like him doing things like that."

"Like talking to people or things that weren't there?" Willow asked.

"Yes." Jia Li nodded. "My father doesn't believe in the old ways."

"What old ways?"

Jia Li grinned self-consciously and wouldn't meet Willow's eyes easily. "Every culture has its mythologies and superstitions, and some of them seem so backward compared to the world we live in. I'm sure you know what I'm talking about."

"You mean like opening an umbrella in the house or walking under a ladder or having a black cat cross the path in front of you?"

"Exactly." Jia Li nodded. "I told you my family lived in Shanghai before coming here?"

"Yes."

"When Lok was just a boy, my parents had many problems with him besides his habit of talking to things. He had seizures and walked in his sleep a lot as well." Jia Li took a deep breath to steady herself, and Willow saw the fear in her friend's eyes. "Once, when he was only four, Lok left my parents' house. I was a baby, so I only remember what they told me. Lok doesn't speak of it. He was gone for two days. My parents searched everywhere for him, at the neighbors' houses, down at the docks where our family restaurant was. They couldn't find him. Then, on the morning of the third day, he was found asleep on our porch."

"Where had he been?" Willow asked.

"No one knows," Jia Li whispered. "Lok told my mother and father that he had walked with the restless warriors, the unburied."

"They were hungry ghosts?"

"My grandfather thought so," Jia Li said. "He said Lok was gifted, that he could see parts of the world that most people could not see." She paused. "But that's ridiculous, isn't it?"

"I don't know," Willow said. *If I could tell her everything I know, she'd be more scared than ever.* So she didn't. "There are some pretty weird things that go on out in life before you start factoring in *guei*. Like when you fall for a guy, right, and your head keeps telling you that he's all wrong for you, but your heart just won't hold back? You know what I'm talking about?"

Jia Li nodded. "Yes."

From the way the other girl said it, Willow knew there was a story lurking there, but they didn't have time to delve into it.

"My mother says that things only got worse with Lok over the next few months," Jia Li went on. "He slipped in and out of catatonic states. Sometimes they would only last for a few minutes, but once it lasted for nine days. They had to put Lok in the hospital and feed him through a tube."

"Didn't the doctors find out what was wrong with him?"

"Nothing, they said. Physically, he was fine. You've seen him play basketball."

"Yes," Willow said. "He's very good."

"And skateboarding. Lok is always best when he is

moving. If he could, I think that he would be the wind. That is the way he was as a child, except for those times he was catatonic."

Willow pulled her knees up and wrapped her arms around them in an effort to stay warm against the chill breeze. Goldfish surfaced repeatedly in the small garden pond, kissing the top of the water, then swimming back below. The ripples spread out, crossing the surface and touching everything.

Nothing passes through life touching without *being touched.* Willow didn't know where the thought came from.

"My grandfather, my mother's father," Jia Li said, "visited Lok in the hospital. He brought my brother out of the catatonic state when everyone else thought him lost forever that time."

"How?" Willow asked. Suddenly the night seemed to press in close around her, making her feel slightly claustrophobic. And she felt as though someone was watching her.

"Through the old ways," Jia Li answered. "My grandfather was a Yao tribesman from the Zhejiang Province. He lived in the Daqi Mountain area. As a Yao tribesman, he was an herbalist, curing the ailments of people with medicines he made. Do you know what I'm talking about?"

"An apothecary," Willow supplied, avoiding the first term that came to mind. "As in alternative medicines. Sure, I'm familiar with that." She brushed her hair back from her face, trying not to look too knowledgeable about the subject.

Jia Li seemed a little embarrassed. "A little of that, yes, but the Yao practice is often called witchcraft even in China."

"Oh, I wouldn't call it that," Willow said. "That has a

negative connotation these days. Herbalism works okay, doesn't it?"

"Not entirely. My grandfather believed mostly in the spirits, that they walked among people, causing good and ill."

"The spirits? You mean ghosts?"

"Yes. My mother was raised in my grandfather's beliefs, but when she came down from the mountain and met my father in Hangzhou before they moved to Shanghai, my father turned her away from those beliefs." Jia Li hesitated, obviously having second thoughts about everything she was revealing. "Although my father doesn't know, I don't think my mother has completely given up those beliefs. There is special incense that she burns sometimes. She tells us that she burns it to remember our grandfather, but I think it's because she practices my grandfather's beliefs."

"How did your grandfather get Lok to come out of the catatonia?" Willow asked.

"My father said it was only coincidence. Grandfather came to the hospital two days before Lok awakened. He somehow knew to come, because there were no phones where he lived at the time."

"But you don't think that's true?" Willow asked.

"No. I saw my grandfather do amazing things with sick people. I know my father believed it, too, but he wouldn't admit it. He doesn't much like being wrong."

"No one does."

"But he knew he was wrong about my grandfather. When Lok was released from the hospital, he went to live with my grandfather."

"Why?" Willow asked.

"I didn't know for a while. My mother and father fought over the decision. Lok was the firstborn son. By rights he should have learned my father's business, but my mother had Lok sent off with my grandfather. Every summer, we got to spend weeks at my grandfather's house."

"Your grandfather took Lok?"

"To protect him from the ghosts. Grandfather said that Lok was one of the special ones, ones who would walk with ancestors, and who would be most abused by the *guei* for things left undone."

A chill gusted over Willow again, no longer held at bay by the blanket. "Was your grandfather able to protect Lok from the ghosts?"

"While Lok lived with my grandfather, he never again was catatonic."

"Wow. That must have made a believer out of your dad."

Jia Li shook her head. "My father still does not believe. He only knows that he lost so many years with his firstborn son. Lok lived with my grandfather till three years ago when my grandfather died." Wetness gleamed in her eyes.

"I'm sorry," Willow said.

"That's why there is so much tension between my brother and father. They hardly know each other, and their views of the world are so different."

"Has . . . has Lok had any catatonic episodes since . . . he came back to live with your family?"

"No, but his mind wanders. Father gets furious at him, which makes Lok very angry in turn. Mother has told my father that when Lok's mind wanders he is seeing things that have to do with the restless spirits. Then they argue, which is something I've seldom seen them do. It doesn't help that Lok has taken such a strong interest in witchcraft."

"He has?"

Jia Li nodded. "From after the time of my grandfather's passing, Lok has sought out the Yao people around Shanghai to teach him of the old ways. The things my grandfather would not teach him."

"What things?" Willow asked.

"I don't know, but when my father found out about Lok's interests, that's when he made the decision to move our family to California. He wanted to get Lok away from their influence."

Oi-Ling's terrified voice called out from the window. "Jia Li, Jia Li! Come quick! There is something in the closet!" Then she spoke rapidly in Chinese.

Willow started to get up, but Jia Li waved her back down.

"It's nothing," Jia Li said, rising easily to her feet and starting toward the door. "Only our brothers scaring her. Oi-Ling has a very active imagination and they know it. I'll be right back."

Willow sat on the small porch and looked out into the empty parking lot. The Rongs' family car hadn't returned. *Do they know where to look for Lok?*

Curious, and wondering how strong her own powers could be, Willow leaned more closely to the small pond and looked into the water. While Buffy had been gone over the summer, she'd taught herself a lot of things and been surprised how easily the craft came to her.

She peered into the pool, staring past the quick, darting movements of the fish. Pale green illumination dawned at the bottom of the pool, spreading up through the water. She raised her hands above the water, amazed at the amount of light shining onto her palms.

When she blinked, movement appeared in the water and she knew it wasn't the fish. Her heart rate increased and a throbbing started at her temples.

Lightning blazed through the water in a heated rush

and the scene cleared, letting her see Lok. Still, his face was blurry, as if it were riding the ripples across the pond's surface.

Look more deeply, a quiet, cold voice ordered from inside Willow's head.

Willow panicked and stopped herself short of screaming, then realized she couldn't make a sound, couldn't even breathe. Whatever force held her kept her tightly under control. She strained against it, but couldn't break it. Her face dipped closer to the fishpond, then she could see Lok more clearly, and she could feel the dark magic swirling around him, threatening them both.

Chapter 8

WILLOW SQUINTED AGAINST THE HARSH GREEN LIGHT streaming from the fishpond. *No*, the voice whispered into her mind. *You will see!* Her eyes opened more widely and the pain ground into them.

Lok was on his knees, his face lit by a patio torch shoved into the ground beside him. Willow got the impression that he was surrounded by earth. Perhaps he was inside a cave, but it felt like a grave. She wanted to tear away from the scene, feeling somehow that it had gone way past the little scrying attempt she'd been after. But she gazed at the unfolding events in hypnotic fascination.

Lok chanted fiercely, cords standing out on his neck. His voice was just beyond Willow's ability to understand, but she heard the fiery cadence of it. He held his hands out, stretching his palms toward the rough earthen wall before him, beseeching and demanding. Perspiration shined his face and gathered in the corners of his eyes. His eyes dilated in fear or excitement.

Suddenly, the earthen wall cracked in front of Lok. Great chunks of earth and rock shot from the wall in successive blasts. Miraculously, or by design, none of those airborne missiles touched Lok.

Skeletal hands, possessing only shreds of decayed flesh, pushed through the opened fissure and flexed. Long fingernails prized at the edges of the crack and pushed out, ripping more rock free. Then a face pressed at the fissure. The yellowed parchment skin drew tightly against the hollows of the skull. The high cheekbones split the weathered flesh, and enflamed eyes sat back deeply in the sockets. A rictus of yellowed ivory showed between prune-wrinkled lips. Empty places showed where teeth had come out. White-gray hair blazed with reddish dust hung to the shambling creature's shoulders.

Lok held a talisman before him, but it was too far away for Willow to recognize. The creature stepped from the fissure in the wall and swiveled its head stiffly to bring its baleful glare to Lok. Without hesitation, the creature started for Lok.

He knows not what he does or what he awakens, the voice whispered in Willow's head. The words shivered into her mind like chipped ice. *He must be protected from them, as he has always been protected. Otherwise, they will have him forever, and this I will not allow.*

In the fishpond, the creature lumbered for Lok. It bent swiftly and grabbed up a rusty miner's pick from the rocks strewn across the cave floor.

You will *protect him.*

Black spots caused by the pain hammering Willow's temples spun into her vision. Her chest was suddenly too tight to cry out in pain. *How . . . how am I supposed to find him?*

You will find a way.

In the depths of the fishpond, the shambling dead thing raised the pickax. Lok remained before the creature on his knees, beseeching it, holding up the talisman.

It's too late! Willow screamed inside her own head.

The dead man held the pickax as high as he could, then brought it sweeping down. Lok lifted his hands and tried to shield his face. The pick pierced his palms, nailing them together, then drove into his head hard enough to shatter his spinal cord. A crimson tide of blood splashed over Lok's ruined features.

Willow screamed, but the sound of it was trapped inside her own head. She went completely blind and deaf, on the edge of passing out from the pain.

It is not too late yet. But soon it will be. What you have seen is that which will be unless the course is altered. You cannot let this happen. There are powerful forces here, things which need more done for them than Lok can help with.

I don't know what to do, Willow insisted.

We all have unfinished tasks, Willow. Rest is never easy and seldom welcome for those of us who work within the world. You know, for you are one of us.

The cold inside Willow's head spread, numbing her body. For a moment she felt as though she were adrift on a freezing, black sea. Then someone touched her arm. She opened her eyes and took an involuntary deep breath.

"Willow."

Cautiously, pain still racking her temples, Willow gazed up at Jia Li's worried face. She felt coolness at the corner of her mouth and her jaw. *I'm drooling on myself!* Embarrassment mixed with the strong fear filling her. Then she realized her head was touching the edge of the fishpond, only inches from going inside.

"Are you all right?" Jia Li asked.

"Sorry," Willow said, pushing herself up on leaden arms. "I don't know what happened there." Hesitantly, she gazed into the water. Only the goldfish swam there now, occasionally kissing the surface.

"Perhaps you should go home and get some rest," Jia Li suggested.

"No, I'll be all right. Thanks." Willow rummaged in her purse and brought out a tissue to wipe away the drool. She checked herself in her compact, surprised at how pale she was.

"Let me get you a glass of water."

"I need to ask you a favor," Willow said.

"What?"

Willow hesitated, trying to think of a way to ask what she was going to and make it sound legitimate. "I need to see Lok's room."

Jia Li drew back and shook her head. "I don't know—"

"Maybe there's a clue there."

"A clue?"

"I don't know," Willow said. "Maybe a matchbook or an address book. Something that might give us an idea of where he's gone. I don't think your parents checked there."

Jia Li caved quickly. "Okay."

Winded, battered and beaten, Xander watched Chris fake one way, then dribble the ball back behind his body and streak to the left. The guy guarding him tried to keep up but was definitely outclassed.

"Get him! Get him! Knock him on his ass!" the guy guarding Xander yelled, breaking off to give chase to Chris.

With the winning bucket on the line, the big man guarding Dave had no choice but to sink back into the lane, intending to cut Chris off. When Chris pulled up and left the ground, obviously going for the game-win-ning twelve-foot jumper, the big man left the ground, too, spreading his arms wide. Chris double-pumped and heaved the ball toward the goal.

"No!" Xander yelled, stumbling forward, watching as the basketball arced way too high to hit the rim. He hurt all over. *Fighting vampires and playing basketball all in the same night—file under Never To Be Done Again!* He pushed himself hard, wanting to get under the goal to at-tempt another rebound. Usually all he got was a sharp elbow in the face, but a couple of times he'd successfully wrapped the ball up for important turnovers. He'd never be Dennis Rodman, he realized, but the saving grace was he'd never be Dennis Rodman.

"Allez—" Chris shouted, falling back from the defender.

Then Dave was there, sailing through the air like he had wings. He shot up after the basketball, caught it in both big hands, and shoved it through the basket. "—oop!" He hung onto the rim for a moment as the ball drained through the metal links, a big grin splitting his face.

The three street ballplayers cursed and spat.

Xander stood up and clasped his hands together be-hind his neck to open his chest more. He breathed deeply. "Thank God."

Dave dropped from the rim, landing lithely even after all the full-court ball. "Pay *me*!" he roared. Sweat rolled off him, drenching his clothing, but his movements re-mained loose and easy. "Stuck it in your eye and broke it off, little wannabes!"

The three street ballplayers bristled at Dave's words.

Xander walked over to Dave and spoke quietly. "You know, Dave, we beat them in basketball, but maybe we're not quite ready for them to go postal on us."

"Them chumps don't wanna go down that street,"

Dave declared, looking at the street guys. "I know that ain't happening."

Xander turned and kept the other team in sight. They bickered among themselves for a little while, then reached into their pockets and shelled out the cash in wet, crinkly bills. Xander breathed a sigh of relief, mopped blood from his bleeding nose with his shirt, and returned his attention to the vampires gathered on the bench at courtside.

Five of them sat on the bench or leaned against the chain link fence. The three guys were hard-faced and the two girls looked vampish—in the sexy, non-blood drinking way.

Maybe we can just pack it in and get out of here, Xander told himself. He glanced at the drugstore and Giles's car. The Watcher was nowhere in sight. *Where the hell is Giles?*

Dave slapped a twenty-dollar bill in Xander's hand, startling him. "Thanks, X-Man. We couldn't have done it without you."

"Yeah," Chris added, grinning, "the way you stop a basketball pass with your face—man, you gotta see it to believe it."

"Thanks, guys," Xander said, conscious of one of the vampires standing up by the bench. "I mean that, really."

"Hey," the vampire called. "You guys want a chance to double your money?"

Chris and Dave swapped looks, obviously drawn into the possibility.

"Look," Xander said, "we really should call it a night." *And I can't see vampires out for just a game of basketball. These guys are not my idea of good losers. Talk about taking your basic pound of flesh . . .*

"Give you two to one odds," the vampire said, shrugging out of his coat and flashing the uniform top of a rival high school. He threw it to one of the girls. "Unless you're afraid you got no real game."

"Oh, we got game," Dave said. "Got so much game you guys aren't even gonna get *in* the game."

"You know," Xander said to Chris and Dave, "maybe we need to dial the testosterone level back down a notch here." He watched the street guys, noticing how they pulled crosses from under their shirts and quickly headed out. *They know the score.* "We really don't need another game tonight. I mean, we all got jobs in the morning, right?"

"You have school in the morning, Xander," Chris said. "Dave and I get to sleep in tomorrow."

If those vampires have their way, you're going to be taking a dirt nap tomorrow. Xander looked at the court exit, noticing how far away it suddenly seemed.

"Me," Dave said, "I want another game. Kinda reminds me of why I stuck it out through high school."

The vampire in the basketball jersey grinned. He motioned to his two friends. "Let's do it then."

The vampires all wore basketball jerseys. Xander didn't know if they had actually been players for the other high school, or if they'd stolen the jerseys from bodies of past victims.

Play began explosively with Dave hitting the top-of-the-key jumper to get control of the ball. Xander glanced back at the drugstore, wishing Giles would get there. The only thing keeping Xander on the court was thinking that Chris and Dave were going to end up as vampire munchies without him. Of course, staying there could make him only one more munchie.

The three vampires played down and dirty, fouling with elbows and knees, showing obvious skill at the game. And because of their vampire strength, all of them could jump as high as Dave even though they were inches shorter.

"Man," Chris said during a brief huddle with Dave and Xander as the vampires retrieved the ball after Dave had swatted it out of bounds, "I never saw guys that could move like this."

"I know. They're only five points behind us." Dave studied the vampires, breathing heavily, sweat dripping from his face. "What I want to know is if they're so good, why the hell ain't we heard of them before?"

"Because you're hearing of us now." The lead vampire had LOOMIS printed on the back of his jersey.

Chris and Dave glanced at each other, and only Xander understood it was the vampires' keener sense of hearing that allowed them to hear the conversation.

"Yeah," Dave said. "Lotta good that's gonna do you. Two more buckets and you clowns are toast."

"You know," Xander said, holding his hands up, "just a thought here, but maybe calling them clowns is a not-good idea." He was beginning to hope that maybe they *were* vampires just out for a game. *Stranger things had happened, right? I know from strange.*

"Clowns," Dave insisted. "You guys ain't got what it takes to hang."

"Dee up," Loomis taunted. "You'll be surprised to see what we got." He grinned.

Silently, Xander slipped the cross he'd stuck into his pocket for patrol into his hand. He panted raggedly, drenched in his clothing despite the cool air.

The three vampires stuck a hand into a brief huddle. "What time is it?" Loomis bellowed.

"Game time!" the other two vampires yelled. And when the three of them turned back, their faces had morphed, revealing their true natures.

"Damn!" Chris swore. "Am I just getting tired, or did they just turn really *ugly?*"

No, Xander thought bitterly, *this whole situation just turned really ugly.* He kept the cross hidden from sight.

The three vampires broke, and suddenly they were everywhere, dribbling, shooting, and stealing the ball. Xander had no hope of keeping up with them. Chris and Dave quickly lost ground. In less than a minute, the game was over and the humans never had the chance to score another point. The two vampire girls broke out into a cheerleading exhibition that would have broken Olympic records as they flipped and jumped out onto the court to congratulate their guys. The two girls had their fangs out, too.

"Looks like you guys are the losers," Loomis roared, taking a platinum blonde into his arms.

"I'm hungry," the girl whined, nipping at his neck playfully.

Loomis laughed. "This is Tandy. She's always hungry." He shrugged. "Me and the guys wanted to play a game, but the girls made us promise we'd get them something to eat after." He smiled, tossed the basketball up and punctured it with a sharp-nailed finger. The sudden detonation echoed over the basketball court. "Dinner; now, that'd be you."

The two girls turned on them with catlike grace and savagery.

Chris and Dave seemed frozen.

"Okay, guys," Xander said, pulling on their elbows. "That would be our cue to exit. Stage left, even." But before Chris or Dave could get it together, one of the girls rushed forward with superhuman speed.

Xander lifted his hand and pressed it palm forward into the girl's forehead. The grin didn't leave her face for an instant; she obviously thought he couldn't stop her. Then smoke curled up from her burning flesh where the palmed cross touched her.

"Shit!" the girl yelped as her bangs and forehead caught on fire. She pulled back, but Xander stayed with her for a few more seconds, burning her as deeply as he could before she broke free. She screamed in agony and fury, looking up into the sky as the top of her head blazed and blistered.

"Now!" Xander yelled, shoving Chris and Dave in front of him, trying desperately to figure out where they could safely go.

The gate swung open suddenly and a half-dozen figures stepped inside the court, creating a solid wall that blocked the exit. Their green and white hair stood out starkly against the dark colors they wore.

Xander came to a quick halt, knowing from the hard set of the faces of the new arrivals that rescue wasn't imminent.

"More meat!" one of the vampires screamed.

The leader of the Asian group drew a pistol from behind his back. Xander threw himself against Chris and Dave and knocked them out of the way. A line of bullets smashed into the basketball court and quickly stuttered up one of the male vampires.

The bullets wouldn't kill the vampire, Xander knew, but it definitely wasn't a painless operation.

The vampire jerked and stumbled back, finally knocked off his feet by the vicious impacts. The first Asian gunman ejected the spent clip and took a fresh one from his jacket pocket.

The other vampires watched in stunned surprise. Before they could react, another of the new guys wordlessly stepped forward and unstoppered a large bottle. He poured fluid on the vampire struggling to get up from the basketball court. The downed vampire screamed and cursed as smoke curled up from his drenched body. In the next heartbeat, the liquid ignited a burning pyre out of the vampire's body. In seconds only ash remained.

"Your days are over," the gang leader said in a harsh voice. "The shadows in this city belong to us now." He swung the pistol toward Xander, Chris, and Dave. "The spoils belong to the victor. We are the victors."

"The hell you are!" Loomis snarled. "There's a lot more going on in this town than you—"

The gunman blasted Loomis in the chest with three shots. Loomis dropped to his knees in pained surprise.

Another man started forward with a bottle, but Loomis jerked to his feet and retreated. The Asian youth glanced at the leader. "What do you want to do with the humans?"

"Kill them," the man answered.

"Wait!" Xander yelled. "Hold it! I was just getting to like you guys! Now it's, 'Kill them!'? That doesn't work for me!"

The Asian leader signaled his troops toward the vampires, assigning one man to Xander, Chris, and Dave. Xander glanced up at the Asian youth's face and saw no trace of mercy or compassion. He raised a pistol, casually gazing down the barrel. His knuckle whitened on the trigger.

Xander knew at that range the man wasn't going to miss.

Then, incredibly, the Asian youth's head leaped up from his shoulders. For a moment, the decapitated body remained standing. The gun barrel dropped first, without firing, followed swiftly by the body as it fell across Xander.

Reaching nearly max gross-out potential, because it was one thing for vampires to dust after they were dead and another for a still-warm and bleeding body to be so up close and personal, Xander shoved the dead man from him. *Who?* Then he saw the swordswoman standing there, the dead man's head still wobbling at her feet.

"Go!" she ordered.

Chris and Dave wasted no time, moving with all the athletic ability they had. The chain link fence shivered and rattled as they hit the gate and went through.

But Xander Harris got to his feet in open-mouthed shock and instant lust.

The swordswoman stood almost as tall as he did, but the curves screamed all woman. Her delicate, almond-shaped eyes reflected a beautiful golden hazel in the lights of the basketball court. The raven's wing black hair was piled atop her head, held in place by long ivory needles with tiny green stones in the ends. Her mouth was generous, curved, and full-lipped, darkly red. A round badge Xander couldn't identify hung around her throat on a black leather cord, holding it tightly up against her flesh. She looked like she might have been twenty years old.

She wore a black silk outfit that barely clung to her. Thin straps ran behind her slender neck and held the bodice in place. Despite the bare shoulders, sleeves covered her arms from mid-biceps to her wrists, a runner of wispy material flaring out into a triangle shape on each arm. The bottom of the outfit was a long skirt with generous pleats that dropped to soft boots. A short, shapeless cape with a high collar draped from her shoulders to the backs of her knees, fluttering gently in the breeze.

The sword hanging down in her right hand was over three feet long and dripped blood. The blade tapered, growing slightly wider as it reached the point. Deeply etched grooves marked the top of the heavy blade. Brass fittings and red lacquered wood made up the handle. A dark red sash attached to the end of the handle wrapped around her wrist.

Another sword hilt stuck up over her left shoulder, evidently sheathed down her back. She held a long-barreled flintlock pistol in her left hand. The heavy barrel gleamed dully in the light.

Without a word, the young woman raised the pistol and pointed it at Xander's face, dragging the hammer back with her thumb.

Chapter 9

"DO YOU WORK HERE?"

Rupert Giles looked at the Asian youth with the green and white striped hair standing before him. His voice was tight when he answered. "No. No, I'm afraid I don't."

The youth turned his attention to Barbara Styles, the woman behind the counter. "Do you work here?"

She hesitated. "Yes."

The youth looked around carefully. "Do you own this place?"

"No," Barbara said. "I only work here."

"Then you have a master." The youth settled his unwavering gaze on her.

"I have an employer."

The youth stepped closer and shoved the telephone on the counter over to the woman. "Call your employer."

"Mr. Torrie doesn't like to be bothered," Barbara said quietly and not very confidently.

Without changing expression, the youth pulled a machine pistol from under his long jacket. He fired without seeming to aim, raking a withering hailstorm of bullets across the aisle Giles had taken his purchases from.

Giles jumped, dropping his small basket and starting for the woman's side.

One of the youths moved inhumanly fast, seizing Giles's tie in one hand. "No. Down on your knees. Place your hands behind your head." He shoved his pistol barrel roughly against the side of the Watcher's neck.

Moving slowly so there would be no misinterpretation of his actions, Giles did as he was told.

The gang leader pointed to the phone as he spoke calmly to Barbara, who was shaking and crying soundlessly. "Call your employer," he ordered. "You can give him a message by speaking with him or I can pin it to your dead body."

Barbara froze, her mouth open as she continued to cry noiselessly.

"Barbara," Giles said quietly. When she didn't respond to his gentleness, he put more authority in his voice. "Barbara." The man beside him kept the pistol pointed at his head. *That,* the Watcher decided, *can be somewhat disconcerting.* "Barbara, listen to me."

The woman shifted her gaze to Giles.

"Good. Now I want you to pick up the phone." After she did, Giles let out a tense breath and went on. "Dial your employer's number."

"What . . . what if he's not there?" she asked fearfully.

"Then we'll leave a message on his damned machine," Giles said. "I'm quite sure that will be sufficient." He glanced at the gang leader.

The young man nodded slowly. "That will be acceptable."

Barbara shook so badly she had to make the attempt

four times before she got the right number. "Mr. Torrie, this is Barbara Styles, from the drugstore. Yes, I know I'm not supposed to call you there."

The conversation at the other end of the phone came across as angry, unintelligible gibberish.

"Dammit, Paul!" Barbara screamed. "I don't give a rat's ass what your wife suspects, thinks or even worries about! I've got a man here with a pistol pointed in my face! Of course I haven't called the police! I don't think he would—" She yelped when the Asian youth effortlessly snatched the phone from her hand.

"Mr. Torrie," the gang leader said in a quiet, firm voice, "you will listen to me."

Giles heard the gibberish over the phone for a moment.

The gang leader raised the phone and held the pistol close to it. He fired three shots, waited for a moment, then began speaking again. "No. The woman is not dead. But if you don't listen, she will be, and I'll come to your home and shoot you through the head myself."

Absolute silence reigned at the other end of the phone connection.

"Very good," the gang leader said. "It has come to my master's attention that you have both a profitable legitimate business in this location as well as an illegitimate one. From now on, you will pay my organization, the Black Wind, twenty percent profit of both businesses. We will examine your books. If you don't do this, we will burn this building down, kill your employees, then track you down and execute you as well. A man will visit you next week. Have both payments ready. Cash, no bills larger than a twenty." He pressed the disconnect number.

Giles waited tensely. Everything about the gang, from what he'd seen on television only moments ago to their actions within the drugstore had suggested nothing but professionalism. *Still, there is nothing that bears out a threat like a dead body.* He waited tensely.

The gang leader approached Giles curiously. "You handled that very calmly."

"Well," Giles responded, "it did seem to actually be the only way to handle it."

A small smile lifted a corner of the youth's mouth. "Yes." He knelt slowly, lowering himself to Giles's kneeling height, staying just out of range. His head cocked to one side. "I feel I should know you."

"No," Giles said. "We've never met. I'm sure I'd remember if we had."

"Yes." The gang leader's head rotated back up as smoothly as though it was mounted on ball bearings. He held up his empty hand only inches from Giles's face.

Giles felt unexpected heat from the hand, as if the man were feverish. He stared into the youth's eyes and watched as they transformed from a dark muddy color to white-silver. They became unfocused, like he could no longer see.

Then a seam opened along the man's palm. Incredibly, the seam twitched, then opened wide to reveal a blood-red eye no bigger than a dime. The eye locked onto Giles's gaze.

The Watcher's mind suddenly felt boiling and leaden. Clawed feet seemed to track through his skull, searching and curious.

The seam closed, covering the eye, and the Black Wind leader's eyes changed back from silver to their original dark muddy color. "You are a shadow man, one who watches."

Giles didn't say anything. His curiosity was immediately aroused. Although he knew from his Watcher studies that there were thousands of demons—purebred, lesser, and hybrid—it bothered him when he found those he couldn't immediately identify.

The Black Wind leader stood. "Beware, shadow man. Always remember that you have no special powers. You can die as any other mortal man." He touched Giles's face, tearing a fingernail painfully through the Watcher's already-split lip. The Asian youth took a drop of blood on his forefinger and licked it off with a pointed tongue. The rasp of tongue against skin sounded like pieces of coarse sandpaper rubbed together. His eyes fired silver again for just an instant. He smiled again, thin-lipped and without mirth. "And now that I have the taste, there is no place that you can hide from me."

Suddenly, the raging din of automatic weapons sounded from outside.

"The vampires across the street," one of the gang members stated.

The Black Wind leader nodded and gestured to his men, calling them to him as he raced toward the door. They tore shelves apart, spilling goods everywhere as they went, a final reminder to those who had been threatened.

Giles waited for a moment, feeling his heart thunder in his chest, then pushed himself to his aching feet. He glanced at Barbara Styles. "Don't just stand there. Call the police."

She looked at him. "Call the police, hell. Like they've ever done any good. I'm calling the first friend I can think of who lives the farthest from this damn town, and then I'm leaving. Haven't you noticed what's going on here tonight? There's some kind of gang war shaping up right here in Sunnydale."

"I'm sure," Giles said, "that's not what's really going on here."

"If it isn't, I'd rather read about it in the paper. From a long way away."

Giles ran to the front of the drugstore. Once he reached the door, he peered out cautiously. All of the Black Wind gang members ran across the street, passing his car. *My empty car,* he suddenly realized. *Where is Xander?*

Flashes flared in the darkness surrounding the basket-ball court. One of the large halogen lights over the court suddenly shattered, plunging a section of the park into total darkness.

Then Giles spotted Xander Harris standing in front of a young woman who had an antique pistol pointed directly at his head. As Giles watched, the young woman's pistol went off, discharging a cloud of rolling, gray smoke and a foot-long muzzle flash.

Xander! Before Giles knew it, he was out the door and crossing the street at a dead run.

Angel forced himself up from the windshield of the racing car, overcoming the centrifugal force that tried to pin him there. He rolled to the left on the car hood, then heard bullets cut the air beside him.

The street scene sped by dizzyingly for a moment as he recovered from the fall off the fire escape ladder. He caught the hood's edge and peered through the spider-webbed windshield. The Asian youth driving the car calmly pulled a pistol from his jacket.

Buffy! Her name echoed through Angel's mind like a thunderclap. He reached for that dark part of himself that would forever be tainted by Darla's dark desires, the part that wedded to his own human frailties and jealousies and made him the vampire.

He took on the full strength and speed of the demon that haunted him as he morphed. His senses grew sharper, and the actions of the youths in the car seemed to slow by comparison. But the ravening beast that his returned soul barely kept in check most days grew closer to the forefront of his mind as well, putting that endless fall from grace that much closer.

Growling with barely restrained rage, Angel gripped the car hood with one hand and shot his other hand through the weakened windshield. The safety glass broke around his hand and the windshield tore from its moorings, falling into the car's interior.

Angel gripped the driver's hand, wrapping his fingers around the pistol as well, capturing the hammer so it couldn't go completely back on double-action and fire. Bones broke in Angel's grip, but there was no mercy even in his human soul. *They tried to kill Buffy.*

The man in the passenger seat fired again. Bullets plucked at Angel's duster, ripping one corner to shreds. Angel held onto the driver's hand, twisted, and kicked the man hanging out the passenger side window in the chest.

The gang member flew from the window and crashed into the street. The man rolled over and over, then lay still on the pavement.

Angel turned his attention back to the driver. His lips pulled back, exposing his fangs.

One of the men in the backseat fired at Angel. The rapid blast of bullets punctured the car top, but they also cratered the driver's head. Angel got a faceful of blood and brains, and one of the bullets cored into his cheekbone. Fiery pain flooded his head, almost causing him to black out. His head snapped back. His balance lost, he rolled over the side of the car and fell.

He slammed onto the pavement and the car's rear tires rushed by only inches from his head. Dazed and hurting, his left eye filled with his blood and the driver's, he forced himself to look up.

The sedan swerved out of control and rear-ended a parked van. The dead driver, unrestrained by a seat belt, hurtled through the broken windshield and bounced from the rear of the van. The corpse, half the head missing, flopped to the pavement like a puppet with cut strings.

Staggered by his injuries, Angel shoved himself to his feet. His cheek hurt, throbbing like it was taking hits from a sledgehammer. Blood ran down his face and dripped from his chin. He focused on the young gang member struggling in the backseat of the wrecked sedan.

Questions ran through Angel's mind about who these men were and why things had turned so personal toward Buffy. He desperately wanted one of the gang members alone for just a few minutes, but already police sirens sounded in the distance.

The young Asian in the backseat of the sedan pointed his weapon at the back glass. Bullets blasted fist-size holes in the glass. The gang member threw an elbow into the fractured glass and punched through, uncoiling from the backseat and stepping out onto the trunk. He raised the strange device lining his forearm, his face a mask of black rage.

Angel threw himself to the right, still managing over a dozen feet with the effort despite his weakened condition. He hit the pavement and pushed off again, wrapping his arms around his head and smashing through the front glass of a diner.

A woman screamed, and Angel was suddenly aware that the diner had occupants. The floor space ran straight back with chairs and tables scattered across it. The kitchen was in the back with a pass-through window that ran all the way across. Men in factory coveralls, women with shopping bags, and two kids were hunkered under the tables or against the walls on the floor beneath framed seascape puzzles. All of the diners and waitresses had wide, anxious eyes. The little boy and girl were crying, and were held by scared mothers.

"Are you one of them?" a gray-haired man asked.

"No," Angel said.

"Oh, my God!" a woman screamed, pointing at Angel. "You've been shot!"

Realizing that the damage was more than could be easily explained away, Angel sat up and covered the side of his face with one arm. He morphed his face back to human. "It looks worse than it is." He twisted his head and looked out the window.

"Who are they?" a waitress demanded.

"I don't know," Angel replied. He focused on the building across the street above the alley where he'd come from, scanning the fire escape for Buffy and Willy, but finding neither of them.

"We were watching those guys on the news," another man said. He held a thick paper towel compress against a leg wound. "They were just out at Peppy's Miniature Golf Park. They shot the mayor."

Tortured rubber shrilled out on the street, drawing Angel's attention. Buffy was still nowhere to be seen.

The man from the wrecked sedan deliberately aimed his weapon at the stricken vehicle. Flashes screamed from the weapon on the back of his forearm and tore into the gas tank, then exploded the sedan into fiery ruin. The vehicle jerked up and slammed back down, wreathed in flames. Without pause, his dark sunglasses flashing reflections of the twisting flames, the young gang member grabbed the decapitated corpse by the jacket back, then flung the dead man on top of the burning car.

Another sedan braked to a skidding stop only a few feet from the man. The guy in the passenger seat got out and took a seat in the back. The man that had shot Angel slid into the passenger seat. The driver peeled out before the door closed.

The police sirens screamed louder, drawing nearer.

Knowing staying there to be questioned by the police was not an option, Angel raised up and walked over to the wounded man. "How bad is it?"

"Not as bad as your face," the man assured him in a shaking voice. "Buddy, you better lie down, because I don't see how you're standing now."

Angel surveyed the man's leg, knowing from the spreading bloodstain that the man had a good chance of bleeding out before an EMT arrived. He could also smell the sweet elixir of the blood, calling out to him seductively. His throat hurt and his mouth salivated. His face trembled, from the pain and from the instinctive urge to morph and feed. The appetite made him a demon, but his ability to turn it down kept him human.

"You're bleeding too much," Angel said in a hoarse voice. "Move your hand."

"If I move my hand, I'm going to bleed more." The man sounded hesitant and afraid.

"You're liable to die if we don't shut the bleeding down." Angel stood up on his knees, spotted the red and white checked tablecloth on a nearby table, and grabbed it. He yanked the tablecloth off with a quick snap that sent the plates and glasses atop it crashing to the floor. He looked at the waitress only a few feet away. "Sorry."

"I think that could be the least of our worries," the young woman said.

Angel shoved the man's hands aside and stuck a finger inside the bullet hole in his pants. He ripped the material easily, taking the pants leg off. Blood pumped with every heartbeat, running across the floor like an artesian well. The scent was intoxicating.

After he folded the tablecloth, Angel wrapped it over the wounds in the front and back of the man's leg. "The bullet went through," he told the man, "but it nicked an artery. When the EMTs get here, make sure you tell them that."

"Sure," the man replied in a paper-thin voice.

Angel studied the man's pasty features and dilated eyes, pinpricks on a field of red webbing. The heartbeat at the side of the man's neck was rapid and irregular. Angel glanced at the waitress. "He's going into shock. We need blankets or coats, something to keep him warm."

She nodded but didn't move.

"Now," Angel told her sharply.

Maybe it was the tone of his voice, or maybe it was getting his mangled face fully turned on her, but the waitress moved, staying low as she crossed the floor.

"Hey," a man said, "Joe's my friend. Is there anything I can do?" He wore the same machine shop shirt as the wounded man.

"I'm going to put a tourniquet on his leg," Angel said. "I've got to get it tight enough to stop the bleeding and give his body a chance to start clotting. But if the tourniquet is kept too tight for too long, he could lose the leg." He leaned forward so he could reach a butter knife on the floor. "So you'll need to loosen it for him every few minutes, just long enough to let the blood back into the leg. There'll be some bleeding, but that can't be helped."

"Me?" the man asked. "I never done anything like that. Why me?"

Angel finished tying the knots, then slipped the butter knife into the tourniquet and turned it to tighten it. Once he had it tight enough, the bleeding stopped. "You'll need to do it in case I pass out."

"Oh. Right."

Angel waved the man over and surrendered his place. Joe was hazy, all but out where he lay. Angel glanced at the kids, still crying and wrapped up in fetal positions. Anger simmered within him, but he kept a tight rein on it. That emotion could be dangerous to him as well. If he slew one of the enemies he faced and drank their blood, even that might be enough to extinguish his soul again. He still wasn't sure about the limits of the Gypsy curse that had been laid on him. He moved for the window and stepped through.

"Where are you going?" the waitress asked as she returned with a pile of coats and jackets.

Angel didn't answer. He stepped out onto the sidewalk in front of the diner. Nothing moved out on the street, and nothing moved on the fire escape by Willy's bar. *Buffy. Did they get her?* He sniffed the air, searching for her scent. Panic welled inside him, hammering at his ribs. *She's the Slayer; she was born to die in battle. And these guys knew who she was.*

Chapter 10

RAPID THUMPING FROM THE DIRECTION OF THE BURNING car drew Angel's attention. At first he thought by some freakish chance the headless man hadn't been dead after all.

Then he stared through the wavering flames and saw a familiar, lithe figure on top of the burning car. The incredible tightness in his chest relaxed and he couldn't help but smile. Unfortunately, that made his wounded cheek explode in renewed agony.

Firelight danced on the burnished gold of Buffy's hair as she reached for the decapitated corpse. She grabbed the dead man by one leg and yanked him down to the sidewalk. The corpse dropped to the pavement, clothing burning in a handful of places. The hair left around the shattered parts of the dead man's head smoldered when they hit.

A crowd had started to gather outside Willy's. Most of them weren't any more eager to meet the arriving Sunnydale police than they were to meet the Asian gang members.

Angel crossed the sidewalk to Buffy. She beat at the flames searing the man with her coat.

"He's dead," Angel said.

Buffy didn't look up. "Kind of looks like an incomplete Mr. Potato Head. Think I got the clue on that one."

The sirens screamed more loudly.

"We don't want to be caught here," Angel pointed out.

Stubbornly, Buffy beat at the flames on the corpse. "They knew me, Angel, and they tried to kill me. I want to know why. I mean, there are questions like, is my mom going to be next that kind of grab my attention about now." She hit the flames in a greater frenzy. "Or am I going to go home and find out that she's already dead?"

"Your mom's all right," Angel said.

"And what makes you so sure?"

"They didn't come for you," Angel replied. "They came to rob Willy's. You happened to be there."

"They also knew who I was."

"Or they were looking for someone who looked like you."

"A lot like me." Satisfied with the extinguishing job she'd done on the dead man's arms, Buffy lifted the left one and pushed the sleeve back. She found the picture nestled inside a leather wrist bracelet.

Angel recognized the picture as Buffy unsnapped and removed the bracelet.

"Junior year." Buffy studied the color photo. "Never did like that picture. Made me look too—" She glanced up and saw his face. "Omigod! Your face!" She reached for him, her fingers stained with the dead man's blood.

"I'm fine," Angel said, pushing her hand away, ignoring the blood smell that tantalized him even more now that it came from her fingertips. "I'll just take a really bad picture for a few days."

Buffy drew her hand back. "Not funny."

"Good," Angel said, "because when I laugh it hurts like hell."

A police car roared onto the scene, turning a ninety-degree angle in the street and stopping in front of Willy's Alibi. Spotlights on either side of the car flared to life and tracked across the front of the tavern, scattering the handful of regulars who hadn't already vacated the premises.

"Show's over," Buffy said. "Time for all the suspicious people to flee the scene."

"That includes us." Angel helped her to her feet.

"If any of those guys are left behind and they have these little trophy cases on their arms," Buffy pointed out, "the police are going to be asking questions I can't answer."

"Maybe they won't think it's a very good likeness either," Angel said. "Plus, the gang members seem to have cleaned up after themselves." He hoisted the dead man back up and threw him onto the burning car. The corpse landed with a thud, throwing sparks high into the air.

"Should have brought the body with us," Buffy said as she started down the alley by the diner.

"Would have looked suspicious."

Buffy sighed and silently agreed. "We might have found out something more about these guys."

Angel glanced back at the blazing pyre, watching as the flames welcomed the dead man back into their hungry embrace. "We'll find out more. We haven't heard the last of these guys."

"Do you know what's going on with my brother?"

Willow froze for a moment, halting her frantic digging through the dresser drawers filled with boy things that she'd never really wanted to know about. Well, actually maybe she'd wondered about them, but it hadn't been an overly compelling *need* to know. *How many jocks can one guy need?* Lok Rong seemed to have them color-coordinated.

She glanced back at Jia Li and felt guilty. "Do I look like I know what's going on?"

Jia Li sat on the lower bed of the bunkbeds the two smaller Rong boys slept on in the room. She'd deliberately avoided her older brother's bed. "You look like you know what you're looking for."

"What I'm looking for," Willow said as she finished emptying the drawer, "is something that doesn't fit. It's kind of a standard police procedure." *But what I'm looking for is actually witchcraft materials, which fits exactly with what I think is going on with Lok. However, those things don't fit in this house, so that's at least kind of right. Right?* She wasn't sure, but the guilt was really bothering her. And, so far, she hadn't found any.

The two younger Rong boys weren't helping. They lay up on the top bunk and watched her with eager eyes, arms folded up to pillow their chins. "Boy, are you guys going to be in trouble when Lok finds out you've been going through his stuff," one of them said.

"Yeah," the other one added, "he's going to kick your butts. He hates people going through his stuff."

Jia Li turned to the boys and spoke rapidly and sharply in Chinese. Both small boys cowed back, pushing away from the edge of the bunk. She sat back down, her face flushed. "Sorry, Willow, but little brothers can be such a pain."

"I wouldn't know," Willow said, moving on to the next drawer.

"Big sisters are worse," one of the boys whispered just loud enough to be heard.

Willow had decided the bedroom was definitely a boy's room. Fantastically colored anime posters decorated the walls and *Gundam Wing* action figures formed militia lines against Batman and the X-Men.

There was hardly anything of Lok in the room except for clothing and a few pictures of him playing sports or skateboarding that he'd left in packages or cheap photo albums. He obviously hadn't cared very much about them. For a guy, he kept his stuff surprisingly neat.

Willow still had the headache she'd gotten from the vision earlier. Thankfully, it had dulled to an almost tolerable level. A small anti-headache potion made with meadowsweet that she had at home would allow her to sleep and ensure the pain was gone by morning. *Unless it's some kind of spell hangover from the vision,* Willow thought. *Or something even more malevolent.* She took a deep breath and squelched the panic that vibrated through her. Sometimes really bad spells had delayed reactions. *Okay, we're not going there.* She turned her attention back to her search.

The small antique brass chest was at the bottom of the third drawer. It measured eighteen inches long by twelve inches wide and two inches thick. As soon as Willow touched the cool metal of the chest and felt the thrill of electricity buzz against her fingertips, she knew she'd found what she was looking for.

"What is it?" Jia Li asked, getting up from the bed.

"I'm not sure," Willow said, "but I think it's part of what we're looking for." She set the chest down on the bureau and hooked a fingernail under the small latch. Grudgingly, the latch lifted and she opened the chest.

Inside was a small, faded picture that had browned with age and turned brittle. Packets of crushed, powdered and dried herbs that Willow instantly recognized also filled the chest. Gotu Kola was used in meditation incenses. Marigolds were used to invoke clairvoyance. Mugwort was good for increasing the powers of magical items, cleaning crystals or scrying mirrors, and to aid in astral travel.

She continued sorting through the packets, identifying them and their uses. Oak leaves and bark aided in binding spells. Sandalwood could be used by a warlock or witch to center and calm himself or herself. Dragon's blood increased the strength of other herbs. Uva-ursi, though Willow had never used it as such, was said to increase psychic powers. Damiana was often preferred to produce visions.

A small wooden flute barely fit diagonally in the case. It was no thicker than a finger, with small holes carved into it. Black Chinese dragons, long and serpentine instead of bulky and heavy like their European cousins, ran down the flute on either side of the holes.

Willow took the delicate instrument from the chest with care. Her fingers slid along the polished surface, finding even the imperfections smoothed over. *It's old.* A spark ignited against her fingertips, surprising her with a stinging sensation that caused her to drop the flute. "Oh."

The flute tumbled from her fingers to the carpeted floor. The black dragons seemed to gaze up resentfully.

"What happened?" Jia Li asked.

The flute doesn't like me touching it, Willow thought, but she said, "I don't know. Must have been some kind of static electricity buildup." Her fingertips still tingled.

Jia Li bent and picked up the small flute. She offered it to Willow.

"Just put it back in the chest," Willow said. Obviously the flute held some kind of power and reacted to anyone who had witch powers. Or maybe it just didn't like her. "Do you know what it is?"

"I've never seen it before." Jia Li replaced the flute in the chest.

"It, uh, goes the other way," Willow advised. "The objective here is to not let Lok know we've been looking."

Jia Li turned the flute the other way.

"It's Lok's magic flute," one of the little brothers said.

"Yeah," the other one added. "He plays it sometimes late at night and talks to the shadows."

"The shadows?" Willow turned to the boys and brushed her hair from her face.

"The shadows on the wall." The boy pointed at the wall near the closet door. "They come when he plays. He only does it when he thinks we're asleep."

"What does he do then?" Willow asked.

"Sometimes he argues. Most of the time he just gets really mad."

"Why?"

The boy shrugged. "The shadows argue with him. They don't show him what he wants to see. And sometimes they laugh at him. Then he gets really mad."

Willow digested that, remembering the shambling corpse Lok had called from the earthen wall in her vision. "How does he call them?"

"He plays the flute and uses the candle from the closet. He keeps it up above the door so no one can find it."

Jia Li approached the closet door and felt up over the frame. Her doubtful look turned to surprise. She brought out a long, slim candle tinted light green. The wick was burned black on the end and cooled droplets from past burnings made it knobby. The uneven striations and thickness were proof that the candle was handmade.

Willow knew the candle's scent would be dandelions and horehound before she smelled it. The flute was made from elder wood, so the candle had to be made with dandelions and horehound. It all added up, and it gave her a clue about what Lok was doing.

"What are these things?" Jia Li asked Willow.

"Did your grandfather do anything like this?" Willow asked.

"I don't know." Jia Li looked at the candle and the flute as if they were strange insects. "My grandfather was an herbalist. He grew a number of plants besides vegetables and fruits. People came to his home to buy them and trade them. Those packages contain herbs?"

"Yes," Willow answered.

"Do you know what they are?"

"Some of them," Willow said. *No way am I getting into my interest in witchcraft at this point. Jia Li's already freaked.* "None of them are illegal, so you don't have to worry about that."

"I hadn't even thought about that," Jia Li said softly.

"It might be better if the candle were put back."

Wordlessly, Jia Li returned the candle to its hiding place.

Willow took the faded photograph out gently, feeling the frailty it had. She turned it over and examined the man in the picture.

The photograph was sepia-toned, indicating that it was a hundred years or more old. The man looked thin, dressed in black pants, work boots, and a white shirt that looked a couple sizes too large for him. He wore an uncertain and nervous smile beneath longish dark hair. He stood near a mule-drawn wagon in front of a ramshackle building whose sign announced SUNNYDALE GENERAL STORE. The road was heavily rutted beneath the horses' hooves.

"I thought at first this was your grandfather," Willow said. "But it isn't, is it?"

"No." Jia Li stood close, staring at the picture perplexingly. "This is a picture of my ancestor. The one who died over here."

"Mei-Kao Rong," Willow said, looking into the young face.

"How did you know that?"

"I heard his name mentioned at the graveyard," Willow reminded. "And I saw the gravestone. You seem surprised to see this picture."

"We thought it was lost," Jia Li said. "It was in the things my mother got after my grandfather died. She had copies of the picture made and passed out to my father's sisters and brother, but she thought the original had been lost during the move here. I can't believe Lok didn't tell them he had it."

"Your mother's father had it?" Willow asked, putting the family connections together.

"Yes."

"Why would your mother's father have this picture? Mei-Kao Rong was one of your father's ancestors, not your mother's."

Jia Li studied the picture with renewed curiosity. "I don't know. I don't think anyone thought to ask."

"The picture must mean a lot to Lok." Willow replaced the photograph in the chest. "What do you know about Mei-Kao Rong?"

"Only that he died here in a terrible accident in the mines," Jia Li replied. "His grave lies empty because they never found the body. There were other men who were killed at the same time."

"Do you know who they were?"

"No. I only know this from stories my father's family has told. There are letters that Mei-Kao wrote and sent back to his family, but only a few of those."

"Can you get copies of those letters?"

"Yes. But why would we need them?"

"I don't know." Willow replaced the photograph in the

chest. "I'm just working on the assumption that more information—instead of less—is a good thing." She closed the chest and returned it to the drawer, hiding it away as Lok had hidden it.

Even with hiding it, though, Willow knew it wasn't going to hide all the things she believed Lok was tampering with. The image of the corpse stumbling from the earthen wall, then smashing the pick through Lok's head filled her mind again. She shivered.

"Are you all right?" Jia Li asked.

"Yeah," Willow said. "Just thought I had to sneeze."

The phone in the living room rang. Jia Li excused herself and went to answer it.

Willow looked around the room, trying to find anything else that called out to her.

"Do you talk to shadows, too?" one of the younger Rong boys asked.

Willow glanced at him nervously. "Why would you ask that?"

"Don't know," the boy mumbled, yawning. "You've got that look in your eyes the way Lok does sometimes."

Jia Li returned to the room looking a little afraid. "That was the Sunnydale Police Department. They have Lok. He's been arrested."

Xander watched in disbelief as the black-clad swordswoman leveled the flintlock pistol only a couple of inches from his head. Heart pounding, he turned to see what she was aiming at, spotting the Asian youth with the green and white hair coming up on him from behind.

The swordswoman squeezed the trigger deliberately as the Asian gang member tried to lift his machine pistol. The flintlock's hammer struck the frizzen and detonated, gray smoke trailing from the flash pan, then exploding from the muzzle as the ball hurtled through the barrel.

The ball struck the gang member between the eyes and shattered, creating a cloud of brilliantly glowing green dust. During the short time he'd become Army Guy, Xander had learned about frangible ammo—bullets designed to come apart on impact to stun rather than kill— and he guessed the ball was a frangible round of some type, though he'd never seen any with a green cloud.

At first, the Asian youth hadn't been that upset about being shot between the eyes and had only stumbled back. But he backed hurriedly away from the green fog that formed, spewing from the neat, round hole in his head. The gassy cloud followed him though, and curled into his nose, mouth, and ears. Tremors started shaking him immediately, driving him down to his knees as he lost motor control. In the next instant, he collapsed and fell forward, becoming a disgusting pile of green glop that leaked across the basketball court.

Xander glanced up at the swordswoman, torn between fear and fascination.

She slid the pistol back into a holster at her back. Xander saw the second pistol butt on the other side now. Before he could move, she swept her sword up under his chin, resting the keen edge against his Adam's apple.

Xander worked hard not to swallow, thinking he'd probably cut his own throat if he moved. He showed her his open hands, hearing the slap of feet closing in on them from behind. "I come in peace," he whispered.

A faint smile touched the swordswoman's lips and turned her entirely gorgeous in Xander's eyes.

Why is it all the really cool chicks not only have bewitching powers over me, Xander wondered, *but they can also kick my ass?*

The swordswoman came closer to him and he smelled the flowers in her hair. The sword never wavered from his throat, but somehow it didn't seem so important as he looked into her golden hazel eyes.

"You smell," she whispered in curiously accented English, "mostly human."

"I am human," Xander assured her self-consciously. "And that off-odor is just because I've been playing basketball. Oh yeah, earlier tonight I killed a vampire with trash I found in an alley. Normally, I'm really a very hygienic guy. I floss. I wash. I even pick up my own underwear and socks." *At least once a week.*

She pushed him, bringing her empty hand across to plant against his chest. It made her arm muscles pump up nicely, Xander noticed. And he also noticed that the necklace she wore had two colors, blue and white, and was in two pieces in a yin/yang design. Suddenly, two seemed like an awfully familiar number. Everything wonderful came in pairs. *Eyes, ears, necklace pieces, shoulders, and those rounded—*

Then he was falling backward an instant before bullets chopped the air where he'd been standing.

The swordswoman leaped up and seemed to take flight. The long panels attached to her sleeves trailed after her, fluttering on the breeze and making her seem larger and faster than she was. The sword flashed, splintering moonlight as she flipped through the air, touched down, then hurled herself to the side and flipped again. The gang member tried to target her, triggering short bursts that struck the chain link fence.

When the swordswoman landed again, she was within reach of the gunner. Her arm flicked out, flipping the broadsword like it was weightless. The blade swept the man's head from his shoulders in a spray of blood, then she flipped away again. One of the other gang members opened up, blasting the headless corpse as it dropped.

Still incredibly aware of where the blade had been touching his throat, Xander got up and scrambled over to the gloppy remains of the gang member the swordswoman had shot. Insects crawled through the green glop and Xander didn't think they'd just gathered there. One quick grab made the machine pistol on the ground his. He stayed down, clearing the pistol's action and coming to a prone position on his elbows, the weapon extended before him.

Loomis the vampire closed on the swordswoman, but she snapped her left arm in his direction. Loomis stumbled back with a slim wooden stake through his heart, falling backward and turning to dust before he hit the basketball court.

The swordswoman was already in motion, running toward one of the gang members. The three surviving vampires fought with the gang members, staggered by the rounds they fired. The swordswoman ran toward one of the gang members as he fired, getting his attention, then jumping high into the air.

The gang member fired, accidentally hitting one of his own people and knocking him down in a spray of blood. Apparently not all of the Asians had green glop flowing through their veins.

Xander aimed at the gang member's legs and squeezed the trigger, intent on just wounding the guy. The machine pistol jerked in Xander's hands, then went silent.

The gang member glanced down at his bloodied legs and torn pants, then up at Xander. If there was pain from the wounds, the guy wasn't showing it. He whipped his weapon around and aimed point-blank at Xander.

Chapter 11

H*E'S NOT HUMAN*, XANDER TOLD HIMSELF AS HE LOOKED at the grinning gang member pointing the machine pistol at him, *and this is definitely not good*. He pushed himself to his feet, knowing there was no way the gang member could miss.

The swordswoman landed only a few feet away, touching down lightly as a bird. She swapped hands with the sword and pulled the second flintlock pistol from behind her back. She dragged the hammer back as she brought the pistol up, curled her finger over the trigger and fired immediately.

The ball slammed through the gang member's forehead, unleashing another green cloud. Vapor tendrils seeped into the gang member's head through his ears, nose, eyes, and mouth. He squeezed the machine pistol's trigger but the hard metal passed right through his now-gelatinous finger.

"No!" he shouted, but a bilious green spray came out with his voice as his liquid knees collapsed under him.

By the time his head hit the basketball court, it spread into mush like an overripe melon. The stench of ripe decay filled the immediate area.

God, that's disgusting! Xander looked up at the swordswoman as she calmly reholstered her weapon.

Two gang members turned on her and raised their weapons. The swordswoman threw her arms high into the air and followed them, tucking her knees into her chest, going so high Xander knew her boots had to be spring-loaded.

Unable to stand by and watch the woman be shot down, Xander ran at the two men from the side. He threw himself at them as a stream of emptied brass erupted from the automatic weapons. Xander hit the first man hard, driving both of them back into the second man standing nearby. They all went down in a tumbling heap.

Knowing the two gang members would turn on him immediately, Xander scrambled to get free of the other man's arms and legs. One of the men grabbed Xander by the shirtfront and rolled him over onto his back, coming up on his knees. He head-butted Xander in the nose, bringing tears to Xander's eyes. The other gang member reloaded his weapon and shoved the barrel toward Xander's head.

Even through his blurred vision, Xander saw the swordswoman turn in the air, almost looking like she was floating, her black silk dress flaring out behind her. Her hand and forearm flipped forward sharply.

A meaty smack drew Xander's attention to the man with the pistol pointed at his head. A spike suddenly jutted from the gang member's left eye, sending him backward screeching in pain. Another spike caught the second gang member in the forehead, crunching home. The gang member dropped lifelessly across Xander's stomach. They'd been human.

The swordswoman landed and crossed the distance at a dead run, twirling her blade over so it pointed down. She thrust it into the wounded man's chest, piercing his heart, then twisted the blade before freeing it.

"Be careful," she whispered to Xander, then she was moving, and a hail of bullets tore through the air where she'd been.

Xander pushed the corpse off of him, totally amazed at the whirlwind of destruction the swordswoman had become. None of the gang members or the surviving vampires dared take their eyes from her. Three other gang members with green and white striped hair ran in through the courtyard gate, attacking from the swordswoman's left.

The swordswoman hesitated only a split second. Then she grabbed the sword hilt in both hands and charged the first of the new arrivals. She leaped and kicked the pistol from his hand, at the same time putting her other foot in the man's chest to drive him back, and used the change in momentum to loop into an aerial roll. She slashed down with the sword, splitting the second gang member's skull before he could get away. She landed slightly off-balance, delaying her sidestroke at the third man.

The gang member leaped over her blow, revealing unnatural quickness and strength himself. He caught hold of the tall chain link fence, hooking the fingers of one hand through the mesh and catching toeholds. He swung his pistol back around, firing immediately. Bullets tore chunks from the basketball court and ricocheted to the other side.

The swordswoman dodged to one side, staggered for a moment like she'd been hit. She struck the pistol from the gang member's hand with her blade with a metallic shriek.

The gang member was already in motion the instant he lost his weapon. He dodged away from her second at-

tempt and crawled across the chain link fence with a
fluid grace that reminded Xander of an insect.

Springing lithely, the swordswoman pursued the man.
She planted a foot on the fence nearly eight feet up and
leaped at the gang member. Fast as she was, though, the
gang member moved even more quickly. The sword's
keen edge missed him by inches as he scuttled higher,
then jumped from the fence, tucking into a back flip with
a half-twist that put him within reach of his weapon.

Xander grabbed the machine pistol in front of him and
thrust it at the man, squeezing the trigger immediately.
The bullets hammered the man but he remained fixed on
his target.

The swordswoman released her hold on the fence and
bounded outward, gaining distance from the fence as if it
were a trampoline. She turned in midair as her attacker's
gunfire drove sparks from the chain link fence. She
landed in a crouch, a wisp of black material hanging
from her right hand. She placed something into the cloth
loop with her left hand, then whipped it in a circle over
her head. Even as the gang member turned on her, she
flipped the sling forward.

The gang member's head rocked back, driven by the
green ball that slammed into his chin. The cloud the impact released swarmed up around his head at once, chok-
ing him down. He was porridge slipping through his own
clothes before he stumbled back two steps.

The swordswoman recovered her weapon and gazed
steely-eyed across the basketball court. The two vampire
girls and the one surviving guy dropped the drained
corpses of the last two gang members. Blood shone on
their fangs and lips.

The swordswoman faced them down silently. For a
moment Xander thought they might actually attack her.

He dropped the empty pistol and grabbed the stake the young woman had used to kill Loomis the vampire, then stood at her side—out of immediate sword's reach.

She acknowledged him with a small smile, but her face remained hard.

"Next time," the male vampire promised Xander fiercely, "you'll get yours."

"Oh yeah," Xander replied, "you can just—just take a number, you orthodontist's nightmare!" *Now that really sounded catchy,* he told himself sourly.

The vampire guy followed the two girls, streaking toward the fence on the other side of the court. "And you'll need a bigger toothpick."

"I've got bigger toothpicks," Xander said. "Plenty of them. Whole boxfuls." He glanced at the young swordswoman, who seemed to be smiling at him. *And that was just so much more brilliant.* He groaned to himself. Then tried to smile. "I'm still working on witty repartee."

"Xander!"

Turning, Xander saw Giles at the court fence near the street.

"We need to get out of here," the Watcher called. "Now. Before the police arrive."

"I'll be with you in just a minute," Xander promised. He dusted himself off and turned back to the swordswoman. Only she was gone. He scanned the basketball court quickly and spotted her near the gang member she'd kicked when attacking the three latest arrivals.

The gang member was groggy, barely able to rise to his knees. His eyes widened when he saw the swordswoman closing on him. He grabbed for his dropped weapon, but her sword slashed against his throat, neatly slicing his chin so that blood dripped down the blade. The gang member froze.

The swordswoman put her face close to the gang member's. "Tell your master to stay away, that the ones he seeks are protected." She spoke in a low voice that was cold and threatening.

"He will kill you."

"Death has never scared me," the swordswoman replied. She lifted her sword, making him tilt his head back into an uncomfortable position so that his blood ran down his neck. "Tell your master to stay away, or I will be his fate. Do you understand?"

"Yes," the man croaked.

"I pay for this message with your life." The swordswoman drew back, taking the blade from the man's throat. Effortlessly, she spun and kicked the man in the side of the head, stretching him out unconscious. She lifted her bloodstained blade and inspected it for a moment, watching as the metal soaked up the crimson fluid. She turned and walked toward the dark end of the basketball court.

"Xander," Giles called again, and this time police sirens could be heard in the distance, though they actually sounded like they were going away from the park.

Xander ignored the Watcher and took off after the swordswoman. Although she walked, he had to trot to keep up. "Who are you?"

"Why?" She didn't look at him.

"Well, I'd kind of like to know who to thank for saving my life."

"You don't have to thank anyone."

"Actually, I feel like I do. I was so toast when you stepped into that little adventure."

She glanced at him then, and a timid smile lighted those golden hazel eyes. "You are very polite."

"And normally hygienic," Xander reminded. *Gotta remind her that you don't always smell this bad.*

"Of course."

Xander looked at her. "So, thank you—" He let it hang, hoping she would supply a name.

"You are very welcome," she said, tilting her head to the side and still smiling slightly.

"My name is Xander." *Okay, drawing on response reflex here.*

"I thank you, Xander, for saving my life. You are very brave."

"I am?" Xander caught himself. "No. I mean, I only did what I had to."

"I think, under the circumstances, most men would have ran."

"I think, under the circumstances, you should let me buy you dinner."

She stopped and looked at him. "You do."

Xander stared at her, loving the way she looked, knowing he'd never get her out of his mind. *How many girls can look that sexy with a naked sword in their hand? That aren't the Slayer?* And then he wondered if the smile she'd been trying to hide was just her way of being polite and not laughing outright at him.

"Yeah," Xander said, looking into her eyes. "Absolutely." He felt like he was suddenly standing on the edge of a chasm, looking into a bottomless pit, and his heart kept accelerating. A little quiet voice in the back of his head insisted he back off and remember how badly things had gone with Cordelia Chase.

He wasn't one to have luck with women, yet he pressed that luck every chance he got. Buffy insisted on looking at him like a good friend. He'd gotten over the good friend thing with Willow just in time to nearly screw up both their relationships instead of just Cordy's and his.

"It would be better," the swordswoman said, "if you were to forget you ever saw me tonight."

"For me or for you?" Xander asked, taking a step closer to her. The lemony smell of her filled his senses.

"For you."

"Too late," Xander told her, grinning. "Can't. Wouldn't even want to."

Her smile took on a hint of sadness. "You might."

For a moment, the seriousness of her words touched Xander. *She's not kidding.* Self-preservation pinged on his overloaded radar then and some of the ardor he felt cooled.

As if sensing where his thoughts were headed, the swordswoman started walking again.

Xander watched her take two steps, the dress seeming to glide around her hips, the holstered flintlocks behind her back clearly visible. *I've been involved with She-Mantis who wanted to eat my head, took Inca Mummy Girl to the school dance and almost got mummified, and well . . . Cordy. World's Worst Dates, been there, done that, and got the tee shirt.* The young woman took another step. *What's the worst thing that could happen? At least this girl saved my life a couple times tonight.*

Xander went after her. "Hey, wait up."

She kept walking.

"Please," Xander said.

Slowly, her stride shortened and she waited. Xander joined her, standing at her side. "You can't just save my life and run off."

"Yes," she replied, "I can. I will be doing a disservice to you, and perhaps endangering your life if I don't."

Xander showed her a cocky grin. "From who? These mooks? I could have taken them." He shrugged. "Maybe

I don't quite have that green glop thing down that you do so well, but I've managed before."

The young woman laughed. "You have a good sense of humor."

"That's a good thing, right?"

"Not really," she told him. "Too many people who die young have good senses of humor."

"And here I was always told laughter was the best medicine."

"It doesn't resuscitate you when you're dead."

Xander stopped cold, unable to work with that statement. "Okay, point. But I'd really like to get to know you better. Do you know how many girls you can take out on a date, have this kind of thing happen to you, and have them not totally freak on you?"

Still amused, the golden hazel eyes glittering, the young swordswoman said, "No. Is this your idea of a fun . . . *date?*" She used the word like it was foreign to her.

"Not really," Xander answered. "I was thinking more along the lines of dinner, a movie, maybe some ice cream. And talk. Lots of getting-to-know-you talk."

"Perhaps," the young woman said wistfully, "in the next turn of the wheel." She ran from him then, gaining speed.

"Hey!" Xander shouted. "Hey!" He started after her, watching as she made another of those incredible leaps that took her deep into the shadows. He spotted the chain link fence in front of him too late to stop and smashed into it with a resounding *clank!*

He only caught another glimpse of the young swordswoman as she hurtled down on the other side of the fence. She hit the ground running and disappeared between heartbeats, her black silk dress blending in with the shadows.

Glumly, Xander peered through the trees in the darkened park.

"Xander!"

Reluctantly, feeling completely bummed, Xander turned from the fence and trotted back toward the Watcher. Despite his brave words, he really didn't want to be at the park in case the vampires came back or other gang members showed up looking for their friends.

Halfway across the basketball court, something glittered darkly in the moonlight. As he neared the object, Xander saw that it was the necklace the young swordswoman had been wearing. The leather string looked aged and supple, and he supposed it was possible that the necklace had slipped off during the battle.

Xander knelt and picked it up, feeling the silver resting almost ice-cold against his skin. He stood and looked back in the direction that the swordswoman had gone, but there was still no sign of her. He closed his fist over the necklace and ran to join Giles in the car.

Not exactly Cinderella's glass slipper, he told himself as he slid into the car. But it was something.

Chapter 12

XANDER STARED AT THE DEBRIS STREWN ACROSS THE
Bronze's small dance floor. Unaccustomed bright lights
replaced the dimness that usually filled the club. Broken
chairs and tables lay in scattered disarray, and the floor
was sticky with drinks and, in thankfully few areas, blood.

"My God," Giles muttered as he surveyed the wreckage. "This is from the concert?"

"Actually," Oz said, carrying a chair with three legs
over to a pile that had been made by the stage, "this is
from the war." He wore a pumpkin orange tie-dyed shirt
that included green and purple pigments, and khaki pants.

"What war?" Giles asked.

"We got invaded." Oz put the chair on the pile. Blood
trickled from a cut over his left eye. "Some kind of gang
broke up the show and held up the bar."

Xander pointed at his hair. "Asian guys with green
and white hair?"

Oz nodded toward a television someone had brought

out and set up on stage. "Yeah. We noticed that those guys seem to have been everywhere tonight."

Xander nodded. He and Giles had listened to news reports on the radio on the way over to the Bronze. With everything that was going on in town, Xander had figured Buffy and Willow would head for the Bronze to check on Oz. "We had a run-in with them, too."

"A couple, actually," Giles said. He gazed around. "Is there anything we can do to help?"

Oz shook his head. "I'm just helping clean up. It kept me from running out looking for Willow. I figure she'll be here as soon as she can, and I wouldn't know where to start looking for her." He looked at Xander hopefully.

Xander shook his head.

"Anyway, we've already got the wounded to the ER," Oz went on. "With everything going on in Sunnydale tonight, the ambulance service was overworked."

"How bad was it?" Giles asked.

"Nobody died," Oz answered, "but a few of the injured people are going to spend some serious time in the hospital." He shrugged. "Those were mostly some of the lowlifes who hang around pushing bad business."

"The Black Wind gang members targeted those people?" Giles asked.

Oz gazed at the Watcher. "Seemed to. Something going on that I don't know about?"

Giles took his glasses off and polished them. "Oh, there's something going on, but I'm afraid we're all clueless at this point. Unless Buffy, Angel, or Willow have discovered something."

"Oh, we might have discovered a thing or two."

Xander turned, spotting Buffy and Angel walking through the rubble that was the Bronze tonight. *Where's Willow?* Concern filled him, but he didn't let it run rampant. *She's okay.* Willow had to be okay; his world wouldn't be the same any other way.

"What have you found out?" Giles asked.

Buffy flipped a small rectangular photograph into view. "Recognize this?"

"Junior year," Xander said. "But I thought you didn't like it because it made you look—"

"It *does*," Buffy interrupted. "And I'm not carrying it around. Those gang members were."

"Maybe you've got an admirer," Xander quipped.

Buffy's gaze let him know immediately that his humor wasn't appreciated. "A bunch of them had these pictures," she said.

"Oh." Xander felt bad, but feeling the necklace in his pocket made him feel a little better. As long as he had the necklace, he felt certain he'd meet the mysterious swordswoman again. "Another Slayerfest?"

"No," Giles said. "This is something else. The Black Wind members appear to be interested in taking over criminal operations, at least some of them, inside Sunnydale."

"Black Wind?" Angel asked. He wore a large gauze pad on his cheek.

"That's what they're calling themselves," Giles said, quickly describing the events that had taken place inside the drugstore.

"Oz!"

Xander looked up and saw Willow enter the room. Her eyes immediately centered on Oz and she ran to him.

"Are you all right?" she asked, touching his forehead tenderly.

"I'm fine," Oz assured her.

Xander looked away, angry with himself for feeling jealous of the care they had for each other. Not that it was Willow, exactly, just that someone he knew could seem to be so involved with someone else he knew. Despite the slip he and Willow had made, her relationship with Oz had endured, seemingly stronger than ever.

Then Xander noticed that Buffy and Angel were holding hands. *Angel kills Giles's girlfriend, menaces her mom and friends, then Buffy kills Angel and sends his soul to Hell for a hundred years or so, and they* still *find a way to make it work.* He made himself breathe out, wishing he could feel happier for his friends instead of feeling the least bit—*okay, maybe more than a little*—jealous of them all.

"How's your friend?" Buffy asked. "Any ghosts show up after all?"

"Actually," Willow said, "I think one did. Maybe." She glanced around, indicating the attention they were getting from the other Bronze survivors. "Want to find a place with a little more privacy?"

"Lok is in jail?" Buffy asked.

Willow nodded. "He was when I left the Rong residence." She hugged herself, chilled against the restaurant's vinyl-covered bench.

They sat at a huge round table in the corner of the all-night diner not far from the Bronze, where the after-concert overflow usually came to grab breakfast before heading home. Both walls that framed the corner were glass, looking out onto the news crew finally covering the attack at the Bronze. Only a few curious passersby watched the live broadcast, all of them a little wary of the dark night around them. The diner's usual night crowd was missing in action.

"Why is Lok in jail?" Buffy asked.

"He attacked someone named Jameson Percivall," Willow replied.

"Why?"

Willow shrugged. "I don't know, and if Jia Li knows, she didn't mention it."

"Jameson Percivall," Giles said quietly, "comes from one of the founding families of Sunnydale. One of the library's collections was donated, and named after, an ancestor of his who made a fortune during the gold boom in California."

"Ezekial Percivall," Willow said, nodding. "I should have recognized the name."

"Well, you've clearly had other things on your mind," Giles pointed out. "But the attack does bear fruit from what Lok threatened before leaving the Rong household."

"The part about Lok hoping Willow's family wasn't related to any of the families who got wealthy from the mining operations outside Sunnydale," Oz said. He held Willow's hand under the table reassuringly, and Willow enjoyed feeling the calm, warm strength of him.

"Yes. Was Percivall harmed?"

"Jia Li told me Percivall was taken to the hospital following the attack," Willow replied. "But I don't think she knew how bad it was."

"How did Lok find Percivall?" Buffy asked.

"I don't know. He may have used a spell of some kind." Willow had told them about the box she'd found in his room.

"Can you do that?" Xander asked. "I mean, if you had something that belonged to someone, could you find out where they were?"

"I can't," Willow said, noticing the unexplained disappointment flicker in Xander's eyes, "but someone that's further along in the craft probably could. I can't use a candle to talk to ghosts either. Lok can. The flute I found? It's made of elder wood, which is used to call up spirits. Dandelions and horehound in the candle are used in spells for calling spirits and for clearer communication."

"Unless Lok is only suffering from psychological trauma the family has yet to find out about," Giles said. "Lok Rong may be somewhat delusional and only thinks he's talking to ghosts."

Willow knew Giles was only playing devil's advocate, so she didn't argue the point. "That doesn't explain the vision I had, or the voice that told me I had to find a way to protect Lok."

"No," Giles said, "it doesn't." He sipped at his tea. "It appears that we have a number of conundrums facing us tonight. Not in the least of which is the sudden influx of this gang."

"The Black Wind," Buffy agreed. "Even the name sounds kind of creepy."

"Not all of them are human," Angel said.

"No," Giles said, "they're certainly not. But the inhuman ones aren't familiar to me either. This will require some research. As yet, we don't know if the gang springs from the demon world, or from the human one. Willow, perhaps we could go over the books first thing in the morning."

"Sure," Willow replied.

Giles emptied his teacup and rubbed at his face. "I think our first order of business would be to identify these demons if we can."

"And find out who gave them my picture," Buffy added.

"Right," Giles said. "Until we do, perhaps it would be better if you kept a low profile."

Buffy gazed at the Watcher levelly. "Giles, I've never exactly been low-profile. Even before I became the Slayer. And if I'm out hunting them, maybe they won't be so eager to take me on. Sitting-Target Girl is not my idea of a fun time."

"I suppose." The Watcher glanced at Angel.

"I'll be with her on patrols," Angel said. "And while you guys are in school tomorrow, maybe I can find out something about the Black Wind gang."

"That," Buffy said, "doesn't sound like an entirely great idea."

"I'll be careful. I've been getting in and out of places without being noticed for a long time now."

"The only other piece of business I believe we need to look into at this moment is the young woman that Xander had the encounter with," Giles said. "She appears to have an agenda of her own with the Black Wind gang."

Xander shook his head and held up a hand. "Don't worry about that. I'll look into it."

Being protective? Willow wondered, looking at Xander's face. *Whoever the swordswoman was, she must have made a big impression.*

Giles cleared his throat. "You may want to keep in mind that she could be just as dangerous to you as any of the Black Wind members."

"She saved my life, Giles," Xander said. "In my book she gets filed under not-dangerous."

Being protective, Willow decided, *definitely.* She hesitated. "Maybe looking for this girl isn't a good idea."

"Why?" Xander asked defensively.

"Maybe you're a little . . ." Willow halted, not knowing how to finish her reasoning without sounding offensive. *Needy* sounded so totally gag-me-with-a-dead-rat, and *fragile* would have been ego-bruising.

The silence hung for a moment over the table.

"Vulnerable," Buffy said, nodding, and everyone immediately agreed with her because it was probably the most innocuous thing that could be said.

Xander laughed derisively. "Me? Vulnerable?"

"The breakup with Cordelia hasn't been exactly easy," Willow said quietly.

"Her mistake," Xander said. "Not mine. Maybe I was just born to be Solitary Guy. Love 'em and leave 'em. Maybe it's on my family crest."

Willow didn't think she was the only one who could see through the front Xander was putting up.

"It's okay," Buffy said understandingly. "We all have our kryptonite, Xander, and for most of us it's relationship issues. There's no shame in that. It's just how this whole hero biz is."

"Yeah, well, it'd feel better if I was a comic book hero dating a rich model," Xander said. "I can handle this. Really. If I can't, I'll be the first to ask for help. At least I'm chasing the one person in this whole thing who isn't trying to kill me."

"Xander does have a point," Giles said. "As long as he keeps his head, he should be all right." He pushed his empty cup away. "And it is getting late. We should talk again tomorrow."

Oz pulled his van to a stop by the curb in front of Willow's house, got out, and came around to let her out. He held her hand as he walked her toward the door.

"So how was the concert?" Willow asked. In the van ride from the diner, they'd talked only a little, listening to one of the homegrown CDs of Dingoes Ate My Baby and pretending it was the end of a pleasant date instead of the beginning of something new and nefarious.

"Good," Oz replied. "The band found the groove tonight. The audience seemed to appreciate it."

"I'm sorry I wasn't there."

Oz shrugged and gave her a small smile. "You were

helping a friend, Will. No foul. I wouldn't expect you to do anything else."

Willow sat on her porch steps. She'd called home and let everyone know she was okay, just running late. The porch light wasn't on and the front of the house was relatively bug-free, almost pleasant except for the chill in the air.

Oz sat beside her. "The vision thing was pretty intense, huh?"

"Yeah. I can't get it out of my mind. It was so real."

"But it wasn't real," Oz said gently, putting his arm around her. "Jia Li said her brother was down at the police station."

"I know." Willow fidgeted, remembering the vision vividly, the pick smashing through Lok's head with a hollow *whock!* "But that doesn't mean it won't be true. You know, sometime later?"

"Could be something to look into," Oz commented. "A favor for a friend."

"I'm supposed to help Giles look for these new demons, though."

Oz shrugged. "How many demons do you think there are with eyes in their hands?"

"Actually," Willow replied, "there are more than you might think. Some of them only have eyes in their hands. But that's only if they've bumped into other demons or found humans and taken the eyes away." She glanced at him self-consciously. "Kind of gross for one-on-one talk, huh?"

Oz grinned. "I don't think about demons with eyes in their hands."

"I suppose it's not something you should be expected to."

"No. What I am saying, though, is that it wouldn't

hurt to invest a little time in Jia Li's situation if you want. The demons will have Giles, Angel, and Buffy hunting them. There's no way they're going to escape that."

"And Xander," Willow added. "If this new mystery girl of his turns out to be connected to them."

"Mystery Girl's hunting them. Stands to reason she's connected."

Willow looked into Oz's eyes. "Really kind of worried about Xander here. In a keenly platonic way, I mean."

"I know." Oz kissed her lightly on the lips. "I'm kind of worried about him, too. In a platonic kind of way."

Willow smiled. "I'm glad to know that." She posed. "See? This is relieved."

"I'll hang around a little with him."

"He may not let you."

Oz smiled. "I'll bet looking for Mystery Girl involves wheels. Xander doesn't have wheels. I do. Once he discovers that, bet I can't chase him away with fur and fangs."

"Good point."

"But he can chip in some gas money."

Willow was quiet for a moment, not knowing how her words were going to sound. "Xander really needs somebody, Oz. And he really deserves somebody. He's a good guy."

Oz nodded, agreeing. "We all need somebody, Will."

"But he doesn't need somebody demonic, you know? Somebody normal; that's what he needs."

"You didn't exactly get someone normal."

Willow smiled at him. "For all but three nights of the month, I did. And I'll bet most people can't make that claim."

"Probably not."

"I'm not normal either. I'm a witch." Willow paused,

then made her voice more sharp. "And that was spelled with a *W*."

"It's the only way I'd spell it," Oz assured her.

Willow nestled against him, feeling safer than she had all night. She still had the images of the vision pasted on the backs of her eyelids every time she closed her eyes, but they seemed far away with him there holding her.

"Come on," Oz said gently a few minutes later. She was almost asleep against his chest. "Time for you to turn into a pumpkin."

"You're talking to just the girl that can do that," Willow said. "Of course, that's only if a spell goes really terribly wrong." She let Oz help her up, held him and kissed him briefly, then said goodnight and hoped for demon-free sleep.

Feeling totally zonked and just this side of cratering, Buffy made her way down the stairs in the Summers home. Even standing under the shower and turning the water as cold as she could possibly handle it hadn't helped.

Finding her mom still at the house instead of at work at the art gallery also threw her off her stride. Joyce Summers stood in the living room watching television, dressed in business attire, obviously late going to her art gallery. The local channel was showing a special about the violence that had swept through Sunnydale the night before.

The Asian gang activity had been more extensive than Buffy had at first realized. As she stood on the stairs, wondering what her mother was still doing home, the Slayer watched as story after story aired on the screen. The robbery at the Alibi bar received only a brief mention, as did the drugstore where Giles had encountered the gang. Nearly a dozen other confrontations were covered, but the main story was still the attack at Peppy's Miniature Golf where the mayor had been.

Joyce watched the stories in silence, and Buffy knew all kinds of thoughts had to be racing through her mom's mind. Joyce knew about her daughter's identity as the Chosen One, and had fought to relieve Buffy of the responsibility at first. Although she didn't really accept it now, she at least acknowledged it.

From her mom's sigh, Buffy knew she was in for the big lecture. Or, at the very least, a variant on the same. Quietly, she turned and started to head back up the stairs. Maybe she could just crawl out the bedroom window, make the second-story drop to the ground, and leave for school like she'd left much earlier.

Before she'd taken two steps, Joyce said, "Buffy, we need to talk."

Why is it, Buffy wondered, *that as the Slayer I can sneak up on demons and slay them without them ever knowing I was there, yet I can't sneak out of a room without my mom knowing? Slayer powers never quite seem to match up against Mom powers.* Steeling herself, she turned and went down the stairs.

"Hi, Mom," Buffy tried brightly.

Joyce muted the television with the clicker she held and turned to her daughter. Worry showed in her eyes. "I didn't hear you come in last night."

"It was kind of late," Buffy replied.

Joyce nodded at the television. "I understand that. But after I saw these stories on the news, I had to wonder if you were all right."

Buffy smiled and held her arms out at her sides. She worked not to show the twinge of pain she got from her right shoulder. Even with her beefed-up constitution as the Slayer, she didn't always completely heal overnight.

"Yep, right as rain." She pointed at the clock on the wall meaningfully. "And about to leave for school so I'm not late to any of my classes."

"I checked in on you this morning."

And why is it moms can sneak up on someone with Slayer powers? Buffy felt a little uncomfortable. Her mom knew more about her life than she assumed most moms knew about their daughters. She even knew about her relationship with Angel—*all* of it. And though they didn't argue about it and her mom even kind of liked Angel, Buffy knew Joyce didn't approve of the relationship. "I'm fine. Really."

"There are a lot of people who aren't fine this morning," Joyce said. "The news is reporting that eighteen people died in the violence that broke out last night."

And that's not counting the demons and some of the people who live in Sunnydale without proper documentation, Buffy realized.

"How bad is this going to be?" Joyce asked.

Buffy looked at her mom and saw some of the fear in her eyes. That uncertainty came from the knowledge she had of Buffy's own calling. Honesty was the best thing that Buffy could give her. "I don't know. This just started."

"What does Rupert say?"

"He doesn't know anything either," Buffy replied.

"Gang activity doesn't seem like something that should fall under the Slayer's purview."

"If it was normal gang activity," Buffy agreed, "probably not." She glanced at the television and saw the footage being rerun of the police officer getting shot down by the gang member with green and white striped hair. "But not all of these guys are human."

Joyce hesitated for a moment. "They're vampires?"

Buffy shook her head. "Demons, mostly. When they're not human."

"What do they want?"

"We don't know yet." *Me, for one thing,* Buffy thought, but she definitely wasn't going to mention that to her mom.

"Have you heard about Chengxian Zhiyong?"

Buffy thought for a moment. The name seemed to ring a bell, but she couldn't place it. "No."

"He's a businessman from Hong Kong. A big player in the shipping business. He was also at the miniature golf course last night when the mayor was wounded."

Buffy thought about that. "Kind of interesting that a new businessman from Hong Kong showed up in Sunnydale at about the same time a new Asian gang decides to hit the streets."

"That's what I was thinking," Joyce agreed.

Looking at the television, Buffy asked, "Why haven't the news people made a bigger deal out of that?"

"Because Zhiyong represents nearly two thousand new jobs opening up in Sunnydale," Joyce answered. "And Mayor Wilkins is backing Zhiyong, which gives him a certain amount of clout with the media and other officials in town. They're not going to go after him as long as he's bringing new money into Sunnydale."

Buffy glanced at the clock on the wall, realizing she was going to be cutting it close getting to school on time. She was going to miss her debrief time with Willow this morning. "You think Zhiyong is involved in this?" she asked her mom.

"I think it would be foolish to overlook the possibility," Joyce stated. "What are the odds of a new Asian businessman coming to Sunnydale only a few days before the arrival of an Asian youth gang not somehow being related?"

"Only a few days?" Buffy asked.

"Three weeks."

Buffy gave that consideration.

"I didn't know if you knew about Zhiyong," Joyce said.

"No," Buffy replied. "We didn't. Demons and big international business don't usually go together. I mean, they haven't before. That's not usually the thing we've . . . been involved with."

"Which is why I thought I'd bring it to your attention."

"I'll tell Giles when I get to school." Buffy indicated the clock. "And if I'm going to make it on time, I'd better get moving."

"I'm taking you this morning." Joyce gathered her bag and a light jacket.

"You don't have to do that," Buffy said. "If I hurry, I can still make it okay."

"I know. I just thought it would be nice if we got the chance to talk."

In case it was the last time? Buffy knew that was what her mom had meant even though she hadn't said it. As hard as it had been for Buffy to accept her role as the Slayer, she knew it had been even harder for her mother to accept it. Buffy remembered how she'd felt about her mother's own recent illness. She hoped she'd never feel that helpless again, but her mother faced that every time she went out on patrol.

"Sure," Buffy said, smiling. "Girl talk."

"And breakfast," Joyce said. "Provided the line isn't wrapped around the building. I know you haven't eaten."

"If I'm late," Buffy said, "Principal Snyder will—"

"Will be quite happy with the note I write him," Joyce promised, "because it will mean he won't be getting a phone call from me."

Buffy grinned. "I see."

Joyce switched the television off. "Also, I'll need to make arrangements to get you out of school at lunch."

"Lunch?"

"If we're lucky," Joyce said as she opened the door and headed out of the house.

Buffy reluctantly followed. Her eyes raked the yard and the surrounding neighborhood. There was no guarantee that the Asian gang they'd confronted last night didn't operate in the daylight. And some of them were human, so they could definitely continue the hunt for one Buffy Summers. But would they try to take her at home or at school? Or was she really that important in whatever was going on?

Her mother's SUV sat in the driveway. Joyce slid behind the wheel as Buffy occupied the passenger seat.

"I have an ulterior motive for getting you out of school at lunch," Joyce said as she started the car.

An ulterior motive? Mom? Buffy looked at her mom as they backed out of the driveway onto the street. "You've been watching old police movies again, haven't you?"

Her mom focused on her driving. "Some nights I don't sleep very well."

Because I'm out on patrol? Buffy wondered. *Or because I'm with Angel?* She decided she really didn't want to go there with the conversation and refrained from speaking.

"My ulterior motive revolves around Chengxian Zhiyong," Joyce said. "He's something of an art collector."

"He's been to your art gallery," Buffy said, understanding.

"On more than one occasion."

"So what do you know about him?"

"Personally? Nothing. I can tell you his price range, which is nothing short of extravagant, and his taste, which is definitely traditionalist with no room for avant garde."

"So why lunch?"

"Because that's when I'm accepting a shipment for him at the Sunnydale docks."

"What's the shipment?" Buffy asked.

"A statue."

Buffy considered that. "If Zhiyong owns a shipping company, why doesn't he just ship it himself?"

"Because it's a registered piece of art," Joyce answered. "There is a lot of red tape involved in those shipments. Proof of ownership, that sort of thing. It's just made easier shipping it through a gallery. Once I get the statue in, he's going to take delivery of it from me."

"O—kay," Buffy replied, still not understanding what her mom was getting at.

"I thought if Zhiyong considered this piece so important and so valuable, it might be worth looking at. Don't you?"

"And I can get a peek?"

"If you go with me for a lunch date," Joyce said, "which happens to be approximately the time I'm supposed to sign for the delivery, I feel confident that could be arranged."

Buffy grinned. "My, my, and aren't you the sly planner?"

Joyce smiled. "Of course, this could be just a piece of art. But if Zhiyong is involved somehow in what the Asian gang is doing in Sunnydale, I thought it might be worth your while to get a look at it."

"Definitely." Then another thought struck Buffy. "But it might also be kinda dangerous."

"I've thought about that, too." Joyce looked at her daughter. "But there's no way you can get close to that shipment without me. They have a lot of security down at the docks regarding art shipments. The people down there know me."

"Which is probably why Zhiyong hired you."

Joyce nodded. "That, and I had access to a couple of Han dynasty pieces that Zhiyong wanted me to acquire for him. I did, and he also asked me to negotiate today's shipment for him."

Buffy's mind whirled as she thought. After discovering the gang members from last night had her picture and probably knew who she was, the statue might actually be part of an elaborate trap. However, since an attack hadn't been made on the Summers household, maybe the gang members had been told to be on the lookout for the Slayer instead of hunting her down. But they really hadn't hesitated about trying to kill her, either.

"So," her mom prompted in a casual voice that sounded only a little strained, "want to do lunch?"

"Sure," Buffy said, only sounding a little strained herself, "lunch sounds great."

"Where can I find something like this?" Xander held the yin/yang necklace in his palm as he showed it. The silver backing was nearly two inches across, not perfectly round but the intention to be perfectly round was there. Carved white and blue stones made up the two inlaid halves.

Teresa Lawton gazed at him in the high school hallway like he was something she'd accidentally found stuck under a cafeteria table. It was the kind of look she gave everyone who didn't travel in her circle. She was brunette and pretty, dressed in a fuchsia minidress. "You expect me to know?"

Xander looked at her. "Look, Teresa, you're one of the fashion mavens here at Sunnydale High."

"Oooh," the girl said, arching a brow and putting a hand on one slender hip, "now there's an unexpected compliment. Of course, considering the source, I'm not going to swoon in delirium."

"Terrific." Xander was getting tired of the insults. Since he'd been at school that day, inquiring about the necklace he'd found, humor at his expense seemed to be the flavor of the day.

"I mean, look at this." Teresa did a short runway platform hip-swivel toss that drew the attention of every girl in the hallway and set guys' hearts into overdrive.

"That—" Xander observed, swallowing hard, "—that should be against the law."

"A dweeb with cute talk," Teresa exclaimed. "Who knew? However, the hip-sashay wasn't what I wanted you to notice."

Right, Xander thought, but he didn't say anything.

"This," Teresa said, running a hand down the tight lines of the dress, "is fashion. Strappy poly-spandex. Shirred bodice, center front. A sheer handkerchief hem. An eye-catcher if I do say so myself." She paused, glancing at the necklace. "What you're holding in your hand, Xander Harris, is junk."

"Junk?" Xander grinned nervously and tried not to let his irritation show through. "This isn't junk. This is a . . . a family heirloom."

Teresa looked at him and shook her head. "Not in this family. Some names the accessory fashion-challenged should remember, Geek Boy." She tapped her purse. "Versace." She tapped her sunglasses. "Oakley." She tapped her tennis bracelet. "Tiffany's." And she tapped her shoes. "Anything Gucci."

"Right. I'll try to remember those."

Teresa sniffed disdainfully. "As for your little trinket,

you could probably find another in a garage sale. If you hit the properly downwardly mobile areas in Sunnydale. In fact, I'd start with your neighborhood." Without another word, she moved on.

A small group of fashionably aware guys and girls moved with her, laughing fashionably at Xander.

You know, Xander thought, *I'm not gonna get out of high school soon enough.* He closed his hand over the necklace and turned to walk down the hallway. At least his luck hadn't gone completely sour. At least he hadn't bumped into—

"Oh my," a familiar voice said.

Xander looked up, his heart stopping on the spot.

Chapter 13

CORDELIA CHASE STOOD IN THE HALLWAY IN FRONT OF Xander, looking every bit the high school beauty queen in silver-white Capri pants and a patchouli drawstring cami that showed a lot of healthy, tanned skin that Xander used to love to get next to. He hadn't even known patchouli was a type of purple color before Cordelia because he'd never had a patchouli Crayola Crayon, even in the big 128-count box. Her dark hair swept back from her shoulders.

"Hi," Xander said, cringing inside because he knew saying even that much these days was enough to draw Cordelia's wrath.

Cordelia glanced down at the necklace in his hand. "New hobby? Or rewards for begging?"

"More like a quest-type event," Xander said. *Think neutral, totally neutral, going stealth-mode here. No biting remarks, no attacks.*

Cordelia looked a bit more curiously at the necklace. "Vampire thingy?"

"No."

"Death spell talisman thingy?"

"Wouldn't be holding it if it was," Xander politely pointed out, just so she'd know it wasn't dangerous.

"Unless it only killed brain cells," Cordelia said. "Or eliminated that faithful trait that shows up more often in dogs than it does in the male species. You could still be safe then." She smiled with cruel charm.

Xander started to respond, but caught himself. "Fair enough. Okay, you've gotten that out of your system."

Cordelia eyed him archly. "That isn't the only thing I've gotten out of my system."

Xander walked away because it was the only nonviolent, nonderogatory thing he could do. "See you around, Cordy."

"That would fall somewhere under the heading of aggravated assault."

Xander didn't look back through sheer force of will. He and Cordelia Chase had never traveled in the same circles—except when they were out slaying vampires and other demonic beings. And that hadn't exactly been a barrel of laughs. Especially for Cordy, when she got ostracized from all the other cools for standing up to them and going out with him. *Things were so much better when she simply despised me from a distance instead of making things so personal.*

He squeezed the necklace in his hand, hanging onto the little bit of hope he'd crawled into bed with last night. *I've met someone new.* The swordswoman's face had haunted his dreams all night, which had been kind of a pleasant experience as far as haunts went.

Reluctantly, he turned his steps toward the library. *When you have to find out stuff, there's really only one place to go around here.* The drawback was that he wasn't quite certain how ready he was to share the mysterious swordswoman with his friends.

Only Giles was in the library when Xander arrived. The Watcher glanced up at him from the main desk.

"Good morning, Xander," Giles said.

"Not exactly," Xander replied. "But I'm hoping it'll pick up. I swear I'm due."

"Oh?"

"Cordy. Hallway. Majorly bad scene."

"I'm . . . sorry to hear that?" Giles tried valiantly.

"Yeah," Xander said. "Me, too." He leaned on his elbows on the countertop. "You know, I'm beginning to think she's never going to get over me."

"Really?"

Xander glanced at the Watcher suspiciously. "Sarcasm?"

"Not at all. It doesn't surprise me that Cordelia is hurt. I actually suspect both of you have been quite hurt over this, and I wish things hadn't worked out as they had."

Seeing the honest sympathy on Giles's face unnerved Xander. It was one thing to take the breakup as a bad joke, but it was another to overinvest in the heartbreaking side of it. "She'll get over it. Her life is nothing but up from here, and she knows it."

Giles remained noncommittal.

"Okay, enough maudlin self-pity, which, by the way, is a shame because I've learned to do it so well." Xander laid the necklace on the counter. "I came here seeking answers, o wise and great oracle."

Giles picked up the necklace. "And this is?"

"The swordswoman's. She dropped it last night. I found it."

"Why didn't you mention it last night?" Giles examined the necklace with mild enthusiasm.

"Last night I wanted it for myself."

"I see."

"I know it sounds kind of weird." Xander suddenly felt more than a little uncomfortable.

"Not really." Giles turned the necklace over in his hands.

"Some people might think it was a fetish of some kind."

"Oh, and do you have a habit of taking girls' personal items for your own gratification?" Giles asked. He looked up quickly. "And if you do, please don't tell me about it."

"No, I don't. She dropped the necklace. I just wanted to return it to her. I thought maybe you might be able to help me find her."

"The necklace is quite old. Pity there isn't a jeweler's or silversmith's inscription on it."

"There are markings on the back," Xander pointed out.

"I saw those, but I can't read them." Partially absorbed by the mystery, Giles reached for a piece of paper and a pencil. "They appear to be in Chinese, but I'm not expert enough in the different dialects to know how to translate it."

"Do you know someone who could?"

Giles placed the paper over the back of the necklace, then took the pencil and rubbed carefully. The inscription materialized on the paper. "I can pass this around and see if anything turns up." He glanced at Xander. "Mind you, most of our efforts right now are directed toward the Black Wind question."

Xander nodded. With the violence that had taken place last night as well as the news coverage, all of Sunnydale was in an uproar over gangs and Asians. The school grapevine had it that some of the Asian students in school had decided not to come today. "Did I miss the morning briefing?"

"No." Giles handed the necklace back to Xander. "I think everyone slept in this morning."

Xander bounced the necklace in his palm, enjoying the solid, heavy feel of it. It was easy to imagine that she hadn't simply dropped it, and that she'd intended for him to find it so he could find her. "What can you tell me about it? How old is it?"

"I'd guess easily four or five hundred years old," Giles replied. "Probably a family piece that's been handed down for generations."

"So she'd want it back?"

"Oh, most definitely, I'd say. Although it may not be overly cosmetically appealing—"

"Glitzy," Xander translated.

"—the age alone is going to make a piece like that a collector's item. But I suspect the personal value she probably places on it would overshadow that."

"What about this yin/yang thing?" Xander asked. "She was really good at martial arts. Maybe I should check out some of the dojos around Sunnydale."

Giles sighed. "Xander, you do know that the yin/yang isn't a martial arts symbol?"

"Sure. Everybody knows it signifies good and evil."

"That's not precisely true, either. What it actually represents are the two polarities of existence that are believed to exist within everything. Yin, the dark half, symbolized evidently by the blue stone in the piece you're holding, represents the female side of existence. It's withdrawn, passive, and receptive, and tends to keep everything moving down and in. The white stone, the male half, on the other hand, represents yang. It is supposed to be masculine, forceful, and expansive, tending to keep things moving up and out. But neither of these two halves occurs without having a little piece of the other within them. That's why each half has a small dot of the other within it."

"And all this means what exactly?" Xander asked. Long explanations were the chief reasons he didn't like coming to Giles for help. He wished there was a way to put the Watcher into *TV Guide* mode.

"That you may not be looking for a martial artist."

Xander shook his head. "You saw how she moved. Even from across the street, you had to see how she moved."

"I did."

"If she's not as fast as Buffy, then she's definitely a close second. And as for jumping, man, she's got Buffy beat hands down."

Giles nodded. "I'd say that's a fair assessment. But what I'm suggesting is that if it's not a warrior per se that you're looking for, it might be a Taoist monk."

"A monk?" The idea jarred Xander. The image that instantly came to mind contained lots of little old guys in robes, shaved heads, and wrinkles. *When you can snatch the pebble from my hand . . .*

"The yin/yang symbol is derived from the Taoist beliefs," Giles continued.

"She didn't call me grasshopper," Xander pointed out.

"Yes, and I'm sure that's probably a very significant observation."

Xander frowned. "Now *that's* sarcasm."

"Definitely."

"Okay, I had that coming. Let's say she's some kind of monk, which kind of creeps me out in its own very weird way, do they all take some kind of vow of chastity or celibacy?"

"No."

"Then that's okay. She can be a monk."

Giles looked at him. "Xander, from the little bit I saw

of this young lady, as formidable as she appears to be, I'd say she's already whatever she wants to be without your blessings in the matter."

Yeah, but no vows means she's dateable, too. Xander said thanks and headed for the door.

"You're quite taken with her, aren't you?"

Xander turned around and kept walking backward, never losing the smile on his face. "Not me, Giles. I'm just a gentleman, trying to return a lost item to a young lady."

"Right." Giles nodded, looking unconvinced. "While you're caught up in this quixotic venture of yours, do be careful."

"Of course," Xander replied, still walking backward as the first bell rang. "Careful's what I do best." He turned around and walked into the wall beside the door.

Angel stood safely in the shadows on the west side of the warehouse away from the morning sun. Forklifts slammed and screeched as they ferried loads to and from the docks and the big ocean freighters sitting in anchorage. Men's voices, mixed with the slap of the waves, echoed around him.

He carried a Styrofoam cup of coffee and a small brown paper bag. A fresh, white gauze patch covered the wound on his face. The pigs' blood he had bought from a butcher he did business with had healed part of the damage from last night's gunshot wound, but a complete restoration was a day or two off. Drinking human blood would have cut the time frame down to hours, but that wasn't an option.

Sunnydale wasn't big enough to have a huge amount of shipping, but what there was went briskly. Vegetables from different nearby farms were taken onto ships while other goods were off-loaded. Huge boom arms carrying cargo netting full of crates containing farm equipment, computers and peripherals, and clothing swiveled over to the docks.

Security teams, provided by the different shipping lines as well as harbor patrol, moved through the dock-workers and ships. Sunnydale police officers were in greater numbers than usual. It was no secret that they were looking for the Black Wind gang members who had terrorized the town the night before.

Angel had walked Buffy home after the meeting in the diner broke up, then returned to his mansion long enough to get a change of clothing. Nocturnal by nature, he hadn't needed sleep. But the day and the wounds wore on him now.

He watched the brown gulls and white terns out in the harbor as they heeled through the blue sky. Their excited squawks signaled the times they found a prize bit of flotsam on the water just before they dove for it.

Then a familiar *squeak-squeak-squeak* of a grocery cart caught Angel's attention. An ancient bag lady trundled her shopping basket along the wooden and concrete walkways of the docks.

The bag lady wore a heavy brown coat against the morning chill rolling in off the sea, a black-watch cap, and dark yellow galoshes that sported strips of gray duct tape applied in layers. She was leathery and wrinkled and thin, only a couple inches over five feet tall. Fingerless black gloves covered her hands. Iron-gray hair hung under the watch cap to her chin.

Her cart was battered and bent, and had the one wheel that continued to protest shrilly. Metal jangled as the basket rolled and shook. Plastic trash bags were only half-filled with the day's bounty, but Angel knew they'd be filled before the old woman gave up.

"Louise," he called softly.

The old woman's head whipped around and she reached for the lead-weighted shark billy she carried in one of her galoshes. Her eyes narrowed as she studied Angel with wariness and suspicion. Her life had never been easy, and it showed in every coiled movement, every scar on her face and arms.

"Angel." Then she recognized him, eyes widening. She smiled and waved. "How are you doing, my boy?"

"Top o' the morning, Ma," Angel said, because he knew saying that always made her smile. She loved his Irish accent, which he usually negated from his speech so he could blend easier in Sunnydale. He walked toward her as far as he could and still remain within the sheltering safety of the shadows. Louise knew what he was, and knew why he couldn't come into direct sunlight.

She turned the shopping basket toward him and pushed it forward. Her bird-bright blue eyes studied him. "It's been a long time since I've seen you." When she drew even with him, she reached out and patted his arm. "It's good to see you."

"It's good to see you, too." Angel offered the coffee and the brown paper bag. "I brought breakfast if you're interested."

She held up a hand, the fingers crooked and bent from hard times as well as age. "You know I don't take handouts."

"I know." Angel had met Louise when he'd first come to Sunnydale at Whistler's insistence, before he'd met Buffy. The sea had drawn him because he'd known vampire predators hunted the shores, and hunting those hunters had been a step in the right direction. He'd saved the old bag lady on one of those restless nights, and she'd invited him into the cardboard shack she'd set up under one of the older pilings.

"Me and old Betsy," Louise said, slapping her cart affectionately, "as long as we can still get up and down this beach, we make do."

"I need some information."

"Well, in that case I'm working." Louise gratefully took the coffee and paper bag. She sat cross-legged in the building's shadow.

Angel sat beside her, admiring her gusto as she prowled through the bag.

"A sausage, egg, and cheese bagel," she said enthusiastically. "Bless you, Angel."

"You're welcome." Angel sat with his knees raised before him, shoes just beyond the searing touch of the sun.

Louise expertly peeled the bagel, took a paper napkin from the bag, and tucked it inside the neckline of the black Metallica concert tee shirt she wore. "What were you wanting to know?"

"Anything you can give me about the Asian gang that hit town last night."

Louise ate as they talked, but when she spoke her words were always clear. Her eyes roved incessantly, bearing the mark of the hunted. The local vampires and demons stayed away from her for the most part, knowing she'd been put under Angel's care.

Every day Louise panhandled her way through Sunnydale, picking up interesting seashells along the beach to sell to tourist shops, collecting aluminum cans to sell to can banks, and scavenging things that other homeless people she knew could put back together and sell somewhere else. In her constant travels, she was generally a good source of information.

"I don't know how reliable this information is," Louise warned.

"It will beat anything I know now," Angel promised.

She looked at him as if to make sure he was telling the truth. "They call themselves the Black Wind."

"That much I knew," Angel said. "But I don't know where they're from or what they want."

Louise nodded and took another nibble from the bagel. "I got this from one of the Chinese sailors on *Ryan's Star.* Do you know the ship?"

Angel shook his head.

"She's a deep-water English transport," Louise said. She often talked about the ships like they were visiting relatives. She traded things she acquired or fixed for items the sailors had, then sold those items in town. "Handles cars and computers shipped out from Singapore. Old Soo-Pheng is a sailor aboard her. He grew up around Hong Kong and was in the merchant marine, so he knows a lot about China. And he knows about the Black Wind."

Angel waited patiently though he was restless inside. Louise was a natural storyteller and couldn't be hurried.

"The Black Wind is an old gang in China," Louise said. "Until 1997 when the Brits gave Hong Kong back over to the Chinese government, they were kept out of Hong Kong proper. Then they spread throughout it. They work behind the scenes like most of the gangs there do. Soo-Pheng says the gangs there are sometimes called triads."

Angel nodded. Triad more accurately described the Chinese organized crime families, but after seeing the Black Wind in action last night, he knew there weren't many who were better organized.

Louise touched Angel's forearm. "Soo-Pheng also says these Black Wind guys are very dangerous, Angel."

"I think so, too."

The old woman nodded. "Just make sure you keep that in mind if you have any dealings with them."

"I will."

"Soo-Pheng says they have some kind of black magic powers."

"Some of them are demons."

"From the way he talked," Louise said, "I thought they might be." During her travels through Sunnydale, she'd encountered her share of demons.

"What are they doing in Sunnydale?"

"I don't know. Soo-Pheng seemed really surprised when we talked this morning. Usually the Black Wind is never seen, and they're always after big businesses. Most of their crimes are blackmail that allows them to make businesses do what they want. Black market shipping, paying off extortion, that kind of thing. He says they've gone in and taken over other triads in the past, and only when the blood hit the streets did anyone really talk about them. The kind of attacks they did last night is unusual."

"They did it to make a statement." Angel's thoughts flickered to Buffy, wondering if they had come for her, then dismissing that because it made no sense to travel to the Slayer when she offered them no threat where they were. "There has to be something here they want. Unless they were chased out of Hong Kong."

"Not according to Soo-Pheng," Louise said. "No one could chase them from Hong Kong because they're too strong. People are afraid of the Black Wind, Angel. You should be too."

"I am," Angel admitted. But the fear was more for Buffy than for himself. He also had the feeling that Louise knew more than she was telling.

"Then you should stay away from them."

"I can't."

"Sure you can."

"They're after Buffy."

"That little girl you're so much in love with?"

Angel nodded. Louise knew, though he'd never told her about the relationship. "They tried to kill her last night. They had her picture."

"Then she's one of their targets."

"Yes. I can't let that go." Angel looked at the old woman. "I won't let that go."

Louise folded the empty bagel wrapper neatly and put it into her coat pocket. "I didn't know they had an interest in Buffy."

Angel waited.

"I don't know what it is they're searching for," Louise stated, "but Soo-Pheng says they're going to try to take over the criminal element in Sunnydale. Perhaps use Sunnydale as a stepping-stone to bigger things. Soo-Pheng may have only been guessing at that part. But they're searching the outlying areas, too."

"For what?"

"Soo-Pheng doesn't know. He heard that from a cousin who handles some of the contraband shipping along the West Coast."

"How did the Black Wind get here?" Angel asked.

"By ship. It would be the only way to move so many people secretly. Illegals get brought in and put into sweatshops in the larger metropolitan areas all the time."

Angel gazed out at all the freighters in the harbor. "Which ship?"

"None of these," Louise answered. "If they'd come in on one of these I'd have known."

"Do you know where I can find them?"

The old woman hesitated, fear showing in her blue eyes. "It will be very dangerous."

"It already is," Angel said softly.

"There's a warehouse at the north end of the docks where contraband goods are sometimes temporarily stored." She gave him the address. "I've heard someone new has moved in there. It could be them."

"I appreciate it, Louise." Angel took her hand and pressed money into it, and was gone before she could protest. He thrust his hands deeply into his pockets, banking the anger that surged within him, letting the demon that still existed within him gnaw at the restraints. For once, the mayhem and destruction they both desired were on the same wavelength.

Chapter 14

"HI," WILLOW SAID, TAKING HER SEAT IN COMPUTER class next to Jia Li. She quickly shuffled her books, book bag, and purse out of the way. "I looked for you this morning."

Jia Li's eyes were puffy and red from lack of sleep, but she looked elegant as always in an ankle-length jade eyelet skirt and a black handkerchief-hem tank. She wore her hair up in a bun. "I got here late this morning."

The rest of the class talked hurriedly around them, swapping stories about things they'd seen themselves, or heard about, or had seen on television regarding the gang attacks last night. The stories were already bordering on the wildly fantastic, and Willow knew with certainty that they would only grow in the telling.

"Is everything okay?" Willow powered up her computer and slipped her work CD into the drive.

"I don't know. My mother and father didn't get Lok home till early this morning. They're going to have to retain a lawyer to represent him. He's going to be formally charged." Jia Li's voice quavered.

"Everything will be okay."

"No," Jia Li said quietly, "it won't be. I saw Lok this morning. He scared my sister and brothers. He was talking out of his head, Willow. Talking about the *guei* and the vengeance they had to have on those who are responsible for their deaths."

"Like the man he attacked last night."

"I don't know. Hardly anything of what he is saying is making sense."

"What do your parents think?"

Jia Li shook her head. "I've never seen them so lost. My parents have always known what to do, even when we first moved to Sunnydale. They bought out the business they wanted, then renamed it and are making a success of it. That is what their lives are like. But this only reminds me of Lok as he was before. When my grandfather had to take Lok to live with him. Only my grandfather isn't here anymore." A tear ran down her cheek.

Willow quickly dug into her purse and handed over a tissue.

"Thank you."

More students entered through the door, the last refugees before the final bell.

"I can't stay after school and study like we'd planned. I have to hurry home to be with my brothers and sister so my parents can make the appointment with the lawyer." Jia Li was silent for a moment, looking at the computer screen. "Lok will be there, and I don't want to be there with him." Fear shone in her eyes.

"You don't have to be there alone," Willow said. "How about some company? We could study there. I mean, if you don't mind the way I just invited myself over."

Jia Li only hesitated for a moment. "I would appreciate that. You're a good friend, Willow."

The final bell rang, only slowing the conversations around them a little. Willow turned her attention to the computer screen, bringing up her assignment for review. However, in the depths of the screen, she got a momentary image of the shambling corpse burying the pick in Lok's skull again. She flinched as the melon-splitting sound echoed in her head.

"Are you all right?" Jia Li asked.

Willow blinked, lost for a moment in the vision and the hollow whisper of words that remained just beyond her hearing. Then she focused on her friend. "Sure. It was just a shiver. They always have the AC turned up really high in computer lab." But she couldn't help thinking that inviting herself back over to Jia Li's house was probably not the smartest move she could make.

Angel stood up as tall as he could in the sewer and pushed the manhole cover up and over. The sewer systems throughout Sunnydale made daylight travel possible in most instances.

The sewer water ran through a channel cut through the center of the huge system. Angel stood on the edge of it, aware of the rats watching him from the shadows. As alive as his senses were, he could feel their hunger and anger. Being hungry and angry seemed to be a rat's whole life.

He paused after he had the manhole cover moved enough, watching and listening intently. The warehouse roof was constructed of beams and crossbeams and fabricated out of corrugated metal covered with pitch and pebbles, one of the older buildings down at the docks.

Dim light glowed through the multipaned windows. The harbor sounds echoed inside the cavernous building. The open and broken windows let in the brine smell of the ocean and the sharp scent of pine that made up most of the crates and pallets. Diesel and oil fumes, both new and old, clung to the warehouse as well.

And there was the definite stench of blood, some of it fresh.

Cautiously, Angel gripped the edge of the manhole and pulled himself up till he could see. The warehouse was less than half full. Stacks of crates occupied the floor with no real organization. Broken boards and empty boxes littered the spaces in between along with straw, Styrofoam pellets, and bubble pouches used as packing.

Angel climbed through the manhole and got to his feet. Startled cooing sounded overhead. He glanced up to see a flock of pigeons along a beam in the corner of the building. They settled down quickly.

Moving quietly, Angel kept the back wall to his right and made his way around the warehouse. A few missing windowpanes allowed direct sunlight into the warehouse along the east side but he easily avoided those. He made his way through the crates, memorizing names to check out later, hoping some of them might offer leads that could be followed up on.

Gravel crunched under tires outside the cargo bay doors.

Angel ducked behind a stack of crates as the bay door rose up on a chain hoist.

A black Camaro rumbled into the building and stopped. A half-dozen Asian youths trailed the vehicle in. They still wore dark clothing, but not the green and white striping in their hair.

Okay, so they do war paint, Angel thought. Without the distinctive hair coloring, they almost looked like anyone else—except they had a predator's habitual scan going, their heads always moving, eyes always alert, bodies evenly balanced for quick movement.

They spoke in Chinese, their voices too low to be overheard. The car doors opened. The driver and a man in the passenger seat got out, both of them holding weapons. The guy on the passenger side reached into the backseat and roughly pulled out a man dressed in black Dockers, a dark gray sports jacket and a black turtleneck. He wore a blindfold and his hands were bound behind him. The Black Wind member tripped him, sending him crashing to the concrete floor.

"Please," the man whispered desperately. "I'll do whatever you want. Just don't hurt me. You don't have to hurt me."

"That is very good, Mr. Collins," one of the gang members said. "We wouldn't want to have to hurt you. We need you alive. If it's convenient for us." He gestured to the other men.

Two straight-backed chairs were brought over from a stack against the nearby wall and placed facing each other. The gang member sat in one as Collins was placed in the other.

"Mr. Collins, you may call me Gao." The gang member reached forward and stripped the blindfold from Collins's eyes. He crossed his knees calmly, as if they were having an everyday conversation.

Collins blinked frantically. "I don't know anyone named Gao."

The gang member nodded. "Then you still do not know anyone named Gao. I only said that you could call me by that name."

Collins started to stand. "You can't do this to me."

Gao slammed a hand against Collins's chest and

knocked the man back into the chair. Effortlessly, he closed his fist and hit Collins in the face with a short jab. Blood sprayed from the prisoner's lips. "Stay seated or I will have your legs broken. Your ability to walk is a luxury for you and not at all a necessity for me."

Blood dribbled down Collins's chin as he nodded. Panicked tears rolled down his cheeks. "Sure. Whatever you want."

"You're an attorney here in Sunnydale," Gao said. "A very wealthy one, judging from your bank accounts and your residence. But you derive most of your income from business that doesn't show up on your books or the papers you file with your country's Internal Revenue Service."

"I don't know what you're talking about."

Gao slapped the man so fast that even Angel almost didn't see the motion.

Collins screamed in pain, but one of the gang members standing around him quickly clapped a hand over his mouth. The gang member held a sharp knife against the lawyer's throat.

Gao leaned forward easily and spoke softly. "We must speak quietly, Mr. Collins. If we were to be discovered here, I'd have your throat slit, then your face stripped from your skull and your hands cut off to make identification more difficult. Do I make myself clear?"

Collins nodded.

"My associate is going to remove his hand from your mouth. What we do next is up to you. Do you understand?"

The gang member removed his hand from Collins's mouth.

"Yes," Collins whispered. "I understand. Please. You don't have to kill me."

"No, and I don't want to kill you, either," Gao agreed.

"You need to understand that. Your security is in your hands. When we are done, you can walk out of this building or we'll take you out in pieces. I would rather you lived. It would be hard to find someone with your connections to replace you."

Collins took a panicky breath, then exhaled. Blood bubbled from his mouth.

Angel glanced around, not wanting to be party to whatever took place next. But he also knew if he was discovered there was a chance they'd kill the lawyer first thing.

"Your out-of-sight business includes procuring certain goods for a specialized clientele." Gao took out a pack of cigarettes, shook one out, then tapped it against the back of his hand. He stuck the cigarette into his mouth and lit it.

The sharp smell of cloves from the cigarette tickled Angel's nose, overriding the scent of blood.

"We want your client list, Mr. Collins," Gao said. "And we're prepared to let you continue your job as middleman."

"I can't do that," Collins replied. "My suppliers would—"

Gao lifted a hand in front of the attorney's face. Collins drew back as the eyelid in the palm opened to reveal the orb within.

"Your suppliers will do nothing to you," Gao commented. "Once they understand that you belong to us. And they will understand that."

"Okay," Collins said, attention riveted on the eye in Gao's palm. "When are you going to let me go?"

"When it is time."

Abruptly, the pigeons in the upper corner of the warehouse left their perch. Angel gazed in their direction and spotted the guard on the catwalk above. Angel shifted, sliding behind the stack of crates as the man watched the flying pigeons.

Around the corner now, Angel watched as the pigeon flock flew across the warehouse to the other corner over Gao's head.

In a blur of movement, Gao focused on the birds. He threw his cigarette away as his head suddenly morphed, allowing his mouth to open nearly a foot across. A thick, saliva-covered black lizard's tongue flicked out with lightning speed and stuck to one of the pigeons.

Gao's tongue reeled the squawking, frightened bird into his mouth with a snap of movement. Only a few feathers escaped devouring. The gang member chewed noisily, crunching bones, then swallowed, turning his face back to its more human aspect.

"Oh, my God!" Collins whimpered. "That was disgusting!" Then he realized he'd spoken out loud and leaned back in his chair.

Gao smiled. "I take no offense at your judgment, Mr. Collins. You don't know enough about me to even begin." He took a deep drag on his cigarette and blew it out, expelling two small pigeon feathers as well. "I, however, hold your future, your very life, in my hands. And as I ask you questions, I'll know if you're lying to me." The eye in his palm blinked.

The two small pigeon feathers drifted through the air and stuck to Collins's jacket.

"Do you believe me?" Gao asked.

"Yes," Collins answered without hesitation.

Gao's mouth flared open again. The long, black lizard's tongue flicked out, seeming to barely touch the attorney's face. But when the tongue flicked back into Gao's mouth, a two-inch patch of skin was missing from the man's cheek.

Blood streamed down Collins's face. He opened his mouth to scream but Gao punched him in the stomach, knocking the wind from him. Collins doubled over and fell from the chair to his knees.

Gao leaned down and whispered mockingly in the attorney's ear. "I'll know when you lie, Mr. Collins. Even when you're telling me what you think I want to hear." He held the palm eyeball out only inches from Collins's own eyes.

Collins sobbed silently as blood dripped from his face onto the scarred and stained concrete.

Angel leaned against the stack of crates and tried to figure out his next move. If he was lucky, and very quiet, he could make the manhole and a clean getaway without being discovered.

But he couldn't leave Collins behind even if the man was involved in every criminal activity in Sunnydale.

Knowing he was going to regret it—if he lived long enough—Angel glanced into a nearby crate. The lid was slightly ajar, a crowbar lying across it. He picked up the crowbar and peered inside the crate. Computer memory chips filled the interior, but the box beneath it was marked VODKA. Another nearby crate was marked SAFETY FLARES. It was open.

You gotta love flammable products. Vampires feared fire; most demons did, too.

Angel took the computer chips down and hooked his fingers under the lid on the case of vodka. He pulled, willing the staples not to shriek as they slid free.

Once he had the lid off, he glanced up to check the guard's progress on the catwalk above. The gang member was still circling, his attention riveted on the conversation Gao was having with the prisoner.

Angel worked quickly. He tore a section of his shirt into strips, not even bothering to take it off first. After uncapping the vodka bottles, he stuffed the pieces of shirt into the necks, turning them upside down briefly to soak the makeshift wicks before returning them to the crate.

As Angel was starting on the sixth bottle, glass crashed behind him, followed by the roaring bellow of an automatic weapon. He whirled as the glass flew around him, spotting the gang member on the outside of the multipaned window that had just gone to pieces.

They had guards outside, too. Desperately, Angel shoved two of the vodka bottles into his duster pockets, then seized a third bottle, a handful of the safety flares, and the crowbar. He ran, twisting around the corner as bullets chipped the concrete floor, tracking him.

At least a dozen rounds chewed through the corner of the crate he took cover behind. Rough splinters peeled back from the wood and pierced his flesh, bringing stinging pain.

Angel glanced upward, knowing the most immediate danger was going to come from the guard above. Tucking the crowbar under his arm, he took out one of the flares, broke it to ignite it, and lit the wick on the vodka bottle. The flame burned blue and yellow, slowly at first because the fire fed only on the alcohol in the rag.

The guard on the catwalk came at a run, yelling. He leaned over the railing and brought his weapon up.

Angel ran toward the back wall, then turned and launched the Molotov cocktail. The gang member was just turning to bring his weapon to bear on the other side of the catwalk when the vodka bottle shattered against the railing.

A spray of blue and yellow flames licked out. Not all of the vodka caught on fire at first. But when the burning bits touched the drenched parts now fed with oxygen as well, they swirled into a conflagration. The gang member turned into a running, shrieking torch. Flaming drops of alcohol dripped through the mesh catwalk floor.

The outside gang member leaped through the shattered window.

By then Angel was in motion, the crowbar tight in his hand. He grabbed the gang member's machine pistol and hooked the crowbar behind the man's foot, then yanked. He pulled the man from the harmful direct sunlight and kicked him in the head when he tried to fight back.

The gang member sprawled bonelessly.

Bullets hammered the wall beside Angel and one cut across his lower back before he threw himself forward in an all-out run. Whether his pursuers had meant to or not, they'd cut off his retreat to the manhole and the sewer system.

Angel cut around the next row of crates, slid to a stop, and jammed the crowbar under the second crate. The row was stacked six high, almost twenty feet tall. He leaned against the stack of crates and grabbed the crowbar in both hands, shoving and lifting with everything he had.

Slowly, then with increasing speed, the stack of crates shifted and tumbled into an avalanche. Most of the gang members went down under the assault. By then Angel was already sprinting down the row. He halted at the end of the stack of crates and peered around the corner.

Gunfire broke out behind him but none of the bullets came close. The gang members had lost him for the moment but the warehouse was too small for Angel to stay lost long.

Gao stood near the Camaro. Collins was huddled at Gao's feet, the barrel of Gao's Glock pressed against his neck. The gang member stood calmly, holding his prisoner, and talked to his men.

Glancing up, Angel spotted the top of the crate ten feet up. Another row of crates stood in front of it, only a few feet taller. Above that was a fire suppression system that hopefully remained operational. Angel leaped to the top of the crates and landed quietly.

Yelling orders, Gao quickly organized his men, getting them to settle down into a search pattern.

Angel lit another vodka bottle, took aim on the open crate of vodka, and threw as hard as he could. The Molotov cocktail arced across forty feet and dropped. For a moment Angel thought he'd missed the crate. Then the heavy vodka bottle crashed into the crate with enough force to break through the wood and shatter the bottles inside.

Glass and wood and vodka poured over the concrete floor. The burning wick caught the racing pool of alcohol on fire with a hissing *whumpf!* Feeding on the oxygen and straw packing that had been inside the crate, the fire quickly spread. The flames sprang up, speeding up the side of the stacked crates.

Gao yelled more orders. Some of the gang members split off to find fire extinguishers. They returned quickly and hosed the fire. Clouds of white vapor rolled against the mass of twisting flames but appeared to have little effect. Thick, acrid, black smoke pooled against the warehouse ceiling. In seconds, the fire had spread down two rows of crates.

Angel waited, watching the gang members search frantically. The smoke rolled across the warehouse ceiling, obscuring his vision and stinging his eyes. As the fire continued to burn, the smoke got thicker, completely filling the warehouse, getting thicker at ground level as the air became saturated.

The fire alarm rang stridently, hooting into the cavernous warehouse. Immediately, thick blobs of white retardant foam sprayed down from the suppression system like a sudden blizzard, adding to the confusion.

Angel listened to the sounds of the gang members coughing and hacking below him. If he still breathed, he'd have the same problems. He gathered himself, sheltered in the smoke, and leaped across the twenty-foot gap between crate stakes, making his way toward Gao and Collins.

Someone below heard him and fired up at the roof. Holes opened in the ceiling, letting in shafts of morning sunlight. Sunlight sizzled the back of Angel's hand, bringing a searing pain as the flesh blistered up. He leaped across to the next row, readying the crowbar in his hand.

At the next row, he turned and dropped to the floor, jumping out toward Gao and Collins. The smoke was so thick in the warehouse now that visibility was limited. Angel's dark clothing helped disguise him as he landed on the other side of the Camaro.

He pushed himself effortlessly up from a drop that would have shattered a normal man's legs and sent shards of pain ripping up into his own body. Without hesitation, knowing he had only heartbeats before the Black Wind members found him, he sprinted toward Gao and Collins.

Gao spotted Angel and brought his pistol up, yelling for the others.

Chapter 15

"THIS WAY, MS. SUMMERS."

Buffy stayed a step behind her mom as they walked through the packed cargo warehouse. Yellow and green forklifts darted through the aisles stacked high with crates and shelving piled with boxes and other containers. Supervisors yelled to get the attention of workers, holding up clipboards with cargo numbers on them. Bright sunlight showed on the other side of the big bay doors that weren't blocked by trailers. Other forklifts barreled into the trailers carrying packages and crates. The noise cascaded inside the warehouse.

"The package arrived safely?" Joyce asked.

"Yes." The warehouse supervisor was a gruff guy in his fifties with broad shoulders and white and gray chest hair that stood out so straight it looked like he'd shoved a cockatoo down his shirt. His name tag read COBEN. He punched numbers into a digital unit held in one big hand and the readout flashed instantly. "Came in on *Blue Tulip* about an hour ago, then arrived here in the warehouse maybe ten minutes ago." He looked at Joyce. "I'm kinda surprised they told you to get here so soon."

"Actually," Joyce replied. "I forgot what time I was supposed to be here, but I knew it was around noon."

Buffy knew that really wasn't true. Joyce had been told to schedule pickup of the statue at one-fifteen that afternoon, but she'd known the statue would arrive around noon.

Coben shrugged. "It's no skin off my nose. If we hadn't of had it, you'd have had to wait. But since you're here now, we'll go ahead and pull it for you." He glanced at the aisles as they passed.

Buffy scanned the numbers painted on the concrete floor at the front of each aisle.

Coben halted in front of 37 and glanced up at the top shelves. He cursed under his breath, then looked at Joyce and said, "Excuse me. It's just that after those gang-bangers drifted through Sunnydale last night, some of the local guys decided not to show up in case there was any leftover flak. We're working with nearly a third of our crew from temp agencies."

Intrigued, Buffy asked, "What kind of flak?"

"We work a lot of Asian guys down here," Coben said. "There was some talk that maybe some of the people down on the docks that lost stuff would be looking for a little payback."

Buffy had heard some of the stories on the radio on the way over from school. Besides terrorizing several businesses in Sunnydale, the gang members had also confronted two different gangs along the docks shortly before morning. At least, that was what the police department believed had happened. Two warehouses had gone up in flames. The fire department was still searching through smoldering debris for corpses. The official body count was now up to twenty-seven, but was expected to go higher.

"I have to admit," Coben said, "some of the Asian guys who work here said they had some trouble coming to work today. Especially the young guys. They got some suspicious stares and a few choice words tossed their way." He spotted a passing forklift, put his hands together around his mouth, and whistled.

The forklift driver stopped.

"Hey, Bobby," Coben yelled. "I need a crate down."

The forklift driver flipped Coben a salute and backed up, swinging easily into the aisle. "Which one?"

Coben read off the number and pointed out the crate.

Buffy stepped back as the forklift driver lowered the crate in front of her. Joyce stepped forward and checked the paperwork against the copies she'd brought to the warehouse.

"This it?" Coben asked.

Joyce nodded.

The crate was a three-foot cube of wooden slats. The paperwork was in English and Chinese. At least, Buffy assumed the second language was Chinese.

"I thought I remembered it," Coben said, pulling a hand truck from under the shelving. "Some guy called earlier from Zhiyong Shipping wanting to know if your package had arrived."

"Really?" Joyce asked.

"Yeah." Coben shrugged. "If the guy really works in shipping, he should know we don't give out information about other people's stuff like that." He glanced around. "Got any place special you'd like this taken?"

"I'd like to confirm the contents first," Joyce said.

"Sure." Coben pulled a crowbar from the front of the next aisle over and set to work on the top of the crate.

Nails screeched as they pulled free of the wood. Styrofoam peanuts floated free of the crate.

Joyce kneeled beside the crate and sifted through the contents, finally unearthing the statue. A fierce dragon's face filled with teeth glared up from the sea of Styrofoam. The face looked like it had been carved from black rock.

Not exactly a poster child for Friendly, Buffy thought. The back of her neck tightened in response to the sight of the dragon.

"Everything look okay?" Coben asked.

"Yes." Joyce stood again. "Can you seal this back up for me?"

"Sure." Coben quickly hammered the nails back in with the crowbar.

Joyce led the way to the Summers's SUV and Coben rattled along behind her. The station wagon was just tall enough in the back to hold the crate. After Joyce had signed the paperwork, she slipped behind the wheel and they took off back toward downtown Sunnydale.

Buffy gazed through the window at one of the burned heaps that had been a warehouse until early that morning. Firemen still pumped water onto the smoldering debris.

"Well," Joyce said, "that certainly seemed to be anti-climactic."

Buffy started to agree, then spotted the van pulling in behind them in the side mirror. The windows were covered in dark Mylar, turning the interior black. "Take a right at the next light," she said as her Slayer senses flared in warning.

"What's going on?" Joyce demanded.

"I think we're being followed."

"Who?"

"Don't know," Buffy answered. "But I'd like to find

out." She reached down into her bag and pulled Mr. Pointy out as she continued watching the van in the side mirror.

Joyce coasted through the yellow light ahead and turned right, driving almost casually. "Maybe you're just imagining things." She started to look over her shoulder.

"Don't look," Buffy said.

"Then how are we supposed to know if they're following us?"

"I'll look. But only through the mirror."

Even though the light had turned red, the van pulled through the intersection and trailed them, slightly closing the distance.

Okay, Buffy thought, wishing her mom wasn't with her, *time to run.* But she had to wonder if the unknown person or persons in the van was after her because she was the Slayer, or because of the crate her mom had picked up at the warehouse.

The van continued following, and the distance shortened between it and the SUV.

Buffy looked at her mom. "Floor it!"

Gao's first two rounds cut the air over Angel's head as he leaped feetfirst and skidded across the Camaro's hood. The fire-retardant foam made the metal slippery. He dropped to a crouch on the other side of the sports car with the crowbar drawn back as flame jumped from Gao's muzzle again. The bullet cored through the Camaro's windshield.

Angel brought the crowbar off his shoulder like he was smashing a line drive. The impact sounded metallic and meaty, mixed with the snap of splintering bone.

Gao yelled as the pistol flew away. He swiveled, setting up in a martial arts stance, then launched his left foot at Angel's head in a roundhouse kick. Moving quickly, Angel shifted and used the crowbar to block the kick, then shifted the hook to catch Gao's foot. Angel yanked, pulling the demon off his feet.

Collins crawled away.

Angel grabbed the lawyer's belt and threw him against the Camaro. "Don't move," he ordered. "If we get out of here, we're going to talk."

"Okay," Collins replied, pressing up tight against the sports car.

Warned by the slither of movement, Angel turned back to Gao. The Black Wind member rolled backward, then swept Angel's feet from under him with a leg. Angel crashed down painfully, watching as Gao got to his feet, moving lithely in spite of his injured hand.

Gao's head fell back as his mouth opened hugely again. The forked tongue flicked out, coming straight at Angel's eyes.

Angel grabbed the black tongue, stopping it only inches from his eyes. The wicked, barbed forks writhed as they tried to reach him. The tongue pressed forward, incredibly strong, forcing Angel's arm back. The tongue's scaly surface burned Angel's palm.

Gao hissed angrily, shifting in a spidery crouch.

Angel rolled and got to his feet, still gripping the tongue. He yanked, getting all of his weight and strength into the effort, pulling Gao forward. Angel snap-kicked, catching Gao under the chin. The demon's teeth sliced through the ropy tongue and blood sprayed.

Revulsion filled Angel as he threw the severed tongue aside. The tongue continued twisting and writhing like a dying snake, tracking blood across the pavement. *That is disgusting.* He glanced at his hand and saw the reddened flesh, still felt the acid burning into him.

Gao stood unsteadily, bleeding profusely from the

mouth and nose. He held his right hand forward and the eye opened in his palm.

Immediately, lethargy filled Angel. His arms and legs felt leaden.

Gao tried to yell for help, but only a bloody, choked cry sounded. Still, it was enough to attract the gang members. Footsteps and yells sounded in the roiling smoke, growing closer.

Focusing, Angel forced himself to step toward Gao, backing the Black Wind gang member against the wall. The eye opened wider in the palm and Angel felt like he was moving through quicksand. He drew the crowbar back, then rammed the sharp end through the demon's palm-eye and the concrete beyond, nailing the hand to the wall. The lethargy dropped away.

Collins hunkered against the car, coughing and retching from the smoke. Angel grabbed the man by his jacket, got him up on his feet, and got him moving. Collins ran unsteadily, banging into the crates on either side of the stack. Angel kept him headed for the sewer opening.

A figure, blurred by the thick curtain of smoke, moved ahead and called out in Chinese.

Angel caught Collins by the jacket and swung him aside, then picked up a small crate full of machine parts. The Black Wind member fired as Angel threw the crate. The stream of bullets cracked the wooden crate open but the machine parts slammed into the gang member anyway, driving him back and down.

Collins collapsed, unable to go on. Sirens screamed outside the building, letting Angel know the police or fire department or both had arrived, drawn by the smoke and alarm. He grabbed the attorney and hustled him toward the manhole.

"C'mon," Angel growled. "Just a few more feet."

Cool, though fetid, air came up from the manhole. Angel helped Collins find the ladder built onto the wall below and guided him down. Rats scattered along the sewer as they entered.

Draping Collins's arm across his shoulder, Angel took long strides down the sewer system, putting distance between them and the warehouse. With any luck, Collins would be able to give him a better lead on what the Black Wind gang intended for Sunnydale. He kept moving, listening for sounds of pursuit.

Joyce hesitated briefly, then put the SUV's accelerator to the floor. The big vehicle shivered in response at first, then started gaining speed. She focused on the traffic, gripping the wheel with both hands. "I hope I don't get a ticket."

"Actually," Buffy said, "a police officer might not be such a bad thing right now." She continued watching the van in the mirror.

The van floated back and forth in the SUV's wake, jockeying for position. The driver no longer tried to remain sneaky.

Buffy swallowed hard. Her mom had been involved in her Slayer activities a few times, and even with Angel after he'd turned evil again for a short time. But that wasn't where moms were supposed to be. As good as she was, Buffy knew she couldn't protect everyone.

"Why are they chasing us?" Joyce asked.

"I don't know." Buffy felt guilty about not telling her mom that the Asian gang members had carried pictures of her. It hadn't broken in the news either, and somehow it just wasn't the kind of thing that lent itself to casual conversation. *Gee, Mom, would you believe the new bad guys in town are carrying around* my *picture?*

"Hang on," Joyce warned, then pulled a hard right again, blitzing around a slower moving car making a right turn as well. Rubber shrilled on the street, drawing the attention of pedestrians and sending them scurrying back for the safety of the sidewalks.

Buffy braced herself, glancing at her mom briefly in surprise. "Remind me never to go up against you in bumper cars at the amusement park." *Mom as wild-eyed woman stock car driver—who knew?* Buffy glanced at the side mirror, thinking for a moment that they had lost the van.

Then the van came barreling around the turn, skidding wildly out into the oncoming traffic lane. Horns blared and the van knocked bumpers with a Sunnydale cab, only rocking it a little where the driver had braked to a halt.

"I should have left you at school," Joyce said. "You're only in danger because I brought you out here."

"I'm in danger," Buffy said, "because I'm the Slayer. There's nothing you could do about that."

"They don't want you," Joyce said. "They want the crate."

"How do you figure that?"

"If they'd wanted you, they would have tried for you at school."

Buffy thought about that. "Okay, point."

Without warning, a sedan in the oncoming lane ahead suddenly slewed sideways, filling the two-lane street.

Buffy glanced around wildly, then spotted what she was looking for. "Alley!" She pointed.

Joyce followed her directions immediately, pulling hard on the wheel and tapping on the brake. The SUV's rear wheels skidded momentarily, then followed the pulling power of the front ones, straightening out as Joyce roared down the alley.

The alley was narrow, covered in a thin, crumbling blacktop that hadn't seen better days in decades. It was sandwiched in between an older apartment building and an abandoned office building hung with signs that promised renovation.

No direct sunlight touched the alley, and Buffy knew that was not good. It also made her more curious about what was actually in the crate. Why would an ugly stone dragon be so important?

Before they reached the end of the alley, another van suddenly pulled into it, blocking the way.

"Brakes!" Buffy said.

Joyce stomped on the brakes, bringing the SUV to a shuddering halt at the end of the alley.

Buffy opened the passenger door and climbed out with Mr. Pointy in her fist. There was barely room in the alley to get to the rear of the SUV. *Not my mom, you creeps. Nobody hurts my mom.* But she knew that wasn't true. She waited by the bumper.

The van trailing them had parked less than twenty feet back. The tinting on the windows was too dark to allow any visibility inside the vehicle. Then the doors opened on both sides.

Two men got out, both of them carrying metal softball bats.

"If you're looking for Larry's Line Drives," Buffy said helpfully, "you missed it by miles."

Both men morphed their features, revealing their vampiric natures. "Step away from the car," one of them ordered. "We only want the crate."

"Right. The crate." Buffy glanced at her mom, then at the three vampires who climbed from the other van.

"The crate's all yours." She walked around the SUV and took her mother's hand. She hid Mr. Pointy in her other hand as she guided them to the wall and out of the way.

The vampires converged on the back of the SUV.

Chengxian Zhiyong glared through the polarized window of his limousine and watched the warehouse burn despite the best efforts of the Sunnydale Fire Department. Four trucks continued to spray water onto the warehouse, but they lost the battle as they had the two others during the night. Even as Zhiyong watched, the warehouse's ceiling collapsed, revealing the structure's metal bones. Smoke continued to curl up into the sky, drifting by the news chopper covering the fire.

"The loss isn't so great, Mr. Zhiyong," the man seated across from him said.

Zhiyong spoke without looking at the man. "Those were not your goods, Mr. Wallace."

"No, I suppose they weren't." Terry Wallace was a model of American efficiency. He was trim and athletic, dark hair in a military cut, six feet five inches tall, and liked using his height to intimidate others.

Zhiyong had learned long ago that the best tools to intimidate others were money and power. When he was much younger, he used to think money and power were one and the same, branched out at times through religion and politics as a person used either of those to acquire wealth.

"I hired you and your people to guarantee things like this would not happen," Zhiyong said. "I do not want to live in a world of acceptable losses."

"I understand that, sir, and I—"

"Yet I find myself on the cusp of a dangerous situation despite your best efforts. Had I not taken proper precautions, and had this event taken place a few hours earlier, I would have risked disastrous exposure." Zhiyong paused and glanced meaningfully at the man. "You know about exposure, Mr. Wallace, and how bad such a thing can be."

Wisely, Wallace didn't say anything.

Zhiyong waited, staring at the man's expressionless face. Before turning to the private corporate sector, Wallace had been with the Central Intelligence Agency. They'd met in Thailand and done business together before and after Wallace's government career had gone down in flames.

Terry Wallace had been shepherding governmental black ops in Asia, and had gotten greedy. Once his sideline business practices had been discovered, the American government had quietly put him out of business, but had been unable to publicly acknowledge the affair. It had left Wallace in a position to deal with a number of people around the world, but always on the outside of wealth and power—looking in. Hungry men were good to have around.

"Mr. Zhiyong," Wallace said with studied seriousness, "I can assure you that none of the local or state law enforcement agencies were involved with this. The payoffs we had were accepted without hesitation."

"Then who," Zhiyong asked, "would have done such a thing?"

Wallace hesitated. "I don't know."

"It is your job to never allow yourself to be in a position to tell me you don't know."

"Yes, sir."

"I pay you very good money for your services and those of your men."

"Yes, sir, you do."

"I expect very good service in return."

"And you'll get it, sir."

Zhiyong looked at the man. "I should have gotten it from the very start."

Wallace appeared as though he was about to argue, then caught himself and said nothing.

"I want the people responsible for this."

"Yes, sir. They'll pay, sir."

"No," Zhiyong said. "I want your people to do nothing other than to find out who is responsible for this."

The firemen around the first truck broke and ran back as the front of the warehouse suddenly exploded, sending twisted metal and flaming concrete chunks through the air. A large amount of the debris landed out in the harbor a hundred yards away. The ships had already been backed to a safer range. Explosions continued to buffet the general area for a moment. The Sunnydale police moved the lines back immediately. The news chopper dropped down lower, swooping through the smoke.

"Munitions?" Wallace asked, a little surprised.

"A few things," Zhiyong admitted. "I knew there would be some resistance from certain parties here. Sunnydale is privy to very interesting business. Did you know the town was built over a Hellmouth?"

"I've never even heard of a Hellmouth," Wallace admitted.

"Pity. I think the subject would fascinate you. There's a lot of power here. For the person strong enough to bend even a part of it to his will." Zhiyong stared through the window and watched the rescue workers rush to the aid of those injured by the flying debris. He had no idea what the casualty rate was. Nor did he care.

"I'm always ready to listen, Mr. Zhiyong."

Zhiyong smiled. "Are you? I know you still have trouble believing in vampires, even after you have seen evidence of them yourself."

"I've seen what I've seen."

"But you don't believe in arcane forces, Mr. Wallace."

"I . . . *struggle* with the idea of magic."

"Not magic," Zhiyong corrected. "Magic is a parlor trick, a sleight-of-hand. I'm talking about true power. Money pales by comparison. Where I see vampires, creatures fueled by darkness and demons, you see what you refer to as madmen or genetic anomalies. You cannot accept what is before your eyes. That's why you will never find yourself in a position as I am." He looked back at Wallace. "I hope I have not offended you, for that definitely wasn't my intention."

"No, sir." But the set of Wallace's jaw indicated otherwise.

Zhiyong didn't care. Money bought Wallace's pride and loyalty twenty-four hours a day every day of the week. He ordered the driver to return to the offices he'd secured there in Sunnydale. He switched on the television set and watched the local coverage of the warehouse fire.

The phone rang and he answered.

"Master, it is Hang-Ki," the voice said in their native tongue.

"Where is Bunseng?" Zhiyong demanded. Bunseng had been in charge of the warehouse operation and the lawyer, Collins.

"He is injured, Master."

"If he is conscious, I want to talk to him."

"Master, his tongue has been shorn from his head. He will need much healing before he is able to talk again."

"What happened?"

"We were spied upon, Master."

"By whom?"

"A vampire."

The answer surprised Zhiyong. He knew vampires could move around in the day as long as they avoided direct light. The surprising thing was that any of them, let alone one, would choose to interfere with the warehouse operation. "Only one?"

"Yes."

"Did you recognize him?"

"No. But I will know him if I see him again."

"What of the lawyer?" Zhiyong deliberately didn't use Collins's name. Wallace understood the language, but he didn't need to know all of the details or the names involved in the Sunnydale operation.

"The vampire freed him."

"Why?"

"I don't know, Master."

"Did Bunseng get the information from the man that I requested?"

"Sadly no, Master."

"Where are they?"

"They escaped into the sewers. We are searching for them, but the fire and police rescue units make things more difficult."

"Did this vampire know our guest?" Zhiyong asked.

"Master, I don't think so."

"Yet, the vampire saved this man at the risk of his own life?"

"Yes, Master."

"A vampire with compassion, then," Zhiyong said. "That will certainly narrow our search. I will be in touch with you soon." He broke the connection and looked at Wallace. "I need you to talk with Mayor Wilkins again. Tell him I'll need those files he offered earlier. Especially the one pertaining to a vampire named Angel."

"Yes, sir." Wallace didn't bother to write the name down. He never wrote anything down.

Zhiyong relaxed in the plush seat and considered the situation. Losing the warehouse was only a minor inconvenience at the moment. With no exposure at risk, all he'd lost was some merchandise and time.

But he had lost Collins as well, and that would slow the search he was presently conducting. However, now that he suspected who Angel was, pressure could be applied in that direction.

"Mr. Wallace," Zhiyong asked, shifting to another potential problem area, "have your men made any progress in identifying the young woman who attacked my men last night?" He knew about the Slayer, but this new woman was completely unexpected.

"Not yet. But give them a little more time. They're very good at what they do."

"Of course." Zhiyong didn't berate the security man over the young woman. She remained a mystery at present, and Zhiyong hated mysteries. However, the woman also represented some of the arcane forces at work in the situation. Her warning to him, about the men he searched for, had come as a surprise. The men he searched for had been lost over a hundred years ago, forgotten by nearly everyone in Sunnydale.

So how is it the young woman knows of them? And why would she champion them?

Silently, Zhiyong gazed out over the city that he was already thinking of as his. Mayor Wilkins had been quite generous. A vampire with a guilt-ravaged soul, a young girl who believed herself to be some legendary force against Darkness, and a few friends did not add up to any insurmountable obstacle.

In his years, he'd faced much worse, and he'd always won. He had no doubts about the outcome now. Then the phone rang again and he answered.

"Master," the voice at the other end of the connection said, "there has been a problem."

"What problem?"

"The delivery you made through the art gallery has been intercepted."

A chill touched Zhiyong's heart. Sharmma's statue was integral to everything that he had planned. He could not lose it. "Get it back! At once! Do you hear me? Get it back!"

Hidden on the third floor of a shipping warehouse less than five hundred yards from the burning building, Angel watched the black limousine as it drove away. He hadn't recognized the Asian man in the back-seat.

Angel watched the luxury car till it disappeared. He also heard Collins quietly trying to sneak off.

"Are you sure that's what you want to do?" Angel asked, turning to the man. Both of them stank of smoke and the sewer. Burn marks seared their clothing.

Collins glared over at him, then glanced longingly at the stairway over his shoulder. "Getting out of here sounds like a hell of an idea to me." Since Angel hadn't hurt the man, the lawyer had gotten cocky. "Why? Are you planning on stopping me?"

Angel unleashed his anger for a moment, allowing his face to morph into that of the demon. He was confused by the situation, and the man in the black limousine definitely offered a new kind of threat. How much of that threat was focused on Buffy remained to be seen. "I could stop you if I wanted."

Collins froze.

"I think we both know that." Angel morphed back into his human features. "What I'm suggesting is that if you try to leave this building by walking through the doorway downstairs, you're going to have a lot of people in your face wanting to know what you're doing out here and what happened to you. Are you prepared to answer those questions?"

Fearful frustration twisted the lawyer's features. "No."

"Good. Then maybe we understand each other." Angel crossed the floor. The third story of the warehouse was primarily for long-term storage, for replacement motors, winches, and supplies seldom used by the facility but kept on hand out of necessity. Spiderwebs glazed the corners of the room. Mildew and mothball stink clung to everything.

"You're not human."

"And you're not exactly on the side of the angels."

"How do I know you're not working for them? That this isn't some kind of trick?"

"You don't."

"What do you want from me?"

"I want my questions answered," Angel replied.

"And if I choose not to answer them?" Collins glared at him like a petulant child.

Despite his flagging strength and the pain that throbbed through his body from the burns and wounds, Angel moved with his incredible quickness, stopping only inches from the lawyer. "You're all out of choices, Collins. I saved your life, and right now I own you." The words came from the past, from the time when Angelus had been the most feared vampire in Europe. Angel regretted the ease with which he slipped back into those words, but he needed the threat.

"Oh, God," Collins choked, crumpling into a seated position.

"You're at my mercy now, not His," Angel growled. "And right now that's what we'd call a limited resource."

Collins wrapped his arms around himself, crying silently. "What do you want?"

"Who is the man in the limousine?"

"Chengxian Zhiyong."

"Who is he?"

"He's a shipping line owner from Hong Kong."

"What's he doing here?"

"I don't know. Zhiyong contacted my office nearly a year ago and had me start setting up his business offices and licenses here in Sunnydale. At that point I thought he was strictly legitimate. Mayor Wilkins asked me to work with Zhiyong, help him get set up."

"Why?"

"I don't know." Collins wiped at his face, smearing soot and baring fresh burns. "I don't always know what's going on. The kind of money I get paid under the table, I can't afford to ask a lot of questions, you know?"

Angel didn't say anything.

"People like Zhiyong, they don't answer questions like that. And God help you once you ask one question too many because the next thing you know your throat's cut and you're bleeding on your own shoes."

"What has the mayor got on you?"

"Enough," Collins replied.

"What is the mayor getting out of this?"

"I don't know. I don't think he counted on things getting this out of hand. We're a small community here, but we have a lot of problems. You must know that. Everybody knows that. Nobody wants to talk about it. It's bad for business."

Angel ignored the guilt being dished his way and focused on getting to the truth because Buffy's life was on the line. "What did those men back in the warehouse want from you?"

Collins shrugged.

Maybe he was cool enough that it would have fooled a jury, but Angel smelled the fear on him. "You're lying."

"You got there too soon. They were only starting—"

"No," Angel said quietly, and the heaviness of his tone shut the lawyer down at once. "Someone very close to me is caught near the eye of this storm. You're not going to lie to me and you're not going to stall me. Otherwise I'll take you back to those demons myself and take whatever they offer in trade. Either way, you're going to be worth something to me."

"All right, all right." Collins took a deep breath. "I do legal work, you know that. And I'm good at it. But I've got alimony, child support, college tuition for a couple kids and a secretary who threatened to tell everybody she was having my baby. I personally think she was lying because the baby didn't look anything like—"

"Move on."

"I need money," Collins said. "That's what I'm getting at. I just need money."

"I don't need the *why,* I need the *what,*" Angel said. "What's the business you're running on the side?"

"I'm a go-between. There are people out there who need . . . certain things that can't be gotten through regular channels. Things that—"

"What kinds of things?" Angel demanded, slamming his hand against the wall beside the lawyer.

Collins jumped. "Things like a right hand cut fresh

from a corpse. A virgin's eyeballs. Dried blood. A two-headed calf, and you'll never believe how hard it is to come up with one of those. *Objets d'art* that are contraband in a dozen countries because people believe they're haunted or possessed or cursed. Things that—"

"Enough," Angel said. It was easy to figure that Collins was a go-between for witches and warlocks and demons needing hard-to-get ingredients for spells.

"I'm not the only person who does things like this, you know," Collins said defensively. "There's a law office in L. A. that specializes—"

"The demons wanted your list of clients?" Angel asked.

Collins nodded. "Either they were planning on taking it over, or they meant it when they said they would be the new suppliers."

Angel turned the information over in his head, trying to find an area that he could turn to their benefit. Maybe Giles could make something of it.

"That's really all I know," Collins said. "Except for one other thing."

"What?"

"My great-great-grandfather practiced law in Sunny-dale back during the gold strike days," Collins said. "He handled a lot of business for the city's founding fathers. And he covered up a lot of bad things they did that they didn't want anyone to know about, paying off judges, victims, witnesses, or hiring people to threaten or harm the ones he couldn't buy off. I've never done that."

Angel waited.

"The thing that Chengxian Zhiyong seemed most interested in was a mine shaft that collapsed in 1853. . . ."

Chapter 16

BUFFY WATCHED THE VAMPIRES OPEN THE BACK OF HER mom's SUV and yank the crate from inside. The crate smacked down on the blacktop in the alley, and the sound echoed between the buildings and mixed with the street noises.

Okay, so we're not into gentle right now, Buffy thought.

One of the vampires hooked his fingers under the top of the crate and yanked. The nails shrilled as they pulled from the wood. The vampire shoved both hands into the Styrofoam peanuts and lifted the dragon statue from the crate.

"Is this it?" he asked, turning the dragon around for everyone to look at.

"Looks like it," another vampire said.

"Unless they decided to mess with us," a young vampire put in. He wore a Grateful Dead concert tee shirt. He gazed at Buffy and licked his lips. "Maybe it's a fake."

A fake what? Buffy wondered. She studied the dragon more closely. Now that she saw the whole body, she realized the statue exhibited some very human characteristics. The dragon stood very erect and its front claws looked more like human hands with elongated fingers. Even though it was a statue, intelligence seemed to gleam in the dark eyes.

"Nah," the first vampire said. "This has got to be the real deal. Why make a fake one?"

"To fool us."

The first vampire shook his head. He traced the statue's lines with his fingers. "You haven't been around long enough to know something that has power when you see it. When you touch it." He grinned, baring his fangs. "This is what we came looking for."

"Then," the young vampire said, "maybe we deserve a little reward." He stepped toward Buffy. A sinister smile curved his lips. No one followed him.

As the vampire closed on her, Buffy turned so that her left side was to him.

The vampire stopped. A puzzled expression filled his face. "Move aside, babe. I'll do the old lady first and save you for dessert."

"Maybe you need to figure on biting something that would be healthier for you," Buffy said.

"Buffy," Joyce called in a small voice.

Buffy heard the fear in her mom and it made her a little madder. Her mom had brushed up against Sunnydale's undead underbelly a few times and knew it existed, and Buffy hated that. Some things about a teenager's life were just supposed to remain unknown from their parents—for their own good.

"That wasn't at all polite," Buffy said.

"Sue me," the young vampire entreated, grinning mockingly. "And where the hell does polite get you these days?" He reached for her.

Buffy uncoiled like a snapped spring. She lashed out with her left foot and drove it into the vampire's face. As he stumbled back, she kicked again and knocked him up against the SUV.

His vampiric nature enabled him to recover quickly. He raked a hand at her, trying to grab her hair.

Buffy ducked beneath the attempt and spun to the right. Staying low, she brought Mr. Pointy up in a back-hand strike. The wooden stake broke through the vampire's rib cage and angled up into the heart.

A sick look filled the young vampire's features as he gazed down. The stake had punched through the grinning skull face on the front of his shirt. "Shit!"

Buffy looked up into his eyes and twisted the stake. "Being impolite," she stated clearly, "especially to my mom—kills."

The vampire turned to dust.

"Now *that's* grateful," Buffy quipped as she turned to face the other vampires. "Anybody else feel like showing a little gratitude?" Before anyone could answer, a chill wind suddenly swept through the alley, prickling Buffy's skin.

Then young Asians with green and white striped hair rushed into the alley. Some of them jumped on top of the vans and the SUV as they made their way toward the vampires clustered around the statue.

One of the gang members leaped at Buffy.

The Slayer spun and dove below the attack. She caught herself on her free hand and shoved herself back up. The vampires and the gang members closed on each other immediately. The yells and growling filled the alley at once.

Two gang members grabbed hold of the statue the vampire held. All three of them yanked on it, breaking it into dozens of pieces that fell at their feet.

By then Buffy was up and racing toward her mother. She took Joyce by the elbow and ran along the apartment building toward the door that led inside the structure. Gunfire cracked in the alley and ricocheted off walls.

Buffy didn't hesitate when she found the apartment building door locked. She stepped back and kicked it open, then pulled her mom inside. A few people stuck their heads out of their apartments on the lower floor.

"Get back inside your homes!" Joyce warned. "There's a gang fight in the alley!"

Buffy paused and glanced back at the doorway. No one was following them. *Which might usually be considered a good thing,* she told herself. Only now she knew it was because the gang members considered the statue more important than she. *And why is it?*

"Buffy!" her mom called urgently. "Come on!"

"Can't," Buffy apologized. "Slayer things to do. You keep going." She turned and ran back to the door before her mom could argue.

By the time she reached the alley, the fight was nearly over. The vampires had lost—big-time. The ones who hadn't been killed were fleeing and the gang members seemed happy to see them go.

Two of the gang members packed the last of the pieces of the statue back into the crate. Then they ran back out into the street to be picked up by vehicles that screeched to halts.

Buffy sprinted toward the van blocking her mom's SUV. She stepped inside and dropped behind the steering wheel. The keys dangled from the ignition. She gave them a twist, shoved the transmission into reverse, put her foot down on the accelerator, and turned to look out the back glass. She watched the cars picking up the Asian gang members and wondered if she'd be able to follow one of them before anyone noticed her.

"—exploded," the radio DJ said as the set blared to life. "Before Sunnydale fire department teams could contain the blaze, the warehouse burned. There are several reports of—"

Buffy cut the steering wheel hard as she roared out of the alley. Driving was never her thing. She slewed wildly, rocking the van from side to side as she tried desperately to control the vehicle.

Then a vampire who had evidently taken refuge in the van during the battle rose up from the empty cargo area behind her and reached for her.

Buffy ducked, then slammed back in the seat as the van collided with something behind it. The vampire flew backward and smashed against the rear doors. The engine shuddered and died.

Glancing around as she scrambled out of the van, Buffy saw that she'd barely steered the vehicle from the mouth of the alley. The rear wheels rested on the sidewalk. The van's rear bumper partially wrapped a street sign posting COMMERCIAL UNLOADING ONLY.

The vampire rushed from the van and came straight at Buffy. His mouth was open wide, revealing the big fangs.

Too late, Buffy realized she was still in the shade of the alley, covered by the shadow of the apartment building. Before the vampire reached her, a horn blared. Startled, the Slayer turned and watched as her mom drove the wagon from the alley, tires spinning. Buffy dodged out of the way just as the SUV's front grille smashed into the vampire.

Joyce drove out onto the street. As soon as the sun's ray's touched the vampire, he caught on fire and burned to death on the front of the SUV. Buffy watched in disbelief as Joyce braked to a stop and threw the passenger door open.

"Come on," Joyce said as flaming bits of the vampire fell to the pavement.

Buffy joined her and glanced up the street, hoping to catch some sign of the fleeing gang members. But they were already gone. She turned to her mom. "What do you know about the statue? Don't you usually work up some kind of history on things that you import?"

"Yes," Joyce answered. "But only on pieces that I'm going to sell. Mr. Zhiyong only made arrangements to ship that piece through my contacts. I wasn't going to sell it, so I didn't ask for any documentation on it." She continued driving.

Buffy worked hard to recall the details of the dragon statue. Maybe Giles could figure something out about it from the description. She hoped. Because for the moment she was clueless about what was going on in Sunnydale and she hated it.

"Willow Rosenberg, I'm shocked!"

Eeep! Recognizing the voice, Willow came to a frantic halt, looking up from trying to juggle her books and her laptop and not look like she'd been speeding through the halls. She turned and smiled. "Hello."

Cordelia Chase had just stepped from the school library, one eyebrow raised in total rebuke.

Okay, what choices do I have? Fake surprise that I was running? Mortification that I was caught? Willow chose a medium path. She approached Cordelia. "I really needed to talk to Giles. I had to hurry."

Cordelia crossed her arms and shook her head. "You know as well as I do that there is no excuse for running in the halls. You didn't used to be such a rule-breaker, Willow.

Once upon a time, I thought I could count on you to be pretty much perfect. A real goody-two-shoes. You were dependable. *Then.* Of course, that was before you and Xander had your little fling and revealed the true you to me."

Willow glanced at her watch and tried not to feel guilty. *I really don't have time for this.* Jia Li had agreed to meet her in the parking lot, but the girl was also in a hurry to get home. If Willow didn't get there soon, she knew Jia Li would probably take the bus.

"Is Giles inside?" Willow asked.

"Yes. He's going over monographs regarding," Cordelia lowered her voice as a group of students walked by and pretended not to be talking to Willow, *"Licharnian demons."* She returned to her normal speaking voice. "I think he's on the wrong track. What you guys are looking for is the Saggitautan demons."

Willow's immediate thought was to defend Giles. Luckily, she curbed her impulse. She also wasn't too terribly surprised that the Watcher had recruited Cordelia to help out with the research. Or maybe Cordy had noticed last night's weirdness all on her own and decided to ask questions. "I need to check in with Giles."

"Of course," Cordelia said, walking away and dismissing Willow all in one move. "But when this turns out to be about Saggitautan demons, don't say I didn't warn you."

Willow chose discretion as the better part of valor and scooted on inside the library.

Giles stood behind the book-littered desk. Huge tomes filled with drawings of demons—insides as well as outsides, some of them looking totally gross and gooey— lay open everywhere. Books were stacked on top of books till they threatened a paper avalanche.

"There you are, Willow," Giles said, smiling at her. "I was wondering when you might wander by. I wanted your opinion regarding the demon I spoke to last night." He swung one of the books around to her as she approached. "Cordelia is of the opinion, mistakenly, I assure you, that the demon was a Saggitautan. Myself, I believe it was a—"

"Licharnian," Willow interrupted.

Giles looked up from his book. "You agree?"

"Don't know. Talked to Cordelia at the door. I don't really have a lot of time to talk right now. Gotta hurry."

"Hurry where?"

Stepping around the counter, Willow pulled out the phone cord for her laptop, and hooked it into the jack under the counter. "Going over to Jia Li's."

"The girl you went to the graveyard with last night? Whatever for?"

"Because she really needs a friend, Giles. And I'm her friend. I take friendship issues very seriously." She flipped her laptop open. She'd turned it on in the hall. She clicked on the newspaper morgue icon and got entry to the site.

"We really need you here tonight," Giles said.

"I'm not going to be lying fallow," Willow explained, checking the computer to make sure the files she wanted were downloading. Luckily, all the newspaper files were zipped, making them much smaller than they normally were. However, they were in graphic format and took a little longer to download than simple text files. It was helpful that her earlier search hadn't loaded many hits, but it was disheartening, too. She added two thick books from the counter to the stack she was already lugging around. "I'm taking *Lucien's Guide to Demon Talents and Traits,* and Jubal Foster's *Demonic Anatomy.* Neither of those is a picnic."

"True," Giles said.

Finished with the download, Willow unhooked her

laptop and shut it down. She took a folded piece of paper from her pocket and handed it to Giles. "That's Jia Li's number. In case you need me." She gathered her things in a firmer grip. "Wish me luck."

"Why?"

"In case Jia Li's brother really can call up demons with his flute and candle."

Giles paused. "Given the vision you had, visiting that house isn't exactly the safest course of action you could follow."

"Maybe. But the vision I saw was of Lok in a cave. As long as I stay in the Rong house, everything should be all right." Willow hesitated and glanced at Giles. "If I turn something up, I'll call. Or you can get me at the Rong number."

Giles nodded.

Willow hurried for the door, on the verge of pure frantic. Looking at the newspaper morgue files while Jia Li was in the house at the same time wasn't going to be easy. And then there was the whole Lok demon-summoning/mysterious voice/vision dynamic going on. *So much for homework.*

Xander came down the steps in front of the school three at a time, immediately spotting Oz's van idling at the curb. Oz had the door open by the time Xander got there. Xander had tracked Oz down at lunch and asked for the favor.

Excitement flared again within Xander as he pulled himself into the van's passenger seat. He felt the yin/yang necklace through the material of his pants pocket. "I really appreciate this, Oz. Walking downtown before the market closed would be tough."

"There's always a cab." Oz checked his mirrors and

pulled out into the heavy traffic inching out away from the high school.

Xander checked his reflection in the mirror, seeing the bruises on his face. Scrapes and more bruises decorated his knuckles. "Not for me. I made twenty bucks the hard way last night and I'm not going to blow it on a cab."

Oz looked at him with raised eyebrows. " 'The hard way.' Wait, I don't even want to know."

"Playing basketball," Xander explained. "That's how I picked up all these cuts and bruises."

"I thought it was from the vampires and Black Wind gang members."

Xander shook his head. "Man, those guys got nothing on street basketball hustlers."

"So maybe you want to clue me in on what we're doing here," Oz said.

"Downtown," Xander said. "We're going to the open market area."

"Ah," Oz said. "Searching. Do we have any clue-type things? Or are we just following pheromones here?"

Xander dug the necklace from his pocket. "Last night, while we were fighting those Black Wind guys, the swordswoman dropped this."

Oz reached for it, feeling it briefly and smelling it. "Lemons. Exotic."

Xander took the necklace back, watching the 'burbs slide by outside the window. "Wait till you see her. She's absolutely gorgeous."

Oz nodded, but didn't say anything.

Xander waited until he couldn't handle it any longer. "What?"

"I didn't say anything."

"No, but you're thinking something."

Oz shrugged. "I'm an internal person. Usually I think a lot."

"So what are you thinking about?"

"Right now?"

"Yeah, right now." Xander felt a little defensive and really didn't want to.

"Willow. Willow and me. You, some, maybe."

"Get to the thinking about *me* part."

"Actually," Oz replied, turning the corner when the light turned green, "I find the whole Willow and me thing much more interesting. You're more like bean sprouts on a vegetarian buffet. A nice addition, but I didn't go there looking for you." He smiled.

"Thanks for that. No, really, I mean that." Xander tried to listen to the music but couldn't concentrate. "You think I'm stupid to be out looking for her, don't you?"

Oz shook his head. "A little impulsive, maybe."

"Then why are you here?"

"Because you asked," Oz replied simply. "And I know you'd go crazier if you were by yourself."

Xander looked away from Oz's honest expression. "I appreciate that. And I would. Go crazier, I mean." He paused, trying to get past the sudden thickness in his throat. "This whole coming graduation thing is getting to be a bummer, you know?"

"Maybe."

"Remember what it was like back in grade school?" Xander asked. "By our senior year, we figured we'd be top dogs. King of the hill. The very best there was in high school. We'd have the coolest comebacks, our pick of the girls, and no homework. It's what we gave all those years up for as underclassmen."

"It's not much fun the second time around, either."

"Sorry," Xander said. "Forgot." Oz had experienced his

own problems with his first senior year, which was why he was repeating it this year. "But you know what I mean?"

"Yeah," Oz replied. "I know what you mean. That's kinda how I felt the first time. Until I found out I wasn't going to make it through. That'll leave you kinda flat, for sure." He shrugged. "But, on a brighter note, I got to spend more time with Willow than if I'd gone to university this year. Sometimes life has a way of working things out for you on its own. You just gotta leave it alone and let it happen."

"I know." Xander blew out a frustrated breath. "I thought I had a handle on this year. Dating Cordelia Chase, who I never figured would give me the time of day, being part of the group with Buffy, and finally getting out of school seemed just around the corner. Then Cordy was gone."

"She had her reasons," Oz pointed out.

"That she did." Xander couldn't look at Oz, knowing both of them knew what those reasons were.

"It might not have worked out anyway," Oz said. "Leaving high school has that effect on people. Willow and I are doing great, but who knows what the future holds?"

Xander shook his head. "Can't see a time when you and she aren't together."

"Me neither. But stranger things have happened."

"Then there's this whole get-out-of-school thing going on. You and Willow and Buffy are already planning college. You know what I'm planning?"

"No."

"Nothing." Xander sighed. "Maybe a road trip. I always wanted to go see stuff, you know."

"What stuff?"

Xander shrugged. "Other stuff, I guess. I've pretty

much seen all this stuff." He waved at Sunnydale. A gray-haired granny lady on the corner waved back.

"So there you are," Oz said, "feeling maybe okay about other stuff when along comes these new demons and Mystery Girl."

Xander glanced at Oz. "How'd you know I was calling her that?"

Oz glanced at him. "You don't know who she is, you don't know where she came from, you don't even know her name. What else are you going to call her?"

"Maybe that *was* a lock." Xander juggled the necklace in his palm. "I just have a feeling about this. She likes me. She told me I was polite and brave, and that I have a good sense of humor." He paused, thinking. "Do you know how many girls have ever told me that? I mean, all three of those things?"

Oz shook his head. "No idea."

"I can count them on—" Xander stopped himself and sighed. "None, Oz, that's how many have told me that. Zipola. And this was only a first date. Kinda. Maybe once she gets to know me—actually, that's kind of scary to think about."

"Then don't."

"Can't think about anything else," Xander sighed.

Oz drove carefully through the crowds, getting closer to the open market area. Farmers put up stands with vegetables, fruits, and flowers. Flea market merchants and craftsmen worked booths or out of the backs of flatbed trucks. There was an old movie theater that showed old science fiction and horror movies for two bucks a head.

"I sound pathetic, don't I?"

"No."

"You'd tell me, wouldn't you?"

"No."

"Because you care about me?"

"Because it might get back to Willow and I don't even want to try explaining that."

Xander shook his head. "You're a funny guy. God, you gotta love that warped sense of humor. Otherwise you'd hate it."

Oz only smiled as he pulled into a parking area only a couple of blocks from the open market.

"Look, before you get into the whole she-could-be-a-mantis-girl-or-a-mummy-or-somebody-out-to-use-me, just know that I've already scoped that whole scene out. I know the risks I'm taking."

"Good," Oz said, switching off the engine. "Because if she's jumping twenty feet into the air, shooting demons with flintlock pistols, and lopping off body parts like it was nothing, I got a news flash for you: she ain't normal."

"That's kind of judgmental, don't you think?" Anger stirred inside Xander and he struggled to keep it under control.

"I know about things that aren't normal. And this is one of them."

"You're the most normal guy I know," Xander protested.

"I'm a werewolf, Xander. Buffy's the Slayer. Willow's a witch. Giles is a Watcher. Angel is a vampire. Not exactly poster children for normal."

"She's normal enough."

"Boy, are you hooked." Oz stepped out of the van.

Xander got out on his side. "Look at what you're saying. Maybe normal just isn't what I'm looking for in my life."

"I know. That's what I'm trying to tell you." Oz nodded toward the market. "C'mon. Let's go see if we can ferret out Mystery Girl's secret identity."

* * *

Most people, Buffy reminded herself, *wouldn't feel safe entering a vampire's lair.* She stepped across the threshold into Angel's mansion, though, and felt like a weight had lifted from her shoulders.

Angel slept sitting up against the wall beside the unlit fireplace. He only wore torn and stained pants, naked from the waist up. The wounds, burns and cuts mostly, stood out against his flesh. His forearms rested on his bent knees, and he didn't appear comfortable at all.

The mansion was huge and rambling, and had high ceilings. The bookshelves held old tomes on demonology and the supernatural. There were couches, a bed, and red velvet curtains. The place wasn't a home; it really was a lair, a place where an animal came to hide from the rest of the world. Buffy felt guilty about thinking that, but she knew it was true. Angel didn't live there; he existed. He lived when he was with her, and sometimes that thought scared her, kind of felt like responsibility. But she knew he felt the same way about her. She invested so much trust and hope in him, yet was afraid of those ties at the same time.

Newspapers lay scattered around him and she wondered what he'd been searching for.

She crossed the room with total Slayer stealth, not wanting to wake him. Easing her backpack from her shoulders, she sat cross-legged in front of him. She propped her elbows on her knees and rested her chin on her fists. She scanned the newspapers. There were a couple local papers, an *L.A. Times,* and a *Wall Street Journal. Not exactly Angel's typical reading material,* she thought.

She studied the various wounds on Angel's body, knowing some of them were fresh and wondering where they'd come from. But she also remembered what it had felt like to lie in his arms, to be totally wrapped up in someone else's flesh. She missed that, was afraid of that, and wanted that all in one heartbeat. Then the feeling burst.

Buffy felt a twinge in her stomach, a note of warning that came from her Slayer senses, and watched as Angel's eyes opened. "Hey," she said.

Angel looked embarrassed. "Didn't hear you come in."

"Slayer skills," Buffy said. "Makes evil things everywhere live in fear."

"Have you been here long?" Angel sat up straighter.

"A couple minutes. What about you?" She touched one of the papers. "I know you've been here long enough to catch up on some reading, but looking at all the new cuts and bruises, you've been elsewhere as well."

"I was following up on the Black Wind gang."

"Clue-type things?"

"I found some of them down by the harbor."

Buffy remembered the newscast she'd heard on the radio at lunch. "Big explosion? Possible munitions storage for gang activity?"

"Yeah. But then I lost them."

"You shouldn't have gone by yourself."

"I had to. These guys have got you marked, Buffy, and I need to know why."

"*We* need to know why," Buffy corrected.

Angel nodded. "I thought you were supposed to be at school with Giles."

"I took a rain check. I knew you'd be looking into this thing and I wanted to make sure you were all right."

"Thanks."

"So give. What did you find out?" She listened intently as he described the confrontation inside the warehouse, looking at the papers regarding Chengxian Zhiyong and the shipping business he was bringing to Sunnydale. Then she gave him the story of the statue in the crate her mother had been responsible for. "If the mayor's involved, which he is, we can kind of fill in the blank about how the Black Wind members had my picture."

"Yeah. The main concern is why Zhiyong is here in Sunnydale."

"Crime monopoly. Zhiyong wants more. Total greed factor."

"Sunnydale isn't exactly the Boardwalk of gangdom," Angel replied.

"Maybe there's more crime-type things going through Sunnydale than we thought," Buffy pointed out. "We aren't exactly crime-fighters. We specialize in demons, who are usually involved in crime-type things, but we don't know all the mundane things that go on here."

"I thought about that," Angel agreed. "And I even considered the possibility that Sunnydale was a staging area."

"Bigger and better conquests from here? Now we're talking Risk, not Monopoly."

Angel got to his feet, not moving as fluidly as normal. The wounds had evidently taken their toll. He paced, thinking on his feet. "There's more to it than that. The lawyer I talked to said that Zhiyong was having him dig up old land claims from a hundred and fifty, two hundred years ago. Some of the paperwork got lost over the years, and Zhiyong's take on it was that some of those files were lost intentionally."

"Why?"

Angel shook his head. "Collins didn't know. He'd started the research, but hadn't gotten very far before he was taken to the warehouse today."

"Did the papers help?"

"No. There's a lot of fanfare about Zhiyong's company, about the number of jobs it could potentially open up here in Sunnydale as well as the effect it might have on some aspects of Pacific Rim shipping."

"But that's not what we're looking for."

"No. And there's very little background material in those articles that doesn't reflect favorably on Zhiyong and his operation."

"We didn't ask Willy about Zhiyong last night," Buffy said. "We didn't know his name last night. We could go there."

"Zhiyong is involved," Angel said. "I was just thinking about making the rounds myself."

Buffy nodded. "When I got here, you looked like you were thinking really long and deep thoughts."

Angel smiled. "Yeah. Let me grab a quick shower and we'll go."

"The sun will still be up for a while longer. Is there a way you can get to the Alibi in the daylight?"

"I can get there through the sewers," Angel said, disappearing into a back room.

"Not a pleasant thought," Buffy said.

"It's a relatively short trip from here."

"Easy for you to say," Buffy shot back. "Only one of us can hold our breath the whole way."

"It's a nice piece. Probably worth a hundred dollars or so. Do you want to sell it?"

Xander took the necklace back from the Hispanic man's hands protectively. "I'm not looking to sell it," he explained. "I wanted to know if you'd seen another one like it."

The man leaned back in his folding chair and put his jeweler's loupe away. Silver rings, bracelets, and necklace chains filled the black velvet-bottomed boxes on the cloth-covered table. "Not today."

"Not today?" Xander's excitement quickened his pulse. "Did you see one like it yesterday?"

"No."

Keeping his impatience in check, Xander asked, "Then when did you see one like it?"

The man shook his head. "I don't know that I have, kid. I only know that I haven't seen a piece like that today or yesterday." He rolled a toothpick in his mouth. "Tell you what, I'll give you one hundred twenty-five dollars for the necklace. Won't even ask you where you got it."

Xander curbed a heated remark. "I'll think about it and get back to you." He turned to leave.

"Go ahead," the man promised, "but you ain't gonna get a better offer here."

Disgusted and starting to get more than a little dejected with nearly an hour invested and nothing to show for it, Xander threaded back through the marketplace. The area was a narrow street with pedestrian-only traffic, open to anyone with goods to sell and a license, from farm products to clothing to jewelry. A few of the stands offered candied apples and cookies. It was a great place to come and hang out during the spring and early summer.

Oz waited by a collection of velvet paintings of Kid Rock, X-Men, and other media stars. "No luck?"

"No." Xander scanned the booths and market areas, trying not to let his frustration sound in his voice. Oz had been a good sport about giving up his time. Xander continued down the lines of booths.

"I've been thinking," Oz said.

"Please don't do that."

"C'mon, you're going to have to lighten up a little bit here or you're going to go into critical meltdown."

"I'm light."

"What I was thinking was that you might want to consider starting your own self-help group. Kind of a *I Can't Help Loving Supernatural* theme. You know, a haven for unlucky-in-love guys and ghouls."

"Har-de-har-har," Xander replied. "I mean, hardly a har-har there."

"It wasn't that bad."

A dragon fluttering on a pennant caught Xander's eye. He made his way down to a booth specializing in Eastern herbal remedies, incense, and kimonos that was at the back of the market area. It wasn't jewelry, but maybe the culture was right.

A young Asian guy worked the counter, hair slicked back and wearing a Bronze tee shirt. He filled jars with different incense sticks. "Can I help you?"

"I hope so," Xander told him, placing the necklace on the glass counter. "I'm trying to find someone who might know about this necklace."

The guy took the necklace and inspected it. "This is very old. Chinese, I think, if that helps." He glanced up.

Xander shook his head. "Not really. I figured Chinese. I met this girl and she dropped it. I found it later. I want to return it to her, but I didn't get her name. I thought maybe the necklace was unique enough I could find out where she got it and who she was."

"Beats me." The guy handed the necklace back and smiled. "Judging by that grin on your face, she must have been pretty."

"Very."

"Wish I could help you. You might ask Master Kim. He knows a lot about old jewelry, and this is definitely not something you're going to find on a shelf somewhere."

A momentary elation filled Xander. "Where do I find Master Kim?"

"Down at the Green Dragon Temple martial arts dojo. It's not far from here."

Xander memorized the directions, which weren't difficult, then headed back to where he'd left Oz. Only Oz wasn't where Xander had left him. The sidewalk in front of the closed movie theater was empty.

While he stood there looking, a strong arm roped around Xander's neck and dragged him back. He grabbed the thick forearm with both hands and tried to fight his way free. He even considered screaming, which wasn't all that macho but could keep a person alive, but he couldn't get any air out of his lungs. Or in. His vision faded around the edges as he kicked. One of the Black Wind gang members grabbed Xander's feet and held them as they entered the theater with him.

They carried him past the concession stand and into the dark area of the theater.

Xander was on the verge of passing out when he saw Oz lying facedown on the carpet in the aisle. One of the Black Wind gangers was securing Oz's arms behind his back with strips of gray duct tape.

Then the guy holding Xander slammed him down on the ground. Xander croaked painfully as air rushed back into his lungs. He tried to get up, but he was kicked in the ribs, which ignited a blast furnace of pain.

One of the gang members placed a foot between Xander's shoulder blades and kept him pinned to the floor. Another gang member wrapped Xander's ankles and wrists with tape. When they were finished, they rolled Xander over on his back.

"Xander," Oz said in a muffled, pain-filled voice, "they want the necklace."

Chapter 17

STUBBORNLY, GLARING UP AT THE BLACK WIND GANG members standing over him, Xander said, "What necklace?"

One of the gang members kicked Xander again.

"Being the tough guy in a situation like this," Oz gasped, "is way overrated in my opinion."

Xander struggled for his breath. The gang member grabbed his hair and yanked his head up so they were face-to-face.

The gang member grinned cruelly. "We want the necklace."

"Don't know what you're talking about," Xander gritted.

The man slapped Xander.

Xander's head whipped around, feeling like angry bees had crawled under the skin. He tasted blood inside his mouth. *Demons,* he reminded himself. *Some of these guys are demons. They're not looking for her to make nice. They'll use the necklace some way, track her down, chew her head off. The usual demon stuff.* And he was the only force preventing that. It made him feel special. In a pain-filled kind of way.

"Give it up," Oz said.

Xander remained silent. It got a little easier when he was convinced that his jaw had been broken and would probably fall off if he opened his mouth. *Why don't they just search me?* he wondered. *They gotta know it's on me.*

The gang member gestured to one of the others. He spoke briefly in Chinese.

The second gang member pulled out a butterfly knife and flicked it open in a practiced maneuver. He ran a hand over Xander's shirt, then found the necklace in Xander's pants pocket. He raked the knife over Xander's thigh.

"Oh, man," Xander cried out, "be careful down there." He watched as his pants split open to reveal his pocket. A slice in the pocket showed the silvery gleam of the necklace.

Grinning, the gang member reached for the necklace. A blue lightning flash exploded against the gang member's hand, throwing him back a dozen feet to land in the seats.

"How did you do that?" one of them demanded.

Xander shook his head painfully. "Wasn't me."

The gang members drew back hesitantly. The one who'd taken charge held his hand out. Even after he'd heard Giles's story, Xander still wasn't prepared to see the eyelid blink open in the man's palm. He held his eye-palm close to the necklace but didn't touch it.

The gang member's head mushroomed as the top half fell back to unleash a thick, black tongue. The tongue's forked ends fluttered against Xander's face, feeling like burning coals.

Oh, man, Xander thought, *now here's a Gene Simmons nightmare come to life.*

The doors to the concession stand area opened suddenly and a man stepped into the theater. "I thought I heard somebody down here. What the hell is going on?"

The gang member leaning over Xander turned his head. The lizard tongue shot out like an arrow. It speared through the man's left eye, popping the orb out, then splintered the back of the man's head with a liquid crunch. When the tongue withdrew, chunks of bloody flesh tore loose with it. The gang member swallowed them whole.

The dead man dropped, a crater where his face had once been.

The gang member turned his attention back to Xander. The forked ends of his tongue fluttered over his lips. He chewed and swallowed. "The necklace has powers. It cannot be taken from the one who has it. It must be freely given."

"Threatening to kill me is freely giving it?" Xander asked.

The gang member smiled coldly. The forked tongue caressed Xander's face, licking around his eye sockets, reminding him how vulnerable he was. "I don't make up these rules. Give it to me."

Xander struggled not to throw up. "It's kind of hard to give the necklace to you when I'm tied up."

"Just tell me I can take it. That's all that's required."

"And if I say no?"

The gang member rolled his tongue out again. "I could kill you."

"That wouldn't get you the necklace, would it?"

The gang member cocked his head sinuously. "No, but I could kill you and leave it here."

Okay, Xander thought desperately, *not too thrilled with that possibility.*

"Or," the gang member said, "I can kill your friend

while you watch." His tongue snapped out, ripping a cut along Oz's jaw.

"Xander!" Oz yelled, bowing up as he tried to escape his bonds. "Really time to assess the new girlfriend campaign!"

"They could kill us anyway. If I give them the necklace, maybe they'll kill her, too."

"She held her own the other night," Oz pointed out. "Give them the necklace and maybe they'll be sorry they ever went looking for her."

"Decide," the gang member ordered.

Xander hesitated, feeling like a real weenie. *Why do I always have the hard decision?*

The gang member's tongue flicked out.

"Wait!" Xander said. *We're tied up here, she's not,* he told himself. But it still didn't make him feel a hell of a lot better.

Abruptly the theater doors opened again and a middle-aged woman came through. "Roger?" She stumbled over the corpse at her feet, saw the gang members, then turned and ran. The gang member's tongue snapped a hole through one of the swinging doors, missing the woman by inches. Her screams reverberated throughout the theater.

Still, Xander knew, it would take a little time before help arrived.

"Decide," the gang member ordered again. "There is no time."

"Take the necklace," Xander said.

Hesitantly, the gang member reached for the necklace. His hand was shaking when he closed his fist over it. Then he ripped it away from Xander, tearing the pocket out as well. The gang member stood, still clutching his prize. "Take them with us. Hurry."

"Wait!" Xander protested. "What happened to, 'Let them go, we have what we want?'"

"We don't have it all," the gang member said. "There is still the matter of your friend, the Slayer."

Before Xander could say anything else, one of the gang members covered his face with a cloth. He smelled a foul chemical smell, then it felt like the world fell out from under him.

Night blanketed Sunnydale when Buffy and Angel left one of the dives on the north side of town. She was amazed, thinking back on it, how many places there were in the city that catered to crooks, gangs, demons and other assorted bottom feeders of society. No one had given them any concrete leads regarding Zhiyong.

"I don't think I could have taken another hour of that," she admitted, referring to the endless tirade of abuse they'd had to listen to. Knowing that a few demons and other lowlifes would be counting bruises in the morning didn't really make her feel any better. Some of the talk had been embarrassing and ego-battering. "And in the end, what did we learn? Zhiyong is rich, owns a shipping company with offices in Hong Kong, Shanghai, Singapore, and now Sunnydale. He likes golf and collects sculpture. Not even a footnote about demons."

Angel walked beside her. "There was some mention of a possible organized crime connection."

"It was never proven," Buffy grumbled.

"Interesting that the reporter who broke the story disappeared and hasn't been heard from since."

"Okay, so we know he likes his privacy. There's still no indication of what he's doing in Sunnydale."

Angel didn't say anything, but he studied the town around them.

"Angel?" Buffy looked around, wondering what had captured his attention.

"Notice anything about the town?" Angel asked.

Buffy studied the streets as they stopped at the corner. Lights reflected from the store windows around them. "There's not many people out tonight."

"No," Angel said.

A police cruiser glided to a stop at the curb in front of them. Two officers rode inside, the one in the passenger seat carrying a shotgun in plain sight. The driver turned his spotlight on Buffy and Angel.

"Hey!" Buffy complained, putting up a hand to shield her eyes.

The spotlight went out. The police officer on the passenger side stuck his head out the window. "If you don't have any business in town, we're advising citizens to go on home for the evening."

"Is there some kind of curfew I haven't heard about?" Buffy's immediate impulse was to rebel, but she kept herself calm.

"No," the police officer replied. "Just an advisory we're putting out." He motioned to the driver and they rolled on.

Angel watched them move slowly down the street. "They were making sure we weren't Asian," he said softly. "If we had been, I get the feeling that encounter wouldn't have gone so easily."

"I know." Buffy crossed the street, keeping her senses open. Anti-Asian feelings had been another thing they'd kept running into during their talks. "Things in school have been kind of tense as well. There were four fights involving Asian students this afternoon." And those were only the ones she learned about after her mom had dropped her back at school.

"Everybody's scared," Angel said.

"I know. Mom really didn't want me out tonight, but what's a Slayer to do? The vampires aren't going to stay inside." She glanced around at the sidewalks and stores as she passed them by, realizing that the attrition rate was higher than she had at first thought. "It's always been kind of scary to be out at night in Sunnydale, but I've never seen it like this."

"They have faces to fear now," Angel stated. "And a lot of faces in their neighborhood look just like the faces they're supposed to be afraid of."

"I guess it's confusing."

"It is. I was in Europe during World War II. Just wandering. I stayed for a while in Romania, looking for answers as to what I was supposed to do."

Buffy stuck her arm through his and matched her step to his. She knew that had been after the Romani had reunited Angel with his soul.

"I saw neighborhoods in turmoil, striving to survive in the midst of Hitler's confusion and racial genocide," Angel continued. "Tonight is nothing like that. Those times were worse than anything else could be."

"There were the riots in L.A.," Buffy said.

Angel nodded. "I saw those on television." He paused as they crossed another street. "But neighborhoods these days don't get to know each other the way they did sixty years ago. They were more interdependent then. They actually knew each other, watched each other's kids play together. Then, they turned on each other, fed each other to Hitler's armies and the concentration camps."

"That must have been hard." Even though she tried, even though she'd seen a number of terrible things in her own life, Buffy knew she'd never see all the horrors that Angel had lived through.

"There was nothing I could do," Angel said. "So I left

one day. And I didn't go back for years. But if you know where to look, know what was there before in spite of all the rebuilding that has gone on since the war was over, you can still see the scars."

They walked silently for a while, and even though Buffy knew vampires and other demonic monstrosities waited out in the night, it was easy to pretend it wasn't so for just a little while. At least, it was until the scream echoed down the street.

Buffy sprang to action only a half-step ahead of Angel. The scream was feminine, high-pitched, thin and frail. She ran hard, staring into the shadows near the closed second-hand clothing shop. Five figures struggled in the darkness, limned against the pool of electric white light from the convenience store a half-block up the street.

Two women, both Asian and one of them at least in her sixties, struggled against three young guys. A paper sack lay on the ground, material scattered in all directions.

"Give me the purse, bitch!" one of the guys snarled. He waved a baseball bat threateningly.

"Carter!" another of the boys said, pointing at Buffy. "Watch out!"

Carter turned immediately, bringing the baseball bat back to his shoulder.

Anger filled Buffy as she reached for the guy, thinking he was a vampire or demon.

"Buffy," Angel called anxiously behind her. "They're human."

Buffy checked her swing. Slayers lived on the edge of life, where there was no margin for error.

Carter swung the baseball bat without hesitation, aiming for Buffy's head. The Slayer set herself and swung the edge of her left hand toward the bat. The weapon splintered only a few inches in front of Carter's hands.

Following her own forward momentum, Buffy kicked Carter in the chest with her right foot, lifting him clear of the ground.

The second guy came at her, punching viciously. Staying on the aggressive, Buffy went at him, blocking his punches rapidly, then punched him in the face, pulling the blow at the last minute so she wouldn't hurt him badly. He fell backward.

Angel dodged the third guy's punch, then caught him by the shirt back and belt and threw him onto the other two.

On the ground now, crying and frightened, the two women looked up at Buffy and Angel fearfully. They held their open hands up to defend themselves.

Hurt and anger thundered like matched horses through Buffy's temples. Her hands shook as she glared at the three young men. She thought she recognized two of them from school.

"What the hell did you think you were doing?" Buffy demanded. Angel stood only a half-step behind her, but she wasn't sure if it was to back her or to shut her down if she lost it. She couldn't believe the three young men would attack two helpless women.

The three guys got up. Carter needed help from both of them. "Did you get a good look at them?" Carter asked. "They're Chinese! Just like those bastards that attacked our town last night! It's time for a little payback! Two of my buddies are in the hospital, and one of them is in a coma! I was there when they told his girlfriend, my *sister*, that he probably wasn't going to make it!"

Buffy took a deep breath. "These people," she said clearly, "aren't Chinese." She pointed at the sign over the clothing store. "Yamamoto is a Japanese name."

Carter held an arm across his stomach, breathing in

short gasps. "Chinese, Japanese, whatever. It doesn't make any difference. This is our home."

"This is their home, too," Buffy said. Willow had brought her to the shop a few times while looking for make-over projects. The Yamamoto sisters had always been friendly and helpful, and they'd been in business in Sunnydale for over twenty years, according to Willow.

"Please," one of the women said, "I think my sister needs to see a doctor."

Angel bent and easily lifted the woman from the sidewalk. "I've got her."

The other Yamamoto sister led Angel back into the shop. "Come. We can call from in here. My sister must be taken care of."

Carter's two friends pulled at him, urging him to leave before the police were called. Even as he was backing away, Carter pointed at Buffy. "They gotta pay. This is our town. They can't come in here and hurt people without getting hurt back."

Sixty-year-old sisters, Buffy thought, watching them go. *Bet they really hurt a lot of people.* For a moment she considered going after the three guys and holding them for the police. Only she was afraid that she wouldn't just stop at overpowering them.

"Buffy." Angel stood inside the shop doorway. His eyes showed his concern.

"Is she okay?" Buffy asked.

"Yeah. A little shook up. She'll have a few bruises. Nothing a few days' rest won't take care of."

"Good." Buffy turned to him. "After the ambulance guys get here, I've got an idea."

Angel looked at her.

"One thing we did turn up during our search was the

location of Zhiyong's offices. Maybe we could drop by there and look things over."

Angel paused. "It might not be the smartest move we could make."

"No, but this is my town, Angel. For good or bad. And I'm not going to let someone come here and crater that little bit of security most of these people cling to. It's not going to happen on my watch."

Rong, Rong, Willow thought, reminding herself what she was looking for as she trekked through the old copies of the *Sunnydale Post,* the bi-weekly paper that had served the Sunnydale community a hundred and fifty years ago. Her eyes burned as she tapped the keyboard, manipulating the graphics so she could read the stories.

She sat in the Rong living room, listening to Jia Li serving dinner to Oi-Ling and her two younger brothers. The conversation was rapid, like a Ping-Pong game, only Willow could understand none of it because it was all in Chinese. But she didn't mind. As long as they were talking, she knew they weren't paying attention to her and not being able to understand the conversations kept her from being too distracted.

Turning her attention back to the latest page of the paper she was working on, Willow tapped the keyboard. All the old issues of the *Sunnydale Post* had been saved off in a graphic format she could read in Adobe Acrobat. Unfortunately, when viewing a whole page, none of the stories, or even the headlines, could be read.

So the process of reading each page was tedious. They had to be sectioned off, stored as separate files, then gone over in detail.

"Would you like some more hot tea?" Jia Li asked, entering the living room with a pot.

And the process was further complicated by Jia Li's constant attempts at hospitality.

"Sure," Willow said, tapping the mouse pad to send the window with the current story she was reading to the bottom of the screen. It left the window with the homework she was supposed to be working on.

Jia Li poured carefully. "More lemon?"

"No, thanks," Willow answered. "I'm fine. How is Lok?"

"I just checked on him a couple minutes ago," Jia Li answered. "He's still sleeping."

"That's good," Willow replied. The Rong parents had called over an hour ago to say that the meeting with the attorney was running late. Then there was a late shipment at the docks, caused by some kind of explosion earlier in the day. Evidently, with everything that had happened in Sunnydale the previous night and that morning, no one's schedule was even close to timely.

Lok had come in that morning, argued with his father for a couple of hours, but hadn't tried to leave the house. After that he'd fallen into a deep sleep and hadn't awakened. Sometimes, Jia Li had said, Lok had slept as much as forty-eight hours after being in an agitated state.

One of the boys called from the dining room. Jia Li excused herself and went back to take care of the situation.

You should just tell her you're trying to find out what happened to her ancestor, Willow chided herself as she brought the window back up. But she knew she couldn't do that. With the state her friend was currently in, Jia Li would probably not deal very well.

Willow ignored the burning in her eyes and scanned the headlines, wishing Oz would call so she wouldn't have to worry about him. *But how much trouble can Oz and Xander get into? They're probably just having a pizza at the Bronze.*

She had initially entered a search based on the parameters of Mei-Kao Rong's name, any Rong name—accidental death, death, and murder.

Unfortunately, the writers and editors of the *Sunnydale Post* hadn't been really thorough on their editing. Sometimes wrong was spelled rong, adding to the number of hits. And accidents, death, and murder were always prime considerations for stories.

When the current headlines came into view, Willow got excited. *MINING TRAGEDY KILLS 37.* She tapped the keyboard again, bringing the story into better focus and started reading.

According to the story, a cave-in had occurred in a mine north of Sunnydale on August 13, 1853. The mine had been owned by Sunnydale Mining, a partnership venture formed by prominent members of the city. A list of eighteen family names followed.

Thirty-five of the men had been Chinese laborers hired to do the excavation. Mei-Kao Rong's name was among them.

"Now you know."

The hoarse, croaking voice behind her surprised Willow. She turned to find Lok Rong leaning on the couch behind her.

Chapter 18

Lok looked pale and hollow-eyed, so weak that he could barely stand. He was still dressed in yesterday's clothes, wrinkled and stained from his stay in the jail.

"Lok!" Jia Li approached Willow quickly, but her face was filled with apprehension. "What are you doing?"

"Spying on your friend," Lok spat, "who is obviously spying on me."

"You're not making any sense," Jia Li said.

"Take a look at her computer. It has the answers." Before Willow could prevent it, Lok snatched her laptop away. He opened the computer so it hung straight down, the screen facing his sister so she could read it.

Jia Li glanced at the screen, then at Willow. "I don't understand."

"I was doing research on your ancestor," Willow replied desperately. "I didn't even know if I would turn anything up. I only now found that."

Lok pushed the laptop back to Willow. He placed his

243

hands against his temples and screamed out in pain. Saliva flecked his bluish lip. He spoke in Chinese, the words coming so fast Willow guessed that they would be almost incoherent even to someone who spoke the language.

"Lok!" Oi-Ling called from the dining room. Her small face was filled with worry. Tears glimmered in her eyes.

Jia Li tried to go to her brother, but he straight-armed her and knocked her down. For a moment dark malevolence filled his eyes and Willow thought he was going to attack his sister. Willow closed the laptop, prepared to use it as a weapon if she needed to.

Veins stood out on Lok's neck as he made himself step back. He turned his baleful gaze on Willow. When he spoke, his voice was inhuman, cold as a gust from the grave. "Stay out of this, *witch*!"

Willow drew back out of range, put the laptop down, and went around the couch to help Jia Li to her feet.

"He doesn't know what he's doing," Jia Li said. "He's not himself."

Oh, Lok's probably himself, Willow reasoned, *but it's probably getting pretty crowded in there.* She felt certain that at least one hungry ghost had taken partial possession of Lok.

Lok crossed the room to the front door and fumbled with the doorknob. Then he finally got it open and lurched outside.

"I can't let him go!" Jia Li cried.

"You can't stop him," Willow replied, reaching for her friend. "He'll just hurt you."

Jia Li evaded Willow, running for the door.

A snarling, white-hot liquid hiss poured through the room. As Willow watched, frost formed on the decorative mirror by the front door. Like everything else in the living room, butterflies adorned the mirror's four corners. The butterflies were dyed scarlet, blue, orange and yellow, their delicate wings positioned horizontally to their bodies.

As the frost spread out from the mirror's center, it touched the four butterflies. Their wings suddenly fluttered as they came to life and sprang from the mirror.

Jia Li screamed and stepped back.

Moving quickly, guessing that zombie butterflies probably weren't a good thing, Willow grabbed throw pillows from the couch and smashed them. Bilious green paste stained the pillows, smoking at first, then eating holes through the fabric. Willow dropped the pillows to the floor.

Wisps of smoke belled out from the frost-covered mirror. Chinese characters suddenly scrawled in blood spread across the mirror.

"What does it say?" Willow asked.

Jia Li shook her head, backing away. "A warning. Do not interfere."

In the next instant, the blood-red characters caught fire, scorching across the mirror, leaving a soot residue. Then the mirror exploded, spreading a shiny glass haze over the living room.

Cautiously, Willow walked through the falling shiny haze. It didn't seem dangerous and she needed to know where Lok had gone. She held her breath till she was outside, just in case. She stepped out beside the goldfish pond and looked down.

Lok ran unsteadily across the restaurant parking area toward a parked motorcycle. He knelt beside it and started cutting wires. Sparks flared and the motorcycle's engine turned over, almost catching.

"He's leaving," Willow said.

"We can't let him go." Jia Li stood in the doorway of the house, a cordless phone pressed to her ear.

"I don't think we're going to have a choice." Still, Willow started down the steps. *If Buffy was here, she could knock him out or something.*

Lok touched the stripped wires again and the motorcycle engine turned over again, catching this time. It warbled a high-pitched keening.

"You have your mother's car," Jia Li said, coming up behind Willow. "We can follow him and get help out to him."

"I don't think that's a good idea."

"Do you have any other ideas?"

"No." Hesitantly, Willow kept going down the stairs. Her mother's station wagon was on the other side of the parking lot.

Lok threw a leg over the motorcycle and walked it backward, getting it turned around.

"Hurry, Willow," Jia Li pleaded. "Whatever has possessed Lok is only going to hurt him."

Willow remembered the vision she'd seen and silently agreed.

You must go, the voice whispered into her mind. *It is too late to stop him at this point. You must do what you can to save him. Things will be much worse if you don't. Your friends will be hurt. The time to move is now.*

Although she didn't know the source of the voice, Willow believed what it said. She ran, listening to Jia Li call out Oi-Ling's name.

Willow reached her mother's car and pulled the driver's door open. She jammed the key into the ignition, surprised to find she still had her purse, not remembering when she'd picked it up. The car started quickly.

Jia Li slapped a palm against the passenger door glass, slipping into the car immediately after Willow unlocked the door. She spoke quickly into the cordless phone she'd carried from the house.

Willow put the car into gear as Lok roared out of the parking lot. Willow pulled out after him, putting her foot heavily on the accelerator. She didn't know what Lok would try to do once he saw them following him. The tires shrilled as she pulled out onto the street, cutting off an SUV and getting an irate horn blast in her wake.

"Sorry," she said, glancing quickly into the mirror, then back at the single taillight of the motorcycle speeding through the traffic ahead.

Jia Li twisted in the seat and kept saying hello into the cordless phone, but it was obvious they'd exceeded the instrument's range. Frustrated, she screamed—just a little, Willow noticed—and switched the handset off, placing it between the seats.

"Do you have a cell phone?" Jia Li asked.

"On my birthday wish list," Willow replied. Lok whipped in and out of the traffic, which thankfully, was pretty light for this time of night. Willow followed suit, having to whip a little slower with the station wagon. But then, people had a tendency to get out of the way when they saw her coming.

"I called Ngan," Jia Li said, watching the traffic and only now reaching for her seat belt. "She's one of the night hostesses at the restaurant. She'll stay with Oi-Ling and the boys until my parents get back or we return."

Willow nodded. "That was quick thinking."

"I couldn't get hold of my parents." Jia Li glanced at Willow. "I'm really scared."

"Me too," Willow said. She pulled hard to the right, going up on the curb for a brief instant to avoid a car waiting to turn left. The station wagon rumbled up and down. *There goes the front-end alignment. I'll never get to drive the car again.* She prayed that the car would hold together and that she didn't kill anybody and that she didn't get a ticket. Getting stopped by a policeman wouldn't be so bad if there wasn't a ticket involved.

"Maybe we can call from wherever Lok goes."

"Sure," Willow answered, but the image of the cave in the vision haunted her. Personally, she didn't think they were going to end up anywhere near a phone.

"When I was younger," Giles said, closing the last book he'd been searching through and sliding it back onto the table, "I used to think I would never grow weary of looking at demons."

Across the table in the school library, Cordelia just looked at him and shook her head. "Eeww! Now there's a positively horrible thought. I came down here to help you and I don't really care to reminisce about things that at one time lived down Demon Lane."

Giles looked at Cordelia. "Why is it exactly that you did come to help me?"

Cordelia looked at him. "Because you asked."

"If you'll forgive me for saying so, but you're not generally this generous, Cordelia."

She rolled her eyes up at him.

"I meant that in the kindest way possible," Giles offered.

"I kind of noticed everything else that was going on last night, too."

Giles nodded, but continued looking at her. "Since you've . . . broken off your involvement with Xander, I'd noticed some reticence on your part to involve yourself in these . . . things."

"There are other things in life than demon-hunting."

"One would suppose."

Cordelia took a breath and let it out. "Look, Giles, if it will make you happy, I'll tell you."

"Happiness doesn't always go along with curiosity."

"Whatever." Cordelia looked at the book in front of her. "Things are not so great at my house right now. I wanted to be somewhere other than there. And I didn't particularly want to be somewhere where I had to be Cordelia Chase, Social Butterfly."

Social Butterfly wasn't exactly how Giles would have termed Cordelia's involvement with the student body—not even with the ones she pretended to like. But he understood the sentiments.

"I just didn't know I was going to have to be Answer Girl tonight," Cordelia said.

"You're right. I'm sorry about prying."

"No, you're not. You're a Watcher. Watcher's watch . . . and they *pry.*"

"I am sorry," Giles said.

"It's okay." Cordelia flipped pages in the book she was checking. "Plus there's graduation coming up. If the world suddenly ended, which it could do if Buffy and her little group of wannabes didn't figure out what to do, then I'd have wasted all that effort on the senior pictures and figuring out how I was going to dress for the graduation, right?"

"Right." Giles glanced at the time and found it was just after eight o'clock. No one had checked in yet, so he chose to view that as a good thing. He reached for another book and blew dust from the cover. It was Taukut's *De-ranged Demonology Demystified.* Primarily the book covered the social stratification of Urgotian demons that had once been bred and raised on farms in an alternate reality, then claimed their own freedom through a bloody, centuries-long revolution. Hence, *De-ranged.* It had been years since Giles had referenced it, but he was getting truly desperate.

Giles stood up, feeling the stiffness in his knees and lower back. He palmed his empty cup. "Could I get you more tea?"

"Ugh," Cordelia responded.

Giles retreated to the small office he kept inside the library and poured. "With all this time we've invested in this, you'd think we'd have turned up something by now."

"You should have kept Buffy here, as well as her friends. We could have gone through a lot more books than these."

"Buffy's on patrol."

"Some get-out-of-jail-free card."

Giles resumed his seat, letting his mind wander. It didn't wander far, trekking through various remembrances of the demons he'd been researching. "There is an angle we haven't pursued."

Cordelia looked at him. "What?"

"The young woman Xander encountered."

Cordelia frowned. "What about her?"

"I wonder if it would be any easier to pin her down. She had a definite interest in the Black Wind demons. Perhaps if we found her, or what group she was with, we might know more about the demons we're currently facing."

"She's seen Xander and he's put the moves on her," Cordelia said. "We'll probably never hear from her again."

That's pretty mean-spirited, Giles thought, then wondered if Cordelia was really that bitter or was dealing with her own sense of loss. He cleaned his glasses and sipped his tea. "This morning, Xander brought me an item that the young lady had dropped."

"The little trinket he was showing out in the hallway this morning?"

"It was a necklace, actually, that the young lady was wearing that night. The yin/yang symbol. Very old, possibly hundreds of years."

"They say some of the garbage we're throwing away now is going to exist in landfills for hundreds of years. Is that ever going to make it more than garbage?"

"The stones," Giles mused, choosing to ignore the sarcastic comment. "The stones were blue and white. Now that I think about it, blue was also used to symbolize water and death." Something was at the edge of the Watcher's mind, something he couldn't quite grasp. "Let's take a moment and see what we can turn up in this venue, shall we?"

"Xander!"

Struggling with sleep, not wanting to wake up, Xander tried to roll over on his side but couldn't for some reason.

"Xander!"

"Hey, hey," Xander mumbled. "Just five more minutes, okay? My head feels like it's going to bust open."

"Xander! Wake up now or you may never get another chance."

This time Xander recognized the voice as Oz's, and there was no way Oz should be in his bedroom. A guy's room was his castle, after all. He opened his eyes slowly, taking in the uneven stone walls around him. He was lying on a cold, stone floor and grit was digging into the side of his face.

"Are you awake?" Oz asked.

"God, I hope not," Xander replied. "This had better be some kind of nightmare I'm going to wake up from any second now." He blinked his eyes. Even though the light was dim, it hurt his eyes, making the headache even worse. And it tasted like something had died at the back of his throat.

251

"Not a nightmare," Oz replied, and his voice echoed just a little, giving an indication of how big the place was that they were in.

Cautiously, wondering if anything was broken, Xander rolled over on his back. When he flopped down so hard, he realized that might have been a mistake because there was no guaranteeing that he would be able to roll back onto his side. His hands were still bound behind his back and his ankles were tied together. "Are you still tied up?"

"What do you think?"

"Okay, just checking. Wanted to make sure I wasn't missing out on anything." Even though the area was dim, he clearly saw the irregular stone ceiling at least twenty feet above. It looked artificial, though, because he could see where power tools had scored the stone. Two battery-powered camping lanterns sat on the two desks in the main area. Large and small rectangles of paper covered the walls. He leaned his head forward, feeling like he was ripping the back of his skull out and shoving his ribs through his side. He breathed painfully. "Do you know where we are?"

"No. But I'm thinking this isn't a tidy little hole in the shire."

"Captured by hobbits," Xander groaned. "Now there's a cheery thought. If we wait long enough, maybe the White Rabbit will put in an appearance and send us home." He laid his head back and hit a stone wall.

"Don't think so."

Painfully, Xander hooked his elbows down onto the floor, pushed with his heels, and inched back toward the wall. With a lot of work and groaning, he finally managed a sitting position.

Oz sat only a few feet away. One of his eyes was nearly swelled shut. He sat against the wall, looking pale.

"Man, you should see your eye," Xander said.

Oz nodded carefully. "Yeah, well, you should see your lip. Actually, you probably can."

Xander glanced down and could see his lip. It was all puffy and swollen and blood-crusted, and wasn't something he generally saw unless he was making monkey faces. His jaw still ached and he thought a few teeth were loose. "How long have you been awake?"

"Conscious, you mean? Maybe ten minutes before you."

"Any idea where we are?"

"Besides a cave?" Oz shook his head automatically, but quickly stopped, eyes narrowing in pain. "I figured, if we woke up at all, we'd be in a dilapidated warehouse or a crack house, or just a really seamy part of Sunnydale. Something that a gangbanger might call home. A cave, now that's where monsters or guys with savior complexes hang out."

"I'm thinking we got stuck with the monsters. Any sign of them?" Xander tried to work his wrists against the rough stone wall at his back, hoping to catch a projection sharp enough to cut what felt like duct tape.

"Not yet."

"Think they just abandoned us?"

"No. Thinking a lot about how that guy in the theater was speared through the head by that tongue."

"Gives a whole new twist to brain food," Xander said. The tape around his wrists caught on a rough surface. He kept rubbing against it, hoping to wear through the tape, and gradually began to feel it give.

"What are you doing?" Oz asked.

"If I'm lucky, getting my hands loose. I found a jagged piece of rock back here."

"Let me know how it works out. I can't even feel my hands anymore."

The closer Xander got to the top of the tape, the more the rough stone abraded his wrist. The pain became torture, made even worse because he was doing it to himself. But he felt certain that if they were going to escape they were going to have to do it on their own. No one knew where they were.

After another moment, the tape binding his wrists parted. "Okay, I'm free."

"If you'd been Harry Houdini, you'd have drowned," Oz said.

Xander pulled at the tape around his ankles and freed his legs, then went over and did the same for Oz. Leaving the cave immediately wasn't an option. After being tied up for so long they were barely able to stand for the first few minutes. A quick exploration of the cave's only exit showed them a narrow tunnel carved through stone.

"Weapons," Oz said, lurching around the room. "Going empty-handed would be totally lame. There's nowhere to run."

"Weapons would be good," Xander agreed. "Kinda lends to that can-do attitude." Only the room was barren of accessible weapons. The chairs and desks were made of steel, neither of which was very useful in fighting vampires. He opened the desk drawer and found a compass, pens, pencils, and a wooden ruler. He picked up the ruler. "Hey, I found something."

Oz looked at him. "It's a ruler."

"It's wood."

"Okay, it might scare them if they were raised in Catholic schools."

A glance at his watch told Xander it was almost eight-forty. Night had fallen over Sunnydale while they'd been unconscious. There was no telling how many Bad Things were going on back home by now. He shoved the ruler and pencils into his back pocket stubbornly. *Wood is wood,* he groused to himself.

Oz took the lantern from the desk he searched. He walked to the wall and played the light over the papers hanging from bulletin boards that had been affixed to the stone with masonry nails. "Have you looked at any of these papers?"

"Don't get me wrong here," Xander said, "but the last time I looked, paper was a little less lethal than even, say, a wooden ruler."

Oz ignored the sarcasm, moving slowly down the line. "They're maps of Sunnydale. Areas around Sunnydale. Some of this stuff goes back to the 1830s."

"Terrific. Really *old* paper is probably even less dangerous than new paper. The chances of getting even a decent paper cut out of old paper are probably astronomical."

"It's new paper, Xander." Oz continued looking.

"Oh, good, then we're talking modern technology here. Moving right on into the nuclear age." Still, Xander's innate curiosity about things that didn't fit, coming from long periods of wondering why he didn't fit in with different groups and events, claimed him. He gazed at the wall.

Oz waved the lantern at the rest of the cave. "The rest of this place puts me in mind of the old bomb shelters people built back during the Cold War."

"Or a smuggler's cave. Lots of Barbary Coast pirates in these waters at one time." Xander could tell Oz liked the bomb shelter idea, so he went with it. "But the Cold War's over. So why new maps?"

"Exactly." Oz tapped the maps in quick succession. "Geographical. Topographical. Street. Inside Sunnydale. Outside of Sunnydale."

Xander tapped one of the street maps. "Look. There's my house."

Oz gave him a look.

"Okay," Xander shrugged, "probably not important." Then he looked at the bulletin boards. "But this is." He yanked the bulletin board from the wall, stepped through the center, and pulled the wooden framing apart. "Stake kits. Some disassembly required."

"Go ahead," Oz said. "I'm going to take a few of these maps. If we make it out of here, maybe they can give us a clue about what they're doing in Sunnydale."

Xander had finished deconstructing the second bulletin board when they heard approaching footsteps out in the hall. Oz returned the lantern he was carrying to the desk. He grabbed four of the bulletin board stakes from Xander and sprinted to one side of the doorway.

Breathing hard, heart pumping frantically, Xander hid on the other side of the door. The footsteps grew louder. Xander gripped a makeshift stake in each hand. *Does wood work?* he wondered, remembering how the swordswoman had used the flintlock pistols and the sword. *Or are we just gonna piss them off?*

Three Black Wind gang members strode into the room. They stared at the shadows at the other end of the room, then spread out. They didn't turn back to the doorway.

Xander swapped looks with Oz, not believing the gang members were moving on to search the empty room. Oz jerked his head toward the door. Xander led the retreat, bolting through the door, turning the corner, running up the high, shallow stairway, slamming back and forth between the walls because the way was so narrow—

—and running into one of the biggest feet Xander had ever seen.

The foot was attached to the Black Wind gang member on guard at the top of the stairs. Grinning, the gang member kicked Xander in the chest, driving him back into Oz.

Together, Xander and Oz thudded, thumped, and thundered back down the narrow staircase. At the bottom, fully aware of all the new bruises and cuts he'd added to his collection, Xander got to his feet. There was nowhere to run, but there was no denying the fight or flight instinct.

The Black Wind gang member at the top of the stairs shook his head, grinned, and lifted the mini-Uzi in his scarred fist. Xander could have sworn malevolent orange light glowed in the gang member's eyes.

"No escape," the gang member promised softly.

Chapter 19

STANDING ON QUIVERING LEGS, XANDER HELD ONTO THE angry frustration that filled him as he stared up at the big Black Wind gang member blocking escape at the other end of the stairwell. It wasn't a true berserker mad-on, but it overpowered the part of him that was so scared. "Hey, Oz," he said in a shaking voice, blowing bubbles in the fresh blood streaming from his nose and busted lip, "you ever see Butch and Sundance?"

"Yeah," Oz replied behind him. "I always hated the ending."

"Every now and then, I used to think maybe they made it." Xander glanced over his shoulder and saw the three gang members inside the room where they'd been imprisoned were walking sedately toward them. *Like we're nothing.*

"I really don't think they're going to just let us go."

"Follow me."

"Fol—"

Before Oz finished speaking, Xander screamed, "*Yaaarrrggghhh!*" and sprinted back up the steps. He knew the move had to have surprised the gang member because the guy didn't unload.

Instead, the gang member stretched out a hand, intending to grab Xander's head. Xander ducked and forearmed the mini-Uzi away. He hit the gang member like a football linebacker, planting his shoulder in the guy's crotch. At first he didn't think the guy was going to fall, then there was a demonic scream of agony.

Caught by the stairs behind him, the gang member toppled forward. But he went too slowly. Before Xander could get to the top of the stairs, someone caught his foot, tripping him.

Driven by his own momentum, Xander skidded over the top of the fallen gang member, kicking out at anyone who tried to grab him again. He pushed himself to his knees, spotted the mini-Uzi in the gang member's hand, and dove. He fisted one of his stakes and drove it into the Black Wind member's arm. When the guy released the mini-Uzi, Xander scooped it up and turned back to the stairway.

Oz was just stumbling to the top stair, his pants legs in tatters, bloody scratches covering his ankles. The gang member behind him grabbed his foot and tripped him.

Reacting instinctively, totally locked in Army Guy mode, Xander grabbed Oz's shirt collar and yanked him the rest of the way up the steps. "Go!" Xander said, and squeezed the trigger, causing the Black Wind members to dodge back.

Click.

"Click?" Xander asked, staring at the machine pistol in disbelief. "All I get is *click?*"

"You're right," Oz said. "I thought *yaaarrrggghhh* had

more style points." He grabbed Xander by the arm and hauled him to his feet.

Together, they ran down the passageway, following the incline. Two more turns and about a million ragged breaths later, they reached a large cave where three black cars were parked under rows of electrical lighting that hung from the cave ceiling. Other Black Wind gang members stood at work stations around the cave or talking in groups. Oz pointed toward the double doors to the left. They ran.

A harsh voice yelled out behind them. Immediately, all the gang members headed in their direction.

Don't have to be bilingual for that, Xander thought. The doors were locked when they reached them. There was no opportunity at all for trying to get through before the enemy overpowered them.

Xander tried to cover up as best as he could, but the gang members didn't hesitate about scoring extra punches and kicks as they dragged him and Oz to the center of the big room. One of the Black Wind members took control and spouted orders.

Two of the gang members brought over chains that were hung from slotted tracks attached to the ceiling. Xander guessed the chains were used to transfer heavy cargo or work on the vehicles. All of the equipment looked new.

In less than a minute, Xander and Oz were trussed up in chains, then pulled off the ground, hanging upside down. The position left Xander on the brink of unconsciousness as blood pounded through his head.

The lead gang member held up the blue and white yin/yang necklace. "I want to know about the girl you got this from."

Dreading what was going to happen, Xander said, "So do I. I think she's really my kind of girl. Do you know how many of you guys she took apart last night? Things were moving so fast I kind of lost count. But I bet it was a lot. I mean, she didn't even slow—"

One of the gang member's slapped Xander.

"If we have to do this the hard way," the leader said, "we will."

"Man, you've been watching way too many action flicks," Xander said, still swinging at the end of the chain. "Tough guy talk isn't needed here. I'd tell you if I knew. I just don't—"

The gang member hit Xander again. This time blood from Xander's split lip struck the leader, who turned and yelled at the other man. However, the blood also landed on the yin/yang necklace he was holding. Immediately, the leader began screaming angrily and trying to wipe the blood from the blue and white stones.

Pale, green smoke drifted up from the necklace, curling and dancing against the bright lights overhead. The gang leader's hand suddenly turned liquid and the necklace dropped through fingers that just oozed away. He screamed in pain. The other gang members drew back.

Still swinging at the end of the chain, Xander watched as the gang members drew their weapons, all of them looking like living shadows at the edge of the light. He glanced at Oz, who was swinging only slightly.

"Can't be good," Oz commented.

The necklace continued to smoke and the scent of heavy pollen filled the air.

The two doors at the cave mouth blew inward and hung haphazardly from the hinges, followed immediately by a thunderous boom that echoed within the cave. Xander could see the sea beyond the small dirt road that led to the cave. The waves rolled in, silver-tipped by moonlight, pushing a gray fog cloud. Cold wind whipped into the cave, pricking Xander's skin with goosebumps and whipping his hair. He squinted against the wind, thinking something was moving inside the fog that shoved into the cave.

The swordswoman stepped out of the fog as coolly as if she was walking down a fashion runway. Her heels clicked hollowly against the stone floor. She wore the same outfit Xander had seen her in last night, except that now she had the hood up on the cape, shadowing her features.

"Is that your girl?" Oz asked.

"Yeah," Xander said, smiling in spite of the pain he was in. "Makes a hell of an entrance, doesn't she?"

"I guess so," Oz replied. "But she'd better have an army at her back if she's going to come in here."

Xander lost some of his smile as he realized how many gang members there were around them.

"And this isn't exactly a primo location for us either," Oz added.

The swordswoman spoke clearly, but it was in Chinese. And even though Xander didn't know what the words were, he knew an ultimatum had been given.

One of the Black Wind members screamed an order, and time seemed to slow down as Xander watched. The gang members brought their weapons up, leveling them at the young woman.

"Noooooo!" Xander screamed, but he knew it was already too late.

"Found it."

Giles looked up at Cordelia's triumphant announcement. "What did you find it in?" He crossed the library to look at the book she was holding.

"Fleming's *An Eccentric Guide to All Things River Daemon*." Cordelia tapped the gilt lettering as she read it, underscoring the words. "It says here that the blue and white yin/yang did not become a symbol for this group until the inception of the yin/yang and Taoism in the Han dynasty. Major score, huh?"

"There are some who believe that the symbol and Taoism actually began in the Shang and Chou dynasties nearly thirteen hundred years earlier," Giles said, peering over Cordelia's shoulder.

"Hey, don't rain on my success here."

"May I?" Giles asked, opening his hands for the book.

Cordelia passed the heavy book over reluctantly. "The group the symbol seems to represent is loosely translated into Spirit Guardians. They were associated with the Celestial Dragon, called . . . let me see. It will come to me."

"The Tien Lung," Giles said as he continued reading. "You know, there is some thinking that belief in dragons springs from sightings of the few demons still left in this world before the arrival of mankind chased them into other dimensions. The early history of China was shaped by much of the flooding that ran rampant throughout the country. There are stories in that book about Yu the Great, the man who is believed to have conquered the flooding problems by cutting inland channels and building dams to control the flooding."

"That's in there," Cordelia said.

"I see that. He was also thought to be the first king of the Xia dynasty."

"Fleming makes a definite case that Yu was," Cordelia said. "He goes on to state that Yu's father, Gun, was first placed in charge of the flooding problems. Gun was supposed to have ascended to heaven and stolen a handful of magic earth—or something like that. Anyway, the magic earth worked well, growing into huge mounds that blocked the floods. Unfortunately, the theft was discovered and the Emperor of Heaven sent the god of fire down to bring back the magic earth. Like you're going to get away with something like that. Right!" She shook her head. "Gun was executed as a sign of the Emperor's wrath, so that all would know to never try such a thing again. Major bummer."

Giles nodded and sat down. As much as he had studied and learned and read, there were still so many aspects of the world—especially the hidden parts of it—which he hadn't heard of.

"The Chinese people believed dragons were responsible for all the rains that flooded their lands," Cordelia said. "Since some of earliest human civilization took place in those areas, maybe the floods were caused by the demons struggling to hang onto their territories."

"I understand that," Giles said. "But what has that got to do with what's going on here now?"

Cordelia shook her head. "Beats me. I suppose that will be answered when we discover what the Black Wind gang is doing here in Sunnydale." She paused. "But whatever it is, you can rest assured that the girl Xander seems so ga-ga over isn't exactly what she appears to be."

"No," Giles agreed quietly, looking over the material, "I would say she isn't at all." *And that would have to be Xander's luck.* The Watcher only hoped that Xander didn't get in so far over his head that he actually lost his head. He glanced at Cordelia. "Well, come on. We've got work to do here."

Xander watched helplessly as the Black Wind gang members opened fire on the swordswoman. But she spun to her right and sprinted at the wall as bullets slammed into the stone floor behind her. She raked her hood back, exposing her calm features, and slid free one of the swords sheathed down her back. The gun blasts were so loud Xander couldn't even hear himself shouting.

Never slowing, the swordswoman ran up onto the wall a few steps, actually defying gravity. Then she arced back, tucking her knees into her chest to flip completely over. She landed on her feet on one of the parked sports cars and swept a flintlock pistol free. She fired, striking one of the Black Wind gang members in the head with the bullet.

Green smoke pooled around the gang member's head for a moment, then he dissolved.

Before her opponents could target her, she was in motion again, dropping out of sight behind the car. One of the gang members yelled out an order and four men ran forward, two to either side of the car. They almost shot each other as they rounded the vehicle.

The swordswoman slid from under the car, streaking out from the front. In one lithe motion, she pushed herself up and charged the line of gang members. She carried her sword pointed down for close-quarters fighting. Before the gang members could fire, she was among them, a hawk among pigeons. By that time, they couldn't fire without hitting each other.

Xander struggled against the chains that held him, shimmying and twisting, gaining a half-inch here and there.

The swordswoman struck and a head left a gang member's shoulders. She continued with her forward motion, breaking through the line. Lashing out with the empty flintlock, she caved in another gang member's skull.

On the other side of the line, she holstered her pistol and took her sword in both hands. Before her opponents could turn or run, she was back among them, slashing mercilessly.

The gang members at the sports car opened fire, shooting into their own ranks. The human members went down, torn and bloodied, but the demons among them only staggered back.

The swordswoman grabbed one of the demons to use as a shield, stepping close in behind him, then shoving him toward them. Even though the bullets couldn't kill him, they must have hurt a lot judging from the way he screamed. She ran her captive at the car, tripping him at the last moment and throwing him into two of the shooters.

She spun left, bullets cutting the flying wedges of material floating from her right arm. She shook her left hand, then came to a spot and threw twice quickly. The throwing knives she carried thudded into the skulls of her targets, dropping them both. Before the demon she'd used to get close to her other attackers could get up, she chopped his head off, leaving him sprawled across the sports car.

She drew her second flintlock pistol and wheeled toward Xander.

Xander turned cold for a moment as he looked down the weapon's large-bore barrel. Then he saw the pistol muzzle move up, saw the powder smoke puff from the frizzen and barrel, and felt the vibration along the chains that held him. He dropped unexpectedly, hitting his head hard. But the chain was loose enough that he could free himself.

"Get out of here, Xander!"

A smile spread across Xander's face. *She remembers my name!* He grabbed the loose chain and began slipping loops from his head and shoulders.

The swordswoman disappeared again, ducking behind some of the crates in the storage area in the cave. The Black Wind gang members, their numbers already down considerably, weren't as anxious to pursue.

Finally free again, Xander slipped over to Oz and reeled him down. His fingers manipulated the knotted chain easily.

"So this is the girl?" Oz asked.

"Isn't she great?" Xander asked.

A gang member creeping around the corner of the crates suddenly stopped, then turned around, trying to hold himself together because he'd been nearly eviscerated. Only in the glance he got, Xander knew the guy wasn't human. Nothing human had internal organs like the ones Xander saw.

In seconds, Oz was free as well, both of them staying low beside a nearby sports car for shelter. Bullets ripped the car body and starred the windshield and windows.

The swordswoman reappeared behind another stack of concrete. She held both flintlock pistols again, both at full-cock. She fired them one at a time with deliberate aim. Two more gang members dropped, their heads wreathed in green smoke.

"Hey," Oz said, crouched down with his back to the side of the sports car, "I think the key's in the ignition."

Xander pulled himself up briefly and checked. A key ring dangled beside the steering wheel. Then a stray bullet took the side mirror off only inches away from his head. He dropped down again. "Okay. I'm thinking now is a good time to leave. You're driving."

Oz nodded. "What about your friend?"

Xander spotted her among the crates, drawing the attention of every gang member in the cave with lethal intensity. Even as he watched, though, another man stumbled back, his head split into halves. "We're not leaving without her." He popped the door and crawled across the bucket seats, painfully knocking his knees, elbows, and head into the steering wheel and gearshift, crowding up against the passenger window so hard that he smeared his bloody lip across it.

Oz followed immediately, sliding easily behind the

steering wheel. He cranked the ignition, and the throaty roar of the engine covered the sound of gunfire for a heartbeat. It also attracted the attention of some of the gang members.

"Duck!" Xander yelled, pulling his own head down. Oz ducked as well, and then the windshield came apart, blowing square chunks of tinted safety glass all over them.

Oz put the transmission in reverse and stomped the accelerator. The tires shrilled against the stone floor, then the rubber caught hold and they hurtled backward. Something slammed into the rear of the sports car, but when Xander dared to turn and look, he thought he saw a man leaping into the air.

A heartbeat later, a gang member, legs broken from Oz's unplanned assault, thumped heavily onto the hood.

Xander's head snapped around as he lifted his hands defensively. Even though his legs were broken, the gang member reached for Xander. The guy's head seemed to stretch, then his mouth flared incredibly wide and his tongue flicked out. Xander dodged just as Oz slammed on the brakes.

The sports car shuddered to a halt, crashing into another vehicle.

The demon's thick tongue penetrated the seat less than an inch from Xander's head. His cheek burned when it brushed against the slimy, fetid tongue. Borderline freaked, Xander raised a foot and drove it into the demon's head. "Back! Back! Back!" he yelled at Oz.

Oz stomped the accelerator again. The sudden movement, combined with Xander's kick, rolled the demon from the sports car's front end.

"Stop!" Xander ordered, watching as the demon tried to get up.

Oz skidded to a halt. "Now forward?"

Xander threw a forefinger forward. "Engage. Warp nine."

The sports car leaped forward like a rocket and slammed into the demon like a battering ram. The demon smashed into the sports car Oz had hit earlier and never made it up before Oz slammed into him again, smashing him in between the two cars as he rolled by.

Xander watched in horrified fascination as the demon's head swelled to three times its size, like everything in his body was being forced upward from the point of impact. The tongue shot into the air like a party-popper, followed immediately by a torrent of blood and chunky parts.

"Plan?" Oz asked, both hands on the wheel.

"Gotta rescue the girl." Xander pointed to where the swordswoman was still taking cover among the crates. However, she was running out of crates.

"Can't finesse this," Oz said as they shot across the cave. "Warn her."

Oz laid on the horn, adding the shrill bleat to the staccato gunfire. He headed the car straight at the swordswoman, taking out two gang members who were in the way. The sports car plunged through some of the crates, cracking wood and scattering contents.

The swordswoman back-flipped out of the way, landing on the first crate beyond the sports car's impact radius.

Xander leaned out the missing windshield area. "C'mon! We're rescuing you! We gotta get out of here!"

The swordswoman smiled and shook her head. "This is a rescue?"

"Okay," Xander admitted, "we've done better, but this is what you get to work with now."

"Weapon upgrade," Oz said. "Rocket launcher at nine o'clock."

"What?" Xander asked, glancing over at his friend. Then he spotted the gang member on the other side of the cave fitting a telescoping tube to his shoulder. He turned back to the swordswoman. "C'mon!" He held out his hand.

The smile only turned a hint more serious. "You can be very forceful." She took his hand and stepped onto the car hood. "That has a certain charm."

Xander wrapped his arms around her, yanking her into the car. "Go!" he yelled at Oz. The seat brackets sheared through from his and the swordswoman's combined weight, stuttering beneath them and suddenly flattening out, leaving the swordswoman lying on top of him. "Man, has anyone ever told you that you have the prettiest eyes?"

Before she could answer, Oz floored the accelerator, swinging around to watch through the back windshield as they broke free from the crates.

Then the rocket collided with the crates in front of them, creating a great, snarling explosion of flames, heated air, and a concussive wave that scaled up quickly, twisting and grabbing at the stone ceiling.

"Taking out the exit doors," Oz warned. "Hold on."

"Be careful," the swordswoman said. "There are cliffs just beyond the doors and a deep part of the ocean."

"Cliffs?" Xander asked. He wanted to ask more, like cliffs how high and ocean how deep, but the sports car slammed into the exit doors.

Chapter 20

ZHIYONG INTERNATIONAL SOUNDED MORE PRETENTIOUS than it was, Buffy discovered. The shipping magnate had his offices in a four-story downtown building with accountants, dentists, optometrists, psychiatrists, a private detective, a palm reader, and a psychic.

All of that information was courtesy of the directory plaque in the foyer and Gus, the security guard who was watching George Romero's *Night of the Living Dead* on a small black-and-white television at the security desk. Of course, Zhiyong's offices took up the entire fourth floor.

Gus was in his late sixties, a thin rake of a man with bitter blue eyes, a rounded back, and an impressive growth of nose hair. "Lemme call Mr. Sledge, make sure he's expecting you."

"Sure," Buffy said. Art Sledge was the detective on the third floor. She hoped he was in because it would make getting to the fourth floor much easier.

Gus had a brief conversation over the phone, then

turned back to Buffy. "Mr. Sledge says you don't have an appointment."

Angel unfolded a hundred-dollar bill and popped it between his hands.

"Hey, Art," Gus said, "they got a C-note here." He looked back at Buffy. "Yeah, Buffy Summers. High school, college maybe."

Buffy felt complimented to be mistaken for a college student. Of course, that evolution was just around the corner.

"Nah, they ain't packing, Art, and they don't look like bill collectors," Gus said. "Okay, I'll send 'em up." He cradled the phone. "Mr. Sledge says you can come on up."

"Great," Buffy said.

Gus leaned authoritatively on the counter. He puffed his chest out. "I help Mr. Sledge out on some of his tougher cases. If you got any problems, you just stop by and see ol' Gus." He smiled and patted the pistol on his hip. "Me and Thelma Lou, we been down a lotta hard roads together, if you know what I mean. And this ain't a normal town."

And sometimes I think there aren't very many normal citizens, either, Buffy thought. But she smiled and said thanks, then headed for the elevators. She entered the cage and pressed three. Angel got in behind her. Gus was watching them from the security desk, feet propped up. She waved at him.

"Real watchdog," Angel commented as the elevator doors closed and the cage jerked upward.

"Thelma Lou," Buffy said.

"I heard."

"Guys and their guns: will the penis envy never end? I wonder if he's got a name for—" Buffy stopped herself. "Okay, don't want to go there." The elevator pinged at the third floor and the doors opened. Buffy walked through.

"They had new security cameras in the foyer downstairs," Angel said as he walked beside her.

"I noticed them." Buffy walked past Madame Zaprola's door, taking in the illustration of a lean-hipped woman dressed in a slinky black dress standing beside a cauldron. She had her hand on a wolf's head. A tree with an owl on a limb in front of a full moon stood in the background. *That would set Will's teeth on edge.*

Judging from the offices, there were a lot of late-evening clientele in need of fortune-telling, accounting and counseling. *Of course,* Buffy realized, *this is Sunnydale.*

She and Angel walked past SLEDGE INVESTIGATIONS to the stairwell at the end of the corridor. She went through the door into the darkened stairwell, glanced briefly up the steps, then started up.

"I don't think the building installed the new security cameras," Angel whispered.

"Didn't need to," Buffy agreed. "They have Gus and Thelma Lou."

"So we have to assume that Zhiyong knows we're coming."

Buffy nodded. "If he's here." She reached the landing and started up the final flight of stairs. The door at the top was locked. She glared at the door. "What? No Keep Out or Beware of Dog signs?"

"Guess not." Angel glanced at her. "I don't suppose you'd consider giving up and coming back later?"

"Nope." Buffy drew her leg back and drove it into the door. The facing tore loose as the lock shattered. The door flew inward and landed at the feet of three men standing in the ornate, picture-studded hallway.

They were dressed in black suits. The man in the middle held a snarling, maddened animal at the end of a heavy chain leash.

Although mostly doglike in appearance, the animal had a wedge-shaped skull and tiny greenish black scales that covered its gaunt frame instead of fur. The eyes were fiery, downturned crescents that wept flames. The fires dropped from the creature's saliva-coated muzzle but winked out of existence only inches above the carpet. Scarring marred the scales, mapping out a history of violent abuse. Huge talons stuck out from feet the size of pie plates.

"Liondog," Angel said quietly. "It's supposed to be one of the three creatures that made up the ancient Chimera."

The liondog bayed anxiously, sounding haunting and insane. Flames belched from its throat, lashing out nearly six feet.

Buffy leaned back from the heat. "Boy, I bet he's no picnic to be around when he's got indigestion."

"Beware of dog," the man holding the leash said. Then he released it and slapped the liondog on the flank, speaking in Chinese.

The liondog ran straight for Buffy, jaws widening in anticipation.

For a moment, Willow thought she'd lost Lok Rong. She'd followed him easily from the restaurant in Sunnydale—though at high speeds she wasn't entirely comfortable with—and didn't have to work at all to keep the motorcycle in sight with the headlight glaring against the night. The ocean rolled to her left, white-capped waves assaulting the beach.

Then Lok had disappeared briefly around a curve in the highway that wound through the hills outside Sunnydale. When Willow made the curve and looked ahead, he'd vanished.

"No," Willow pleaded, although she was really uncertain what she was going to do if she caught up with Lok. The main thing, she supposed, was to keep him in sight so they could tell his parents—or the police. She stared desperately into the darkness.

"Over there!" Jia Li exclaimed, pointing across Willow toward the beach.

Willow barely made out the dirt road that led from the highway down the decline to the beach. She only got a brief glimpse of the overturned motorcycle lying at the bottom before she raced past it.

"You saw the motorcycle?" Jia Li asked.

"Yeah." Willow checked the rearview mirror, side mirror, then looked out the back glass. Seeing no one, she braked quickly and cut the wheel. The station wagon slid sideways for a moment, then came to a stop. "Okay, sorry. Maybe I'm a little tense."

"Hurry," Jia Li urged. "The motorcycle was turned over. He may have wrecked."

Willow put her foot on the accelerator and made the turn, zipping back up the highway in the direction they'd come from. She turned sharply onto the dirt road, oversteering for a moment and skidding through the brush beside the road. Then she recovered and sped down toward the motorcycle. When she stopped, a dust cloud coiled up around them for the moment, obscuring the motorcycle.

Jia Li was out of the station wagon before Willow could even warn her to be careful. The crash of the surf echoed against the big, craggy hill in front of Willow. When she'd been on the highway, it hadn't looked very big at all. The station wagon's headlights showed the mouth of a small cave near the waterline.

You must go, the voice whispered in Willow's mind.

The time draws near. If Lok should perish at this time, much evil will be unleashed. You can help him. You must.

Willow wanted to disagree, but somehow she knew that the voice spoke the truth.

"He's not here!" Panic-stricken, Jia Li gazed out at the ocean. "Willow, he's not here!"

Willow took a deep breath as she went to her friend. "If he's not here it only means that he ditched the motorcycle and walked away."

"Where?"

Willow pointed at the cave ahead of them. Small curlers rolled into the mouth. "Maybe there."

"Why?"

"I don't know. Maybe you should go call the police."

"What are you going to do?"

Willow pulled her hair from her face, not liking the answer she was going to have to give. "Go look for Lok, I suppose."

"I can't leave, Willow," Jia Li said. "Not without knowing if he's all right."

"Let me get a few things out of the car, then we'll both go." Willow didn't like the idea of Jia Li going with her, certain that there were things about to happen that she didn't want her friend around to see. In fact, Willow was pretty certain she didn't want to be around, either. Whatever held Lok in its thrall was powerful.

Images of the dead thing lurching free of the earthen wall kept looping through her mind. She noticed her hands were shaking slightly as she took the heavy-duty camper's flashlight from the back of the station wagon. She also took up the spare bag of herbs and witchy things she kept there for emergencies.

When she turned off the car's headlights, the dark shadows surrounding the beach seemed to rush in at her like rabid beasts. *Okay, definitely the wrong place for wigging out.* She took a deep breath and switched the flashlight on. The cone of light only helped a little, seeming to vanish almost instantly.

Resolutely, she led the way into the cave, following the waves washing inside. Slick stone turned downward immediately and the crashing waves sounded thunderous inside the passageway. *At least we won't be heard,* Willow thought. Then she realized that they wouldn't be able to hear anything lurking in the darkness inside the passageway, either.

When the sports car bucked against the doors to the cave mouth, Xander covered the girl in his arms protectively. Metal screamed and screeched as Oz kept the accelerator pegged and the huge doors gave way. Sparks flared on either side as the hinges scraped the length of the sports car.

"Brake!" Xander yelled, knowing at any moment he was going to feel the gut-wrenching twist of freefall. "Brake!"

"Got it!" Oz yelled. The Camaro skidded to a halt, slewing sideways. Then it dipped slightly like a bucket on a Ferris wheel.

Xander glanced at Oz, who was looking in the rearview mirror. "Over the edge?" Xander asked.

"Maybe a little." Oz shrugged.

And the car rocked again.

"Everybody just stay still," Xander advised. "Think ground thoughts." Anxiously, he craned his head around and looked through the back glass. The dark Pacific Ocean stretched out behind the car. Something crunched under the tires. "We are *not* going to panic here."

"They're not staying still," Oz said, staring ahead.

Xander looked and spotted a dozen Black Wind gang

members charging out of the cave like a boiling mass of hornets. "Okay, it's official: now you can panic."

"Got to go for it," Oz said, shifting gears.

"Do it." Xander waited, holding onto the swordswoman. *This dying thing won't be so bad. I won't be alone. I'm with Oz and—* He still didn't know her name.

Oz punched the accelerator and the front tires spun. "There's not enough traction."

"Hang on."

"Sure," Oz replied. "Hanging."

Gingerly, Xander moved from under the swordswoman, not believing what he was about to do. He glanced at the approaching Black Wind gang members, spotting the muzzle flashes from their weapons, hearing the explosive chatter, and knowing it wasn't mosquitoes cutting the wind around him. Nowhere near calmly, he climbed through the shattered remnants of the windshield and flattened himself on the hood. "Now try." He gripped the hood tightly as a line of bullets chewed holes in the fender only inches away.

This time the tires gripped the dirt road, pulling the car back on level ground. Oz cut the wheel hard to the right, sliding back toward the cave for a moment.

Xander tried to scramble back into the car but lost his grip. He slid sideways, scrabbling hard to find something to hang onto. Then the swordswoman and Oz grabbed his legs and hauled him back inside the car. He landed in the swordswoman's lap, which wasn't an entirely bad place to be.

"Thanks," Xander said, looking into those golden hazel eyes that had haunted his sleep the night before. "But this has gotta be really uncomfortable."

The swordswoman smiled. "I find it curiously . . . tolerable."

Oh, my God, and she thinks I'm tolerable, too, Xander thought. Then he bumped his head on the doorframe as Oz drove. He glanced behind them, seeing the Black Wind gang members pursuing them on foot. It wasn't going to do them any good because they couldn't run as fast as the sports car. They quickly disappeared in the dust clouds left by the Camaro.

"You know," Xander said, "I'd like to introduce you to my friend, Oz. That's him driving." He jerked his thumb in Oz's direction.

Oz shot Xander a look. "Since there's only the three of us, I bet she had that figured already."

Xander ignored the comment, concentrating on the woman. "And I would introduce you to Oz, except that I don't know your name."

Moving gracefully, the swordswoman somehow managed to dump Xander onto the front seat while she slid into the back. She hesitated only a moment. "My name is Shing."

Xander grinned. "Oz, meet Shing. Shing, Oz."

Oz glanced up at the rearview mirror. "Hi."

"It is very nice to meet you, Oz."

"Thanks for the big rescue scene back there," Oz said. He steered fiercely, keeping the car just barely under control as they rocketed down the dirt road. Rocks and gravel pinged constantly against the undercarriage.

Then the car skidded out of control, hitting a high spot in the road and going airborne for just a moment. Oz got the vehicle back under control just in time to keep them from piling into a large tree. They went cross-country for a moment till Oz spotted the thin sliver of highway ahead. They raced up the embankment and went airborne again in front of an oncoming eighteen-wheeler.

Xander yelled as the big truck bore down on them. It

missed them by less than a foot, then the slipstream caught them and rocked them up on two wheels for a moment. They settled down with a harsh thump.

"You are welcome, Oz," Shing said calmly.

"Screaming?" Oz asked, lifting an eyebrow.

"I thought I had time," Xander said. "Anyway, that wasn't screaming. It only sounded like it. That was a family battle cry."

"A family battle cry."

"I can see where you'd get the two confused, if your ear isn't trained for the difference." Xander grabbed the branches that had broken off and fallen into the car during their cross-country trip.

"You face gangbangers, demons with these incredible tongues of death, but you're afraid of trucks?"

"I have a problem with head-on collisions," Xander admitted. "Too many episodes of *World's Most Incredible Police Chases,* maybe. Do you have any idea where we're headed?"

Oz pointed at the sign ahead.

SUNNYDALE   3 MILES

"Once we get there," Oz said, "I'm thinking Giles will probably be at the library. If not, we'll go by his house."

"Sounds good. Maybe we could stop and get a pizza on the way." Xander looked at the swordswoman, who was busy pouring more gunpowder into her pistols. "Do you like pizza?"

"I don't know," she said. "I've never had pizza."

"Really?" Xander grinned. "You're in for a treat."

She dropped balls into the pistol barrels, then seated them with the ramrod. "Do you think we have time for pizza? There is much evil about to be done if we don't stop it."

We? Xander decided he liked the sound of that *we.* It

really sounded promising. "There's always time for pizza. It was designed for on-the-go people."

As the liondog lunged at her, Buffy leaped, drawing her feet up just out of the creature's reach. Flames torched the area where she'd been, peeling paint from the wall and doorway behind her. In the next instant, she had Mr. Pointy out of her jacket pocket and in her hand.

One of the men opened his mouth—no, his head, she decided—and lashed out with his tongue. She turned in midair, feeling the tongue glide slick-wet over her jacket. She fell forward, not trying to land on her feet, trusting Angel to keep the liondog off her as she went for the three men facing them.

Landing on the floor, she rolled toward the first man, using him as cover as the other two brought up their pistols. She caught a brief glimpse of Angel going down under the liondog's assault. Angel had both hands on the creature's head, controlling the direction its mouth faced.

A huge bellow of flame spewed forth, narrowly missing Angel. He levered an arm under the liondog's muzzle, his other hand gripping the back of the dog's neck.

Then Buffy lost sight of them, rolling over to face the first man. She kicked hard and swept his feet from under him; she was up and moving again even as he fell. Striking from a crouched position, she drove a foot into the side of one man's knee and heard bone shatter just before the agonized scream.

The third man got off three shots before Buffy drove her stake into his heart. The impact shivered along her arm, letting her know she'd struck solidly. The man stumbled back, slammed against the wall, then looked down at her and grinned.

"Wrong."

"Not human, not vampire," Buffy reminded herself. "Forgot with you guys it's the heads." Before she could yank Mr. Pointy free, the demon punched her in the face, driving her back across the hallway.

The demon lifted his pistol and fired.

Buffy launched herself at her attacker, listening to the wind of the bullet whip past her ear. She grabbed the man's gun arm and yanked him off-balance, threw a hip into him and flipped him onto his butt. Even as he landed with his back to her, she hooked a forearm under his jaw and her other hand behind his head. She tightened her grip and twisted, listening to the popping ratchet sound of the demon's skull separating from the spine.

The demon dropped, turning into greenish slime on the way down.

Breathing hard and already moving, Buffy watched one of the two surviving demons suddenly burst into flames as the liondog belched again. *Walking that thing must involve a really big pooper-scooper and a fire extinguisher.*

Angel locked his legs around the liondog's lower quarters and strained against it, bowing it backward. Then the liondog's spine broke with a rolling crunch. It blew out a final gust of flames, shuddered, and died.

Bloodied and torn from his battle, Angel forced himself up, staring down the barrel of the third man's pistol.

Buffy attacked without warning, launching herself into a flying kick. Her foot collided with the base of the demon's skull, breaking it free of the spine. He was soup by the time he hit the floor.

"Kinda like Battling Robots," Buffy said, referring to the boxing game she'd sometimes played with her friends. Her mother had insisted they'd been called Rock 'Em Sock 'Em Robots in another generation.

Applause sounded behind Buffy, causing her to turn at once, her fists raised in defense.

"Very good, Ms. Summers." Zhiyong looked a lot like the pictures Buffy had seen on the school library monitor Giles had dug up earlier, but he probably paid to look that way.

Buffy gave the man a hard look, noticing the half-dozen other men standing behind him. "Gee, the Bad Guy generally doesn't give me a standing ovation when I whack the help."

"Perhaps not, Ms. Summers, but I believe that anyone fool enough to die at another's hands deserves it."

"You only say that," Buffy replied, "because you've never died at another's hands." She and Angel both had.

"There are too many of them," Angel whispered low enough that no one other than Buffy could overhear.

"I know. Plans?"

"Run like hell when we get the chance."

Zhiyong permitted them their quiet conversation, obviously thinking he was in complete control of the situation.

Which, Buffy had to admit, *it definitely looks like.*

"Up until this point, Ms. Summers," Zhiyong said, "I'd not believed the esteemed mayor's insistence that you could become an insufferable thorn in my side."

"Wait until I figure out what you're really up to," Buffy promised, "then you're gonna find out how lousy I can get with insufferance." She glanced at Angel. "Insufferability? One sounds like an insurance and the other sounds like a superpower."

"I think you mean you're going to be really insufferable," Angel said.

Buffy shook her head. "That doesn't sound very threatening. I mean, not like a hero-threatening-a-villain threatening. More like you're going to be annoying than threatening."

"Sometimes," Angel said, "it's better to just say nothing at this point."

"No," Buffy said. "The staring thing never works for me. People just think I'm being quiet."

"For myself," Zhiyong said conversationally, "at this point I generally deal with those who get in my way in only one fashion." He turned to the demons. "Kill them."

The demons raised their weapons.

Knowing they'd never reach the stairwell before getting cut to ribbons, Buffy stamped the very end of the machine pistol the last demon she'd killed had dropped. The weapon popped up from the floor and the Slayer caught it, cradling it in her arms like she'd been doing it all her life. She pointed the machine pistol at Zhiyong.

"I've already been dead once," she said coldly. "Didn't care much for the experience. Me, I'm thinking this could be your first time."

Zhiyong turned slowly.

"Maybe now would be a good time to do a little renegotiating," Buffy suggested.

Chapter 21

THERE IS NO WAY YOU COULD EVER MAKE A CAVE FEEL *homey*, Willow thought as she negotiated another switchback turn in the passageway. She played the flashlight over the rubble ahead, picking a path carefully. Jia Li followed closely behind her, hampered by losing the light occasionally when Willow blocked it from view.

Water trickled down through the rocks, keeping a majority of them wet and slippery, causing the girls to go even more slowly. Of course, that meant any need to escape quickly would be just as hampered. Willow tried not to think about that, but after everything she'd seen while hanging with Buffy, it was impossible not to think about it.

Candy wrappers and Coke cans, even fast-food containers in some areas, showed that kids at least came down into the cave. That was a little reassuring, except when Willow realized that a lot of vampires liked to feed in areas like this.

"Do you see Lok?" Jia Li whispered.

"No." That bothered Willow. Either Lok could suddenly see in the dark or he was so far ahead they couldn't see him. Or maybe he was waiting just around the next switchback, a pick in his hands and an insane gleam in his eyes. She swallowed hard.

The passageway widened another sixty or seventy yards farther on, then leveled out in a cavern that was too big for Willow's flashlight to completely shine across. But a light burned steadily on the other side. Willow took a deep breath, then turned and followed the wall to the right. When she worked mazes, she'd learned to always keep a wall to her right. Eventually, all the walls would lead to the center.

At least, that was the way it worked in the physical world.

However, since entering the cave Willow could sense the presence of Power with a capital P. It was the kind witches and warlocks and some of the fey creatures used. Of course, demonic things used it as well. That was the problem with power: it never really questioned who used it or whether it was being used for good or evil.

"What is Lok doing here?" Jia Li asked.

Willow concentrated on the rocky ground, knowing if she turned her ankle badly enough she might be stuck there. Not a good thought to be having in a dank, dark cave. "I don't know."

"You know more than I do," Jia Li accused.

Guilt flooded Willow. "I'm sorry about looking into things behind your back."

"You could have told me."

"I didn't know how."

"Then why did you?"

"Because when the time got right I wanted to be able to tell you."

"Tell me now."

Willow stopped at the edge of a narrow stream. It ran through the cave they were presently in, nearly a yard wide, until it disappeared under the cave wall. "Mei-Kao Rong was a laborer. When he first came to California, he worked on the railroads. I can't tell you any more than that. Sorry. The information I found was kinda skimpy."

"He had a small obituary."

"Actually, there was no obituary. I looked for one."

Jia Li was silent for a moment. "The lives of Chinese laborers at that time were very cheap."

Willow didn't argue. Most history—of any country—was filled with unpretty moments. Empires, kingdoms, and nations generally got ahead of everyone else by taking advantage of someone. High school had the same kind of pecking order, and the socially privileged got more respected and feared by taking advantage of those who weren't. However, time changed power, even in high school.

Taking a big step, Willow hopped across the small stream and almost fell into the mud on the other side. "In 1851 or '52, the newspaper article wasn't certain, Mei-Kao Rong settled in Sunnydale and started working in the mining camps. In 1853 he was trapped in a cave-in with thirty-six other men."

"All Chinese?"

"There were two caucasian company foremen among those lost," Willow said. She continued following the wall, grazing it with her fingertips. She could see the weak light better now, and realized that it was coming from another passage.

"They died in the accident?"

"Yes." Willow turned to her friend. "I'm sorry."

"Thank you, but I did not know my ancestor. My worries are about Lok."

Willow continued toward the other passageway. Images of the vision swirled through her mind, pushing her panic levels up. *Voice? Whoever you are? I'd really like nothing more than to leave right now.*

But there was no reply.

Despite her feelings, Willow knew she couldn't leave. Even if Lok was a jerk, she knew he'd been possessed by whatever *guei* had haunted him and wasn't totally responsible. Being a jerk was one thing, but getting killed was another. And she was certain she'd never get Jia Li to leave.

"Why is Mei-Kao Rong not in his grave?" Jia Li asked after a moment more.

"The mining company just closed the mine," Willow replied. "They left all of them buried there."

"Then what is Lok doing here?"

"I don't know." But Willow was afraid she really did know. The flute and the candle Lok had made had been dead giveaways.

"Where was the mine?" Jia Li asked.

She's starting to put it together too, Willow realized. "Not far from here."

Chanting reached their ears, a lilting singsong that sounded thin and strained and frantic.

Willow switched off the flashlight at the mouth of the next passageway. Shadows covered the way, but she thought she could see well enough to continue. She glanced over her shoulder at Jia Li.

The wavering light streaming from the cavern below highlighted Jia Li's face, making her appear ghostly.

Or maybe, Willow decided, *I'm just prepared for ghosts.* "We don't know what Lok will do if he finds us here," she reminded.

Jia Li nodded. "I know."

"If he wigs out, we've got to go. At least we know where to find him."

"Yes."

"I need you to know I mean that," Willow said.

Jia Li took her by the hand. "I'm scared of him, too, Willow. Can't you see that in me?" Her eyes held a wet gleam.

"Yes," Willow said.

"But I need to know what he is doing here. It might help."

Willow nodded. "Okay. We'll get a little closer." Slowly, she turned and crawled farther down the passageway. She spotted a concave ledge to the right, almost buried in the shadows on that side. As she crawled toward it, having to duck under the low ceiling, Lok's voice grew louder. At first she thought it was because he was speaking more forcefully, then she realized it was the structure of the concave area that amplified his voice. She hunkered down behind a boulder that was three times larger than she.

Jia Li slid in beside her.

From her vantage point, Willow had a good view of Lok. He kneeled, his arms spread out before him, palms toward the earthen wall. A patio torch was stuck into the ground beside him but instead of the fuel reservoir, the candle Jia Li had found hidden in the closet burned there.

"He's praying to the *guei*," Jia Li whispered. "Calling on them to come to him."

Though Willow couldn't understand the words, she understood the intent. Sensitive as she was to magic and spells, she felt the power growing around her. It was a force, savage and primeval and tainted with darkness.

It is tainted with selfishness, the voice whispered into Willow's mind. *Part of that selfish need comes from Lok himself, because the young are always selfish, and always most selfish as they step through the threshold of adulthood. The guei feed on Lok's need, and he feeds on them in turn. They fulfill a darkness inside him that he was born with.*

What am I supposed to do? Willow asked. *This is way out of my league.*

For the moment, young Willow, you can only watch. There are things you must learn before doing can begin.

Waiting really bites, Willow thought, then realized she probably didn't have a private thought to herself. *Oooops. Sorry.*

Maintain vigilance. Lok is in grave danger. His spell will be too weak to control that which he calls forth. You will need to aid him.

Hands shaking, Willow reached into her bag of herbs and took out a few leaves of burdock root. She readied a protection chant in her mind, saying it under her breath.

By strong and persevering Earth, mother to the
    First and our home,
By quick and warlike Fire, stolen and seduced that
    we might light the way against those who would
    harm us,
By Water moving swift and still, which cleanses
    and makes us whole again,
By Air's sweet breath and gentle caress, which
    nurtures us and lifts us up,
I call upon you as a sister to the moon,
As one of those who would seek understanding
    rather than destruction,
As one who both knows how to give love and take it,
As one who is in need.
Take my strength and love,

Take my knowledge,
Take that within me that is always at rest and
   never still,
Take the breath I take and share and give to the next.
Come to me now, spirits of protection.

Willow felt the power grow within her, lost in a semi-trance for the moment, barely aware of Jia Li staring at her. She turned to the girl, feeling light-headed, like she was on laughing gas from a dentist's office. All uncertainty and fear was gone from her. She was calm, collected.

"It's okay," she told Jia Li. "I know what I'm doing."

Abruptly, the candle in the patio torch fizzled, creating a miniature nova that turned all light within the cave green.

It's started, the voice said.

Willow knew. She felt the power of Lok's spell thrumming inside her, vibrating her flesh as winds suddenly whipped to life inside the cave, becoming a dervish that took on the flesh of sand and small rock. The dervish banged repeatedly against the cavern walls, sounding like a trickling stream.

With a final cry, Lok shoved his hands out toward the earthen wall. Just as it had in Willow's vision, the wall shattered, bursting out in great chunks, only this time the trapped smell of decades-old death erupted into the room. Just as in Willow's vision, the corpse stepped out from the wreckage of the wall, the mining pick clasped in its skeletal hands.

Willow! the voice cried loudly. *You must help!*

The shambling mockery of death gazed around for a moment, then spotted Lok. Lok still had his hands raised, and the candle burned bright green, the flame jerking and wavering against the whirling dervish.

The corpse moved jerkily toward Lok, raising the pick high above its head.

"No!" Jia Li shouted, pushing herself up and running toward her brother. "No!" She tripped and fell, skidding across the rocks and down the incline, initiating a small avalanche.

Willow raised her hands, holding her palms up in supplication, concentrating on the two people in the corpse's path. She scattered the powdered burdock root into the winds that seethed inside the cave.

Spirits of protection,
Heed my plea.
Circle once, circle twice, circle thrice,
Protect those whom I would protect.

Willow shoved her palms toward the corpse and felt the gathered power empty from her body. The force she summoned slammed into the corpse, hammering it back against the wall just as it started to bring the pick down. The rusty point missed Lok's head only by inches.

Jia Li pushed herself up and ran to Lok. Lok maintained his kneeling position, staring hard at the unmoving corpse. His sister threw her arms around him, holding him tight, talking to him rapidly in Chinese, smoothing his scarlet-tipped hair like she would a child.

Feeling totally and completely drained, Willow slumped, unable to find the strength to get to her feet. She gazed into the hole the shambling corpse had come from, spotting the tunnel that lay beyond. The candlelight changed from green to weak yellow again. The wind died away.

And in the fluttering candlelight, Willow saw the withered bodies of the other men who had been buried in the mining accident that had taken Mei-Kao Rong's life. She listened for the voice inside her head, even called out to it, but there was no response. *Are we done here?* she wondered.

Head still swimming, she tried to push herself up. Her knees trembled and barely took her weight. She didn't dare move so soon.

Harsh voices gave her only a moment's warning before she heard feet pounding down the passageway. At first Willow thought it might be Buffy or Xander. Then she spotted the Black Wind gang members entering the cave with machine pistols and flashlights in their hands.

Willow froze against the boulder, hoping it was enough to hide her. Two of the gang members grabbed Lok roughly, binding his hands behind his back with tape. Lok offered no resistance, but Jia Li fought them. One of the gang members screamed at her and she stood up to him, yelling at him. The gang member backhanded her, dropping her, unconscious, to the floor.

Willow started to go forward out of reflex.

No. The voice sounded far away and extremely weakened. *Not time. Waaaiiittt . . .* The voice faded completely, nothing but dead air.

Which maybe, Willow had to admit, *isn't a completely bad comparison.* She hid in the shadows, hardly daring to breathe. And as she sat there, the Black Wind gang members set to work.

One of them brought out a box of lawn and leaf-size garbage bags and they began piling the bodies of the dead miners into them. That intrigued Willow, because the Black Wind gang members didn't really strike her as totally dedicated to neat-freakishness.

* * *

Zhiyong stared at Buffy across the short length of machine pistol that separated them. The extra twenty feet from actual barrel to bad guy didn't matter to the man, Buffy knew.

"Wait," Zhiyong ordered the demons around him. They froze in place, their weapons still trained on Buffy.

Buffy didn't move, knowing Angel had her back covered. "Okay, we've got one of those moments going here," she said. "I guess we can start talking or start shooting. Which would you rather do?"

"You," Zhiyong said, "would shoot me?"

"Fully automatic weapon," Buffy responded. "I guess there's a chance I could miss. Or maybe I'll only shoot off the big pieces and you'll live. I'm not exactly Gun Girl. Of course, you could ask yourself if I've actually got any bullets in the bullet thingy. I mean, maybe this pile of glop here at my feet that used to be one of your demons shot up all the bullets before I punched his ticket."

Zhiyong made a point of glancing around the bullet-riddled hallway. "A lot of bullets have been fired."

Buffy kicked a metallic object embedded in the glop that used to be a demon. The object skidded across the hallway carpet, thudding to a stop against Zhiyong's shoe. "Empty bullet thingy. Maybe I got him just after he reloaded."

"I guess," Angel said quietly, "it boils down to how lucky you believe you are, Zhiyong. Standing here in this doorway, I have to wonder if you've got any other demons making tracks this way, hoping to take us from behind."

That one, Buffy admitted to herself, *I had not thought of.*

"Or maybe one of the other demons will happen to pop in at a really bad moment," Angel continued, "not knowing you're already engaged in an awkward moment. Either situation will get you killed. From where I'm standing, you smell really human."

Buffy watched the shipping magnate, knowing that getting one-upped was really bothering him. Zhiyong wasn't used to getting beaten. Or even stalemated. His face radiated pure attitude.

The sudden, strident ringing of the cell phone startled them all.

"Excuse me," Zhiyong said, opening his jacket widely so Buffy could see he didn't have a weapon underneath. He unclipped the digital cell phone from his belt. He opened it and spoke briefly. Looking very pleased, he folded the phone closed and put it away. He gazed at Buffy. "My life in exchange for yours."

Buffy waited, thinking. She badly wanted to know more about Zhiyong and what he was doing in Sunnydale. "Don't you have one of those speeches to make?"

"What speeches?"

"The ones where you kind of laugh at everybody and tell us how your nefarious, evil plans can't be stopped. Especially the part where you detail everything that you're doing."

Zhiyong smiled and shook his head. "You Americans and your TV. Always thinking you have to have all the answers."

"Not really," Buffy said. "Just like some majorly clue-type ones."

"No."

"No?"

"No," he repeated. "I am not a villain. I am a man seeking compensatory satisfaction for investments I've made. A businessman."

"Greed," Buffy said, "is one of the seven deadly sins. That's kind of a criteria for bad guyness."

"And that makes me the villain?" Zhiyong seemed genuinely amused. "By your definition perhaps, Ms. Summers. And perhaps by the definition of Joseph Campbell. But not by my definition." He paused. "Now I must be going or you must start shooting."

"Going," Angel said quietly.

But Buffy couldn't simply leave, not with Zhiyong smugly thinking he'd won. And the man did think that because she saw it in his eyes. "This town," she stated, "is mine. I live here. I protect it and take care of it. I'm not going to allow you to hurt it anymore."

Zhiyong lifted an amused eyebrow. "This town isn't big enough for the both of us?"

"Works for me," Buffy declared.

"You have until dawn, Ms. Summers. Then everything here you will lose. I trust that's properly a clue that you were looking for."

"Okay," Buffy said. "Deadlines are a good thing to know when there are evil plans."

"Curious, isn't it?" Zhiyong asked. "Have you ever wondered how they came to be called deadlines? It seems a most apt expression in your language."

Okay, so he gets the last word, Buffy fumed, *because I can't think of something properly heroically threatening.* She backed through the doorway, following Angel, keeping the machine pistol leveled.

Angel paused at the railing. "If we go down the stairs we're going to be slowed. They could chase us, maybe catch us before we hit the street."

"Okay," Buffy said, glancing over the railing. "It's only three stories. We can jump. You go first." She held up the machine pistol. "I'm Cover Your Ass Girl at the moment."

"Right. Hurry." Angel leaped over the railing and

dropped like a stone. His duster fluttered around him, then he landed three stories below and rolled out of the way.

Taking a deep breath, knowing she'd done incredible things since becoming the Slayer, Buffy swung over the railing and dropped as well. She didn't know if the sudden thumping she heard was the sound of demon feet slapping carpet or only her heart going speed metal on her.

Buffy landed hard in the stairwell, bending her knees to take up some of the shock, letting her strength and constitution take care of her. She rolled to lessen the impact and in case any of the demons decided to jump as well.

"Hey!" a voice called. "Over here, you two. They're not going to just let you walk out of here after bracing Zhiyong like that."

Chapter 22

Buffy glanced over her shoulder.

A big man filled the doorway at the bottom of the stairs. He looked like he was in his forties, with short-cropped black hair just starting to get peppered with gray at the temples. His face was squared-off and blunt, showing four or five days' growth of whiskers. He wore jeans, motorcycle boots, and a sleeveless navy blue sweatshirt crossed by a double-holster shoulder rig. He had a .45 semiautomatic pistol in each hand.

Footsteps pounded down from above as Zhiyong's minions gave chase.

"Damn," the man growled, "I'da known you guys wanted to wait and party with these freaks, I'da brought a cake. You wanna make an escape, or what?"

Buffy glanced at Angel. The man stood in the only doorway out of the stairwell. She looked back at him. "And you would be?"

"Art Sledge. The private eye you guys said you came

up here to see as an excuse to get into the building."
Sledge gestured up the stairwell with one of the pistols.

Then a demon dropped through the stairwell and
landed with a loud smack against the floor in front of
Buffy. Sledge fired both pistols at once. Both bullets
caught the demon in the head and knocked him backward.

"Let's go," Angel said.

Another demon landed beside the first. He swept his
hands out at Buffy and snared her shoulder.

Twisting immediately, Buffy shrugged out of the
fierce grip. She seized the demon's wrist and yanked.
Bone snapped in her grip but she didn't let go. When she
tugged, the demon fell over her hip. A heartbeat after the
demon landed flat on his back, the Slayer snap-kicked
the demon in the head, popping the skull free of the
spine. The demon puddled at once.

Buffy sprinted for the doorway as Sledge fired another
round farther up the stairs.

Bullets chewed into the walls at the bottom of the stairwell. Noise and plaster dust filled the small enclosure.

Angel paused to open the emergency fire hose compartment and spill the hose out into the stairwell. He
turned the water on and the high pressure turned the
hose into a writhing battering ram.

Sledge led the way toward the other end of the hallway, yelling at people who had dared stick their faces
out of their offices. "I've got a car outside."

Buffy looked behind as Angel bolted from the stairwell. The firehose danced inside the small area, battering
demons aside as if they were nothing. She paused, then
grabbed one of the vending machines from a nearby
nook. Setting herself and using all her Slayer strength,
she yanked the vending machine from the wall and sent
it scooting across the floor toward the stairwell door. The

vending machine caught one of the demons trying to leave the room and knocked him back inside.

Angel waited for her, but Sledge hadn't slowed at all. Buffy ran, catching up to the private eye swiftly despite the fact that the guy was pretty fast in his own right.

Sledge raced across the small parking lot outside and toward a thirty-year-old Cadillac convertible that had seen better days. It was gunmetal gray for the most part, but there were big patches of sea mist green that masked rusted areas.

"Get in!" Sledge bellowed.

Buffy halted at the side of the car, really wondering what the empty drink cans and Doritos bags might be masking. Then a handful of bullets sprayed across the back of the Cadillac. She leaped over the side and landed in the passenger seat as Sledge crawled in behind the wheel. Angel vaulted into the backseat.

"Hurry!" Angel suggested.

Buffy kept her head down. A bullet smashed into one of the red, fuzzy dice hanging from the rearview mirror and shredded its cotton guts all over Buffy. The windshield spiderwebbed around the bullet hole.

Sledge twisted the key in the ignition. The Caddie's engine turned over sluggishly. "C'mon, baby," the private eye said. "Twenty years in this business and you ain't never let me down yet. It's no time to start now!"

Another bullet starred the windshield. At least three more ricocheted from the broad trunk.

Just as Buffy was about to abandon the car and attempt to escape on foot, though exactly where she'd have gone was a mystery, the engine spun and caught. Sledge put his foot down on the accelerator and the powerful V-8 slammed Buffy back into her seat.

"Oh yeah," Sledge crowed in triumph. He roared

across the parking lot, skidded over the short curb, and bounced out onto the street with squealing tires. Horns blared as he narrowly missed cars.

"So how did you know we were there?" Buffy asked.

"He's got the building wired," Angel said from the backseat.

Sledge nodded. "Zhiyong went through the building putting in his new systems, I went right behind him, tapping into those systems. He doesn't know I'm there, but nobody does business in that building without me knowing about it."

"Isn't that against the law?" Buffy asked.

"In every state that I can think of, sure. But that building back there doesn't exactly do biz with upstanding citizens. Me included."

"Why did you help us?" Angel asked.

"I've always favored the underdog," Sledge answered, glancing into the rearview mirror. "A vampire with a soul and the Slayer, I figure that's probably about as underdog as you can get."

Buffy and Angel swapped looks.

"Oh fer crying out loud," Sledge exclaimed. "I work out of the shadows in this town, too. If you're going to live here, you have to know who's who and what's what. And you mix in the right circles, you're gonna hear about you guys."

The Cadillac rushed through the streets like a runaway juggernaut, but Sledge drove with his fingers barely brushing the wheel. The private eye craned his head over his shoulder and looked back.

Buffy looked, too, spotting the two cars that raced after them. "We're getting chased."

"Only for a minute," Sledge said. "See, those two guys are getting antsy. In a minute, one of them is going to pull up beside the other one and I'll have them right where I want them."

"You're sure?" Buffy asked.

"Kid," Sledge sighed, "I been working this town since before you were born. Mostly divorce cases and missing persons, but you think I ain't seen weird before?"

Buffy looked into the madman's gaze that was fostered in Sledge's eyes. "You've probably seen weird before."

"Tons of it. You wouldn't believe some of the divorces I've worked."

"They're making their move," Angel reported calmly.

"Yeah," Sledge replied.

Buffy glanced back and watched the car behind the first one suddenly pull up alongside. The way was cleared because everyone in front of the rampaging Cadillac had pulled to the side of the street.

"See?" Sledge said. "I told you. Now hang on." He stomped the brake and slewed the big luxury car around, barely making the right turn onto a side street. The Cadillac kept turning, coming around sideways. Sledge pushed himself up from the seat, taking up both pistols again.

When the two pursuit cars tried to take the corner, Sledge opened up with both pistols. The right front tire on the car nearest them suddenly went to pieces and threw rubber in all directions. Out of control, it slammed into the car beside it and both of them crashed into the diner on the corner.

Sledge casually slipped behind the wheel again. The tires shrilled as they took off.

"You realize," Angel said, "that Zhiyong is going to know what you did."

"Yeah. I figure, so what. I know what he did, too. And I don't like none of it. This is my town. Maybe I don't always see the better side of it with all the work that I do, but this is still where I like to hang my hat. I get the feeling that if Zhiyong gets his way, there ain't going to be much of Sunnydale left."

Buffy silently agreed.

"Pop open that glove compartment, darling," Sledge suggested.

Darling? Buffy held her immediate response in check. Sledge *had* maybe saved their lives. Inside the glove compartment were a dozen CD jewel cases. "CDs?"

Sledge shook his head. "Nope. Those are DVD. Strictly state-of-the-art stuff. I not only kept an eye on Zhiyong, but I recorded everything he's been doing." He pulled one of the disks out. "I suggest you start with this one. It's definitely interesting."

In the school library, Buffy stood in front of the TV/DVD player Giles had brought out to view the disks Art Sledge had given them. Cordelia watched quietly, tacitly avoiding Buffy. Angel stood on the other side of the room.

Silently, they watched Zhiyong enter a hidden room behind his personal office. The doorway was secreted in the wall.

The hidden room held nothing except shadows.

Zhiyong carried the wooden crate Buffy recognized from the docks earlier that day. He sat the crate on the floor and knelt beside it. His lips moved constantly, but Buffy didn't know if it was a prayer or cursing. Sledge's spy equipment hadn't contained audio.

Again, as they'd watched three times in a row, Zhiyong held his hands over the top of the crate. Slowly, the fragments of the statue lifted from the crate and reformed. Incandescent red light glowed from the statue as it reassembled.

In less than a minute the statue was whole again, as if it had never been broken. Gently, Zhiyong carried the statue to the small wooden altar at the back of the room. He remained kneeling before it, his lips moving constantly.

"Well," Giles said just before Zhiyong got up and left the hidden room on the recording, "we definitely need to find out what that dragon represents."

Buffy silently agreed. "Have you had any word from the others?"

Somberly, Giles shook his head. "Not yet. But I'm certain we will. In the meantime, I'd suggest we all get busy." He crossed over to a table. "I've a few dozen books over here I thought we might begin with."

Chapter 23

"OZ SEEMS AGITATED," SHING SAID QUIETLY.

Xander lounged in a back booth at Happy's Pizza, waiting for the order they'd turned in. Shing sat at his side, picking at a vegetarian pizza slice he'd bought for her from the buffet. He glanced at Oz, who stood near the front of the building at the pay phone. Oz didn't look happy.

"He's talking to Giles," Xander said. "That's not going to be a happy speech. We've got demons and gang-bangers in Sunnydale. Not a good time to be had by any."

"Perhaps we should go meet your friends."

Xander shook his head. "Pizza's five minutes away. And you know how these last-minute-save jobs work out if you don't do something about it."

Happy's Pizza was pretty dead. Only three other people waited at the small tables out front. The pizza was never great, but it was generally hot and was on time. Pictures of Happy Tilson, the owner, a beefy man with a waxed mustache and a chef's hat, decorated the walls.

Xander sometimes worked there as a delivery driver. The place was so laid back they didn't say anything about Shing's swords and pistols. Or maybe, since she was dressed as she was, the workers thought she was a television extra on her way home. Home from where, Xander had no clue.

Shing looked into Xander's eyes and Xander felt happier than he'd felt in a long time. "No," she said in a low voice, "I don't know how these last-minute-save jobs work out."

Xander tentatively slid his hand across the tile tabletop and covered hers. "You know," he said, sliding a little closer, "the hero meets the girl and everything gets all hectic, then she rides off into the sunset and he's stuck kissing his horse."

"It sounds terribly sad," Shing said. A slight smile touched her lips.

"Depends on how you feel about the horse, I guess." Xander grinned.

"You are funny. You make me laugh."

"You look good laughing."

Shing looked away from him briefly. "I'd almost forgotten how it felt to laugh."

"So," Xander said, "how long has it been since you've had a really good laugh?"

She gazed at him with those golden hazel eyes. "Years," she whispered.

Years? The answer jolted Xander and he almost asked how many years, but he breathed in her lemony fragrance and leaned closer. Before he knew it, her lips were brushing his and skyrockets were going off in his head. He pulled back, breathing hard and a little embarrassed about the intensity of the kiss.

"Wow," he gasped.

"Yes," she replied. "Wow."

"It's been a while since I've been kissed liked that."

"Me too."

Xander felt her hand in his, slightly cold to the touch, yet strong and callused like an athlete's. But it was in no way the same as holding hands with a jock. "So, have you ever felt chemistry like this before?"

"Chemistry?" Her brow wrinkled.

"The way certain things," Xander said, fumbling, "uh, chemicals just kind of attract each other."

"I don't know chemicals."

Xander thought frantically. *C'mon, words, you've always been there for me before.* "Kinda like recipes. For baking cakes. Gunpowder, maybe."

Shing smiled. "Ah, alchemy."

Xander considered her answer. "Okay, I guess calling it alchemy is fine."

"No."

"No?"

"No, I've never felt an attraction for another like this before." Shing glanced down. "And I shouldn't let it be happening now." She tried to draw her hand from his. "It wouldn't if I wasn't so weak."

"You're not weak," Xander said, gently hanging onto her hand. "I've seen you fight. You're one of the best fighters I've ever seen, and I've seen the Slayer kick butt everywhere."

"Thank you," Shing said. She looked at him again, and there were unshed tears in her eyes.

"What's wrong?" Xander asked.

"This feeling," Shing whispered. "I've never felt something so strong and so true. Yet, in my heart, I know that it cannot be."

"Why?"

"Because we come from two different worlds, Xander."

"They say opposites attract."

"I should never have stepped over that line." Shing looked at him, squeezing his hand again. "But it was so easy with you, and I have been lonely for so long."

"Me too," Xander said. "But there's nothing wrong with us getting to know each other a little better."

"Oh, no," she said. "There is plenty wrong with that."

Xander shrugged. "I've been wrong before. It's kind of the family motto. Or curse. You pick."

"I'm here to combat the evil Zhiyong tries to bring into this city," Shing said.

"So am I," Xander said. "See? Already we've found something in common." He smiled.

Then someone slapped him in the back of his head. "Hey, Harris, what's kicking, man?"

I'd know that voice anywhere, Xander thought, turning to look at the speaker.

Victor Marquez stood beside the booth. He was a little taller than Xander and about twenty pounds heavier, all of it honed in a gym lifting weights. During the last five years of school, he'd taken every opportunity possible to make Xander's life miserable. Luckily, their paths didn't often cross.

"Look," Xander said with stern politeness, "I'm here with a date and I'd like a little privacy."

"Yeah," Victor said, grinning, "well, homes, people in hell want ice water, too. Don't mean they're going to get it."

"High school visiting hours are over," Xander said. "Real life is going on right now and I'd appreciate it if you'd just move along."

Victor's eyes narrowed the way they always did when he wanted trouble. "You threatening me, Harris?" His three buddies all cracked up, like it was the funniest thing they'd ever heard.

Xander swallowed hard, totally uncomfortable. Despite everything he did with Buffy, all the sheer evil he faced, dealing with the high school crowd wasn't easy. *Demons and gang members are crawling all over Sunnydale, and Victor Marquez has to come into Happy's Pizza tonight?*

"I said, are you threatening me, Harris?" Victor asked again.

"The answer to that would be no," Xander said.

Victor nodded happily. "Now that's a good thing. Keep your fat head from getting all busted up."

Xander didn't say anything and tried to avoid eye contact.

Victor leaned heavily on the booth table. "Hey, homes, how is it you're out with some fine looking fox like this? All dressed up like she's gonna be on *Xena* or something." Then he smiled sarcastically at Xander. "Or is she some kinda damn loser you're dressing up to get yourself all revved up?"

"I really wish you wouldn't say insulting things like that," Xander said.

"Why? Now we got to go back to this whole threatening me issue."

"Not threatening," Xander replied.

"You get yourself all worked up, homes, maybe gonna get your head busted." Victor put his face close to Xander's.

The clerk at the counter dinged the bell. "Harris, you're order's up."

Xander looked at Victor. "I've gotta go."

"Why? Your momma calling you or something?"

Xander made himself smile. "Yeah, I think I hear her."

Victor laughed, then looked at Shing. "Maybe your

girl don't want to go with you. Maybe she'd rather stay here, get a real man on the menu instead of taking mystery meat." He paused, smiling at Shing. "How about it, *Star Wars*? You want a real man in your night?"

"I don't want you anywhere near me," Shing replied coldly.

Now that kind of bluntness, Xander thought, *that tells you she hasn't been to high school around here.* A sick feeling started in the pit of his stomach.

"That was the wrong damn thing to say," Victor bellowed. "I ain't gonna be dissed by no hootchy-looking—"

Before he could stop himself, Xander hit Victor in the face hard enough to knock him back. *Now that—that was just stupid!* He stood up from the table, watching Victor get to his feet, blood running down his nose.

"Big mistake, homes," Victor snarled. He wiped at his bleeding nose, then pulled a lockblade knife from his pocket. "Now I'm gonna carve my name on your face."

Shing suddenly stepped in front of Xander. "No," she said. "You've been disrespectful, and you have received what you had coming. No more. You won't be allowed to harm him."

"You planning on stopping me, girlie?" Victor challenged.

When Shing went into motion, Xander hoped she left Victor alive. She drew one of the swords in a fluid motion, stepped forward, and swung quickly. The first swing sheared Victor's knife blade with a metallic *ting*, leaving a short stump. The second swing didn't seem to touch Victor at all. Shing stepped back and sheathed her sword before the broken knife blade hit the tiled floor.

Then the loose folds of Victor's shirt covering his stomach fell away, cleanly sliced from the rest of the garment. The skin beneath was unblemished.

A dark stain spread across the crotch of Victor's pants.

"Victor," Xander said coolly, "I'd have that bladder problem checked, buddy. Never too early to start having that prostate looked at." He glanced up and saw Oz cradle the phone and start toward them.

"Are we okay here?" Oz asked.

Victor's three buddies nodded and moved back.

Oz looked at Xander. "We've got to roll. Got a whole dead-by-dawn deadline to beat now. Giles didn't give me all the specifics, but it sounds pretty heavy."

Xander retreated to the counter and grabbed the pizza boxes. The guy at the counter looked totally stunned. Xander passed by Victor. "You're going to get a chill if you keep standing there. Then we're talking shrinkage problems on top of embarrassment."

He joined Oz and Shing outside as they were getting into Oz's van. When they returned to Sunnydale they'd driven down to the open market and found it still parked there. They'd ditched the Camaro with the keys in the ignition, knowing that it would disappear in seconds and never be seen again.

As soon as Xander crawled into the backseat with Shing, Oz pulled out of Happy's Pizza parking lot. Xander felt incredible. Shing was incredible. The thing she'd done with Victor had been incredible. He'd actually punched Victor in the nose, which was incredible. And the pizzas smelled incredible. It was just simply an incredible night.

Then he noticed that Shing and Oz were both quiet and withdrawn. "What's wrong with you guys?"

"If Zhiyong is already planning to attack before morning," Shing said, "I may have already waited too long."

"Willow hasn't made it in," Oz said as he drove swiftly. "Giles checked over at the Rong residence and found out Willow and Jia Li took off after Lok some time ago. Nobody knows where any of them are."

"She is in danger," Shing insisted, "if she is around Zhiyong or those he is searching for. He will not allow himself to be stopped."

So, Xander thought, *maybe the night is going to be a little less incredible than I'd thought.*

After the Black Wind gang members had gathered up the last corpse from the mine shaft revealed on the other side of the cave, Willow waited ten minutes to see if they would come back. She breathed shallowly, shaking all over from the strain of being silent and wondering if she could get out of there alive. *And free. Free is important.*

When the ten minutes passed and she sat alone in the dark cave, she added another five minutes to be even more certain, then two more before she felt comfortable enough to move.

She switched on the flashlight she carried and went up the passageway carefully. It really wouldn't do to break a leg now, she thought.

The Black Wind gang members had taken Lok and Jia Li, carrying brother and sister unceremoniously from the cave with the corpses. Lok had never come out of the catatonic state he was in and Jia Li had remained unconscious. The voice that had been in Willow's head also stayed quiet, or it had gotten so weak that it could no longer make contact.

What if they took the station wagon or did something to it? Willow suddenly realized. It was a least a couple miles back to Sunnydale.

But in a few minutes more, she reached the beach. No gang members or demons were in sight. And the station wagon was right where she'd left it, not a mark on it.

She went to it and climbed behind the wheel, then made tracks for Sunnydale only minutes away.

"The demon's name is Sharmma. In old China, he was also called the Dread Dreaming. He was the chief demon among the Wryhrym. They were some of the last of the purebred demons who were thought to be dragons."

Buffy stood off to one side, watching Shing as she studied the frozen picture of Zhiyong kneeling before the altar in his hidden room on the television screen. Even though Buffy had been reminded of what the Spirit Guardian had looked like, she hadn't been prepared to meet her in the flesh.

Shing stood a few inches taller than Buffy, almost as tall as Xander. *Okay, so maybe I had been predisposed to petite*, Buffy admitted to herself. And the barely-there outfit was definitely something guys couldn't ignore. The only one who seemed immune to the look that Shing had pulled together was Oz, who was tensely worried about Willow's continued absence.

"What do you think of her?" Xander whispered at Buffy's elbow. He carried pizza on a napkin with him. All of them ate something, but the meal definitely wasn't as appreciated as much as it should have been.

Buffy hesitated for a moment. *Well, she's not human.* Like she was one with any room to talk the way she was with Angel. "She's tall," she said, nodding. "Definitely tall."

"And cute," Xander pointed out.

"Gotta admit cute, too," Buffy agreed.

"And wait until you see her in a fight. Man, she is like nobody else I've ever seen. She—"

Buffy froze Xander with a look. "Motor down, Fan Boy." The homecoming queen competitive edge was ingrained within her and she didn't try to ignore it. Not with Xander. Some people just needed to remember who they were dealing with.

Xander nodded. "Well, okay, so she's like no one else I've ever seen with a sword." He held his hands open. "Better?"

"Acceptable," Buffy said. "Barely. I do occasional sword."

"The best thing of all," Xander said, "is that she likes me."

Buffy looked at him and felt bad. Someone needed to tell Xander about Shing, but she just didn't have the heart. *Want star-crossed lovers? Take Xander and add any girl.* "That's really good, Xand," she said instead. "Mutual liking is nice."

"The only problem I see," Xander said a little sadly, "is what it's going to be like post-crisis."

"Post-crisis?" Buffy asked.

"Yeah. Like after this morning. You know, after we kick Zhiyong's butt and break all his creature toys."

"We haven't exactly figured out how we're going to do that yet," Buffy pointed out.

"Well, if Zhiyong wins, which I really don't want to see him doing—even though this whole thing he's done has let me meet Shing, which is not a bad thing but doesn't make up for all the evilness—that kind of takes care of all the post-crisis wondering."

"True," Buffy admitted. She looked at Xander. "Don't you maybe ask yourself if you're rushing things?"

"Rushing?" Xander shook his head. "We've seen each other a couple of times now. Both times while kicking creepy creatures' butts. Not exactly the dinner and a movie getting-to-know-you thing, but those who fight together tend to bond more quickly."

Buffy acceded the point reluctantly.

"And in our little group, those who slay together tend to stay together. You and Dead Boy. Willow and Oz."

"You and Cordy?" Buffy reminded.

"I blew that one," Xander said. He gazed back at Shing. "But I'm not going to blow this one."

"Xand," Buffy said carefully, "sometimes things are just beyond our control."

"Are you trying to tell me something here?"

Yes. "No." *Your girlfriend's not human.* "Seeing you in heavy . . . *like* has just brought out the protective, nurturing side of me, I guess. I just want you to be safe."

"Well, I appreciate that," Xander said testily, "but I was looking more for a friend who could be excited for me rather than a big sister. I mean, I finally find a girl who's *not* a demon, *not* trying to eat my head, carve out my heart, drink my blood, sacrifice me to some dark demon-god, or even talk bad about me in the halls, and you can't simply be happy for me." He took a deep breath. "I find that very confusing. Excuse me." He walked away, returning to the main group.

Oh, Xander. Buffy's heart went out to him. She considered again telling him about Shing's true nature, but she knew it wouldn't do any good. Xander was a dreamer and didn't admit anything when he didn't want to—until he had no choice. Like the fact that his and Cordy's relationship dissolved not just because of the Willow/Xander attraction, but because the relationship just wasn't meant to be. It had been a near-miss, and Buffy knew those were the most painful to bear. It was one-degree separation, a small adjustment would make everything truly fantastic, but that one degree of separation gradually affected everything else.

Quietly, Buffy went to stand with the others, but she stayed on the other side of the group from Xander.

"As you may have guessed," Shing was saying, "the dragon mythology that shaped much of ancient China came from the demons that still dwelled there at the time. Gradually, they were phased from our world and exiled to other worlds. Sharmma was among the last of the pure-breds to go, fighting against the arrival of mankind with every power he possessed. For many demons, this world is paradise, and they want nothing more than to get back from the places they were exiled to."

Buffy knew that was true from the times she'd glimpsed those other worlds.

"Then dragons—the Wryhrym, actually—did cause the flooding of ancient China?" Cordelia asked.

"They didn't cause it," Shing replied, "but they took advantage of it. They tried to make a stand, tried to push back encroaching mankind. Sharmma was the worst of them. He unleashed the Dread Dreaming."

"The hopping vampires that came after the floods and killed the survivors, you mean?" Giles asked.

"Yes."

"Did Sharmma create the hopping vampires? Some of the texts Cordelia and I perused suggested that he might have."

"No. The hopping vampires have been around since the emergence of mankind. Actually, they're more ghosts than vampires, though the terms have become interchangeable. We believe that when a person dies, their *po*—their main soul—is released. If that person has lived a good and full life, their *po* ascends to heaven where he or she takes his or her place as a representative of the family. This is why ancestors are so highly prized in our culture. However, if the person died a tragic and untimely death, his or her *po* is trapped here in this world and doomed to be a destructive entity with an intelligence just a step above an animal's."

"The *guei*," Buffy said, remembering what Willow had told her only last night in the Emerald Lotus Cemetery.

"Gooey?" Xander repeated, looking slightly miffed that she'd interrupted Shing's presentation.

"*Guei*," Buffy said. "Hungry ghosts. They kind of wander around tearing up things, punishing descendants who haven't seen to it they were avenged or properly laid to rest. In general, they're just mean and vindictive."

"Exactly," Shing said. "In this state, the *po* can also be called a hungry ghost. But there is one more transformation the *guei* can make. If their corpses are still available to them, they can be returned to them and make a more forceful presence among the living. In ancient China during the days of the dragon floods, this state was called the Dread Dreaming. Sharmma collected the *pos* of those who perished in the flood, bound them back to their decaying flesh, and directed their anger at those who had survived. You can imagine the horror of those survivors when they were hunted through the flooded lands by those they had only just lost."

The image caused Buffy to shiver.

"Have you heard of the Chung Yuan Festival?" Shing asked.

"The Ceremony of Universal Salvation," Cordelia said quickly. "It happens in the seventh lunar month. Our October. It's during the Ghost Month."

Shing nodded. "During that time every year, festivals are held to honor and free the *guei* that still walk through this world. These lost *po* don't just come from accidents, they also come from wars. So you can see there are a great number of them. The Chung Yuan Festival invites these lost *po* to a feast and ritual where Taoist and Buddhist priests conduct the ceremony. Once the ceremony is completed, lit candles are placed in boats or lanterns and floated down a river, or on a lake or ocean."

"To guide the *guei* out of this world," Giles said.

"Yes. You have to remember, though, that these are the bodiless *po*. The others, the ones who have bodies—either their own or bodies of living persons they have possessed—remain here until they are destroyed."

"Destroying the corporeal body frees the soul?" Angel asked from the edge of the room.

"Yes."

Buffy looked at Angel, thinking back to Christmas when Angel had sought release and gone to destroy himself. Only he had been saved.

"Following the lights during the Chung Yuan Festival leads the hungry ghosts to an underworld called the Yellow Springs, ruled by the Lord of Hell," Shing said. "They remain there until they are reabsorbed back into the Tao, and their families no longer have to worry about them or the trouble they will make."

Buffy turned her attention back to the television set. "The Spirit Guardians were responsible for putting Sharmma out of business?"

"Yes."

"So if he's gone, why is Zhiyong chanting to him?"

"Zhiyong is descended from a man named Gun," Shing said. "He was the first man King Shun ordered to solve the flood problems. Gun tried to appease the dragons, the Wryhrym demons, and in doing so, he lost his soul. For nine years Gun toiled in the valley of the Huanghe River. You know it as the Yellow River. Some years were better than others, but still the floods came and still people died. During that time, the power of the

Wryhrym increased. But Gun did not willingly give in to the demons. They lied to him."

"Boy," Xander said, "that's one of the things you can always count on from demons."

Shing smiled at him and Buffy saw a little of the chemistry between them.

"Gun tried to take the demons' power away by stealing a magickal material the demons used to build their own homes among the flooded lands," Shing said.

"The magic earth referred to in the legends," Cordelia said.

Shing nodded. "Only even in this he played into Sharmma's hands. Instead of trying to drain the lands, Gun tried to contain the waters by dikes, building them bigger and taller. With the demon material, he was able to construct them even more quickly and bigger than ever. But it only made the problem greater, saving up more and more water for when the demons chose to strike again. Still, the people believed in what Gun was doing. They came back down from the mountains and built their homes in the valleys again. One day, the first of those dams broke, which caused the others to break, until a huge mountain of water cascaded through the valleys, destroying everything that lay in its path. Including Gun."

"King Shun appointed a man named Yu to the flooding problem after that," Giles said. "He solved the problem by digging channels and draining the water rather than holding it back."

"Exactly," Shing said. "Tien Lung, the demon who helped found the Spirit Guardians, was also known as a dragon named Yinglong. He gave Yu the plans to drain the valleys. In the years that followed, the floods were eliminated and the demons' strongholds were broken. They were forced from this world."

"How does this relate to Zhiyong being a descendant of Gun?" Cordelia asked.

"Gun's bloodline was tainted by the demons as part of his bargain," Shing said. "There has always been a link between Gun's descendants and Sharmma."

"Zhiyong is human," Angel said.

"Yes, he is human," Shing agreed. "And as such, he belongs to this world. Only one of Gun's descendants out of every generation has the link to Sharmma. As long as it lasts, Sharmma has a conduit back into this world."

"Do you think Zhiyong is trying to call Sharmma back into this world?" Giles asked.

"I don't think Zhiyong is that strong." Shing hesitated. "Zhiyong is also the last of his line. He has fathered no children, no future possible vessels to carry on Sharmma's link."

"Now that," Buffy said, "sounds like pressure."

"Yes. Zhiyong has become more powerful, wealthier than any of Sharmma's past links. And he is the first to actively seek Sharmma's blessings, the first who was truly evil. Gun was not an evil man, only a gullible one."

"But what is Zhiyong doing in Sunnydale?" Buffy asked. "China sounds like it would be the hot spot for him."

"I have not been able to uncover much," Shing said. "Zhiyong is very powerful, very hard to get next to. And he has an army of demons surrounding him. Those lesser demons are descended from demons that once served the Wryhrym. For thousands of years they have been out of the sight of most men. Until Zhiyong called them into his service."

"But something brought you here," Giles stated.

"I followed Zhiyong," Shing said, "after it was discovered that he had bridged a link to Sharmma. The others followed me."

"Other Spirit Guardians, you mean," Giles said.

"Yes."

"So what brought Zhiyong to Sunnydale?" Buffy asked again. "Besides all the tourist attractions."

"In 1853," Shing said, "a mining accident killed thirty-seven men. Thirty-five of them were Chinese laborers. Zhiyong came here looking for them, but I don't know why. So far, their bodies have never been found."

"That's not exactly true anymore," a familiar voice said.

Chapter 24

BUFFY TURNED AND SAW WILLOW—TRUE, A DISHEVELED, dirty, and fatigued Willow—but a welcome sight nonetheless. Despite the whole ticking clock thing, Buffy smiled and joined the others in welcoming her friend back.

Oz made it to Willow first, sweeping her up in his arms and holding her tight. Then Xander was there. Buffy did manage to beat Giles. Angel, as usual, stayed apart, but the relief was evident on his face even if he did try to remain taciturn. Cordelia smiled broadly, but didn't join in the group hug.

"I would have called," Willow apologized after the welcoming back was done, "but I thought we might be cutting it close on time."

"Dawn," Oz said, not letting go of her.

"As in this dawn?" Willow asked.

"Yup."

Willow took a deep breath. "Okay, nothing like pressure to keep you going."

"Will," Buffy reminded, "you said something about the bodies of those miners being found."

"They have been," Willow said. "I watched Black Wind gang members sack up the corpses and carry them away."

Willow told her story while the rest of the pizza Xander had brought was scarfed down with renewed enthusiasm. They sat around the big table in the library. They'd pooled their change together to get canned beverages from the vending machines in the lounge.

"Why would they look for the bodies in the first place?" Giles asked.

"The *pos*," Shing answered, her brows knitted in contemplation.

One thing the Spirit Guardian did have working for her was that intense look, Buffy decided. Studious just seemed to come naturally for her.

"What about the *pos?*" Buffy asked.

"They have been trapped within the bodies buried deep in the earth," Shing explained. "That's why Lok Rong's ancestor reached out to him so strongly and for so long. They've been locked up all this time, going more and more insane."

Okay, Buffy thought, *bad enough to have malicious ghosts without having demented malicious ghosts*.

"Why haven't those ghosts reached out to other people?" Oz asked.

"Not everyone is as susceptible to them as Lok apparently is," Shing answered. "Willow is also susceptible to them because of her ability in witchcraft."

"Zhiyong has the corpses now," Buffy said, "the big question is what he's going to do with them."

Shing shook her head. "I don't know. I only found out that he was searching for them here. I came hoping to prevent him from using them. They deserve their chance at eternal rest."

"But now Zhiyong has the corpses, and the *pos,* and a plan that comes together by dawn," Giles said. "What we need is a way to find him."

"Storming his offices is out," Buffy said. "They'll be more prepared this time, and I doubt he's there."

"There may be a way," Willow said quietly.

Everyone around the library table looked at her.

"But it might be kind of risky," she added.

Willow sat on folded legs in the middle of the library, and in the middle of the chalked pentagram she'd drawn while chanting protection spells. Candles burned in the five points of the star and she hoped it didn't accumulate enough to set off the sprinklers.

"Are you sure about this, Willow?" Oz asked from outside the circle. He was barely visible in the shadows that wreathed the pentagram since Giles had turned the lights off.

Willow nodded. "It's what has to be done." And she was always better at things that had to be done. Even if she later regretted them.

Shing stepped to the edge of the pentagram but she didn't cross over. Her face showed concern. "You should not do this by yourself, Willow."

"It's okay," Willow said. "I can do this."

"The forces you're inviting into this room, into your-self, they're strong. The one who contacted you has a fierce need to save his grandchild. He may try to possess you in order to do that."

"I don't think so," Willow replied.

"You're not sure."

Willow tried to hold her gaze, wanting to handle the

risk on her own as much as she could, but she couldn't win against Shing's knowing gaze.

"You are the first line of defense against those spirits," Shing stated. "If they get through you, they will be at every person in this room. The doors you open to the rooms you will visit don't contain only friendly forces. False pride or thinking that you're the only one who faces danger here will not help you succeed."

How does she know so much about this stuff? Willow wondered.

"She's right, Will," Buffy said. "Let one of us act as your anchor."

"Two," Shing said.

Willow saw the look of irritation Buffy shot Shing. The chemistry there was off, but Willow didn't know why. Of course, she wasn't entirely sure what the job of a Spirit Guardian entailed either.

"Two," Buffy said. "I'll be one of them."

"No," Shing said. "It can't be you."

"Why not?" Buffy demanded.

"It must be Oz," Shing said. "He best represents the emotional and physical motivation Willow has to fight against anything that would stop her safe return."

Oz moved instantly, crossing the pentagram lines without touching them and sitting down in front of Willow.

"It could be dangerous," Willow apologized.

"Dangerous can sometimes be exciting," Oz said. "As in aphrodisiac."

Even though the moment was serious and he'd said it without a lot of eyebrow waggling, Willow couldn't help but be amused. Oz could be like that, could move her right out of a serious moment into fun. "You," she said distinctly, "are a doof."

"I'm *your* doof."

"Okay," Xander said, "the doof gets one of the seats on this wicked little ride through the Other Side. That leaves a seat open, and I'm claiming it."

"No," Shing said, looking at Xander. "Your presence would complicate the mix and prove distracting."

Willow's face colored a little at the reminder of the hormonal spark that had passed between her and Xander not so long ago.

"Then it's me," Buffy said.

"No."

Buffy's hands closed into fists and she turned on Shing. "I'd be the best choice. I've been friends with Willow for a long time. It only makes sense."

"If it made sense," Shing replied, "I would agree."

Giles stepped between Shing and Buffy, and Willow thought that was one of the bravest things she'd ever seen the Watcher do. "If I may intercede for a moment."

"Sure," Buffy said coldly, folding her arms and not looking at Giles at all.

"Shing, if I may ask, who is the third person that you would recommend?" Giles asked.

"I should go," Shing stated quietly. "I can provide guidance that none of you can."

"Oh," Buffy said with a trace of snideness, "that's right. I forgot that you had intimate experience with this aspect of things."

Willow didn't know what Buffy was talking about, but the intensity was getting extreme. "Uh, guys?"

They looked at her.

"Calm. It's kind of a key issue when you're doing stuff like this. The spirits really don't like having their jollies disrupted if they're in a quiet place, and going in after them while you're angry or upset is the equivalent of wearing a *Kick Me* sign on the first day of school."

Shing moved closer to Buffy and spoke more softly. "You know what I'm saying is true. And I will take care of her. I swear this to you."

Angel joined Buffy, taking her by the elbow to let her know he was there. They didn't say anything. They didn't have to.

Willow watched the uncertainty play across Buffy's face but didn't know where it came from. *What is it about Shing that gets under Buffy's skin so much?* Willow guessed that it probably had to do with the way Xander was fawning all over her, but how serious could that get in two days? Then she remembered that it *was* Xander.

"Okay," Buffy said, relaxing a little. "You go. But I want my friend back. Whole. Healthy. Sane. All the things I like best about her."

Shing bowed her head, then stepped inside the pentagram.

When the swordswoman entered the protected circle, Willow felt the temperature drop to something just short of freezing.

"What—?" Willow began.

Oz shook his head. "Later. We're okay here."

Shing sat, carefully positioning her weapons so they wouldn't be in the way. She took Oz's and Willow's hands, and Willow felt fingers so cold in her own.

Willow began chanting, drawing on the well of power that she had found within herself.

Guide to borders dark and light,
Grant to me the path I seek.
Not to wreck the barrier,
And ever wanting to be meek,
Show me to the one who needs me,
Show the one to me that I need.

Let our needs be one.
One to one.

In the past when going exploring on the Other Side, Willow hadn't had much luck. At least, she hadn't shown a consistent ability to succeed in contacting something or someone. But tonight, with Oz and Shing holding her hands, she lost herself completely between heartbeats.

Buffy watched the séance tensely. Static electricity filled the room, pulling at her hair. She reached out and took Angel's hand, letting him be her anchor.

"Hey," Xander said to Giles, "what's with the worried look?"

Buffy looked at her Watcher. Giles shook his head.

"You know," Giles commented, "she's under. I've never seen anyone go under so quickly outside of an actual possession. And this isn't exactly safe here, given the dynamics of the group inside that circle, or what's lying out there that Zhiyong is interfering with. She could go so far into the Other Side that she can't find her way back."

"What do you mean she might not find her way back?" Xander demanded.

"Every time a living person crosses over to the Other Side," Giles said, "there's that risk. The places they find themselves in, or the people they talk to, might prove to be too much of a lure. Paradise. On the other hand, there are malevolent spirits that—"

"Giles," Buffy said. "Perhaps now isn't exactly the proper time for a lesson on séances."

"Right."

Buffy turned and looked at Willow. *Don't be gone long, Will. It wouldn't be the same without you.*

* * *

Willow blinked and the pentagram, Oz, and Shing went away. When she opened her eyes again, she stood high on a mountain looking down onto a slow-moving river. Verdant forest surrounded her, shading her from the noon sun.

"That is the Fuchun River," a pleasant voice informed her.

Spinning quickly, weirded out because her previous explorations of the Other Side hadn't included such sharp sensations, Willow stared at the man standing behind her.

He was short and small-boned, reminding Willow of a sparrow. A gray fringe of hair surrounded his head. He wore dark gray robes, contrasting with his parchment yellow skin. "I am Pak-lah, Lok's grandfather. That is Tonglu County where I make my home these days."

"Home?" Willow asked, confused. "But you're—" She stopped herself.

"Dead?" The old man smiled. "Of course I am dead for now. How else would I represent my descendants?"

"Okay," Willow said. She glanced back at the river, watching the small sailboats cutting across the blue waters. *Everything* seemed so real.

"You came here because of my grandson," Pak-lah reminded gently.

Willow started, jarred by the persistence of problems here when everything was the epitome of tranquillity. "Yes. You know what happened?"

"Of course. I spent much of my strength helping to protect you from the sight of Zhiyong's lesser demons. But without you, there would be no chance for Lok."

"I failed," Willow admitted. "Back in the cave, I didn't try to follow them. I should have. But something told—" She stopped, feeling like there was no need to explain further.

"You thought your friends might know where to find Zhiyong," Pak-lah said.

"Yes. And now Jia Li is in as much danger as Lok is."

The old man nodded. "I know, Willow. I brought you here to set this to right. When I chose you, I knew your strengths and your weaknesses." He smiled. "I chose wisely, and for you to fault yourself in any way would be to insult my own choice."

"I'm sorry," Willow said.

"No," the old man said. "I am sorry that your life had to be intertwined with Lok's fate. But there was no other way. I protected him for many years from the ghost of his ancestor."

"Mei-Kao Rong," Willow said.

"Yes. It was a most arduous task. I, myself, was familiar with spirits and ghosts, now I find that I am one." Pak-lah grinned. "Or perhaps I was a spirit or ghost who for a short time found himself to be human."

"Why is Lok so sensitive to the *guei?*" Willow asked.

"It would be just as simple to explain why the sun rises in the east," Pak-lah said. "Or why you have the gift for spellcraft or how it is that your friend Buffy is the Slayer. Some things just are. Lok is sensitive to the *guei*. However, Mei-Kao Rong's hold on him is far stronger than any other ghost will ever have. Once Lok gets his ancestor properly laid to rest, he will be able to handle the burden that has been laid on him."

"That's good to know."

"Time is growing short, Willow," the old man said. "I would have my grandchildren back home and safe."

"If we can find Zhiyong," Willow replied, "I promise you we'll try."

"That is all I can ask." Pak-lah reached out his hand.

"Come, I will show you where to find Zhiyong."

Willow took his hand and the world went away again.

Oz, tense and nervous and maybe more than a little bit scared, watched Willow. He held her hand tightly, feeling no grip at all coming back from her. The candles flickered, throwing uncertain shadows across her face.

Then she jerked and inhaled sharply.

Oz started to speak.

"Don't call out to her," Shing whispered. "Don't speak. She will know your voice and listen to it when she needs to be paying attention to other things."

Oz turned to Shing. He'd known from the very first that something was different about her. As a werewolf, even in human form, his senses were usually sharper than a normal person's were. And his senses now were telling him Shing was anything but normal. He looked at her, silently demanding.

"She is fine," Shing replied, her eyes focused totally on Willow. "Things on the Other Side are often not what a person would expect. Willow is finding surprises there, but no harm. Not yet."

Not feeling a whole lot better, but having to trust Shing's judgment, Oz turned back to Willow and watched her carefully.

When Willow opened her eyes again, she was in a graveyard. Not a cemetery, but a junkyard, a place where old used cars came to die. Stacks of smashed cars made rows ahead of her, creating a maze. The moon burned down, clear and bright, and drew hard-edged shadows against the ground.

"I know this place," she said. "It's McCrory's Salvage Yard, just east of Sunnydale." They stood just inside the front gate. A ten-foot-high wall made of hurricane fencing and sheet metal topped with barbed wire strands enclosed the junkyard. Gravel-covered one-lane roads twisted through the stacks of cars. Potholes, some of them nearly ten feet across, held pools of cloudy gray water, runoff from the limestone rocks.

"Yes," Pak-lah replied, starting through one of the rows that lay ahead of them. He walked across the pool in front of him, not even stirring up a ripple.

"When I was a kid," Willow said, choosing to walk around the pool because she didn't know if she'd sink or not, "we used to tell stories about this place. You know, involving murders and ghosts and stuff."

"This salvage yard," the old man said, "is big enough for the spell Zhiyong is working on. And it is a nexus for power upon occasion. The Hellmouth manifests its power in different areas. The purebred demons, when working through the proper avatar in this world, can use that power at times."

A cold certainty filled Willow. "Tonight's one of those nights, isn't it?"

"Yes."

"Kind of convenient for Zhiyong to find the bodies of Mei-Kao and the others tonight," Willow said. She glanced up at the tall stacks of cars on either side of her, wondering how much wind it would take to topple them. *Not a good thought,* she told herself. *Too much squishiness involved.* She tried to concentrate on Pak-lah.

"This place doesn't just hold the power tonight, Willow," the old man said. "For twenty-four days, beginning five days ago, the power existing in this nexus can be tapped. Zhiyong knows that because Sharmma told him."

"Zhiyong could have waited."

"He is not a patient man." Pak-lah turned left at the next

intersection. "Nor would Sharmma let him be patient. For everything that Sharmma has given Zhiyong, wealth and privilege and power, Sharmma has also demanded. Any power that comes from without a person leaves that person vulnerable, no matter how strong. An individual must build power within himself or herself to fully attain it."

"I know," Willow said, talking even though she wanted to just be quiet, but she couldn't because she was so nervous. "That's how it is with witchcraft. Sure, there are the herbs and things, but those are just to set the mood. I tap into the power I have."

The *scritch-scritch-scritch* of tiny claws on metal drew Willow's attention. She glanced to the side and spotted a half-dozen huge rats lined up inside a burned-out car. Their eyes glowed red. One of them stood suddenly, rearing up on its hind legs, jaws open wide. Then it leaped, tail whipping from side to side and fangs flashing for Willow's throat.

Willow dodged back frantically, trying to escape, and fell into a pothole pool without disturbing the water, just sinking into it.

Pak-lah moved quickly, but it looked like he was moving in slow motion. His forefinger darted in and touched the leaping rat's nose.

The rat froze in midleap, hanging in the air.

Pak-lah gestured at the other rats and they all froze as well. He peered carefully at the rat stopped in midair. "One of Zhiyong's sentries," he stated quietly. "It is only a minor demon, but it proves Zhiyong is being very careful." He stroked the black fur gently, then stepped back. In the next second, the rat was a yellow-green Luna moth.

When Willow looked, the other rats were moths as well.

"Given new forms," Pak-lah said, "these minor demons will find new things to do, be more a part of the yang in the world than the yin." He extended his hand and effortlessly pulled Willow from the pothole.

Even when Willow stepped from the pool, the water remained undisturbed. She felt her clothing, surprised to find that she was completely dry. Tentatively, she stuck her foot into the water. Her foot passed through the water and touched bottom. She felt cold but not wet. Glancing up at the old man, she asked, "How?"

"You are still a part of the flesh world, child," Pak-lah said. "Your mind insists on certain constraints. Do not fret. Only the most trained mind can enter this place and make it bend." He stretched a hand toward the pool.

Twisting like a bashful and happy puppy, a gray tendril of water came up from the pool and threaded through the old man's fingers. He smiled up at her. "None of this is to be feared, Willow. Only Zhiyong's machinations on this plane are harmful." He pulled his hand back and the tendril slid smoothly back into the pool. "Come."

"I want to learn how to do that," Willow said, following him.

"In time, perhaps you will. The forces that you can call on are very strong, and you are still yet growing. Be patient."

Be patient? I really would love to learn how to do that. Willow gazed back at the pool.

Then a great roar reverberated throughout the salvage yard.

Willow's head snapped around and she spotted Pak-lah standing still ahead. "What is that?" she asked.

"Sharmma," the old man whispered. "Zhiyong has awakened the demon." He started forward again. "We must go quickly."

Willow ran after him. "But I already know where Zhiyong is. I can lead my friends back here."

"There is more that must be done. Zhiyong is closer to finishing the spell than I had thought." Pak-lah's legs flashed under the robe and Willow had to struggle to keep up.

They ran between the stacks of dead cars, past rats that turned to moths as they passed. Willow's breath rasped at the back of her throat. "I'll never remember the way," she gasped.

"You will," Pak-lah promised. "You'll remember the way and more."

They turned three more times, then the old man waved Willow into hiding beside a crumpled SUV.

Eerie green light filled the open clearing ahead, coming from the eyes and mouths of seven jade-carved dragons arranged in a circle. Inside the circle of statues, the thirty-five bodies of the lost miners were carefully arranged, feet toward the statues, heads toward the center. They were dressed in black-and-white silk robes, most of them only skeletons now with bits and pieces of dead flesh and wild hair hanging off of them.

Zhiyong, dressed in red silk ceremonial robes, stood in the middle of the clearing next to the black onyx altar Willow recognized from the DVD footage Buffy and Angel had gotten. He chanted, his arms straight out at his sides, short swords in his hands. Jia Li, bound and gagged, and Lok, still held in an apparent state of catatonia, lay at his feet.

Kneeling, Zhiyong touched Jia Li with one sword, barely cutting her forehead. Carefully, still chanting, Zhiyong captured a drop of blood on the sword and flicked it onto the altar. When the drop of blood touched the altar, it burst into a brief blue flame that sent a tower of cobalt-blue smoke up into the air before it extinguished. Zhiyong did the same with a drop of Lok's blood, getting the same effect.

"He is offering them as a sacrifice," Pak-lah whispered. "Taking their lives will make Sharmma stronger."

Pure fear ran through Willow's veins, driving her heart into overload. "We've got to stop him."

"There is little time," Pak-lah said. "You must hurry. And you must know what it is that Zhiyong hopes to accomplish here tonight."

The smoke gathered and eddied above the altar as Pak-lah told her. Even as the old man's words filled her with sick disbelief, the gathering smoke filled her with apprehension.

Something's moving in there, Willow thought as she watched the smoke. *I can see it.*

The eddying smoke suddenly stilled, then it coalesced into a serpentine shape twenty-five feet tall. Cold blue fiery eyes formed near the top, then two clawed appendages that could serve as arms or legs lower below. Twisted horns jutted from the top of his head. Beard fringe dangled from the wide chin.

"Oh mighty Sharmma," Zhiyong chanted, "know that your child stands before you, ready to serve your will."

"Greetings, Zhiyong," the smoke-creature rasped in a deep voice. The nostrils filled delicately, testing the air. "There is a human among us."

"You must go, Willow!" Pak-lah urged, pushing her back the way they had come.

The creature struck quick as lightning, stretching out and snaring Pak-lah and Willow in those fierce, clawed paws. A malicious grin framed the huge, dragonlike face as he pulled them in. "You are a spirit," Sharmma said to Pak-lah. Then the demon turned to the struggling Willow. "But you are human. Still alive, still fresh. I can smell the blood and the stink of fear within you. It is indescribable. Ambrosia."

Willow tried to free herself from the incredible grasp.

The polished claws were as strong as steel, holding her.

"Free yourself!" Pak-lah said, twisting and jerking in the demon's other hand. "Free yourself, Willow! You are not part of this place! You are only visiting! Return to your friends! Return to your body! You are not trapped here! He is only making you believe that!"

"Too late!" the great demon howled in delight, cocking his head so he could glare at Willow with one huge eye. He brought her closer, till she could almost have reached out and touched Sharmma's scaly face. "Too late! I have won! The girl is mine!" He opened his giant maw and tossed Willow inside.

She landed on his tongue, feeling the coarse texture of it rasp against her cheek and exposed skin despite the slick film of saliva that covered everything. The fangs were jagged and pointed, three feet long, and there were dozens of them in double rows.

"Willow!"

On her knees, trying desperately to get to her feet, trying desperately to not believe this was actually happening, Willow peered through the demon's open mouth at Pak-lah in the clawed paw.

"Return, Willow!" the old man told her. "Return and you will be safe! Don't let Sharmma convince you—"

The demon's mouth slammed shut, the fangs razoring closed with grating noises.

Willow slammed her fists against the ivory columns that were the creature's fangs, feeling the top of the demon's mouth pressing down against her head and shoulders. Only the open lips permitted any of the baleful green lights to enter the demon's mouth. Then they closed.

And there was only darkness.

Willow screamed, but she was certain no one heard her.

Chapter 25

"**W**ILLOW!" OZ WATCHED AS WILLOW SCREAMED again, an agonized, despairing scream that he never wanted to hear her make again. Her hand suddenly went limp in his. Then her whole body slumped.

"Will!" Buffy called.

Shing stood quickly as Oz reached out and caught Willow before she could hit the library's floor. "Don't break the circle!" Shing ordered, holding up a hand toward Buffy.

Buffy halted just outside the circle, totally on the edge of wigging out.

Oz felt the same way. Neither of them had been part of something like this, and watching Willow fall dead—*Don't say dead, dammit, never say dead!*—deadweight was unnerving.

"She's my friend," Buffy said.

"Then listen to me," Shing said sternly, "and you will help save her life. Willow is gone far from this place,

338

and she is in a demon's thrall. The only thing that offers her any protection at all is the sanctity of the circle she created and warded. If you break the circle, the protection will be broken, too."

Oz patted Willow's cheek and tried to keep the fear inside him under control. "Willow, can you hear me? Willow? Willow, come on back to me." He felt the chill of her against his skin, surprised that she'd gone so cold and he hadn't noticed.

"You did this to her," Buffy accused. But she stayed outside the circle.

"Hey," Xander said, stepping up. Anger twisted his bruised and bloody features. "Don't you think you're being a little harsh here? You're just upset because you're not in that circle."

Buffy whirled on Xander. "It's more than that. Shing manipulated Willow's spell, made her go further than she could have on her own. That's why she wanted to be with Willow."

Xander shook his head. "No. *No*, you're just being jealous, Buffy. You may be the Slayer, but you're not perfect. You've made mistakes, and you're just as guilty of poor judgment as anyone in this room. Blame yourself if you want to for this, but leave Shing out of it. She was only trying to help."

"Poor judgment?" Buffy repeated angrily. "You brought Shing here, and you don't know anything at all about her."

"She saved my life," Xander argued. "Twice. That buys a lot of respect and loyalty on my part."

"But why did she do that?" Buffy asked. "Was it because you're as cute as you think you are, or was it because she wanted to use you to get to Willow?"

"Take that back," Xander demanded.

"Not until you prove me wrong."

Angel stepped between them. "Maybe we can sort this all out later. We've still got a problem." He pointed at Willow. "And it begins right there in that circle. It ends with wherever Zhiyong is now and whether we can stop whatever it is he's doing."

"Guys," Oz said, a note of hysteria in his voice, his fingers pressed against Willow's neck, "I'm not finding a pulse."

Xander and Buffy broke away from each other, worried looks on their faces.

Oz slid his fingers around on Willow's neck, holding her upper body against his chest, cradling her as he would a child. He stopped somewhere just short of pure panic. "No pulse. No pulse."

"Oz," Shing said, kneeling down next to him. She looked into his eyes, and somehow he felt just a little better. "She's not gone from you, not gone from us. She's only paused, stuck somewhere in the middle."

"Can you help her?"

Shing shook her head. "Not me. You. It has to be you. You fulfill her in so many ways the two of you haven't even dreamed of. One anchors the other. No matter where your lives take you, whether together or separately, you will always be together, one a part of the other. Trust this that I tell you now."

"What do I need to do?" Oz asked, looking down at Willow. *You can't leave now! There's so much we haven't done, so much I haven't told you or shown you.*

"Fill your heart with her," Shing whispered. "Fill your heart with her and reach for her, bind her to you that she may find her way."

Vision blurred by tears that fell now, tracking down his cheeks to land on Willow's unmoving face, Oz remembered Willow. He thought of her the first time he saw her, the first time he held her, the first time he kissed her.

He remembered what he felt like up on the stage at the Bronze, playing or singing, and looking out to see her in the audience. God, nobody smiled like Willow Rosenberg. Had he ever told her that? Suddenly, he couldn't remember what he had told her, couldn't remember if there were words for all the ways he felt about her.

"Willow," he said, but his voice came out in a painful croak. "Hey, Will, you need to . . . to listen to . . . me." His voice kept breaking and nothing had ever hurt his throat as much as simply talking to her now. How could anyone even in this world follow a voice like that?

He tried to clear his throat, but only a dry hiss came out. He swallowed, trying desperately to calm himself and reach out for her. God, everything hurt, and there was a growing emptiness around his heart. *Does that mean she's going away, getting farther from me?* He didn't know.

"Willow!" What was the one thing that he did that guaranteed her attention every time? What was it about him that enabled her to pick him out of a crowd at any moment? What was the one thing he had given her that she would always remember?

How long has it been since she stopped breathing? He wanted to know, but he knew he couldn't bear to ask. It didn't matter. He wouldn't let her leave him.

Music entered Oz's head. Before he'd gotten himself mellow with life and the unplanned things that had a habit of going on in it, the one thing that he'd always been able to do that enabled him to keep on had been music. He could never imagine a time in his life that it wouldn't be there. Maybe it was because music soothed the maniacal beast within him, but he felt it was more than that.

For him, music was pure and clean and the truest thing he'd ever known. Opening his mouth, Oz began to sing. It was a song he'd written for Willow, for Willow alone, one that had never been heard by another living person. He'd written it and sung it to her one night, and he'd felt how still the whole world had gotten around them. Time had stopped.

The hoarseness faded from his voice, and the pain in his throat went away. He stroked her hair and sang the words.

Then he felt her pulse jump under his fingertips. She took a sudden, sharp breath. Her eyes opened and she looked up at him.

"Hi," she said weakly.

"Hi yourself," Oz said.

"How did Zhiyong find the bodies of the miners?" Giles asked.

Willow sat in a chair at the table. She was wrapped in a blanket Giles had gotten from somewhere in the back of the library. She sipped hot chocolate from a Styrofoam cup, her hands still shaking badly with the cold. "Zhiyong had men working near the area where Lok found his ancestor. When Mei-Kao Rong, that's the ancestor by the way, burst out of the wall and tried to kill Lok, the location kind of popped up on whatever spell they were using to search. Kind of like magical radar."

"The wall sealed them off from Zhiyong's spells?" Giles asked.

"Yes."

"Why weren't they able to find the mine's location through their search of old land records?" Giles asked.

"The records had been buried," Willow replied, remembering what she'd found out from the old newspaper articles she'd found in the *Sunnydale Post* and from what Pak-lah had told her. "See, eight of the biggest landowners and city fathers in Sunnydale went in together to develop the mine. They'd found a few traces of gold and hoped they were onto a major find. One of them had discovered some kind of Spanish exploration diary that talked about the Sunnydale area, and a gold mine that the Spaniards had found when they were in California. They hired a mining crew to go into the mine, but safety codes weren't in effect then and a minor trembler shut the mine down."

"They didn't try to rescue the men in the mine?" Angel asked.

"Oh, they tried." Willow sipped more hot chocolate, feeling a little warmer now. "But it didn't do any good. Too much of the mine had fallen in for them to get to the men in time. Some of the miners had families who petitioned to get the bodies back, but the mine owners wouldn't reveal where the mine was."

"So they left them there?" Giles asked.

"Yes." Willow shivered, remembering the way the shambling corpse had attacked Lok. "And for the last one hundred fifty years, those *guei* have had nothing but vengeance on their minds."

"Against the men who sent them there?" Buffy asked.

"Yes. And the families who didn't come for them. You've got to remember, when they become ghosts like that, they're not exactly sane or generous. No Caspers in that bunch. If they could have reached out to any other families, they would have. As it was, Mei-Kao Rong was able to contact Lok. He'd basically been haunted all his life. Until his grandfather was able to shield him."

"Okay," Xander said, "the big question is what Zhiyong is going to do with these dead guys he dug up."

"Zhiyong is going to harvest the *pos* from the

corpses," Willow said. "Then he's going to help them possess thirty-five of the descendants of those eight men who bought that mine. The sins of the fathers pass onto the sons. That kind of thing. And it makes the descendants more vulnerable to *guei* attack."

"The hungry ghosts will be able to do that?" Cordelia asked.

"Pak-lah said yes."

"What happens to the descendants?" Oz asked.

"They're evicted. Kind of dispossessed of their bodies."

"So the *guei* will live again?"

"Not exactly. They'll live in the descendants' bodies, but they'll be like puppets. Going through the motions, but Zhiyong will be pulling the strings."

"Kinda like Stepford Wives," Buffy said. "Only I guess it'll be more like Stepford Kids or Stepford: Next Generation."

"Why would Zhiyong want to do that?" Xander asked.

"Maybe you don't look in the society and business pages," Willow answered, "but most of those descendants control a lot of wealth and are in the big corporate circles. That gold mine was one of the few things their great-great-great-greats went bust on."

"Zhiyong would control more money," Giles said, "which would give him more power."

"Especially here at the Hellmouth," Willow said. "Since Zhiyong has no children, Sharmma's chances of coming back to our world are limited. And if Zhiyong doesn't bring Sharmma back to this world before he dies, the demon will have his soul to torture for a very long time."

"Now there's an incentive plan," Xander commented.

Giles glanced at the clock, looking very tired. "Okay, I suggest we get on the road. Since Zhiyong is moving the timetable up with his two sacrifices, we no longer have till dawn. I'll unlock the weapons closet."

"Sharp things," Buffy said semicheerily. "Head loppers. Remember, people, the heads do have to leave the body at all times to destroy them."

As Willow watched them getting ready, she noticed the way Xander and Buffy stayed away from each other.

Oz stayed at her side for the moment. "Hey, it'll be okay. They'll work it out."

"I hope so," Willow whispered. "This group has been through a lot, but you know sooner or later something's going to happen to bust us up."

"No," Oz said. "It'll never happen. Not if we don't let it."

Only the hum of tires on pavement filled the Gilesmobile as it rocketed—*almost*—through the latest intersection against a red light. Luckily, it was almost three in the morning and not many people were out. *They're all home hiding*, Buffy thought. *They don't know Zhiyong has most of the gang down at the junkyard working on his latest demon spell.*

"Not a very lively rescue party, are we?" Buffy asked. She sat in the backseat with Angel.

The Watcher glanced up in the rearview mirror as they raced through Sunnydale toward McCrory's Salvage Yard. "Given the circumstances, no."

"I guess I kinda blew it back at the library."

"It was a tense situation," Angel stated quietly. "That tends to bring out the worst in people. Especially when they're working on the same goal and have different ideas on how to get there."

"Xander certainly wasn't a neutral party in the event," Giles offered.

"I attacked his new girlfriend," Buffy said. "Definitely no style points there."

Giles cleared his throat. "His relationship toward Angel is sometimes a little less than tactful."

"True. But that doesn't make me feel any better." Buffy glanced behind them, spotting Oz's van following closely behind. Oz, Willow, Xander, and Shing rode in the van.

"He'll be okay," Angel said. "Just give him some time."

"And once he finds out about Shing?"

Angel shrugged. "Then you can give him some more time."

"I keep feeling like I should tell him, you know?"

"It's there right in front of him," Angel said. "He's just not ready to see it."

"He's going to have a hard time dealing."

Angel gazed at her. "We all do. I think part of it is meant to be that way."

"Get through the bad parts and it makes all the good parts better? That kind of thing?"

"That's the kind," Angel said.

Buffy stared down the street, spotting the big McCrory's billboard up ahead. The billboard showed a man bending over deeply under a raised car hood. The slogan read: NEED A PART? IF IT'S BEEN WRECKED, MCCRORY'S HAS THE PIECES!

Xander paused at the hurricane fence around the junkyard and looked up. "Now that's going to be a long climb," he whispered. He carried a double-bitted battleax over his shoulder as casually as if it were a Louisville slugger. "Do you see a ladder?" He looked up and down the fence, then realized a ladder being left outside the fence would have been just too much of an invitation.

"Perhaps I can help," Shing suggested. She stood beside him in the darkness. The trees and brush had been cut back at least ten feet from the wall the whole length, but the grass was deep.

"How?"

Shing hooked her fingers together and bent down. "Step into my hands."

Xander had to grin. "Do you really think you can boost me over the fence?" He glanced over the top at the stacks of cars on the inside. Somewhere toward the center, he saw the green glow that had to be coming from the stone dragon statues Willow had described. Anxiety filled him.

"We could try to find out," Shing suggested, holding her hands together.

Feeling entirely stupid, especially since they were supposed to be attacking the junkyard from three separate directions and no one had really given any thought to breaking into the place, Xander put one foot into Shing's hands. "You know, you could hurt yourself."

"No. Drop the ax. I don't want it falling on you."

Xander dropped the ax. "And I wanted to apologize for what Buffy said back in the library. You know, when she accused you of getting Willow too far on the Other Side." He stepped onto her interlocked hands.

"I did," Shing said. "Willow would not have gotten that far without me. Buffy was right to hold me accountable. Balance yourself on my hands."

Still somewhat amazed at Shing's strength, Xander balanced himself on one foot. She seemed to hold him without too much trouble. "But how did you help Willow? You're not a witch."

"No," Shing agreed, "but I've been there."

"To the Other Side?" Xander almost yelped in surprise when Shing tossed him into the air. He tumbled, fighting to find his balance, expecting to crash into the fence at any moment, waiting to feel the barbed wire rake into his flesh if she got him that far.

Moonlight twinkled on the barbs as he sailed over, missing by at least two feet. Before he could get over his shock at her reply and the fact that she'd cleared the fence with him, the ground rushed up at him. He hit hard, trying to go loose so he wouldn't break anything. His breath rushed out of his lungs in a barely concealed moan.

He glanced around, groaning on the inside. Old Man McCrory was rumored to keep really mean junkyard dogs. According to legend, the junkyard owner fed them table scraps, orphans, and whomever he found crawling over his fence.

Silent as a whisper, Shing landed in front of him with about as much strain as stepping down from a porch. She carried all her gear and Xander's battleax as well.

"Look," Xander said, "I know you're not exactly normal. Leaping tall buildings in a single bound and being Ginsu chef with demons were the first clues. Oh yeah, and the whole Daniel Boone thing with the pistols."

"There's more." Shing handed him the battleax as he climbed to his feet. She started moving instantly, a sword in one hand and a flintlock pistol in the other.

"More?" Xander asked, following her. "I can deal with more. In fact, I think I need to know more so I can deal with it."

Shing turned quietly and put her face next to his. "Xander, please, now is not the time."

Xander paused, inhaling the lemony freshness of her. "Okay. No problem. I'll wait until it's time. Time to discuss more. I'm a patient guy. No pressure here."

She kissed him, her lips pressing coolly against him, making skyrockets blaze through his head. He kissed back, cupping the back of her head and pulling her to him, letting her know how much he wanted her. Things had a tendency to happen fast with him. That trait had gotten him into trouble before. Cordelia Chase had happened fast, the thing with Willow had happened fast.

But nothing had ever felt so right.

At least, that was what he was thinking now. He could even hear his heart *pitty-pattering* like the sound of running puppy feet—

Puppy feet? Those are big puppies. In fact, those are probably—

Xander broke the kiss and glanced toward the car stacks, watching the canine figures break free of the shadows. There were three of them, running low and hard, moonlight glazing their eyes white.

"Dogs," Xander said in warning, pointing.

Then the lead dog breathed out a huge gout of flame that set the patchy grass nearby on fire.

"No," Shing said, turning quickly and dropping into a fighting stance. "Those are liondogs!"

Oz tossed the thick car mat he'd brought from the van over the barbed wire. He glanced worriedly at Willow. "Think you can make it?"

Willow took a deep breath. Despite the hot chocolate she'd had, she still remained chilled and headachy from her experience. "I can make it. I'll just need a boost up."

Oz caught her foot and lifted her within easy reach of the mat-wrapped barbed wire. She carried a short sword across her shoulders. With the mat protecting her from the barbs, she scrambled over the fence, slid down to arm's length, and dropped. She landed on the ground and banged gently against the hurricane fencing before she got her balance.

"Man," Oz whispered from the other side of the fence, "I forgot how tall ten feet was."

"Can you make it?"

"I've got to."

Willow peered through one of the gaps in the hurricane fencing and saw Oz run toward her. He leaned into the wall, got a foot on it, and pushed up.

Even then, Oz barely caught hold of the top of the hurricane fencing. He pulled himself up and over. He was breathing hard when he landed.

"Okay," he said, "which way?"

Willow gazed around the salvage yard, getting her bearings. Everything looked familiar, but it looked kind of different, too. But there was no mistaking the green glow toward the center of the junkyard. She gazed around, looking for the tallest stack of cars she could find that overlooked the area. She was terribly conscious of time passing by. The others were moving toward the eye of the storm as well, and if she didn't get into place, they wouldn't have a chance.

"There," she said, pointing. She took off immediately, knowing Oz was at her back. She ran quickly but tried to keep from making any noise.

The moonlight in the real world wasn't as bright as it had been on the Other Side when she'd been a ghost and walked through the junkyard. She stepped into one of the potholes by accident. Her shoe and pants leg got soaked, and this time the water was cold and wet. Her foot squished as she ran.

Willow weaved back and forth in the maze of wrecked cars, deep into the stacks of flattened vehicles. When she reached the stack she was searching for, she started to climb.

"Are you sure about this?" Oz asked. "Why can't you do your spells from the ground?"

"Because these are complicated spells," Willow said, pulling herself up, then looking for the next handhold higher up. She touched jagged metal and moved her hand to a new spot. *Should have brought some gloves. I knew I was going to be climbing on this stuff.* "I have to be able to see what I'm doing."

Something *scritch-scritch-scritched* over her head, the sound way too familiar.

Willow glanced up and saw the dozens of bright, beady eyes staring down at her. A wiper fell from above her, making slight clanking noises as it dropped. She froze. "Rats!"

"It's okay," Oz said. "I don't think anyone heard that."

"No!" Willow exclaimed, cringing back down as the eyes poured out of the car hulks. "Rats! Lots of them!"

Then the rats plunged over the edges of the cars above them, dropping on them like a heavy, writhing, biting, bloodthirsty blanket.

Senses alert, the Slayer crept through the tangle of wrecked cars. Angel followed at her heels, both of them moving like shadows. Giles and Cordelia held fallback positions a little farther back.

Buffy carried a halberd. It was a lot of weapon for close in-fighting. The halberd was over seven feet long and built along the lines of a spear. The haft was thick oak, hand polished till it was smooth, then smothered in shellac and sanded again so it could be easily gripped.

The business end of the halberd carried a triangular blade nearly a foot long. The design delivered thrusting cuts that would leave an opponent bleeding from a wound that wouldn't close on its own. Below that was a double ax head, one small side and the other large. The large head could be used for battering attacks and for lopping off the big pieces. The small head could be used to trip or seize an opponent, as well as chopping attacks.

Angel stood beside her, carrying two single-edged battleaxes that Xander had insisted on calling tomahawks.

The chanting sounded strong and steady now. It was in Chinese, or another language that Buffy couldn't understand. Zhiyong wasn't chanting by himself anymore. Other voices had joined his.

Buffy crept forward again, moving carefully, alert to every sound. The chanting had a strong cadence to it now, and she could sense the growing power. *How much time is left? Please, don't let me be too late. Being too late really blows.*

Someone rushed at her from the shadows as she rounded the next stack of cars.

Chapter 26

BUFFY SPUN, GOING LOW TO THE GROUND WITH THE HALberd extended before her and held horizontally. Angel was already in motion, coming around to her left.

A Black Wind demon fired the machine pistol he held. Orange and yellow muzzle flashes tore away the night as the rapid string of detonations killed the silence.

Well, there's one greeting you won't find at Hallmark. Buffy dodged to the right, staying out of Angel's way, aware of the bullets tearing up the ground between them. She stepped forward, swinging the halberd up and back, then launching it spear point first with everything she had.

Other demons raced to their position. Zhiyong's chanting came to a stop.

I hope that's a good thing, Buffy thought, *and not that we got here just in time for the end.*

Although not normally a missile-type weapon, the halberd sailed straight and true over the twenty feet separating Buffy from the demon. The triangular blade punched through the creature's throat, severing the spinal cord. The demon dropped to the ground in a green gloppy puddle.

Still on the move, Buffy ran to the halberd and scooped it from the ground, trying not to think of the glop that streaked it. She picked the weapon up and ducked into a crevice between the nearest stack of flattened cars.

Bullets drummed the wrecks, hammering out staccato thunder followed by strident ringing. Sparks flamed out into the alley between stacks.

She glanced back at Angel, wanting to make sure he was all right.

Angel used the two hand axes like he'd been born to them. A demon had stepped from hiding near his position. Before the creature could bring his machine pistol up, Angel chopped the weapon from his hands with one ax, then spun behind the demon and chopped deeply at the base of the skull, dispatching the creature instantly.

"Lost the element of surprise," Buffy said.

"Yeah," Angel commented, glancing around the corner where he hid from the renewed gunfire, "well, they still looked pretty surprised to me."

The gunfire died down and the demons chittered to each other in words Buffy couldn't understand. But it was clear they were telling each other to move up while denying the suggestion themselves.

Buffy glanced up the narrow chimney of space between the cars. The top was twenty feet up. There were plenty of easy hand- and footholds along the way. She climbed, using one hand and the hook half of the battleax blade.

Seconds later, she was at the top, her knees resting against the rusting metal, hoping that it didn't suddenly bow in and let the demons know where she was. Angel was nowhere in sight. The demons continued chittering, sounding more anxious now. There were five of them, Buffy saw, all spread out so they wouldn't be easy to get to.

Beyond them was the opening leading to the area where Zhiyong conducted his spell. The first of the stone dragons Willow had told them about was in view, the mouth and eyes gaping, spewing the rancid green light. Fog gathered inside the open space, thin wisps of white that somehow carried a blood-red tint.

The demons fired at the spots where Angel and Buffy had disappeared from, blasting holes in the rusting metal.

Taking a deep breath, knowing she'd have hardly any time at all, Buffy gathered herself and leaped toward the nearest demon. She landed on the ground behind him, then rammed the spear point through the back of his neck before he even knew she was there.

She pulled the halberd from the demon puddling at her feet, slid her hands to the end of the haft, and swung, taking the next demon's head from his shoulders, sending it spinning like a badly hit grapefruit.

One of the demons shouted a warning, bringing his weapon around immediately.

Buffy threw herself forward, tucking into a roll, the halberd held horizontal so it wouldn't hang her up. She drove up from the ground less than two feet from the next demon, swinging the halberd haft up to break the demon's wrists. He squalled in pain, dropped his weapon, and tried to get away. The Slayer swung an overhand blow, splitting the demon's head like a melon, driving the blade deeply into the spinal column to destroy her opponent.

Bullets chewed into the ground, throwing dirt clods up.

In motion again, her movements following instinct and training, Buffy went after the next demon, using the halberd haft to block his weapon, then grabbing his duster and shoving him back. Bullets from the last demon slammed into the captured demon, causing him to stutter-step.

Wow, Buffy thought, *I bet this guy runs out of friends during fights.* Luckily, the bullets didn't penetrate the demon she was using as a shield. He screamed in pain, sounding human and inhuman at the same time.

Buffy pushed the demon back toward the last one faster, tracking him by the sound of the gunfire. Giving him a final push, she drove the spear point of the halberd into the ground and used it to pole-vault, pushing herself high into the air over the line of bullets. The remaining demon was less than ten feet away. Buffy covered the distance easily, arching her body so that her feet came up over her head.

She laced her fingers together, then reached down and caught the demon under the chin. She yanked, using all of her body weight and snapping the demon's neck like a twig. Off-balance, she fell, barely landing on her knees and missing her feet entirely.

Bullets cut the air above her head. She ducked lower, doubling back for the halberd and the nearest stack of cars. Breathing hard, she pressed up against the cars, taking cover. Glancing around the corner, she spotted a group of demons streaking for her position. Buffy prepared herself, knowing she wasn't going to get out of the attack without getting bloody.

Then a dark figure seemed to appear from nowhere behind the demon, moving inhumanly quick, inhumanly vicious. Twin blades raised and fell, chopping down opponents like wheat before a scythe.

One of the last three fell, tripped by the falling, glopping body of the demon behind him. He rolled to his side on the ground and brought his weapon up, firing steadily.

The bullets caught Angel in midstride, knocking him off-balance, ripping through his flesh. He turned his face up toward the moon in agony. His human features washed away in the moonlight, replaced by those of the demon within him. The bandage peeled from his face, revealing the older wound.

Fangs flashing, Angel dodged to one side, then hacked off the demon's arms with one ax blow. Hands and machine pistol dropped to the ground. As the demon reeled back in horror, Angel struck again, driving his other ax deep into the demon's head, shattering the skull, burying the ax head inches down into the spinal column. The demon melted away from Angel's arm and ax.

The other two turned on Angel, lifting their weapons.

Buffy sprinted from cover, bringing the halberd back. The demons fired, trying to track Angel as he dodged to the side. The bullets struck fire from the cars behind him.

Without breaking stride, the Slayer dropped into a balanced stance and swept the halberd around. She felt the dual contacts, harder cleaving through the second than the first.

Angel turned to her, the axes covered in demon blood, his face awash in the blood of his enemies and his own, pain showing mixed with the rage the change had brought with it.

For a moment, Buffy honestly thought he didn't recognize her, lost somewhere in the dark side of himself. "Angel," she called in a soft voice, knowing the temporary respite was about to be broken by the arrival of more demons.

Angel's mouth worked for a moment. Blood dribbled from the corner of his mouth and down his chin. His clothing was covered in blood from the wounds he'd sustained. "Buffy." Recognition locked into the name.

"Are you going to be okay?" Buffy asked.

Angel's eyes closed for a moment. "Hurts. Been better before." He coughed against his forearm and it came away bloody. "Been a lot better before."

Gunfire rang out.

Buffy looked back toward the clearing, seeing that more demons were taking up protective positions. *Where are Xander and Shing?*

"C'mon," she said to Angel, "we've got to move." She slid under one of his arms, offering support, knowing they'd never get clear of the area before they were overrun by the demons.

The rats clung to everything.

Willow dropped to the ground, bumping into Oz and knocking them both off their feet. Rats crawled across her head, claws digging fiercely into her hair. They tried to crawl down the back of her shirt, scratching eagerly. They stank of sewer and filth and blood. And their fur was matted, slimy and coarse. At least two thick, hairless tails partially wrapped around her neck.

She wanted to scream, but she was afraid if she did, a rat might try to run into her mouth.

Oz growled in fear and anger, brushing frenziedly at the rats that crawled on him, slapping at them and trying to avoid their sharp teeth at the same time. Then he noticed Willow's plight and turned his attention to getting the rats off her.

Take care of yourself, Willow silently pleaded, hoping he could see it in her eyes. More than a dozen rat bites already showed on his face, neck, and hands.

The rats continued squeaking excitedly.

It is only a minor demon. Pak-lah's words echoed in Willow's head. She hung onto them, trying to focus. She slapped away a rat that nibbled on Oz's left ear, watching as blood trickled down his jaw from the slight wound. Then she reached into the small bag of herbs and witchy things she carried.

A rat ran along her arm, evidently intending to search out the contents of the bag. But when it reached the opening, it turned back.

Willow found the rat's retreat encouraging. She pulled out a packet of agrimony, feeling the rats' sharp teeth slice into her flesh. She poured some of the crushed leaves into her hand, then spread them over Oz and herself. Agrimony was used in spells to repel evil.

By the bright light of the cleansing moon,
I name you as demons.
With the cool shadows of autumn,
When all things must end so they may be born anew,
I drive you from my person.
I drive you from my friends.
I drive you from my home.

The spell swelled into being around Willow. She felt the electricity of it thrill through her. A rat lunged at her right eye, rotted yellow teeth closing in. She screamed, and a rattail caressed her lips.

"It's okay," Oz said, knocking the rat away before it could sink its fangs into her eye. Both of them looked like they were wearing fur coats.

In the next instant, the rats squealed in terror. They jumped from Willow and Oz, their fat bodies slapping the ground when they hit. Once they were on the ground, they wasted no time running away through the grass. Seconds later, they'd completely disappeared.

Willow wiped her lips. *Eeeuwww! I'm never gonna feel clean again!*

"You okay?" Oz asked, looking her over carefully, touching her face with his fingertips.

"You look terrible," Willow replied. "I mean, not you personally, but all the rat damage. They kinda chewed on the parts that were already pretty banged up from the demons."

"Yeah." Oz looked at her. "Well, you look great." He leaned in and kissed her.

Then they heard the gunfire.

Anxiously, Willow glanced back toward the green glow. "We've got to climb."

"Okay," Oz said.

She started up.

When they reached the top of the stack and stood on the last flattened car, she saw the lights of Sunnydale in the distance. If they lost here, the city might well be lost, too. She also had an unobstructed view of the clearing where Zhiyong was conducting his ritual.

Zhiyong stood at the altar near Lok and Jia Li, staring toward the area where all the gunfire was coming from. Jia Li struggled against her bonds, throwing herself repeatedly against them. Lok remained unmoving.

Willow wasn't certain if Zhiyong had finished his ritual or if he was only distracted. *He hasn't sacrificed Jia Li or Lok.* She gazed down at the thirty-five corpses circling Zhiyong and the altar. None of them were walking around, but she didn't know if that was a good thing or not.

Maybe he's already finished, Willow thought, hoping that wasn't the case. She laid out her herbs and brought out the candles she'd packed. She pulled the hair out of her face, feeling the matted blood in it, and calmed herself, seeking her center. Witchcraft worked best if the caster was calm.

Serene, however, was entirely out of the question.

"Once I light the candles," Willow told Oz, "we're going to be targets."

"Got it," Oz said, nodding, blood still leaking down his face. "Targets. Not good, but I can deal." He held the short sword he'd chosen as his weapon.

After taking a deep breath, Willow lit the candles, then started to chant.

And some of the demons below started climbing up after them.

Oz set himself, waiting.

Xander thought he was fried. He dodged to the side as the lead liondog blew its fiery breath at him. The heat washed over him, almost hot enough to blister.

Shing turned, her sword whipping out and catching the liondog across the back. The blade cut deeply into flesh, muscle and bone. The liondog erupted into a snarling ball of fire, consuming itself as it burned.

When the second liondog leaped at him, Xander threw himself flat under it. As it went over him, he swung the double-bitted ax, cutting through the liondog's midsection, reducing it into a flaming comet that passed over him.

By the time he got to his feet, Shing had dealt with the remaining liondog and it lay in a crumpled, burning heap.

"Wow," Xander said, looking at the three burning corpses, "crispy critters. It's not just a breakfast cereal anymore." Then the stench of burning liondog hit him and he thought he was going to be sick.

Gunfire sounded a moment later, instantly elevating in intensity.

"Buffy," Xander whispered.

"Yes," Shing replied. "We have no time to waste." She took off running.

Xander gripped the double-bitted ax close to the head so it wouldn't swing as he ran, and followed her as quickly as he could. She seemed to have an unerring sense of direction. They ran through the twists and turns of the maze of cars.

In less than a minute, they reached the clearing where Zhiyong and the altar to Sharmma were. Xander gazed at the altar, watching the smoke eddying above it, remembering Willow's story about Sharmma appearing to her in the smoke and then swallowing her. The smoke was thick enough to obscure the moon and stars above it, but didn't seem to hold anything within it.

"The statue, Xander," Shing instructed. "It needs to be broken."

Stepping over to a stone dragon statue, Xander swept his battleax up in both hands, then brought it crashing down. Sparks jumped when steel met stone, but the stone gave. Shattered, the stone dragon tumbled to pieces and the green light winked out.

Shing was already at the next one. She raised her sword and swung it down, breaking the stone dragon to pieces. The green light disappeared.

A mournful howl full of anger echoed over the clearing, drawing Zhiyong's attention. He spotted Xander and Shing at once, then shouted for his demon henchmen.

Okay, Xander warned himself, *we just popped up on their radar.*

Some of the demons pulled back from the group blocking Angel and Buffy. Many of them threw their pistols aside, evidently finally out of ammunition. But they carried long knives and swords as well.

At the altar, Zhiyong returned to his chanting, calling on Sharmma, the only word Xander recognized. As he chanted, wisps of color suddenly floated up from the thirty-five corpses. The wisps looked flimsy, barely holding together in the breeze.

Then they coalesced, joining Zhiyong at the altar, whipping into a cone of whirling force that moved faster and faster. It turned into a dancing tornado and mournful howls came from it.

C'mon, Willow, Xander thought. *Time to bring out all the witchy secrets and put the kibosh on this.* Trying to think only good, positive thoughts about the situation they were in, he ran to join Shing. He gazed at the approaching Black Wind demons. *Damn, that's a lot of demons!*

They'd planned on dividing the demonic forces and hopefully spreading them a little thin. They just hadn't figured on how huge Zhiyong's guest list would be.

Shing pulled out one of her pistols and shot the lead demon through the head, causing him to fall only a few feet short of her and trip some of the demons behind him, taking three others down. She holstered her pistol and took her sword in both hands, running at the crowd of attackers. Her blade blurred, then turned bloody.

Xander joined her, mostly finishing killing off the demons she'd left hacked to pieces but not quite dead. Blood covered him, feeling warm against his skin. But the dancing tornado seemed to suck the heat out of the area, turning it cold. He shivered and his teeth chattered, but he kept swinging, aiming at heads and throats, but mainly necks because the blade easily severed the spinal cords.

During one momentary lull, when they had to step back from the pile of melting demons Shing had dropped so they wouldn't get caught up in them, Xander glanced at the direction Angel and Buffy were supposed to come through. He saw nothing except the thick knot of demons defending that area. *Are they just held up?* Xander wondered. *Or is it worse?*

"We need to break the other stone dragon statues if we can," Shing said. Despite her battles and the aggressive manner she pursued, not a mark was on her.

The demons climbed over their dead comrades.

"Sure," Xander said. "First chance we get." Then he lifted his ax and swung again.

Chapter 27

"THEY'RE GOING TO BE KILLED."

Giles glanced at Cordelia. "Very possibly, yes. That's what happens to Slayers." Then he returned his attention to the large four-wheel-drive pickup that sat beside a small machine shop.

"If they get killed and we're still here," Cordelia commented, "there's a good chance we'll be killed, too."

"Yes," Giles agreed distractedly. Besides having four-wheel-drive and sitting very high off the ground, the pickup had a snowplow-type assembly on the front that the Watcher assumed was used for pushing wrecks and scrap metal around. A rollbar backed the cab between the twin exhaust stacks.

"What are we going to do?" Cordelia asked.

"What would you like to do?" Giles tried the pickup door. It opened.

"Help, of course," Cordelia answered. "If there was a way."

"There might be." Giles looked under the seat but didn't find any keys. Then he looked in the ashtray and behind the sun visor. *It's going to have to be done the old-fashioned way.* He dug into his pants for a pocketknife, something he tried to carry anytime they were on patrol. It came in handy for putting decent points on anything wood.

"They're not shooting as much anymore," Cordelia observed.

"They probably ran out of bullets," Giles said. "In movies, firearms never need to be reloaded or heroes are allowed to carry an infinite number of clips and magazines. This is real life." He pulled himself up into the pickup and slid behind the seat.

"What are you doing?" Cordelia asked.

"Absconding with this truck," Giles answered. He stripped the plastic covering from the hot wires, then found the ones he wanted. He touched the bare wires together and they sparked. Then the engine rumbled to life with a throaty, powerful roar. "There." The Watcher smiled.

"Where did you learn that?" Cordelia asked.

"I was not always a good boy," Giles replied. "Are you coming?"

Cordelia raced around the truck and climbed in on the other side.

Giles glanced over his shoulder, over the huge propane tank and toolbox in the bed, then put his foot down on the accelerator. All four tires dug into the earth. Before he could stop the truck, he backed over a low-slung sports car sitting on the ground without tires.

Nervously, Cordelia pulled her seat belt on. "You have driven one of these before, right?"

"Not entirely like this." Giles ground the gears, searching for first. "But one that should have been close enough." He shoved the transmission into gear and let out on the clutch. The four tires grabbed hold quickly and shot the truck forward.

Giles steered with a little difficulty, amazed at how much power the truck had. They bounced across the potholes and the rough road, inadvertently slamming into stacks of cars twice. "It's okay," he said. "I'm getting the hang of it." He found a control he wasn't familiar with, pulled it, and found that it moved the snowplow-like plate in front of the truck.

"I can't see," Cordelia said, "and if I can't see, I know that you can't see."

"Just a small adjustment," Giles said. He caromed off another stack of cars. The snowplow assembly dropped slightly, permitting him to see the way again. "There." He peered through the darkness, then realized he had lights as well and switched them on. However, only one of them had survived the earlier impacts. He aimed the truck at the knot of demons working to get at Buffy and Angel.

Buffy and Angel had taken up positions within a cul-de-sac made by metal stacks, unable to advance against the heavy demon troops. Zhiyong definitely wasn't a man to go half-measures.

The demons turned and looked in Giles's direction. He bore down on them. Then their eyes got wide and they turned to run. It was too late for several of them and they went down under the oversize tires. Others slammed off the snowplow blade, arcing up and slamming down on the hood behind it, leaving blood smears on and cracks in the windshield.

Giles braked to a halt in front of the cul-de-sac.

"Giles," Buffy called incredulously.

"Not much of a cavalry, I'm afraid," Giles responded. "But we are under some time pressure here."

Buffy and Angel fought their way to the pickup.

Giles swore, watching as the demons regrouped, planning on taking advantage of the pickup's immobility. The demons started for the truck, and some of them had found a few extra bullets.

"Duck!" Giles advised.

Gunfire took out a side window, spilling chunks of safety glass across Giles and Cordelia.

Someone pounded on top of the cab. "Go!" Buffy yelled.

"Hang on!" Giles yelled back, putting the accelerator on the floor. The tires spun for just a moment, then gripped and threw the pickup forward. The snowplow assembly smashed through the ranks of the demons.

Once through the thickest part of the demon resistance, the going got considerably easier. Giles steered confidently, aiming the pickup at the altar area.

Buffy stuck her head around the cab and by the window. "Hey, Giles, nice save. Mucho props."

Giles jumped. "Please do give me some kind of warning before you do something like that."

"Sorry," Buffy replied. "Willow and Oz are in position." She pointed at the car stack ahead, indicating the two small figures on top of it. Willow sat in the center of the stack while Oz beat back the demons that climbed the stack to get to her.

"Yes, well, we had hoped she'd be able to start her binding spell to tie the *guei* to their corpses before Zhiyong had united them." Giles pointed to the swirling tornado dancing above the altar. "Because that's definitely what that is."

"We'll work with what we've got," Angel said through the hole in the back of the cab's rear window. "Get us as close to Zhiyong as you can. When he goes down, maybe the rest of this will go away."

Giles nodded, steering directly across two of the miners' corpses and leaving only mangled bones behind.

Without warning, a demon who had obviously been hanging onto the snowplow after being hit pulled his head up above the blade. The head folded back, and the demon spat his barbed tongue through the front windshield, exploding safety glass in all directions.

Buffy jabbed the demon with her halberd, spiking the creature through the head and twisting violently enough to break the neck. The tongue turned into a long line of glob as the demon slid down the snowplow blade.

Incredibly, Zhiyong stood his ground beside the smoking altar. Giles drove straight for the man, avoiding Willow's friend and her brother lying on the ground. No matter what, at least breaking the altar should have some effect.

Then Zhiyong raised his hand and gestured at the pickup. In the next heartbeat, a wall of undeniable force slammed into the pickup, blowing all the glass from the windows and stopping it dead in its tracks.

Giles peeled himself off the steering wheel, amazed that he hadn't killed himself. The safety belt had probably saved his and Cordelia's lives. He struggled to breathe, noticing that Angel and Buffy had been thrown forward, sprawling out across the hard-packed earth only a few feet short of Zhiyong.

Rabid screaming reached Giles's ears. He glanced around and saw the remnants of Zhiyong's demon army closing in for the kill. "Now this is going to be a problem."

"So, Miss Summers," Zhiyong said triumphantly, "we meet again."

Still winded from the impact against the ground, Buffy stood unsteadily and wiped the dust from her clothing. "Had to. Haven't finished kicking your butt yet." She wiped her mouth with the back of her hand, tasting blood and seeing the scarlet stain along her hand.

Zhiyong grinned. "Really, all this self-aggrandizing is foolish. You're outnumbered and I control the life force of those thirty-five unfortunate souls who want nothing more than to take vengeance on those people who condemned them to their deaths, then didn't allow them to be properly interred."

"Of course, they're going to settle for the descendants, and listen to what you want them to do."

"Yes. A vengeful spirit will take that vengeance wherever it might. I'm in a position to channel that force."

Angel groaned and staggered to his feet. He swayed uncertainly.

Buffy watched the tornado whirling, listening to the howling streaming from it. *C'mon, Will. Be the spell, be the spell.* "And I'm in a position to put an end to it." She shifted her hands along the halberd. Then she saw Shing closing in on Zhiyong from the side.

Zhiyong grinned, pointing at the demons now running toward them. "Against the power and demons you see before you?"

"Yeah," Buffy promised, watching Shing creep closer. "I've got you right where I want you." *At least, one of us does.*

Zhiyong laughed.

Shing leaped at Zhiyong, her sword raised high above her head as she swung it at him in a move designed purely to decapitate him.

Almost casually, Zhiyong gestured toward her. She froze, hung in midleap. "You're foolish," Zhiyong addressed the swordswoman. "Given your very nature, you should have at least had an inkling of the power I would have over you at this time." He gestured again and Shing blew backward like she'd been shot from a cannon.

Shing struck a pile of wrecked cars nearly two hundred yards away hard enough to kill a normal person. Shing staggered back to her feet. Metal creaked. She glanced up just in time to watch a ton of scrap cars come tumbling down on her. A huge cloud of dust belched out from under the fallen vehicles.

"Do you still have those high hopes, Miss Summers?" Zhiyong taunted.

When she finished the chant, Willow felt the power of the spell surge from her. As strong as it was, she didn't doubt that there had been help along the way. Dizzy and nauseous, she watched as Shing smashed against the stack of cars to her right. The thunderous boom echoed over the clearing, through the ragged alleys of the salvage yard.

"They're going to fall," Oz said. Then he kicked one of the demons climbing up at them in the face just as the creature tried to fire his tongue. The demon fell back from the stack just as the smashed vehicles tumbled and dropped onto Shing, driving her into the ground.

"No," Willow breathed weakly, knowing nothing human could have survived.

Then she heard Xander's anguished shout from somewhere below. *"Nooooooo!"*

A sudden flare of bright white light ignited inside the whirling tornado of souls. The flare expanded, filling the tornado, then blowing it into individual wisps again. All of the wisps returned to the corpses of the miners.

"The spell worked, Will," Oz commented, relaxing a bit because the Black Wind demons seemed less interested in scaling the stack after them.

"I know," Willow said. She looked down, watching as

Xander ran to the pile of metal that had crushed Shing. "But it didn't work in time to save everyone."

Xander stared in hurt and disbelief at the smashed vehicles that had buried Shing. He was battered and bloody from fighting the demons. Together, they'd managed to smash the last of the glowing stone demon statues.

But now there was no together.

Strength left his legs as he stood there. The ax dropped through his fingers. Agony squeezed his chest. He hadn't known her for long, but what he'd known he'd liked, and there had been the promise of so much more. Tears ran down his cheeks. Except for the pain, he felt completely empty—alone again. He closed his eyes and his chin hit his chest.

Buffy watched the tornado disperse, watching the individual wisps track back to the corpses. She looked at Zhiyong coldly. "Oooops. Looks like maybe things aren't going to work out the way you thought they were."

"No," Zhiyong breathed hoarsely, looking out over the corpses.

"My guess?" Buffy said. "Sharmma's not going to be very happy with you after this. You're his last chance to come back to this world." She paused. "And guess what? You tanked it."

Giles and Cordelia came forward and cut Jia Li and Lok free. Lok was still out and Giles had to carry him, but Willow's friend could walk on her own. The Watcher and Cordelia escorted the pair away from Zhiyong.

The Black Wind gang members backed away uncertainly.

Zhiyong turned to Buffy. "Do you know what you've done?"

"Beaten you," Buffy answered. "Ruled out having Stepford Kids in Sunnydale. Pretty much tore down your playhouse. Actually, I feel pretty good about that, if you want to know."

Suddenly, more smoke swirled up from the black altar. It formed a cloud around Zhiyong's head, slipping into the man through his nose and mouth. Zhiyong went into convulsions at once, dropping into a fetal position. Then his body started growing, expanding as flesh ripped and bled, then healed only to rip and bleed again.

Buffy stepped back, not sure what was going on. She looked at Giles, who only shrugged. *Oh, now that's what every Slayer lives to see their Watcher do.*

Zhiyong uncurled from the fetal position, only Buffy knew at once it wasn't Zhiyong anymore. The creature was a fifteen-foot long and less than half that high Eastern dragon.

"Sssslayer," the dragon said in a deep basso voice. "Know me. I am Sharmma, called the Dread Dreaming by those who learned to fear me." He padded forward, light glistened from the five toe talons. "All learned to fear me, as you will now learn to fear me."

"Nope," Buffy said. "All out of fear." She moved the halberd in front of her, keeping it loose and ready in her hands.

"You have destroyed my avatar," Sharmma growled.

"And your chance of getting back to this world," Buffy agreed. "Bet I get bonus points for that."

Sharmma unleashed an angry growl, spewing flames in a cloud nearly twenty feet long. Buffy left the ground as soon as the massive jaws opened, throwing herself up and to the right. As soon as she hit the ground, she started forward.

The demon-dragon turned toward her, mouth opening again.

Buffy swung the halberd, burying the ax head deeply into the side of Sharmma's head. The sharp blade grated on bone, cutting a large flap of skin free but not doing any serious damage because the skull was so thick.

Sharmma breathed flame again, and this time Buffy narrowly avoided being cooked.

Angel came up from the other side, still not up to full speed, but moving very fast. He swung the first ax and buried it deeply into Sharmma's right eye. The demon-dragon whipped around immediately, screaming in rage, blood trickling from the ruined socket. Lashing out with a clawed foot, Sharmma raked Angel across the midsection, knocking him back through the air. He flew nearly thirty feet.

Shelving her concern for Angel for the moment, Buffy sprinted forward. She carried the halberd in one hand, reaching up with her left hand to grab the dragon's shoulder.

Buffy pulled herself up, feeling the demon-dragon's muscle twist and writhe under the rough scales. She kicked her feet against Sharmma's side and straddled her opponent.

Sharmma twisted his head and breathed fire.

Buffy ducked low, becoming a layer of skin over the scales. The demon-dragon's wings beat at her with bruising force. The Slayer slid slightly to the right, trying to stay on the creature's blind side. Sharmma bucked and writhed under her, trying to dislodge her.

The Black Wind demons stayed back, obviously afraid of getting caught by a flame-blast or being stomped underfoot.

Buffy slid forward, having to duck under another blast

of flame-breath. Then she was at the base of the dragon's skull. Sharmma swung his head rapidly, shaking it like a wet dog. Buffy locked her legs around the dragon's neck and held on. She gripped the halberd in both hands, then drove the spear point into the demon-dragon's neck.

The point dug deeply down into the demon-dragon's spinal column. Buffy sawed frantically, trying to cut through the thick bone and muscle.

Sharmma reared up suddenly, standing on his two back legs. Then he came crashing back down on his front two feet.

Unable to hang on, Buffy flew off. She slammed into the ground, stunned. She looked up, trying to get her feet under her, watching Sharmma bear down on her, blood weeping from the eye Angel had destroyed.

"No mercy, Sssslayer," Sharmma promised.

"Xander."

Surprise filled Xander when he heard Shing's voice. He opened his eyes, thinking he was imagining things. Then he watched Shing step through the flattened car hulks. He looked at her, not understanding. "I saw you die," he whispered hoarsely.

She knelt beside him, reaching out to cup his chin in her palm. Her skin was cool to the touch. "No, Xander," she said softly. "You didn't see me die. You can't kill someone who is already dead. That's what Buffy wanted to tell you about me. That's why she wanted to keep me away from you."

"Dead?" Xander felt like he was hanging onto comprehension with his fingernails.

"I died," Shing whispered, "a long time ago. Hundreds of years ago. I wanted to tell you, too, but I couldn't. I've never felt with anyone the way I've felt about you in these past two nights. Forgive me, but for the time it lasted, I wanted that. I wanted you. Please don't hate me." Tears shone in her eyes.

"I . . . I could never hate you." Xander's voice was strained.

"Hate to break this little Kodak moment up," Oz said, climbing down a nearby stack of cars, "but we've got problems." He reached up and helped Willow down. "The dragon has Buffy on the run, and the Black Wind demons are kind of regrouping."

Xander glanced over his shoulder and saw Giles and Cordelia battling the Black Wind demons, definitely in danger of being routed. Angel was down, struggling to get up.

And Buffy was on the run, scrambling for her life with one badass dragon on her trail.

Xander looked up at Shing as he grabbed his battleax. "When we get through with this, we gotta talk."

"Okay," she said. Then she led them into battle.

Okay, Buffy thought, *running out of places to hide.* She ached all over as she ran, part of it from the injuries she'd experienced and part of it from the sheer, driving pace Sharmma maintained. *And hiding from a demon is not exactly what a Slayer is supposed to do.*

But even Giles didn't expect her to beat every demon she encountered. *Did he?* Sometimes, the Watcher seemed genuinely surprised.

She ran toward the narrow alley between stacks of dead cars ahead. It looked too narrow for the dragon.

The rasping breath warned her about the next coming furnace blast. She flipped to the left, landing on her feet, watching as flames licked the ground, so hot they glazed chunks of glass out of the dirt.

With the sudden change in her direction, Buffy barely made the mouth of the alley. She caught the edge in her hands and pulled herself through, collecting a few more small cuts. Then she was running down the alley between the stacks of cars.

Sharmma came after her, sending vibrations through the ground with his immense weight, staying close to Buffy. His gait made him bounce from side to side in the alley, slowing him a little and collapsing stacks of wrecked cars in his wake.

Buffy glanced over her shoulder, knowing she wasn't gaining any ground on the dragon. And the way her lungs and legs were feeling, she couldn't run much longer.

Once Shing was back in pure battle mode, the surviving Black Wind demon numbers dropped in a hurry. Xander couldn't help looking at her, wondering why he hadn't known she was a ghost like everyone else had. He felt kind of stupid about it, but actually it was a good kind of stupid. The attraction was there, and it was real, but the whole ghost/human dynamic was a little weird.

Still, Oz and Willow seemed to be working through it. Then there was Buffy and Angel. *Probably,* he told himself, *the weirdest relationship any of us have been through has been Cordy's and mine.*

He chopped the head from another demon, glancing in Buffy's direction as she disappeared into an alley running through the junkyard. *She can't keep running forever.* Then he spotted the truck Giles had driven at Zhiyong.

And in the bed of the truck he spotted the propane tank.

"Shing," he called.

She looked at him, sword dripping blood. "What?"

"Cover for me. I gotta go get Buffy."

"Of course."

"Xander," Angel called. He lay on the ground, barely able to move, defended by Oz and Willow. He tried to get up but couldn't. Xander knew what the vampire wanted him to do.

"I'm working on it," Xander promised. "Hell, I've almost got a plan." Seeing that there was no key in the ignition, he touched the wires hanging below the dashboard, surprised and relieved when the engine started. He brought the truck around, mowing down another demon as he sped toward the other side of the junkyard where Buffy had disappeared.

Buffy ran, driving her feet hard into the packed earth. Her breath burned her lungs and the back of her throat now. Spots swam in her vision. The shadows in the alley made it hard for her to see. And she kept thinking she heard—

A horn?

She ran through the next intersection, and the honking horn sounded louder. She glanced through the cross-alley on the right.

The pickup Giles had driven flashed by with Xander at the wheel. "Buffy!" Xander yelled, waving.

Buffy turned, her feet sliding out from under her for a moment, catching herself on one hand. She almost dropped the halberd, but managed to hang onto it as she lurched back to her feet.

Sharmma blew a fiery blast at her that missed by inches. The flames coiled on the metal, staying for a moment. The demon-dragon tried to turn as well, but the alley was too tight. Still, the creature was large enough and strong enough to knock the stacks out of the way.

Sharmma crashed into the left row of mashed vehicles, starting a chain reaction that chased Buffy. Cars and trucks dropped from the row, slowly catching up with her even though she was running as fast as she could.

Then she reached the next alley where Xander was waiting with the four-wheel-drive truck.

"Passenger seat," Xander yelled, pointing.

Unable to take the halberd into the truck, Buffy placed it into the bed, then scrambled into the passenger seat.

Xander put the truck into reverse, placing a hand along the back of the seat and peering through the back. "Shing is a ghost."

Glancing through the empty front windshield, Buffy saw Sharmma crash through the last intersection, knocking wrecked cars ahead of him. He glanced around balefully with his remaining eye, then spotted the pickup. He took up pursuit immediately.

"I knew that," Buffy said.

"You should have told me."

Buffy looked at him in disbelief. "I should have told you?"

"Yeah."

She held up her hands, angry now. "This is *not* going to be my fault, Xander Harris."

"What's not?" Xander stayed focused on his driving.

"You and Shing. Getting kind of involved these past couple days."

"I didn't say that was your fault."

Buffy faced him, her arms crossed over her breasts. Despite the fear she felt at Sharmma chasing them, maybe even actually gaining on them, she felt mildly irritated. "Then what are you saying?"

"What I'm saying," Xander said, "is that you should be able to tell me the girl I'm kind of interested in is dead. I mean, that's like one of the top items on a Must Tell list."

"I agree," Buffy agreed. "So you're okay with this? You and Shing, I mean?"

Xander shrugged, then slammed into one side of the alley, screeching for a little while before he pulled back into the center of the alley. "I know that I like her, and she likes me. Don't know what that makes it, but it does make it nice."

"That's good." Buffy returned her attention to the demon-dragon. "Are we clear?"

"Not quite," Xander replied.

"The dragon *is* catching up."

Xander started to turn his head.

"Don't look!" Buffy yelled.

"I'm not done yet," Xander said. "I wanted to apologize for blowing up at you."

"No, I should apologize to you. I should have told you your girlfriend was dead."

"You didn't know you could tell me then," Xander pointed out. "I probably wouldn't have listened. So I should apologize to you."

"I could have been more tactful," Buffy said.

"Hey look," Xander said, "you're messing up my apology. Don't make me turn this car around!"

Buffy smiled, feeling good again now that the tension between her and Xander was better, and that no one had died who wasn't already dead. "Okay, we need a plan for how to handle the demon-dragon. The *Wacky Races* approach isn't working for me."

"Actually," Xander said, "I do have a plan."

"I apologize for not telling you your girlfriend was dead," Buffy said. "Now what's your plan?"

"And I apologize for getting cheesed off at you for

wanting to protect Willow," Xander said. He hooked a thumb over his shoulder at the big tank in the back. "That's propane. *Highly* combustible."

"We're driving around in a bomb, and you're bouncing off the sides of the alley?"

Xander paled a little. "Okay, so maybe I didn't think about that part too well. What I did think about was luring the demon-dragon to the propane tank, then blowing it up."

"Suppose the demon-dragon likes propane explosions? It does have fiery breath."

"Then we're screwed," Xander said. "Because that's as good as I've got."

"It's not bad," Buffy admitted. "I like it."

"Good. Then when you're ready, we'll bail."

"Ready," Buffy said.

Xander jammed the brakes on. The four-wheel-drive shut down immediately, shuddering as it bounced across the uneven ground. The truck turned partially sideways, skidding, then rocked to a stop.

They bailed out the doors, watching Sharmma closing on them. Buffy grabbed the halberd. The demon-dragon blew fiery breath at them, peeling the paint from the truck and setting the cab's interior on fire.

Buffy ran, staying with Xander instead of maxing out. She kept an eye on Sharmma. When the demon-dragon reached the front of the truck, gathering his legs to make the jump over the vehicle, Buffy turned and set herself, drawing the halberd back. She threw the halberd with everything she had. The blade twirled as it shot through the air.

Sharmma leaped, clearing the truck easily. Then, when the demon-dragon was in midleap over the truck, the halberd struck home, piercing the propane tank and throwing off sparks from the metal on metal contact.

The propane caught, roiling up in a super-hot fireball that caught the demon-dragon squarely in its grasp. Shrapnel from the propane tank ripped into Sharmma and reached whatever fuel the demon-dragon used to supply his fiery breath. There must have been pockets of the fuel inside the demon-dragon, because at least a half-dozen explosions followed on the heels of the first.

The concussion knocked Xander and Buffy to the ground. Then it rained flaming bits and pieces of Sharmma for a minute or so.

Xander raised his head tentatively. "Wow," he said. "Poof! The massacred dragon!"

"Good plan," Buffy said.

"Good throw," he replied.

Without a word, they hugged each other.

Epilogue

Buffy found Xander sitting out at the lunch tables alone the next day. All of them were worn out from staying up demon-hunting the night before, but Xander had seemed more down than any of them.

Willow was spending her time with Jia Li. Lok didn't remember any of the possession and had made a full recovery. He still wasn't exactly a pleasant person, but Willow said Jia Li and her parents were relieved.

The papers and media were filled with reports on the mysterious disappearance of Zhiyong, but no one was stepping forward to say what had really happened. And no more Black Wind members had put in an appearance since yesterday.

"Hey," Buffy called.

Xander looked up without much enthusiasm. "Hi. Don't want any company."

"That's too bad, because I do."

"Get with Will."

Buffy shook her head. "She's off with Jia Li."

"There's always Oz."

"Helping Giles file books in the library. And getting rid of empty pizza cartons from the little gathering last night."

"You could always go look up Dead Boy."

"I wanted to eat outside today. He doesn't feel like working on his tan."

That almost got a smile from Xander.

"I heard about Shing," Buffy said more quietly. "She went back to China, huh?"

"Yeah. It appears a Spirit Guardian's work is never done, and Sunnydale isn't exactly her neck of the woods." Xander pulled his knees up a little closer to his chest.

"I thought you looked lonely."

"Me?"

Buffy held her thumb and forefinger up a fraction of an inch apart. "Maybe a little. Thought I'd come share my lunch with you."

"Lunch?"

Buffy held up a brown paper bag.

"You made lunch today?" Xander smiled and shook his head. "I never thought I'd see that."

"Actually," Buffy said, "you still haven't. I bought this particular lunch from Jake Knickmeyer."

"You bought his lunch?"

Buffy nodded. "Cost me ten bucks." She reached into her bag and pulled out two soft drinks. "Had to buy the sodas, too."

Xander looked at the brown paper bag. "So what do you have?"

"Don't know. It's kind of a mystery lunch."

"Jake's mom used to make some of the best peanut

butter and jelly sandwiches," Xander said. "Greg Barrows used to beat Jake up some days just to take his lunch."

"Well, maybe we'd better hurry and eat this lunch before Greg finds out we got it today."

"Jake always got Twinkies, too."

Buffy shook the bag again, teasing. "Maybe we have a Twinkie today."

Xander patted the table beside him. "Okay, you've got me salivating."

"Good." Buffy joined him on the table.

"A mercy lunch," Xander said, taking the bag.

"Not mercy," Buffy insisted. "I get half. Including the Twinkie. Not accepting dibs today."

Xander reached into the bag and took out one of the fattest peanut butter and jelly sandwiches Buffy had ever seen. He grinned in anticipation. "Did I tell you his mom makes her own jelly?"

"No."

Xander nodded as he tore the sandwich in half. He dropped his eyes. "You know, the last couple of days I thought I really had something."

"You did. Shing liked you a lot."

"We're still not together."

"Doesn't always work out that way."

"I know. I'm just tired of it not working out for me," Xander said.

Buffy took her half of the sandwich. "I know."

"I'm going to miss her, Buffy."

"I know that too," Buffy said, "but I'm here and so are the others. You don't have to miss her alone, or be alone, or feel alone. We've all got each other."

"I just feel all busted up inside, you know?" His voice sounded pained and hoarse all of a sudden.

"Xander," Buffy said quietly.

"Yeah."

"We're still going halves on the Twinkie."

"Okay." Xander sounded more normal, a grin on his face. "Didn't get the sympathy vote, did I?"

"Nope. But it was a nice try."

About the Author

Mel Odom lives in Moore, Oklahoma, with his wife and five children. He's the author of several books, many of them including novels in the *Buffy the Vampire Slayer, Angel, Sabrina the Teenage Witch,* and other television shows. He's done the novelizations for *Blade* and the upcoming *Vertical Limit*. He's also done books in the fantasy and science fiction field, including the *Threat From the Sea* trilogy from TSR. His e-mail address is <u>denimbyte@aol.com</u>.

"Wish me monsters."
—Buffy

Vampires, werewolves, witches, demons of nonspecific origin. All of them are drawn to the Hellmouth in Sunnydale, California. And all of them have met their fate at the hands—or stake—of Buffy the Vampire Slayer.

This volume catalogs and explores the mythological, literary, and cultural origins of the endless numbers of ghoulish creatures who have tried to take a piece of the Slayer in the first four years of the hit TV show.

THE MONSTER BOOK
by
Christopher Golden
Stephen R. Bissette
Thomas E. Sniegoski

AVAILABLE NOW FROM

POCKET BOOKS

Everyone's got his demons....

ANGEL™

If it takes an eternity, he will make amends.

❖

Original stories based
on the TV show
Created by Joss Whedon
& David Greenwalt

Available from Pocket Pulse
Published by Pocket Books

. . . A GIRL BORN
WITHOUT THE FEAR GENE

FEARLESS™

A SERIES BY
FRANCINE PASCAL

FROM POCKET PULSE
PUBLISHED BY POCKET BOOKS

3029